THE FUSE

VOL 2 · GRIDLOCK

WRITER · ANTONY JOHNSTON

ARTIST · JUSTIN GREENWOOD

COLORIST · SHARI CHANKHAMMA

LETTERER · RYAN FERRIER

image

fusecomic.com

FUSE CREATED BY JOHNSTON & GREENWOOD

IMAGE COMICS, INC.
Robert Kirkman – Chief Operating Officer
Erik Larsen – Chief Financial Officer
Todd McFarlane – President
Marc Silvestri – Chief Executive Officer
Jim Valentino – Vice-President

Eric Stephenson – Publisher
Kat Salazar – Director of PR & Marketing
Corey Murphy – Director of Retail Sales
Jeremy Sullivan – Director of Digital Sales
Randy Okamura – Marketing Production Designer
Emilio Bautista – Sales Assistant
Branwyn Bigglestone – Senior Accounts Manager
Emily Miller – Accounts Manager
Jessica Ambriz – Administrative Assistant
David Brothers – Content Manager
Jonathan Chan – Production Manager
Drew Gill – Art Director
Meredith Wallace – Print Manager
Addison Duke – Production Artist
Vincent Kukua – Production Artist
Sasha Head – Production Artist
Tricia Ramos – Production Assistant
IMAGECOMICS.COM

THE FUSE VOL 2: GRIDLOCK. First printing. June 2015.

ISBN: 978-1-63215-313-5. Contains material originally published in magazine form as THE FUSE #7-12.

Published by Image Comics, Inc. Office of publication: 2001 Center Street, 6th Floor, Berkeley, CA 94704.

THE FUSE™

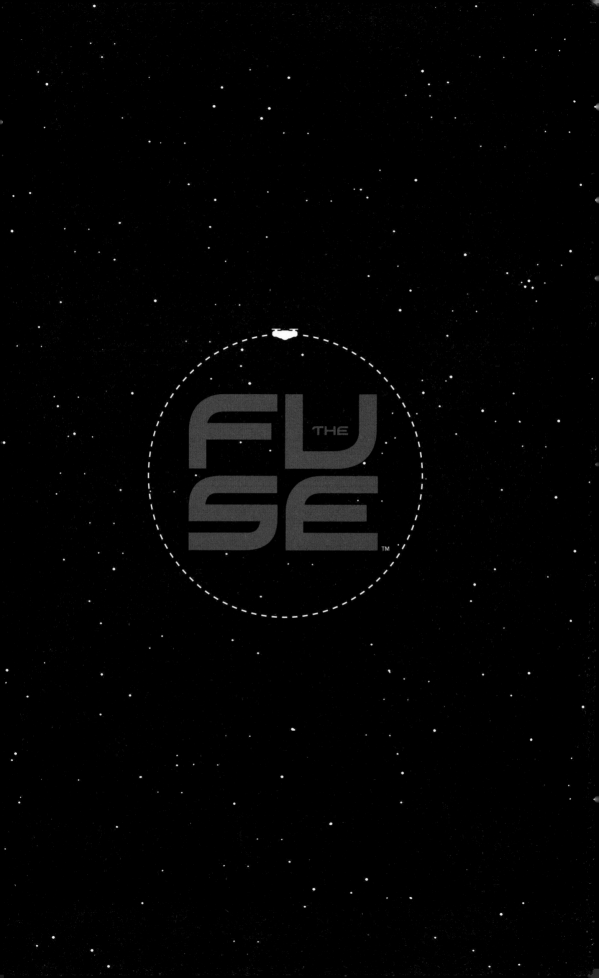

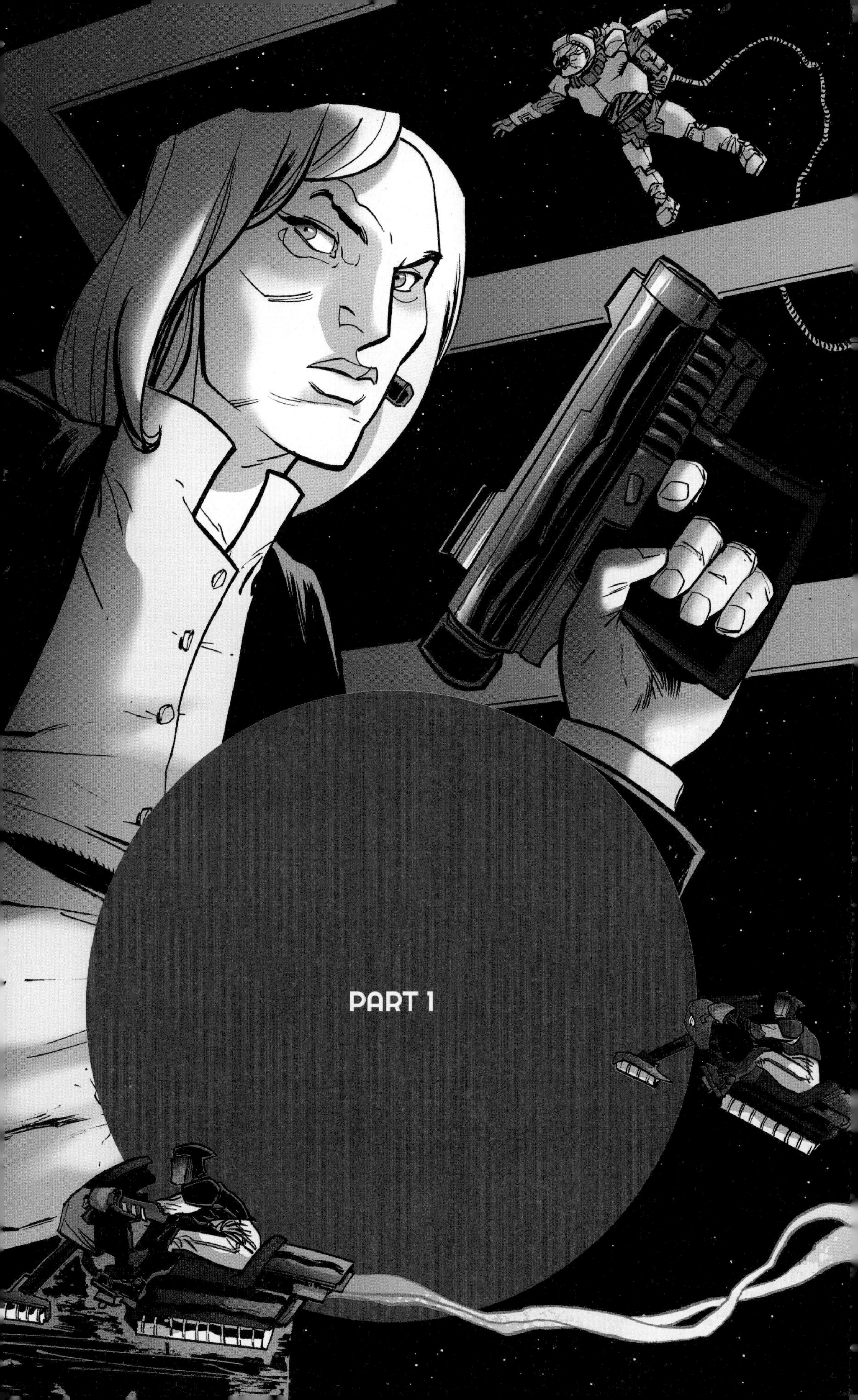
PART 1

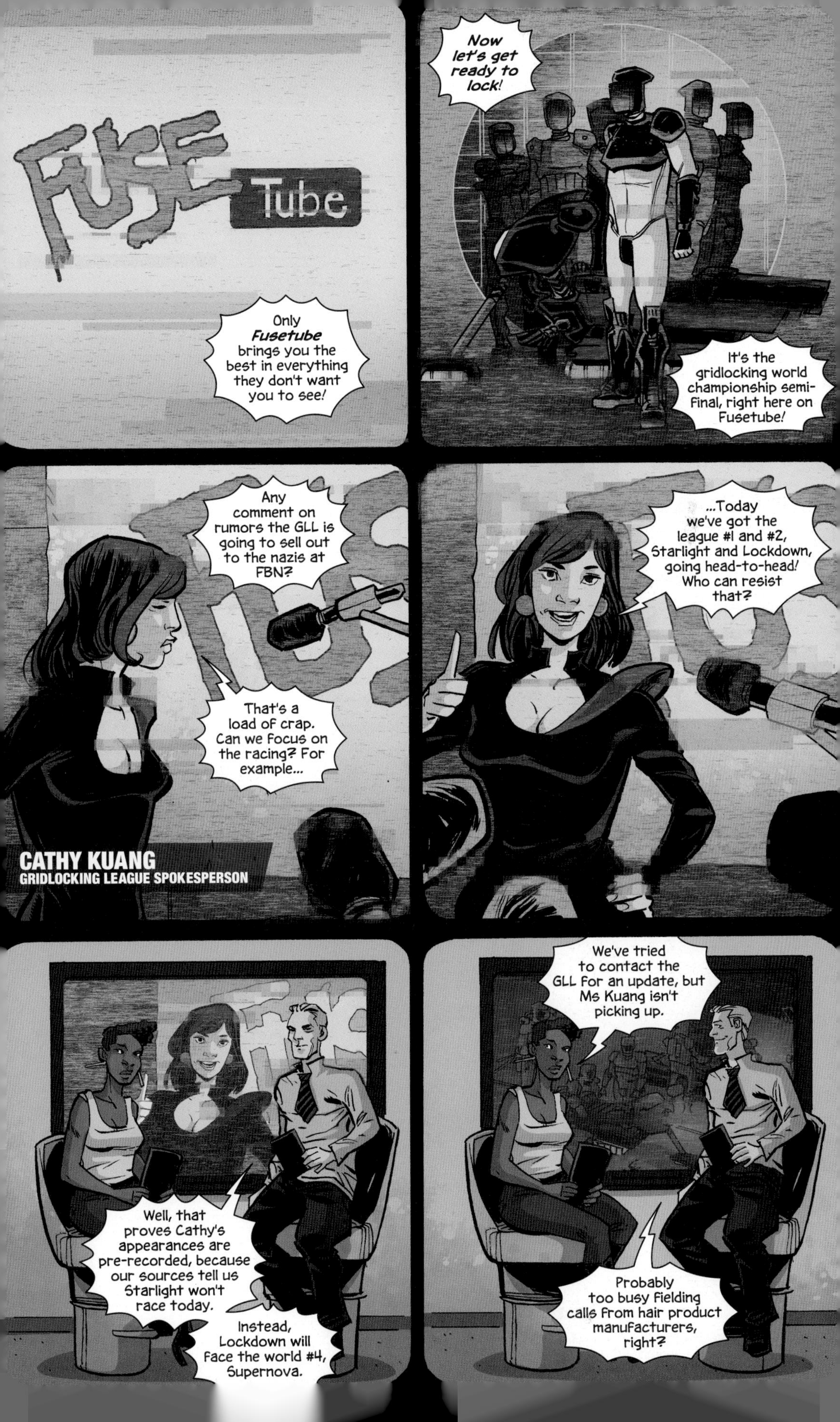
FUSE Tube
Only Fusetube brings you the best in everything they don't want you to see!
Now let's get ready to lock!
It's the gridlocking world championship semi-final, right here on Fusetube!
Any comment on rumors the GLL is going to sell out to the nazis at FBN?
That's a load of crap. Can we focus on the racing? For example...
CATHY KUANG
GRIDLOCKING LEAGUE SPOKESPERSON
...Today we've got the league #1 and #2, Starlight and Lockdown, going head-to-head! Who can resist that?
Well, that proves Cathy's appearances are pre-recorded, because our sources tell us Starlight won't race today.
Instead, Lockdown will face the world #4, Supernova.
We've tried to contact the GLL for an update, but Ms Kuang isn't picking up.
Probably too busy fielding calls from hair product manufacturers, right?

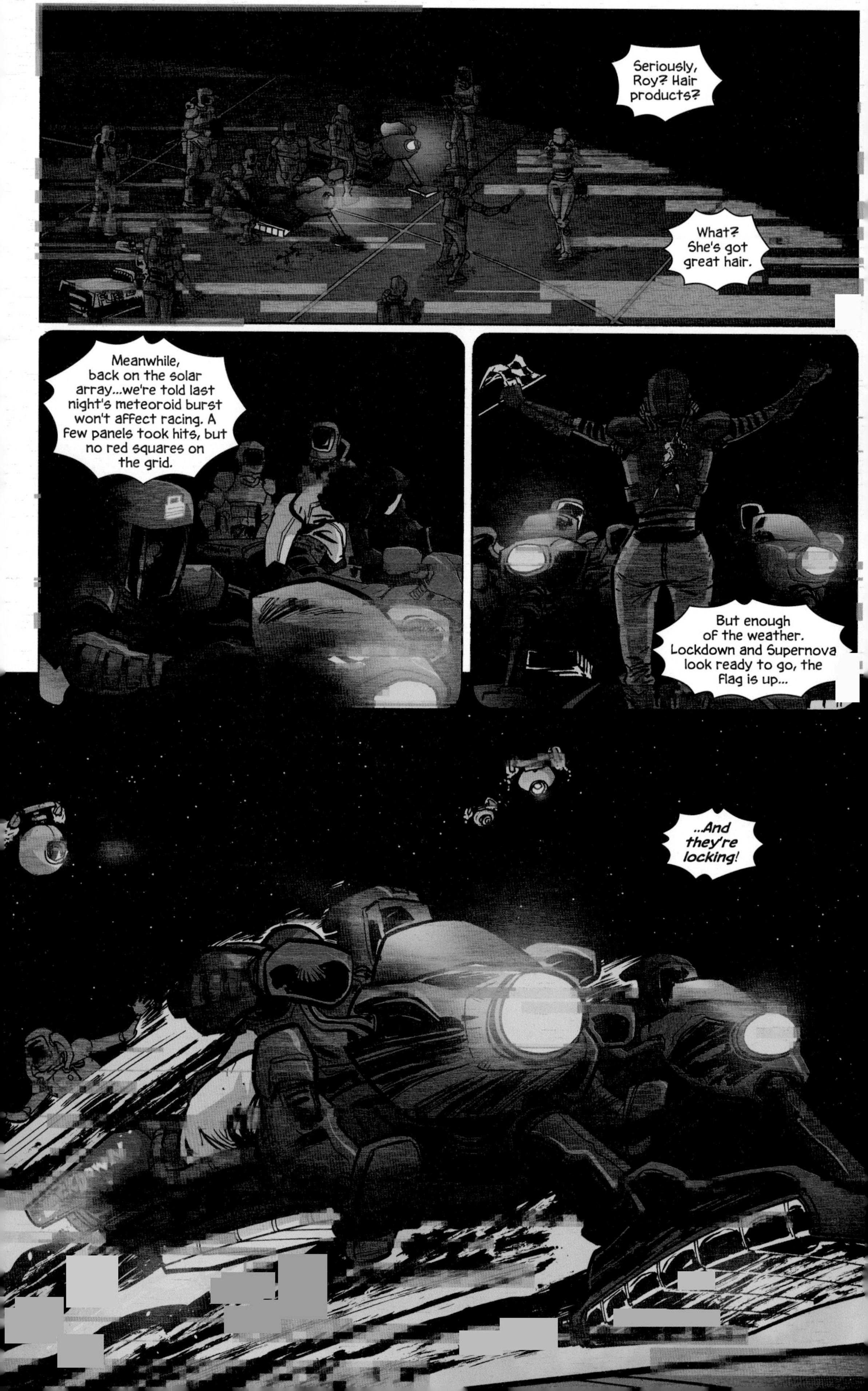
Seriously, Roy? Hair products?
What? She's got great hair.
Meanwhile, back on the solar array...we're told last night's meteoroid burst won't affect racing. A few panels took hits, but no red squares on the grid.
But enough of the weather. Lockdown and Supernova look ready to go, the flag is up...
...And they're locking!

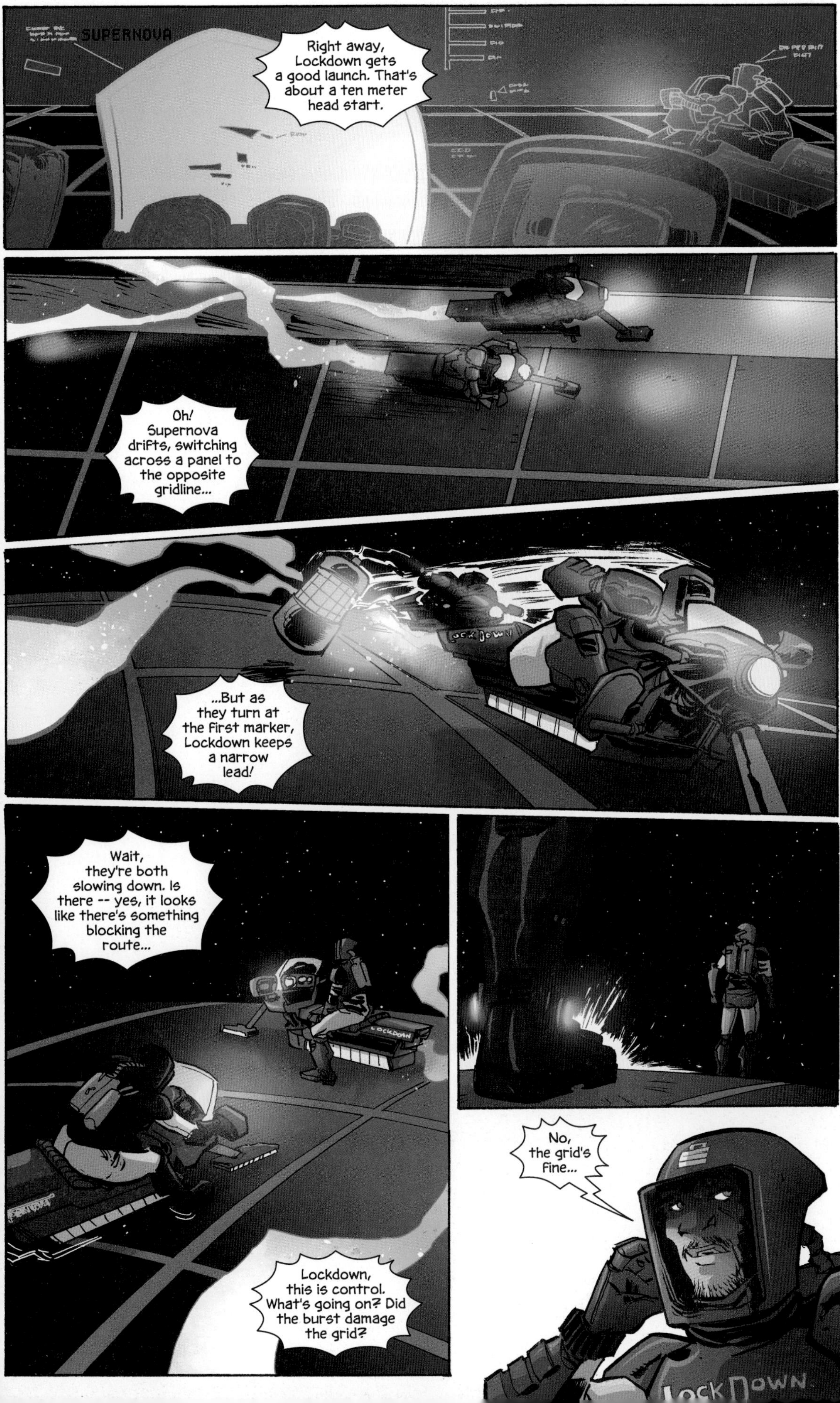
SUPERNOVA
Right away, Lockdown gets a good launch. That's about a ten meter head start.
Oh! Supernova drifts, switching across a panel to the opposite gridline...
...But as they turn at the first marker, Lockdown keeps a narrow lead!
LOCKDOWN
Wait, they're both slowing down. Is there -- yes, it looks like there's something blocking the route...
LOCKDOWN
No, the grid's fine...
Lockdown, this is control. What's going on? Did the burst damage the grid?
LOCK DOWN

THE FUSE

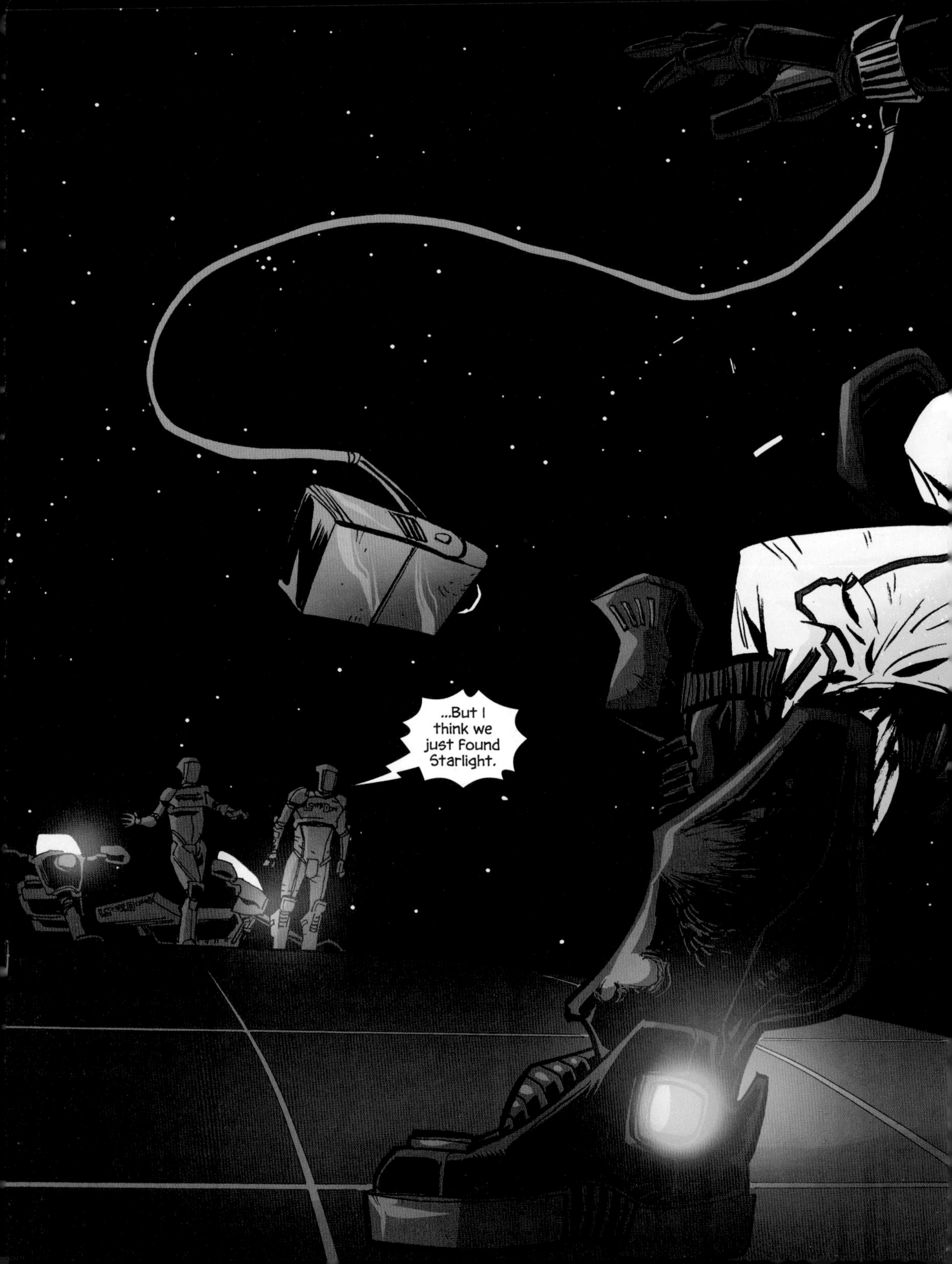
...But I think we just found Starlight.

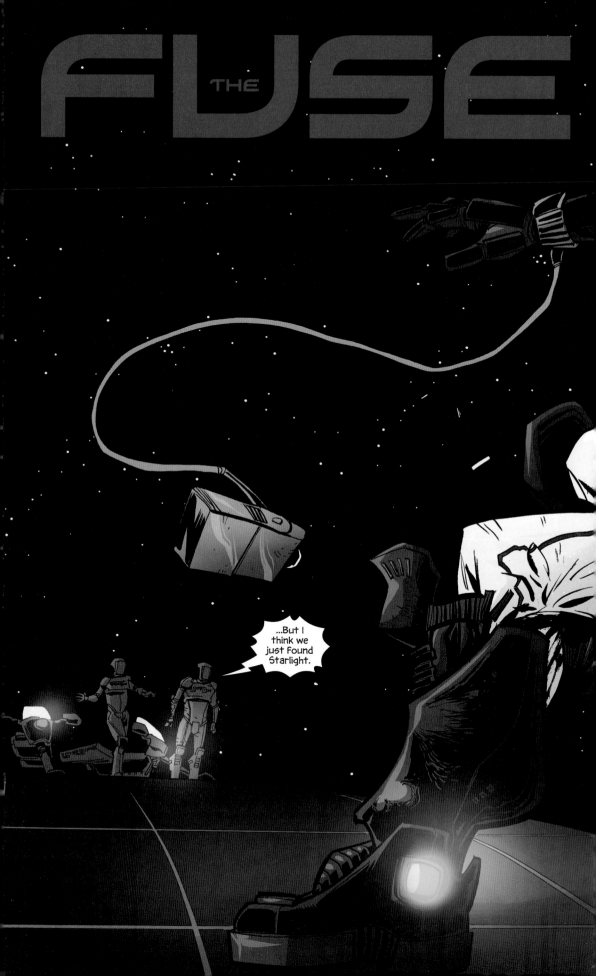

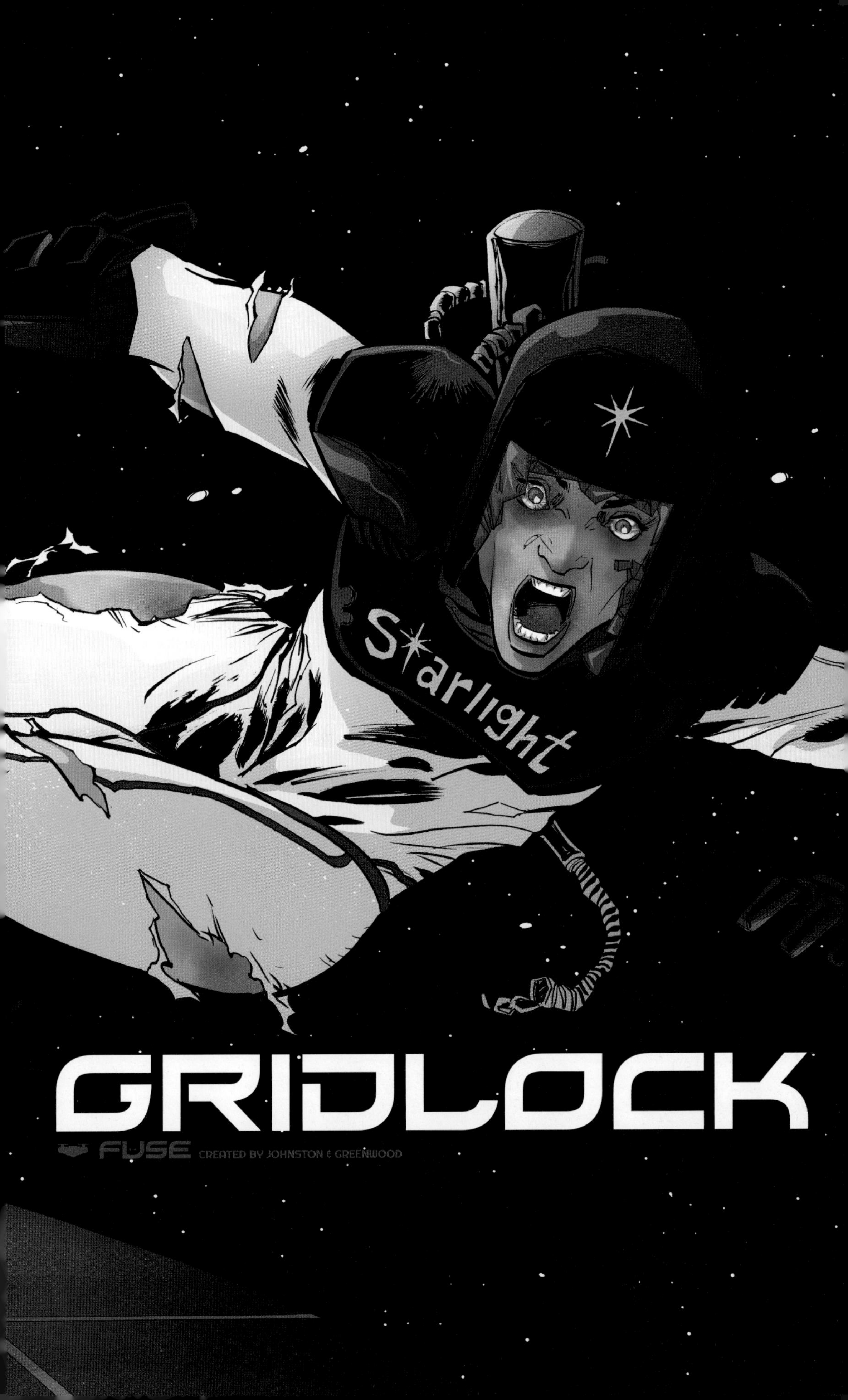
Starlight
GRIDLOCK
FUSE
CREATED BY JOHNSTON & GREENWOOD

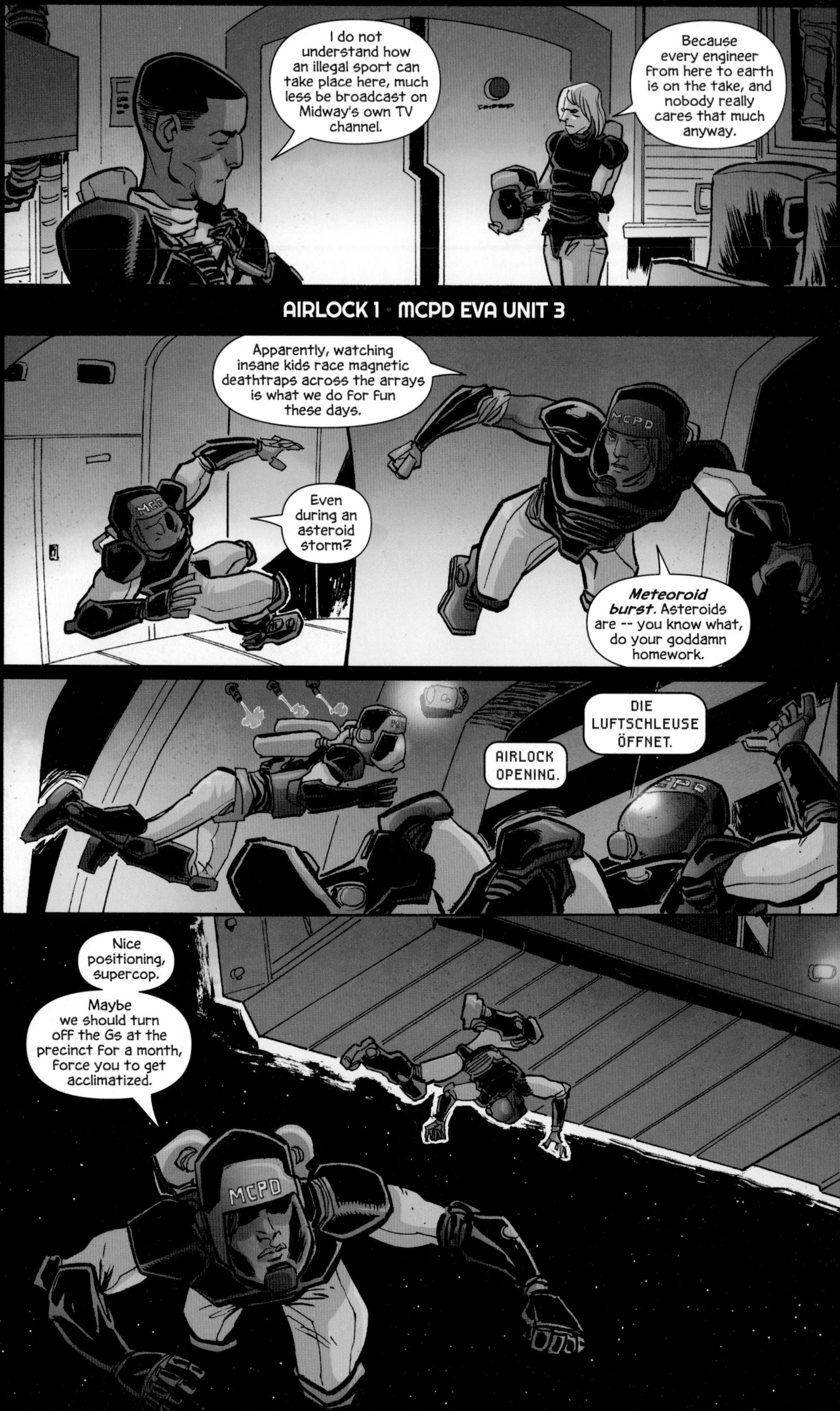
I do not understand how an illegal sport can take place here, much less be broadcast on Midway's own TV channel.
Because every engineer from here to earth is on the take, and nobody really cares that much anyway.
AIRLOCK 1 · MCPD EVA UNIT 3
Apparently, watching insane kids race magnetic deathtraps across the arrays is what we do for fun these days.
MCPD
Even during an asteroid storm?
MCPD
Meteoroid burst. Asteroids are -- you know what, do your goddamn homework.
AIRLOCK OPENING.
DIE LUFTSCHLEUSE ÖFFNET.
Nice positioning, supercop.
Maybe we should turn off the Gs at the precinct for a month, force you to get acclimatized.
MCPD

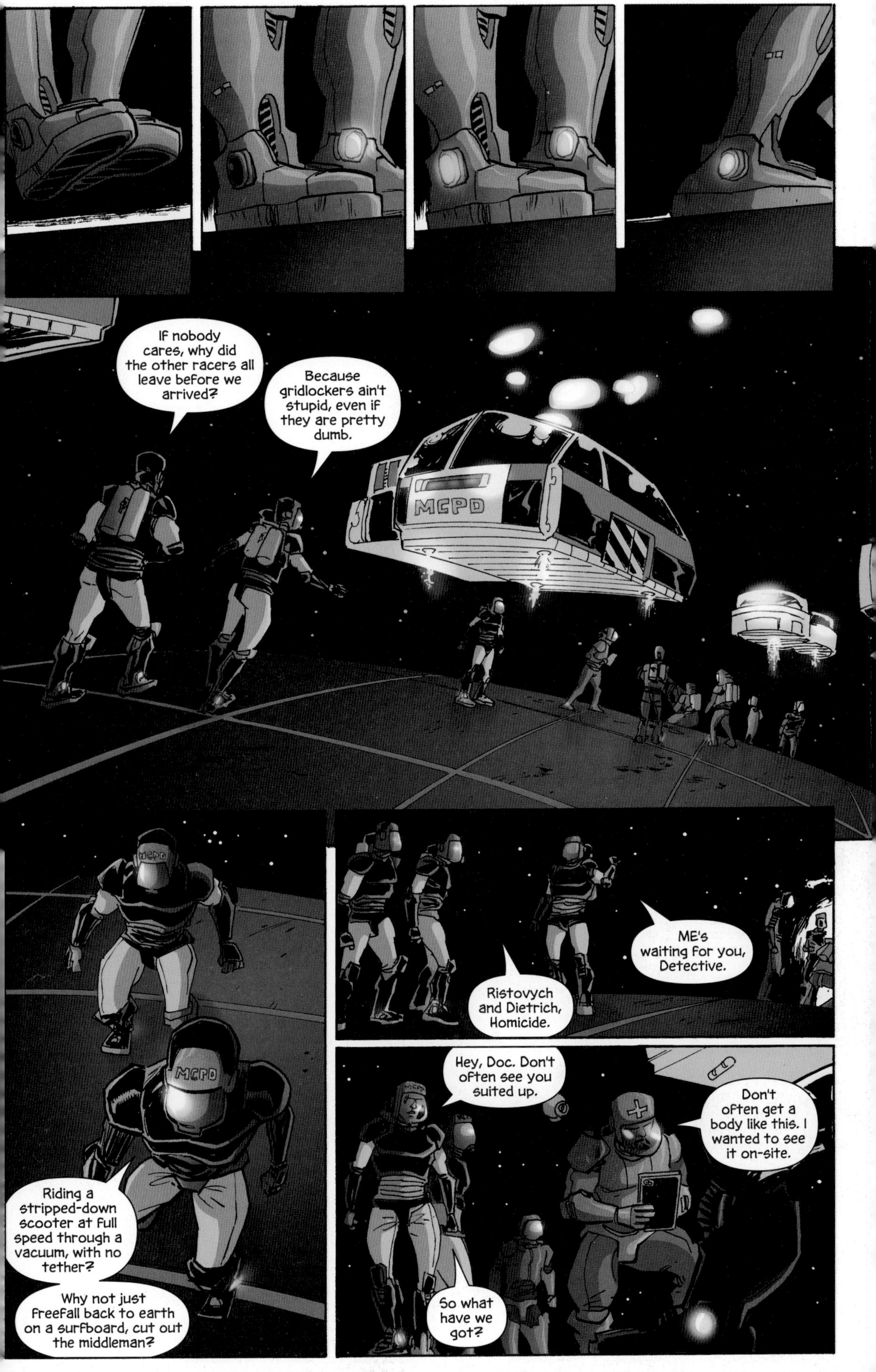

If nobody cares, why did the other racers all leave before we arrived?
Because gridlockers ain't stupid, even if they are pretty dumb.
MCPD
MCPD
MCPD
Riding a stripped-down scooter at full speed through a vacuum, with no tether?
Why not just freefall back to earth on a surfboard, cut out the middleman?
Ristovych and Dietrich, Homicide.
ME's waiting for you, Detective.
Hey, Doc. Don't often see you suited up.
Don't often get a body like this. I wanted to see it on-site.
So what have we got?

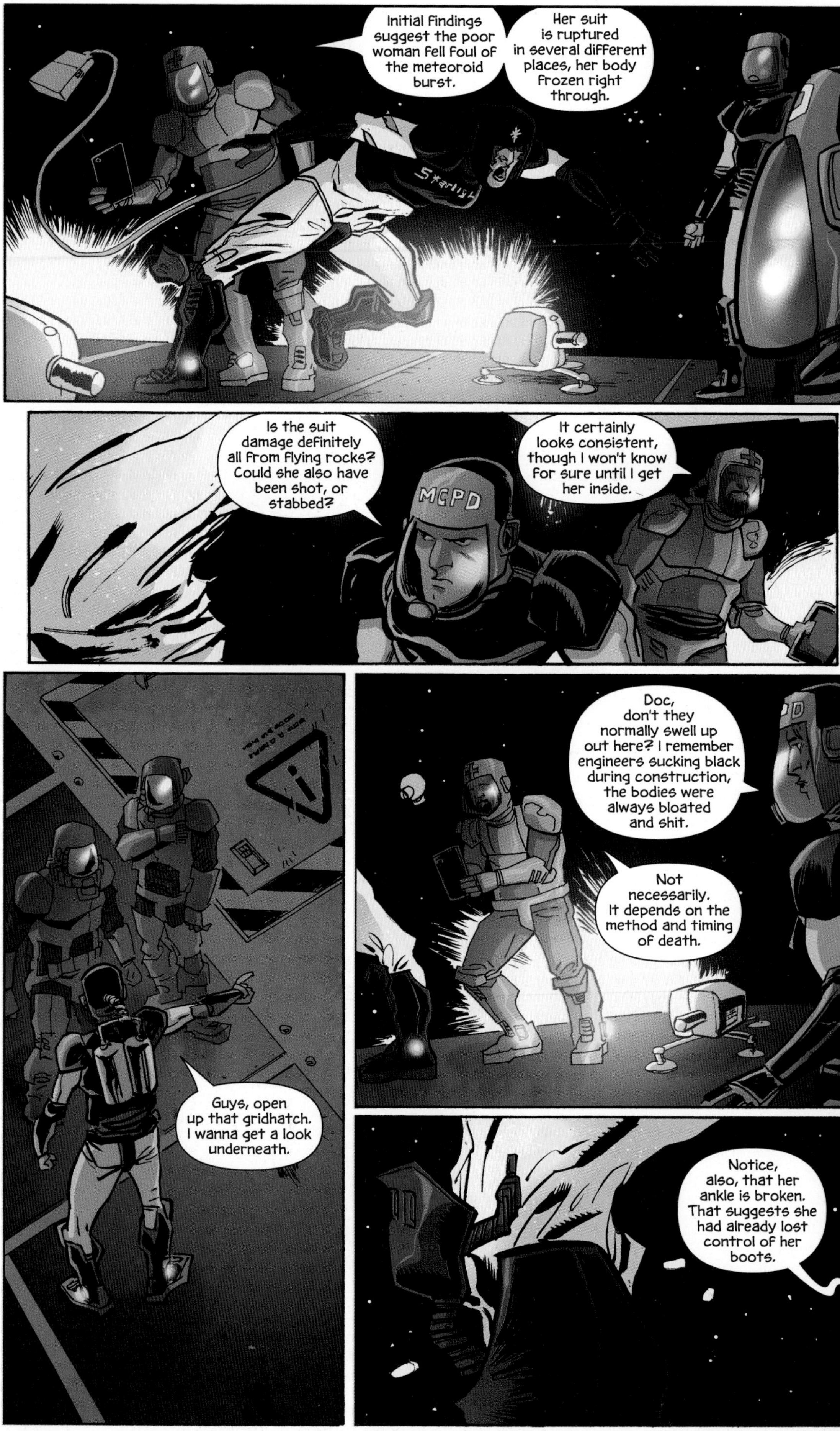
Initial findings suggest the poor woman fell foul of the meteoroid burst.
Her suit is ruptured in several different places, her body frozen right through.
Is the suit damage definitely all from flying rocks? Could she also have been shot, or stabbed?
MCPD
It certainly looks consistent, though I won't know for sure until I get her inside.
Guys, open up that gridhatch. I wanna get a look underneath.
Doc, don't they normally swell up out here? I remember engineers sucking black during construction, the bodies were always bloated and shit.
Not necessarily. It depends on the method and timing of death.
Notice, also, that her ankle is broken. That suggests she had already lost control of her boots.

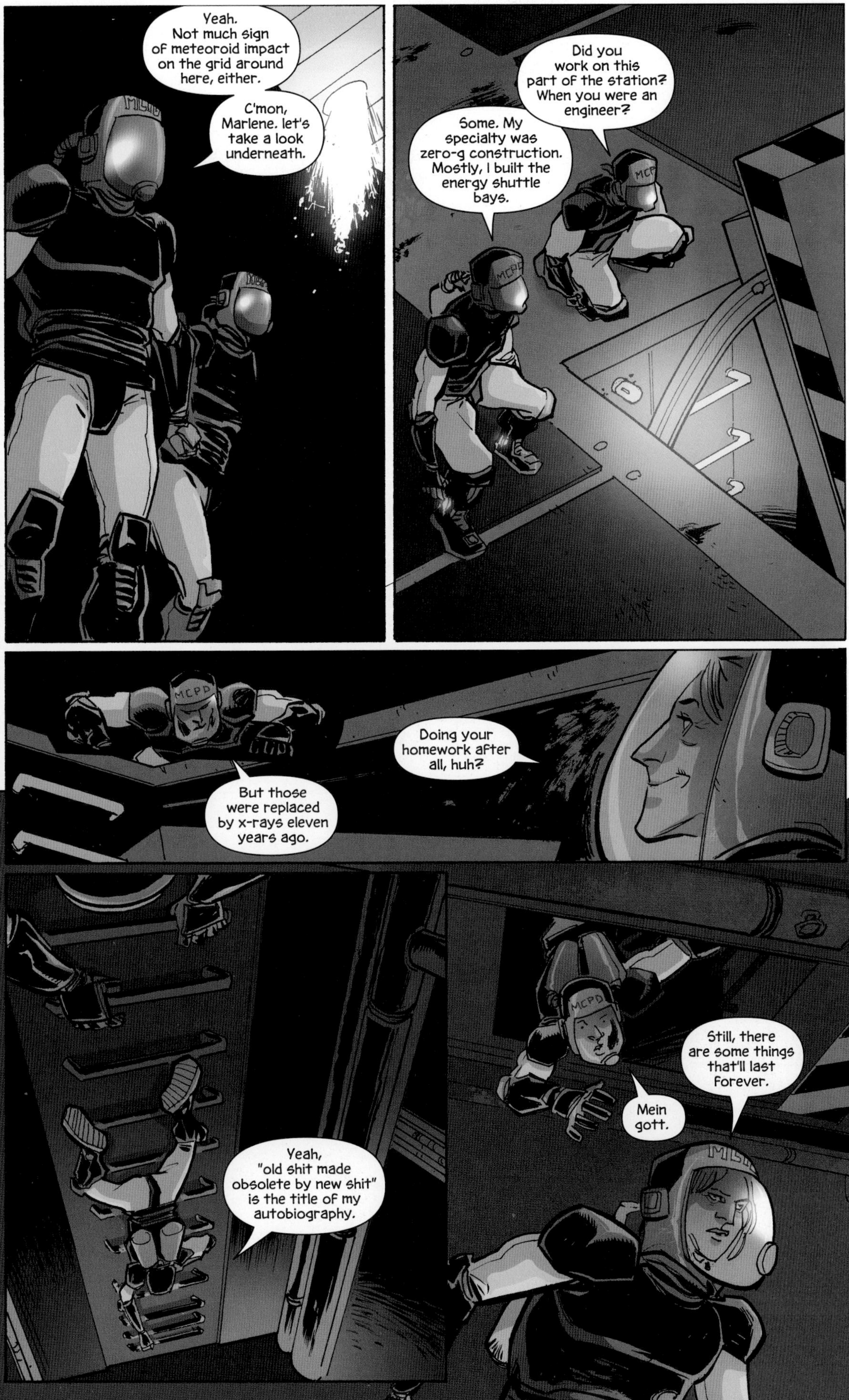
Yeah. Not much sign of meteoroid impact on the grid around here, either.
C'mon, Marlene. let's take a look underneath.
Did you work on this part of the station? When you were an engineer?
Some. My specialty was zero-g construction. Mostly, I built the energy shuttle bays.
But those were replaced by x-rays eleven years ago.
Doing your homework after all, huh?
Yeah, "old shit made obsolete by new shit" is the title of my autobiography.
Mein gott.
Still, there are some things that'll last forever.

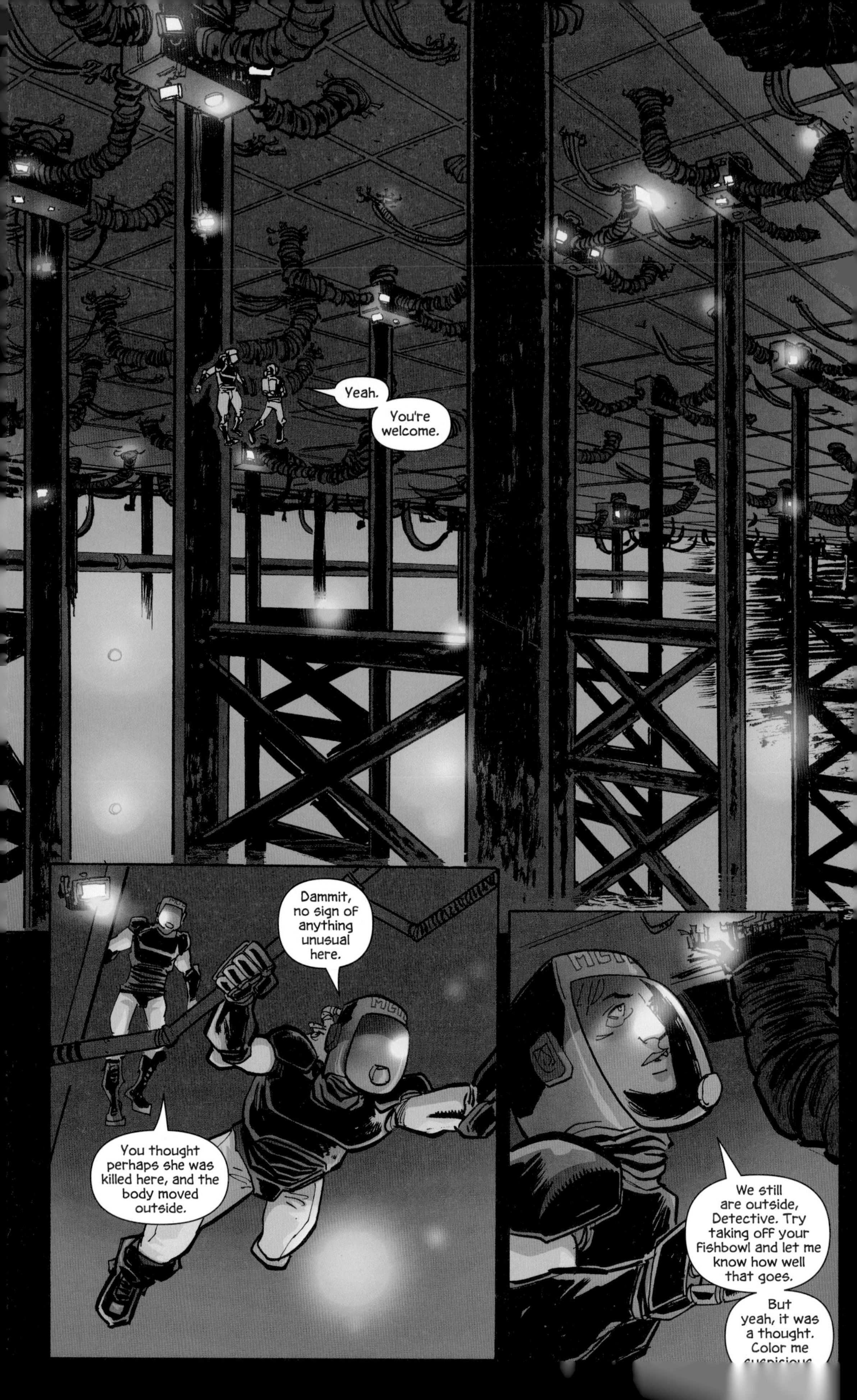
Yeah.
You're welcome.
Dammit, no sign of anything unusual here.
You thought perhaps she was killed here, and the body moved outside.
We still are outside, Detective. Try taking off your Fishbowl and let me know how well that goes.
But yeah, it was a thought. Color me

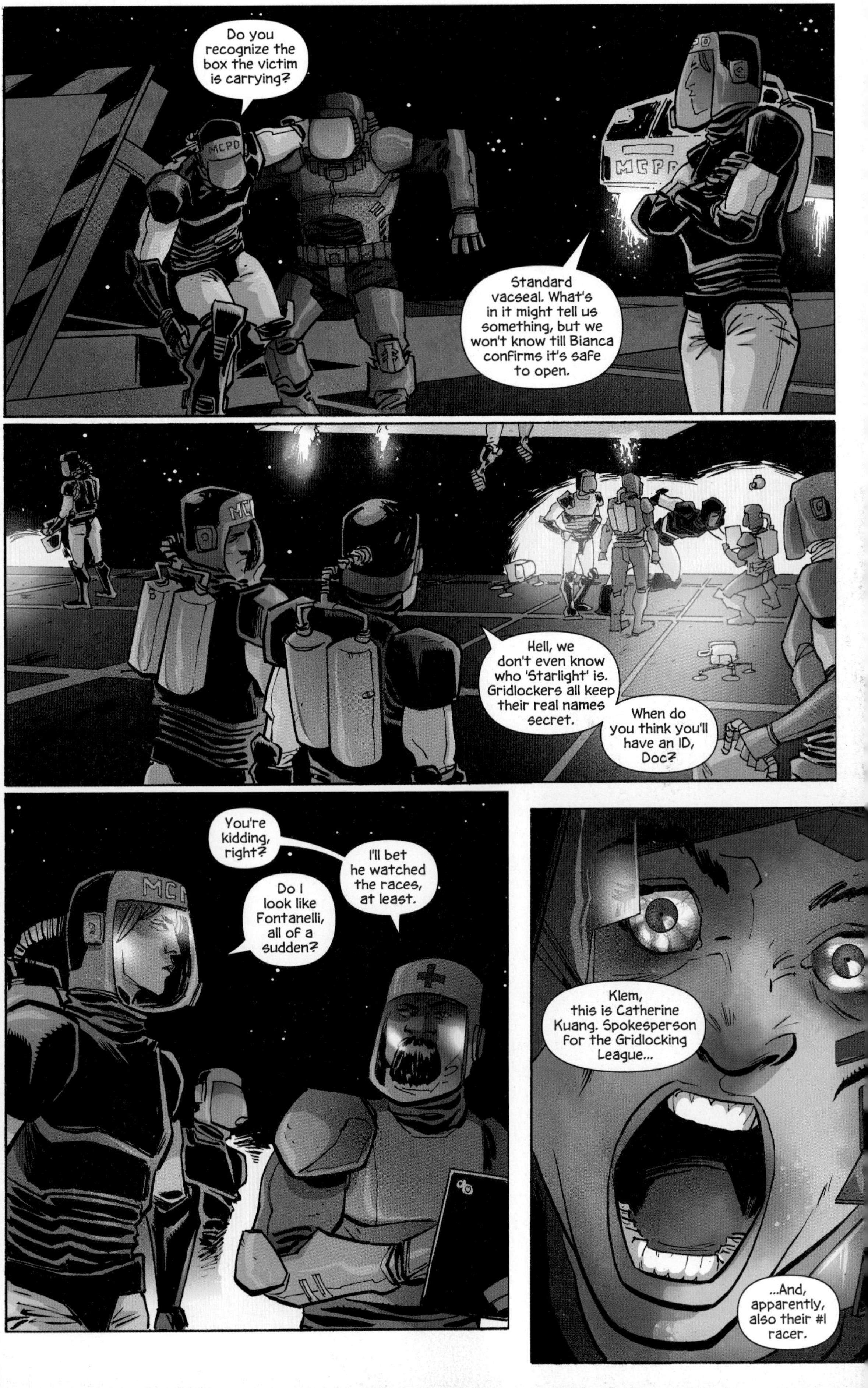
Do you recognize the box the victim is carrying?
Standard vacseal. What's in it might tell us something, but we won't know till Bianca confirms it's safe to open.
MCPD
Hell, we don't even know who 'Starlight' is. Gridlockers all keep their real names secret.
When do you think you'll have an ID, Doc?
You're kidding, right?
I'll bet he watched the races, at least.
Do I look like Fontanelli, all of a sudden?
Klem, this is Catherine Kuang. Spokesperson for the Gridlocking League...
...And, apparently, also their #1 racer.

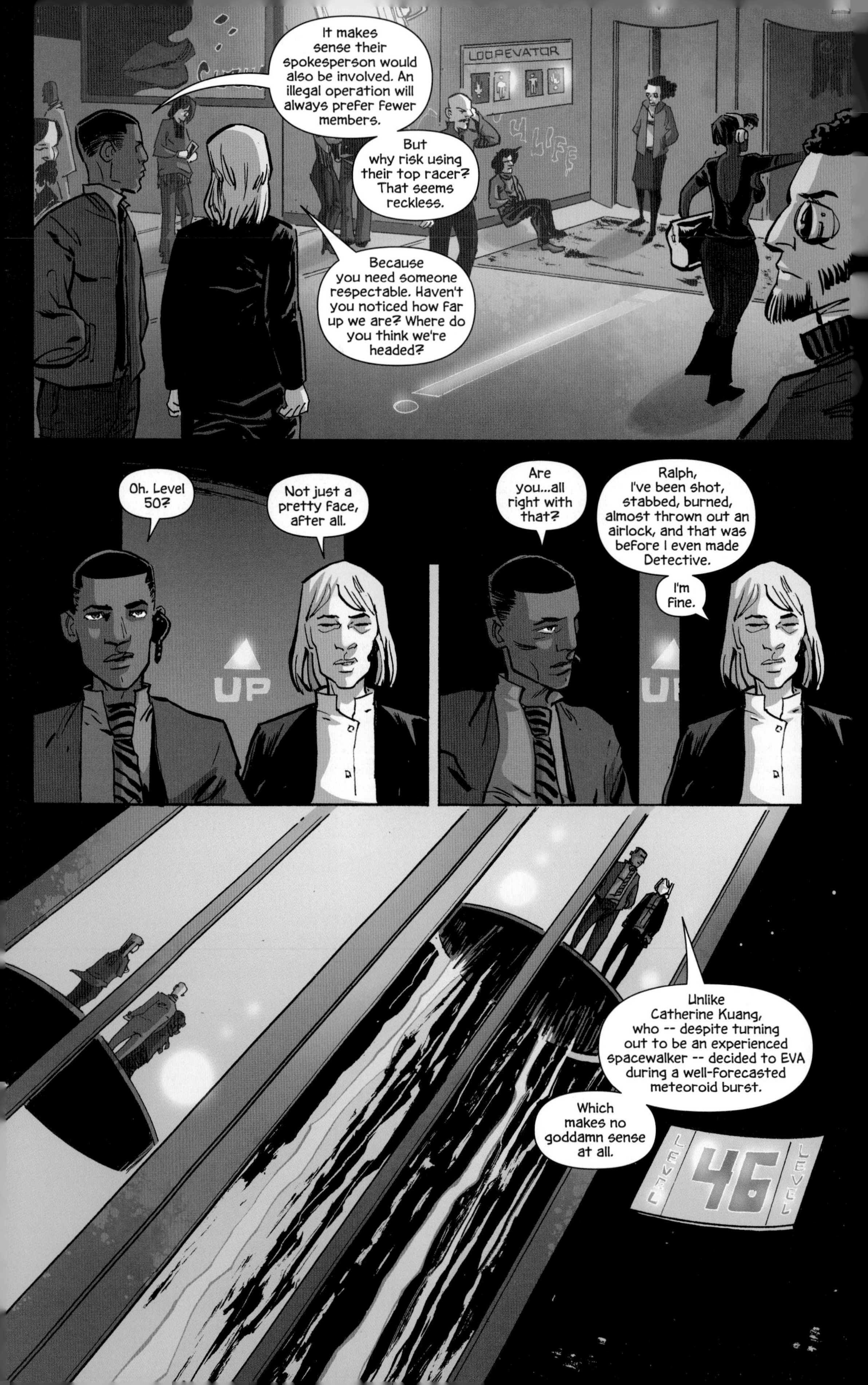
LOOPEVATOR
It makes sense their spokesperson would also be involved. An illegal operation will always prefer fewer members.
But why risk using their top racer? That seems reckless.
Because you need someone respectable. Haven't you noticed how far up we are? Where do you think we're headed?
Oh. Level 50?
Not just a pretty face, after all.
UP
Are you...all right with that?
Ralph, I've been shot, stabbed, burned, almost thrown out an airlock, and that was before I even made Detective.
I'm fine.
Unlike Catherine Kuang, who -- despite turning out to be an experienced spacewalker -- decided to EVA during a well-forecasted meteoroid burst.
Which makes no goddamn sense at all.
LEVEL 46 LEVEL

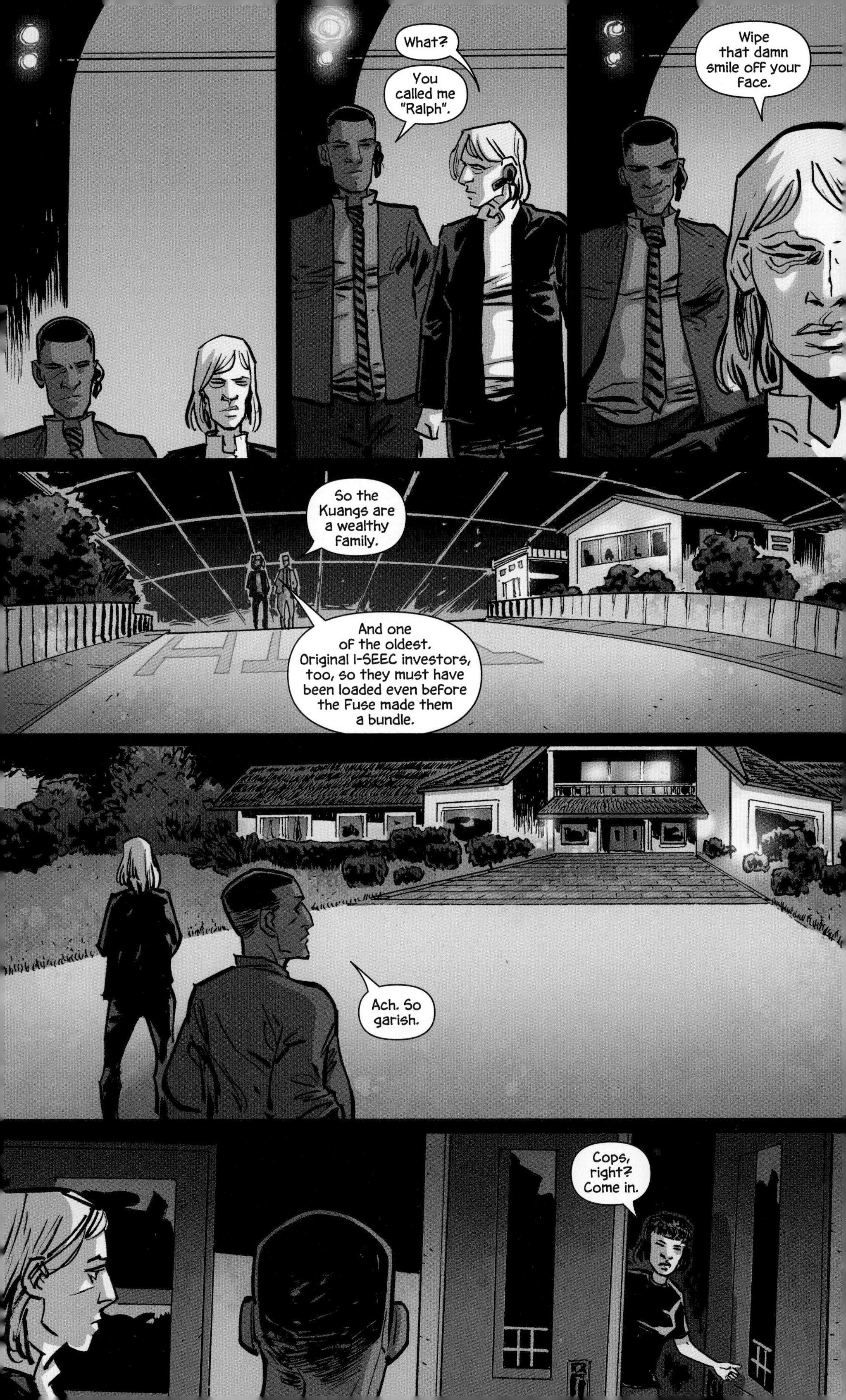
What?
You called me "Ralph".
Wipe that damn smile off your face.
So the Kuangs are a wealthy family.
And one of the oldest. Original I-SEEC investors, too, so they must have been loaded even before the Fuse made them a bundle.
Ach. So garish.
Cops, right? Come in.

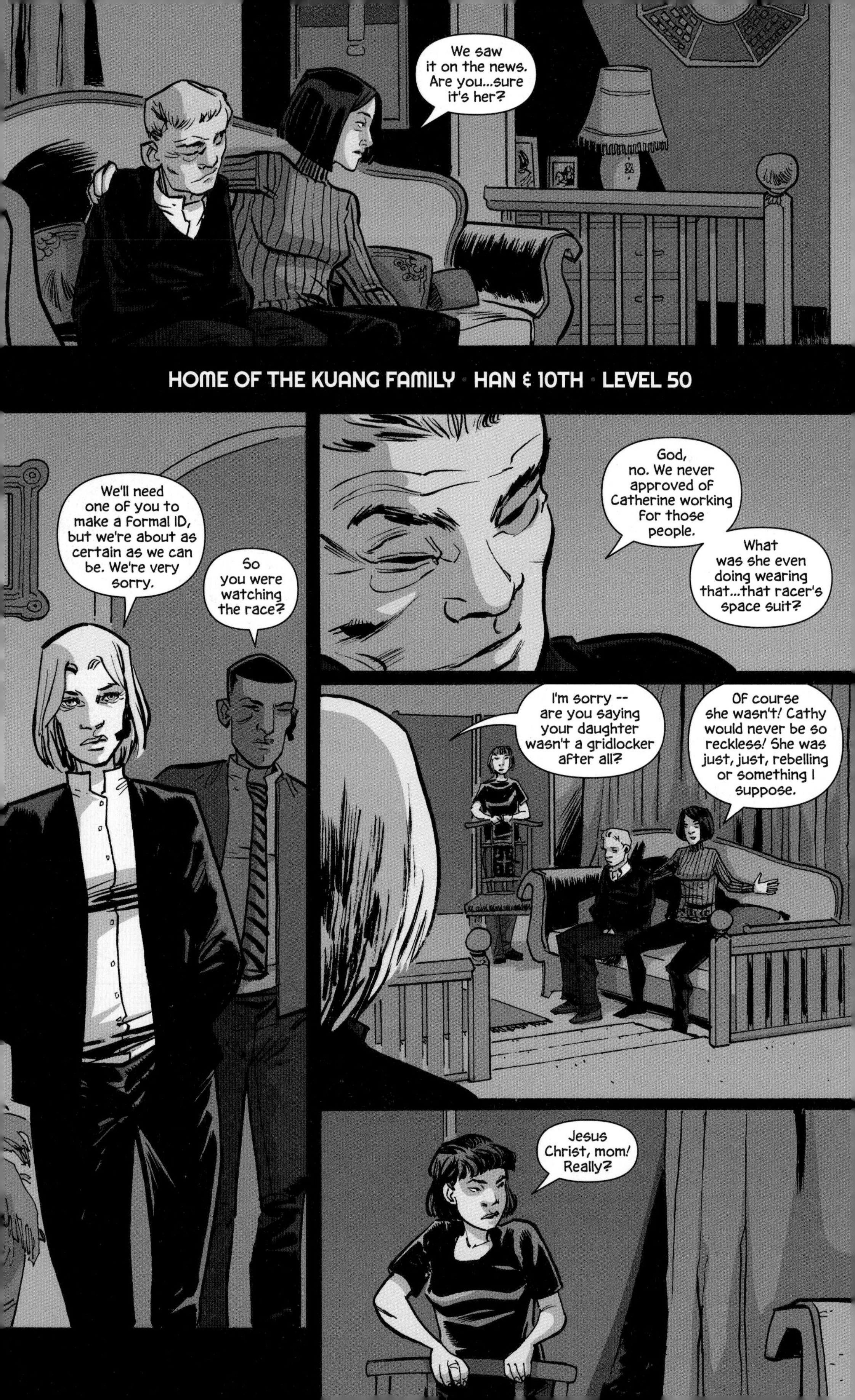

We saw it on the news. Are you...sure it's her?
HOME OF THE KUANG FAMILY • HAN & 10TH • LEVEL 50
We'll need one of you to make a formal ID, but we're about as certain as we can be. We're very sorry.
So you were watching the race?
God, no. We never approved of Catherine working for those people.
What was she even doing wearing that...that racer's space suit?
I'm sorry -- are you saying your daughter wasn't a gridlocker after all?
Of course she wasn't! Cathy would never be so reckless! She was just, just, rebelling or something I suppose.
Jesus Christ, mom! Really?

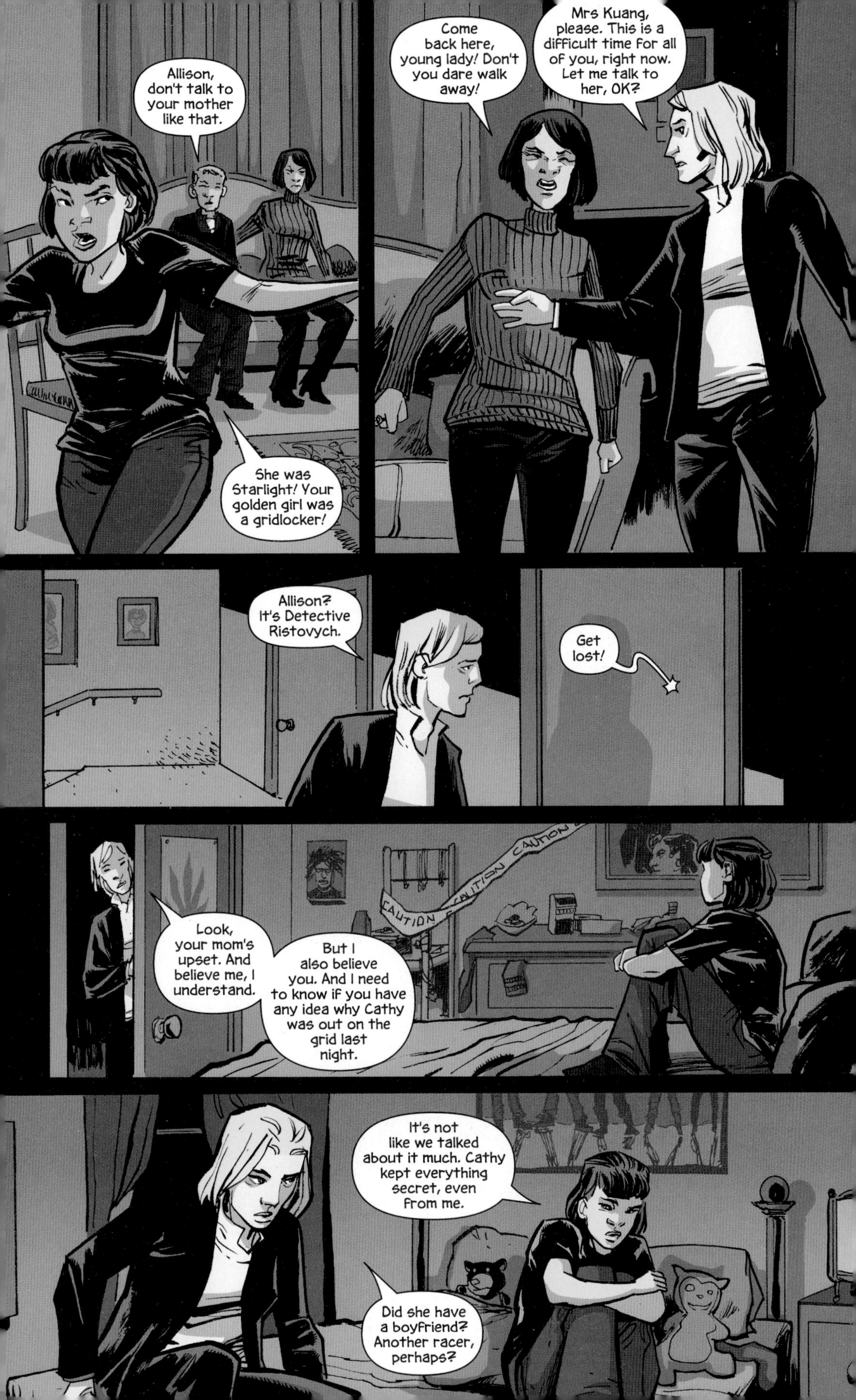

Allison, don't talk to your mother like that.
She was Starlight! Your golden girl was a gridlocker!
Come back here, young lady! Don't you dare walk away!
Mrs Kuang, please. This is a difficult time for all of you, right now. Let me talk to her, OK?
Allison? It's Detective Ristovych.
Get lost!
CAUTION
Look, your mom's upset. And believe me, I understand.
But I also believe you. And I need to know if you have any idea why Cathy was out on the grid last night.
It's not like we talked about it much. Cathy kept everything secret, even from me.
Did she have a boyfriend? Another racer, perhaps?

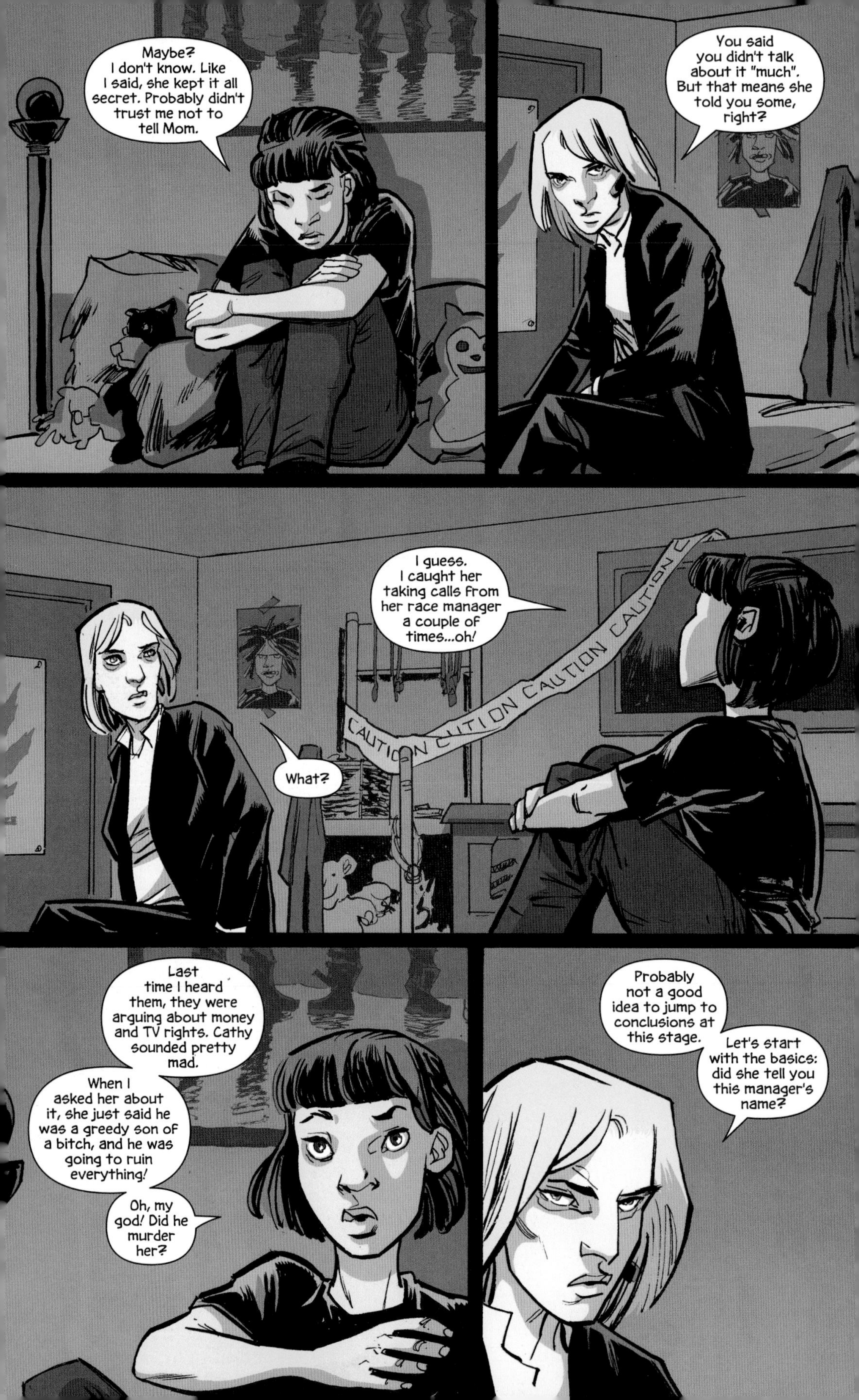
Maybe? I don't know. Like I said, she kept it all secret. Probably didn't trust me not to tell Mom.
You said you didn't talk about it "much". But that means she told you some, right?
I guess. I caught her taking calls from her race manager a couple of times...oh!
What?
CAUTION CAUTION CAUTION CAUTION CAUTION
Last time I heard them, they were arguing about money and TV rights. Cathy sounded pretty mad.
When I asked her about it, she just said he was a greedy son of a bitch, and he was going to ruin everything!
Oh, my god! Did he murder her?
Probably not a good idea to jump to conclusions at this stage.
Let's start with the basics: did she tell you this manager's name?

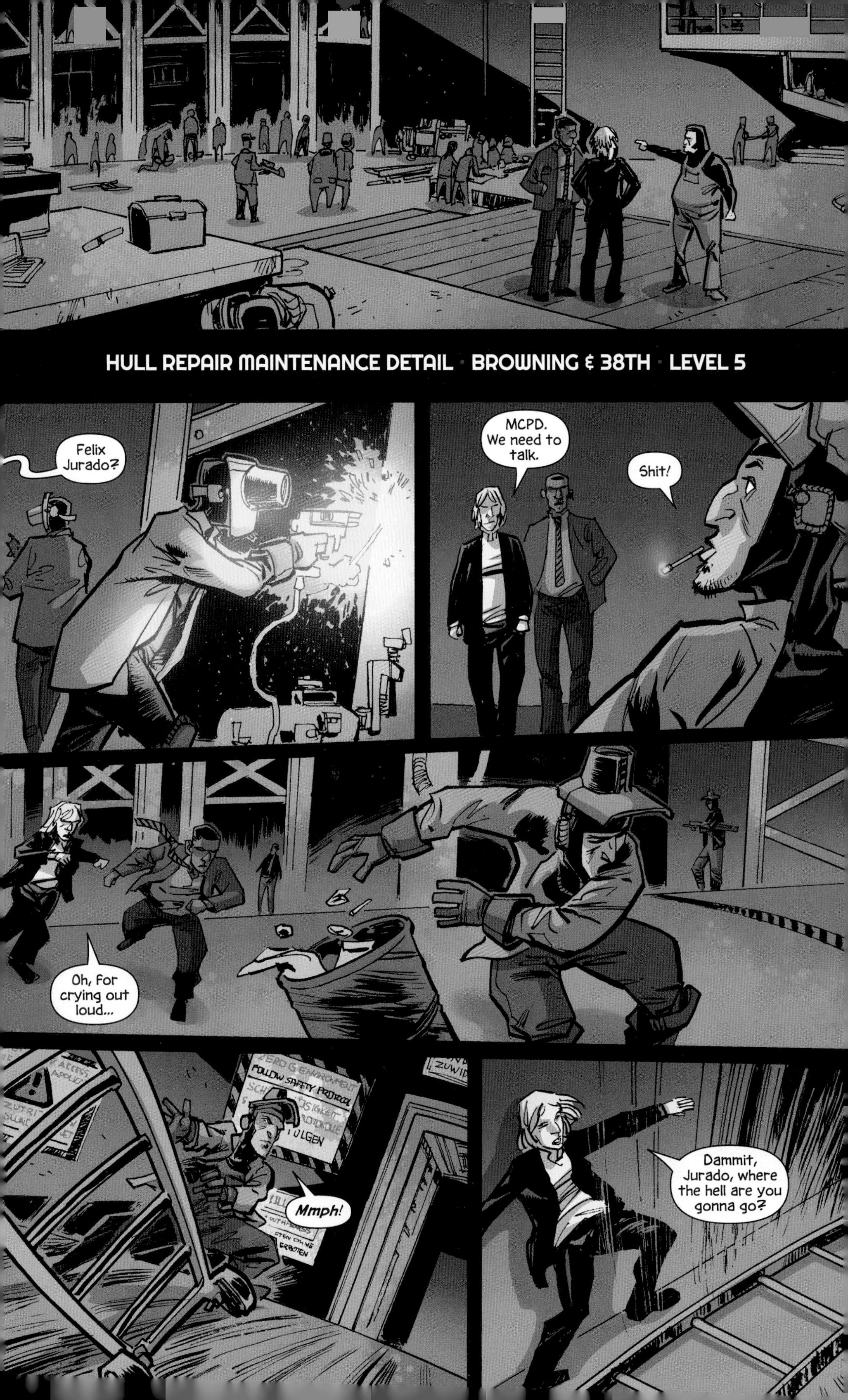
HULL REPAIR MAINTENANCE DETAIL • BROWNING & 38TH • LEVEL 5
Felix Jurado?
MCPD. We need to talk.
Shit!
Oh, for crying out loud...
Mmph!
Dammit, Jurado, where the hell are you gonna go?

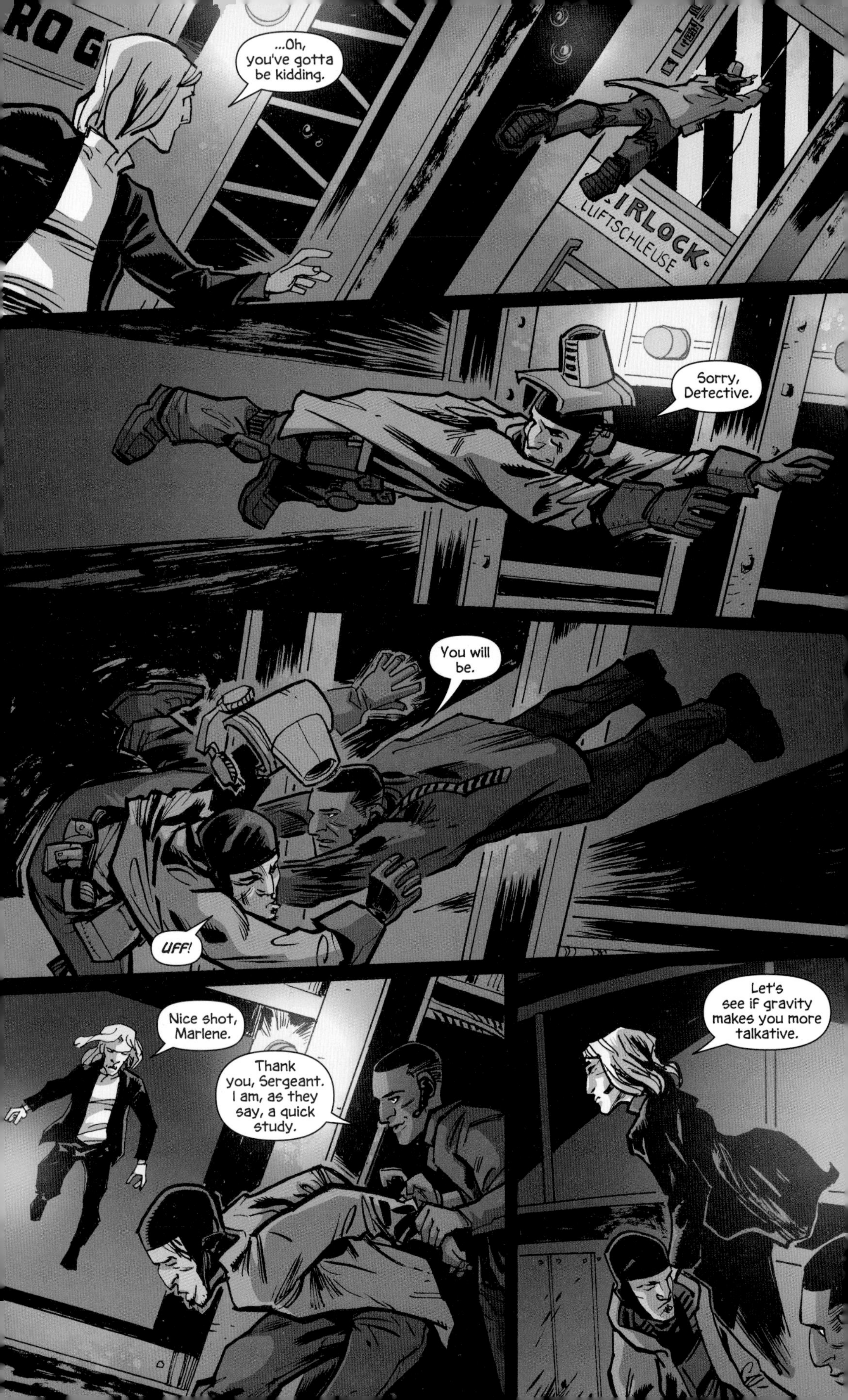
RO G
...Oh, you've gotta be kidding.
AIRLOCK
LUFTSCHLEUSE
Sorry, Detective.
You will be.
UFF!
Nice shot, Marlene.
Thank you, Sergeant. I am, as they say, a quick study.
Let's see if gravity makes you more talkative.

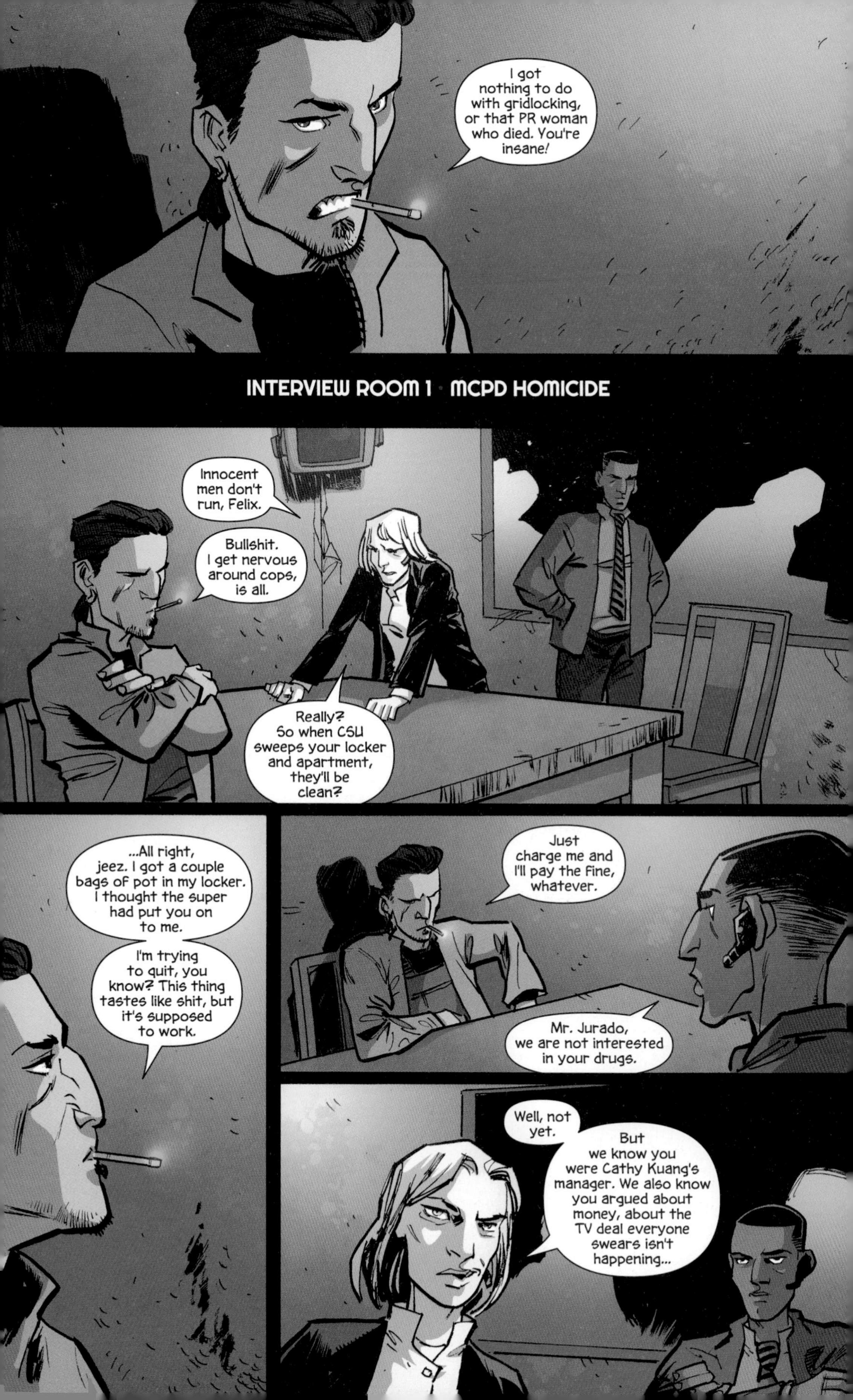
I got nothing to do with gridlocking, or that PR woman who died. You're insane!
INTERVIEW ROOM 1 · MCPD HOMICIDE
Innocent men don't run, Felix.
Bullshit. I get nervous around cops, is all.
Really? So when CSU sweeps your locker and apartment, they'll be clean?
...All right, jeez. I got a couple bags of pot in my locker. I thought the super had put you on to me.
I'm trying to quit, you know? This thing tastes like shit, but it's supposed to work.
Just charge me and I'll pay the fine, whatever.
Mr. Jurado, we are not interested in your drugs.
Well, not yet.
But we know you were Cathy Kuang's manager. We also know you argued about money, about the TV deal everyone swears isn't happening...

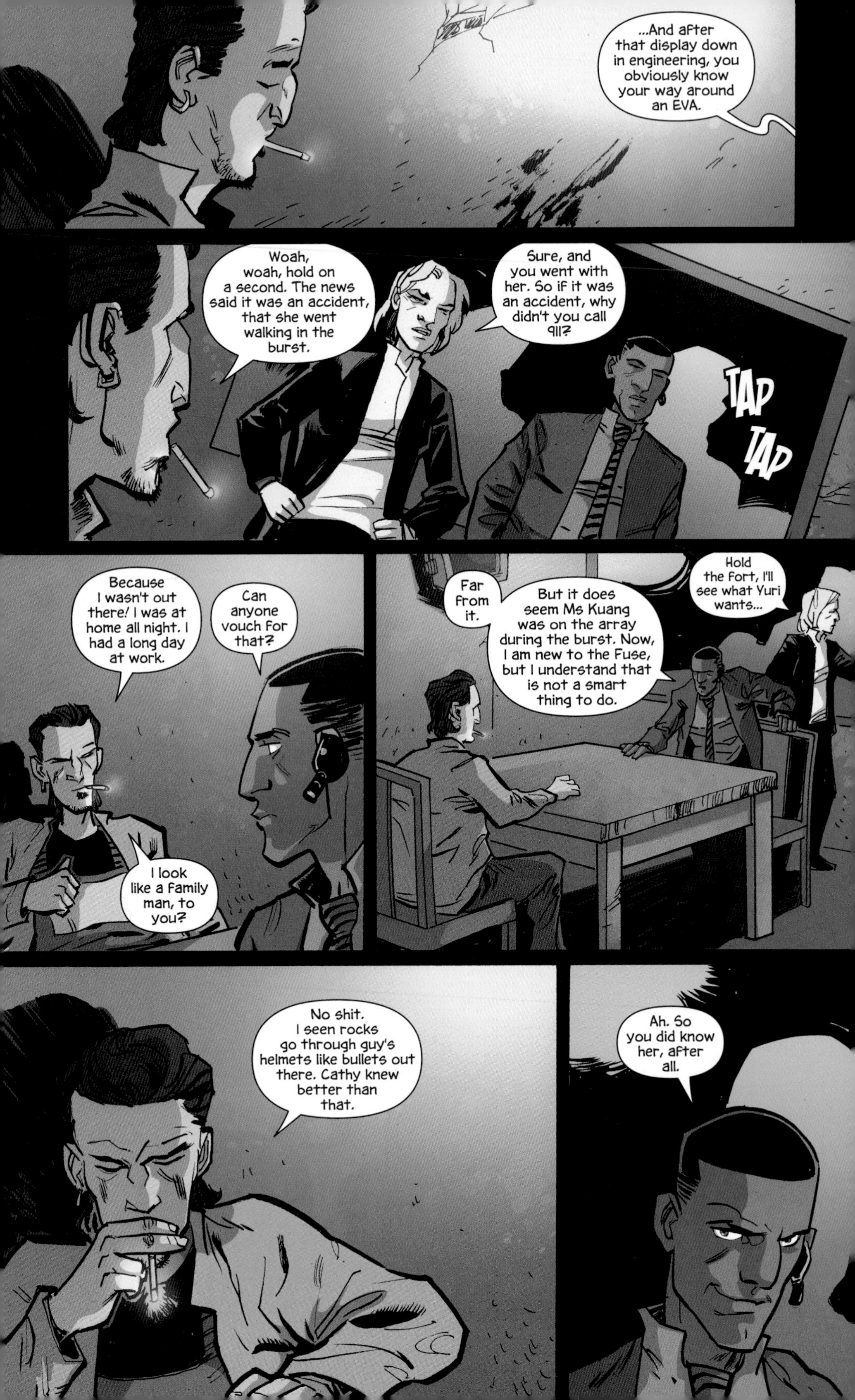
...And after that display down in engineering, you obviously know your way around an EVA.
Woah, woah, hold on a second. The news said it was an accident, that she went walking in the burst.
Sure, and you went with her. So if it was an accident, why didn't you call 911?
TAP
TAP
Because I wasn't out there! I was at home all night. I had a long day at work.
Can anyone vouch for that?
I look like a family man, to you?
Far from it.
But it does seem Ms Kuang was on the array during the burst. Now, I am new to the Fuse, but I understand that is not a smart thing to do.
Hold the Fort, I'll see what Yuri wants...
No shit. I seen rocks go through guy's helmets like bullets out there. Cathy knew better than that.
Ah. So you did know her, after all.

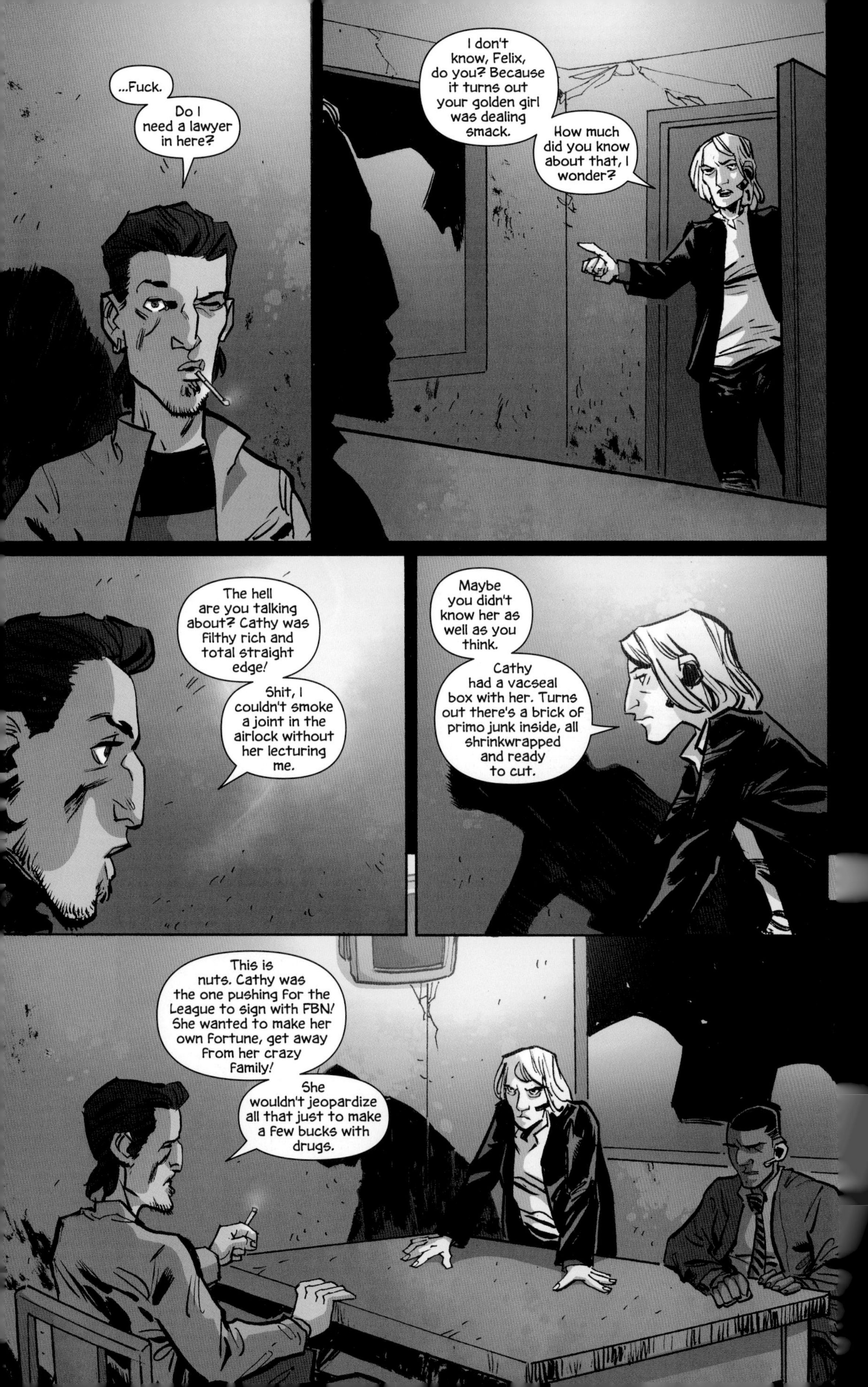
...Fuck.
Do I need a lawyer in here?
I don't know, Felix, do you? Because it turns out your golden girl was dealing smack.
How much did you know about that, I wonder?
The hell are you talking about? Cathy was filthy rich and total straight edge!
Shit, I couldn't smoke a joint in the airlock without her lecturing me.
Maybe you didn't know her as well as you think.
Cathy had a vacseal box with her. Turns out there's a brick of primo junk inside, all shrinkwrapped and ready to cut.
This is nuts. Cathy was the one pushing for the League to sign with FBN! She wanted to make her own fortune, get away from her crazy family!
She wouldn't jeopardize all that just to make a few bucks with drugs.

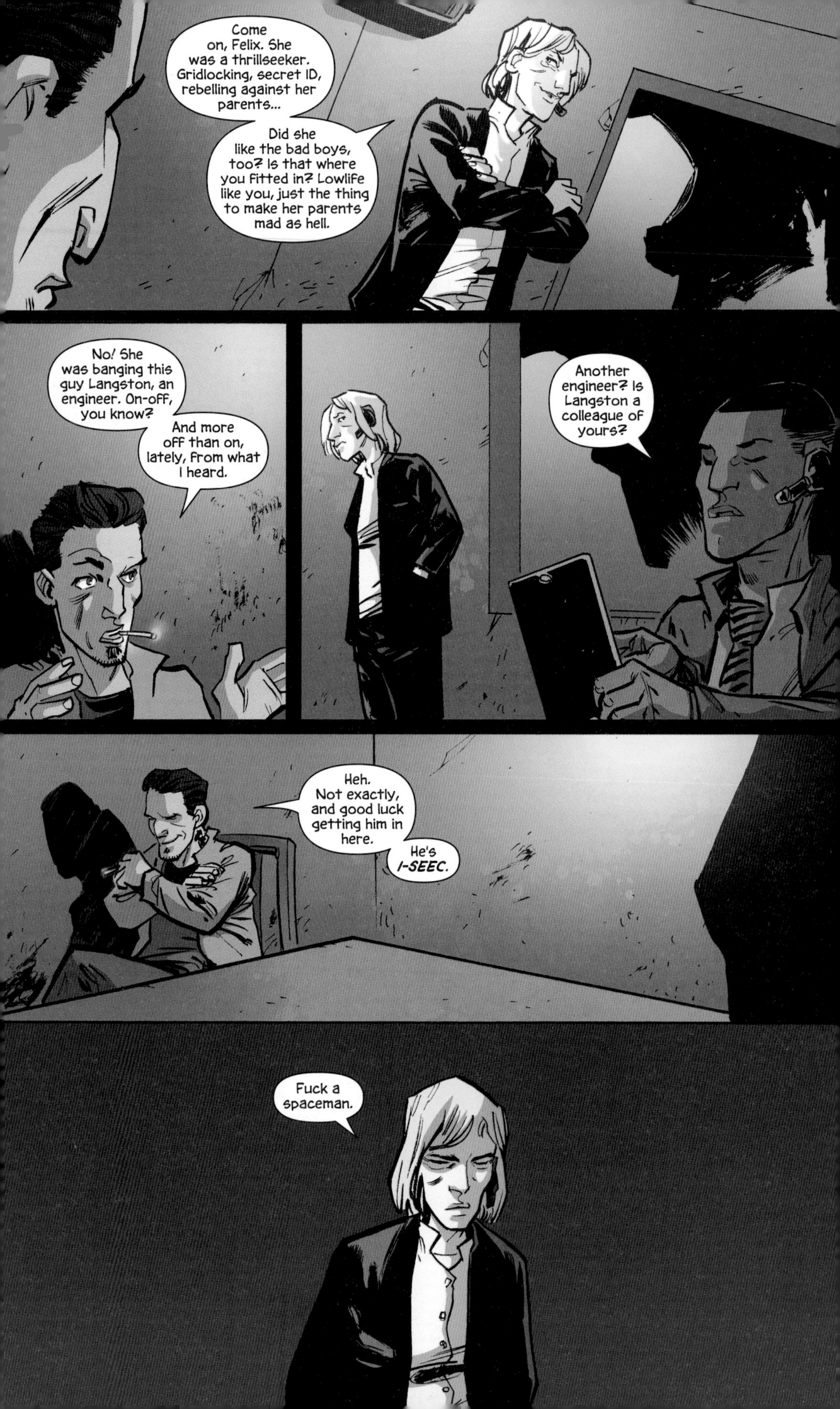
Come on, Felix. She was a thrillseeker. Gridlocking, secret ID, rebelling against her parents...
Did she like the bad boys, too? Is that where you fitted in? Lowlife like you, just the thing to make her parents mad as hell.
No! She was banging this guy Langston, an engineer. On-off, you know?
And more off than on, lately, from what I heard.
Another engineer? Is Langston a colleague of yours?
Heh. Not exactly, and good luck getting him in here.
He's *I-SEEC*.
Fuck a spaceman.

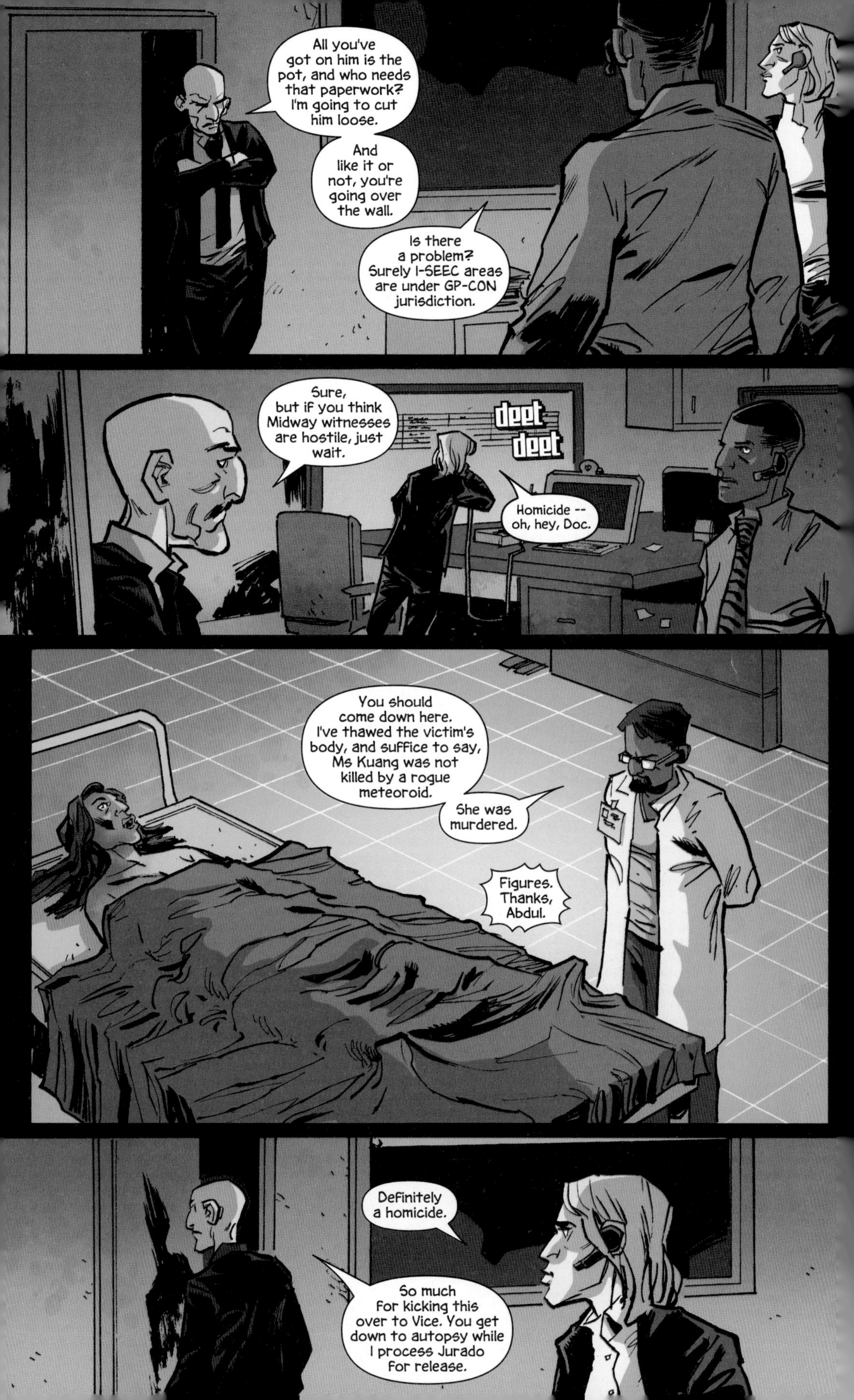
All you've got on him is the pot, and who needs that paperwork? I'm going to cut him loose.
And like it or not, you're going over the wall.
Is there a problem? Surely I-SEEC areas are under GP-CON jurisdiction.
Sure, but if you think Midway witnesses are hostile, just wait.
deet deet
Homicide -- oh, hey, Doc.
You should come down here. I've thawed the victim's body, and suffice to say, Ms Kuang was not killed by a rogue meteoroid.
She was murdered.
Figures. Thanks, Abdul.
Definitely a homicide.
So much for kicking this over to Vice. You get down to autopsy while I process Jurado for release.

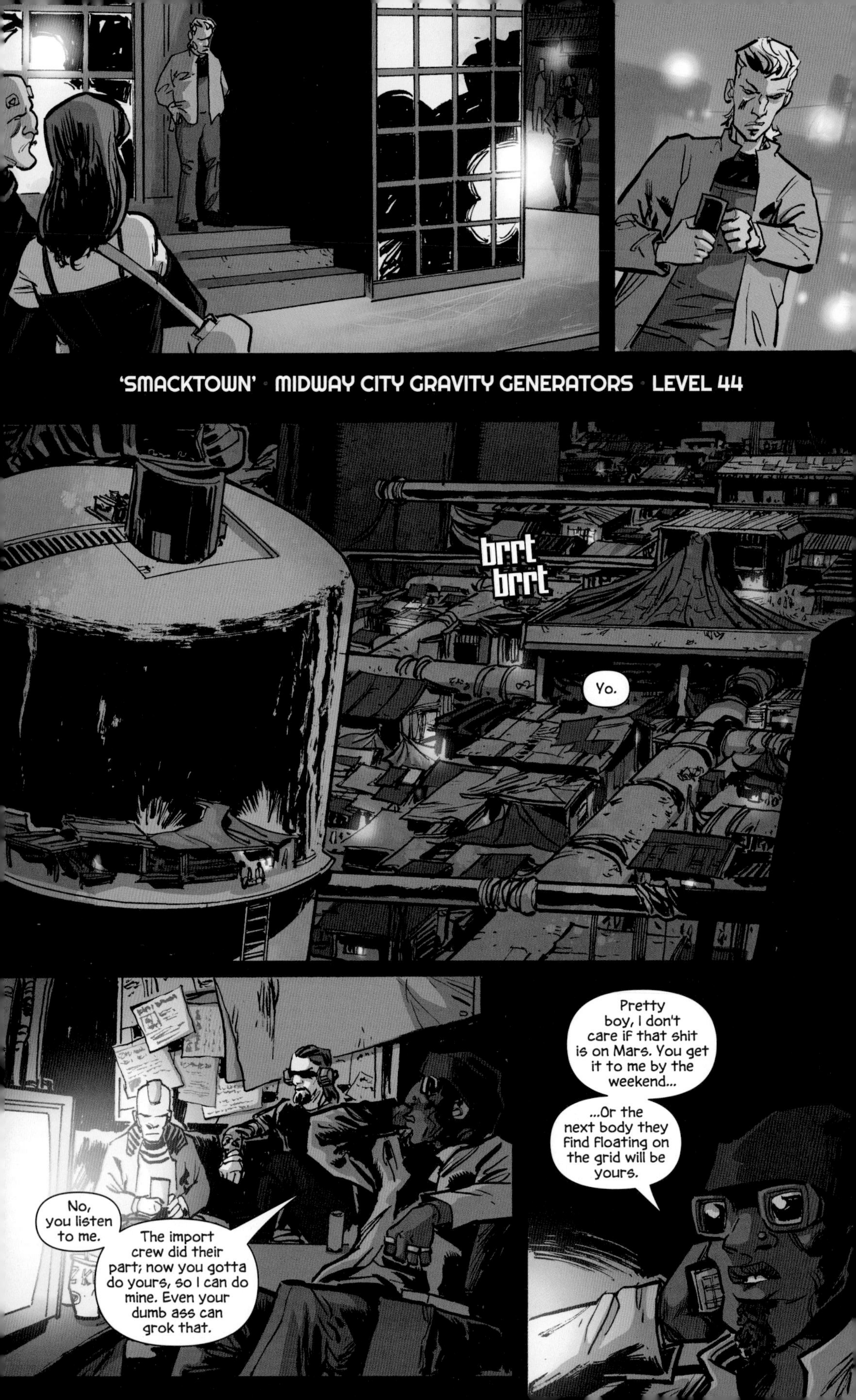
'SMACKTOWN' · MIDWAY CITY GRAVITY GENERATORS · LEVEL 44
brrt brrt
Yo.
No, you listen to me.
The import crew did their part; now you gotta do yours, so I can do mine. Even your dumb ass can grok that.
Pretty boy, I don't care if that shit is on Mars. You get it to me by the weekend...
...Or the next body they find floating on the grid will be yours.

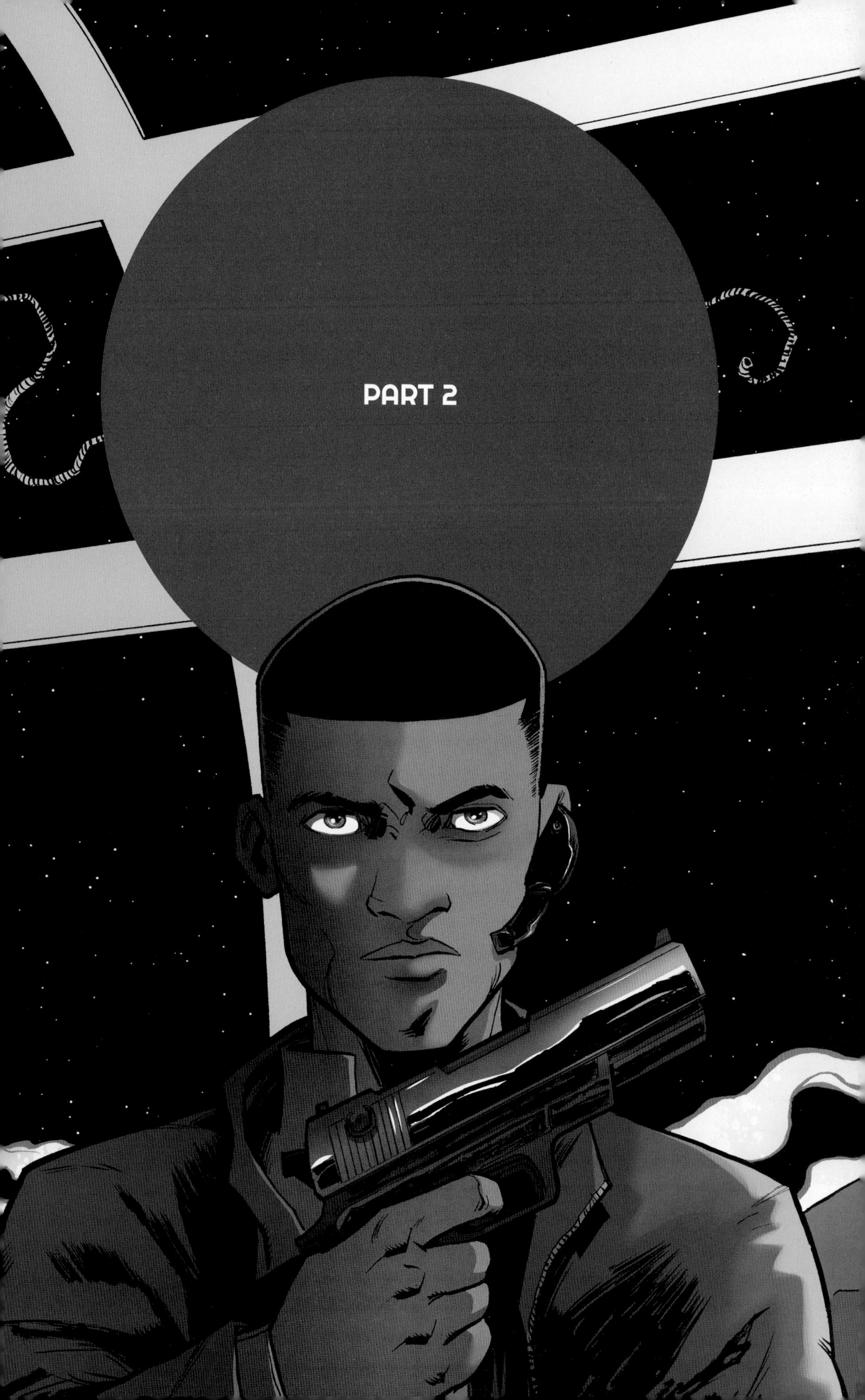
PART 2

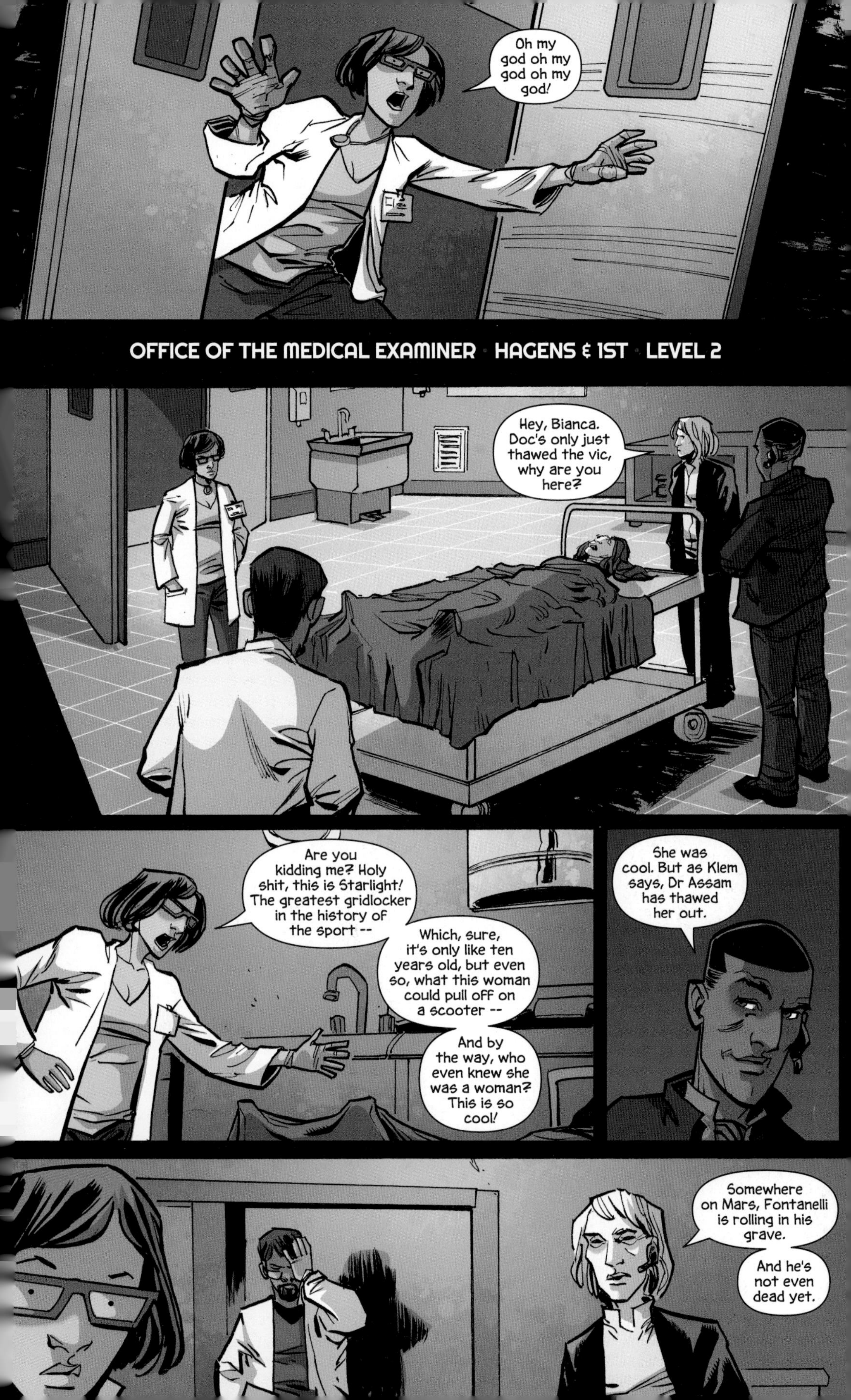

Oh my god oh my god oh my god!
OFFICE OF THE MEDICAL EXAMINER · HAGENS & 1ST · LEVEL 2
Hey, Bianca. Doc's only just thawed the vic, why are you here?
Are you kidding me? Holy shit, this is Starlight! The greatest gridlocker in the history of the sport --
Which, sure, it's only like ten years old, but even so, what this woman could pull off on a scooter --
And by the way, who even knew she was a woman? This is so cool!
She was cool. But as Klem says, Dr Assam has thawed her out.
Somewhere on Mars, Fontanelli is rolling in his grave.
And he's not even dead yet.

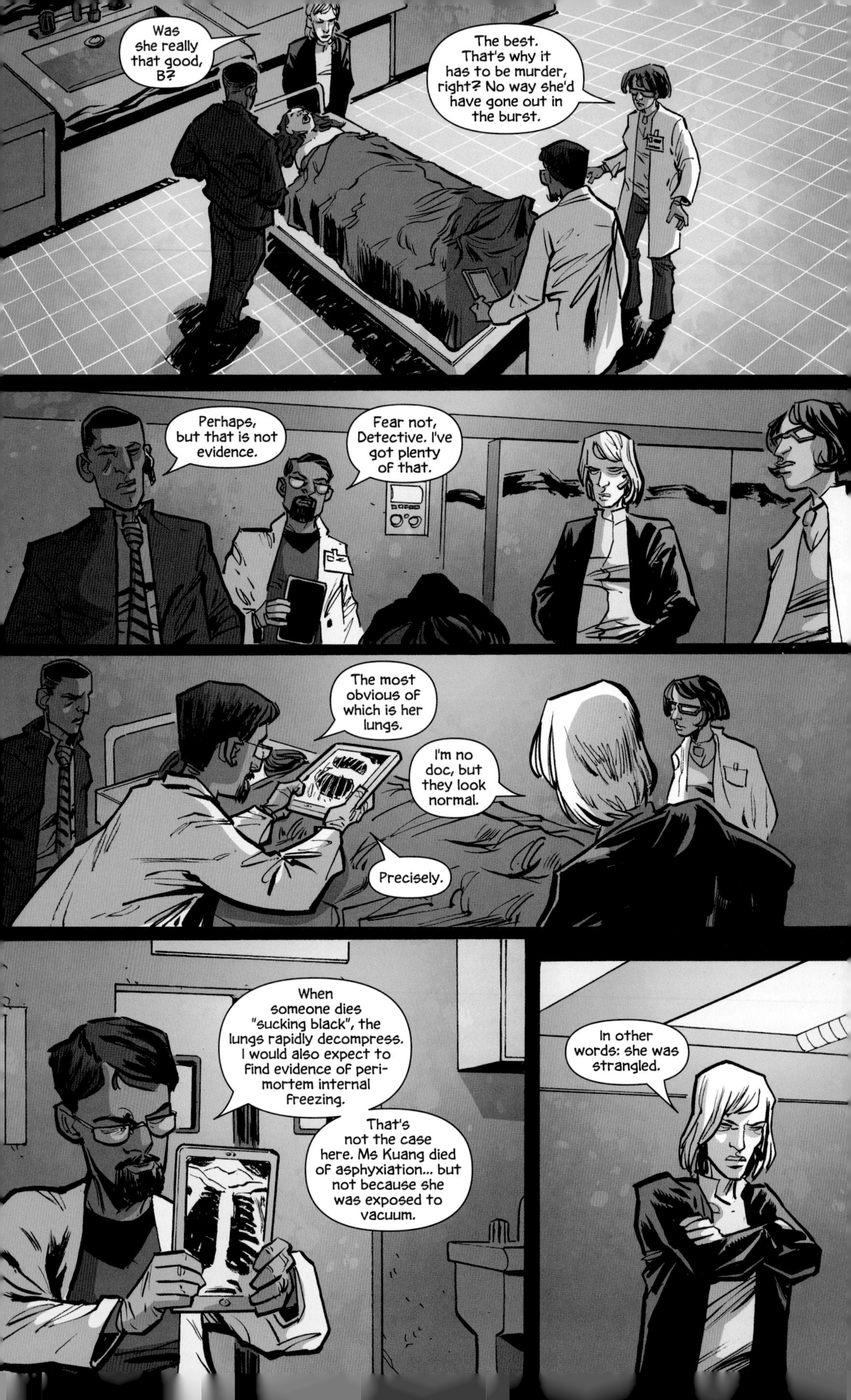
Was she really that good, B?
The best. That's why it has to be murder, right? No way she'd have gone out in the burst.
Perhaps, but that is not evidence.
Fear not, Detective. I've got plenty of that.
The most obvious of which is her lungs.
I'm no doc, but they look normal.
Precisely.
When someone dies "sucking black", the lungs rapidly decompress. I would also expect to find evidence of peri-mortem internal freezing.
That's not the case here. Ms Kuang died of asphyxiation... but not because she was exposed to vacuum.
In other words: she was strangled.

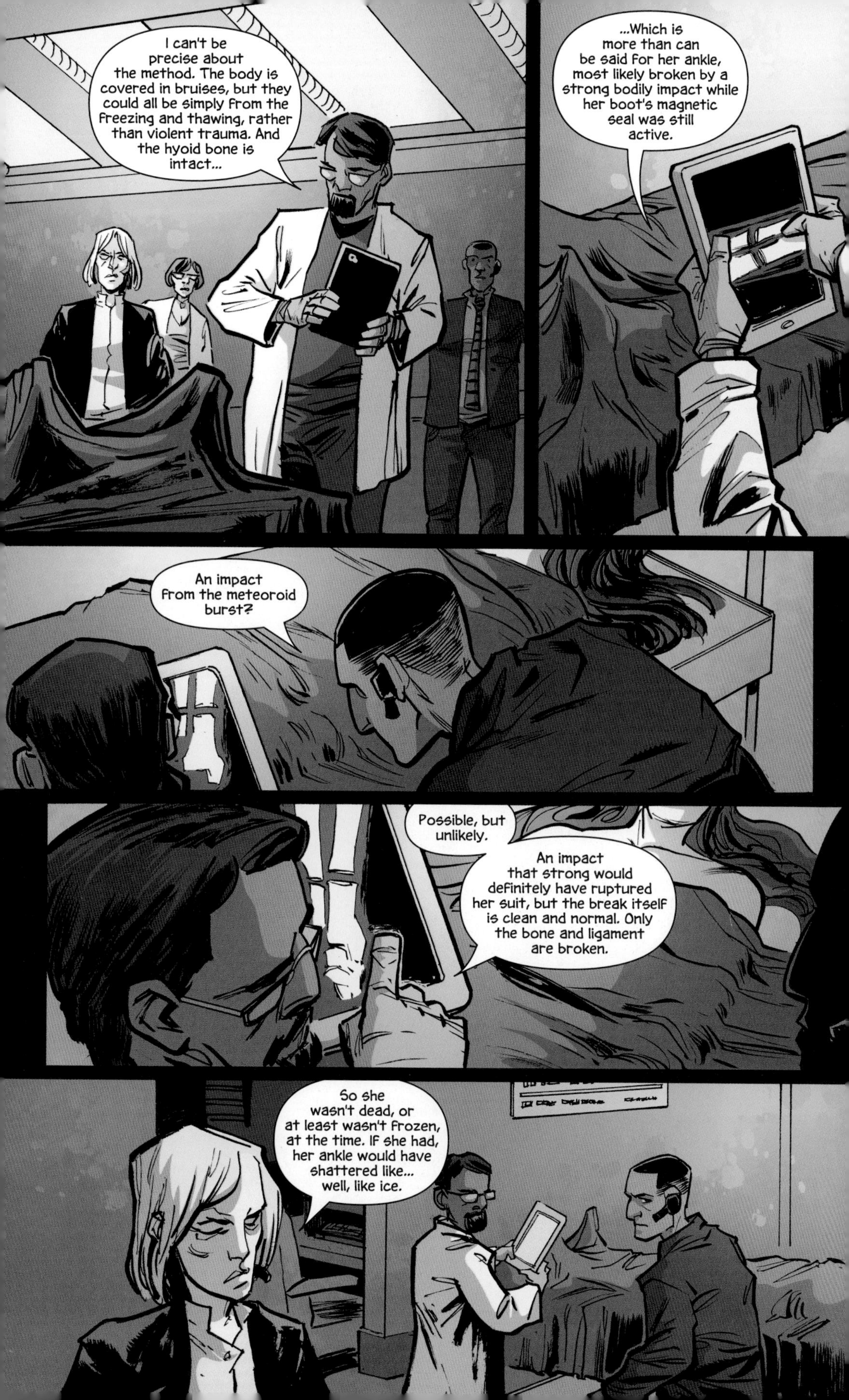
I can't be precise about the method. The body is covered in bruises, but they could all be simply from the freezing and thawing, rather than violent trauma. And the hyoid bone is intact...
...Which is more than can be said for her ankle, most likely broken by a strong bodily impact while her boot's magnetic seal was still active.
An impact from the meteoroid burst?
Possible, but unlikely.
An impact that strong would definitely have ruptured her suit, but the break itself is clean and normal. Only the bone and ligament are broken.
So she wasn't dead, or at least wasn't frozen, at the time. If she had, her ankle would have shattered like... well, like ice.

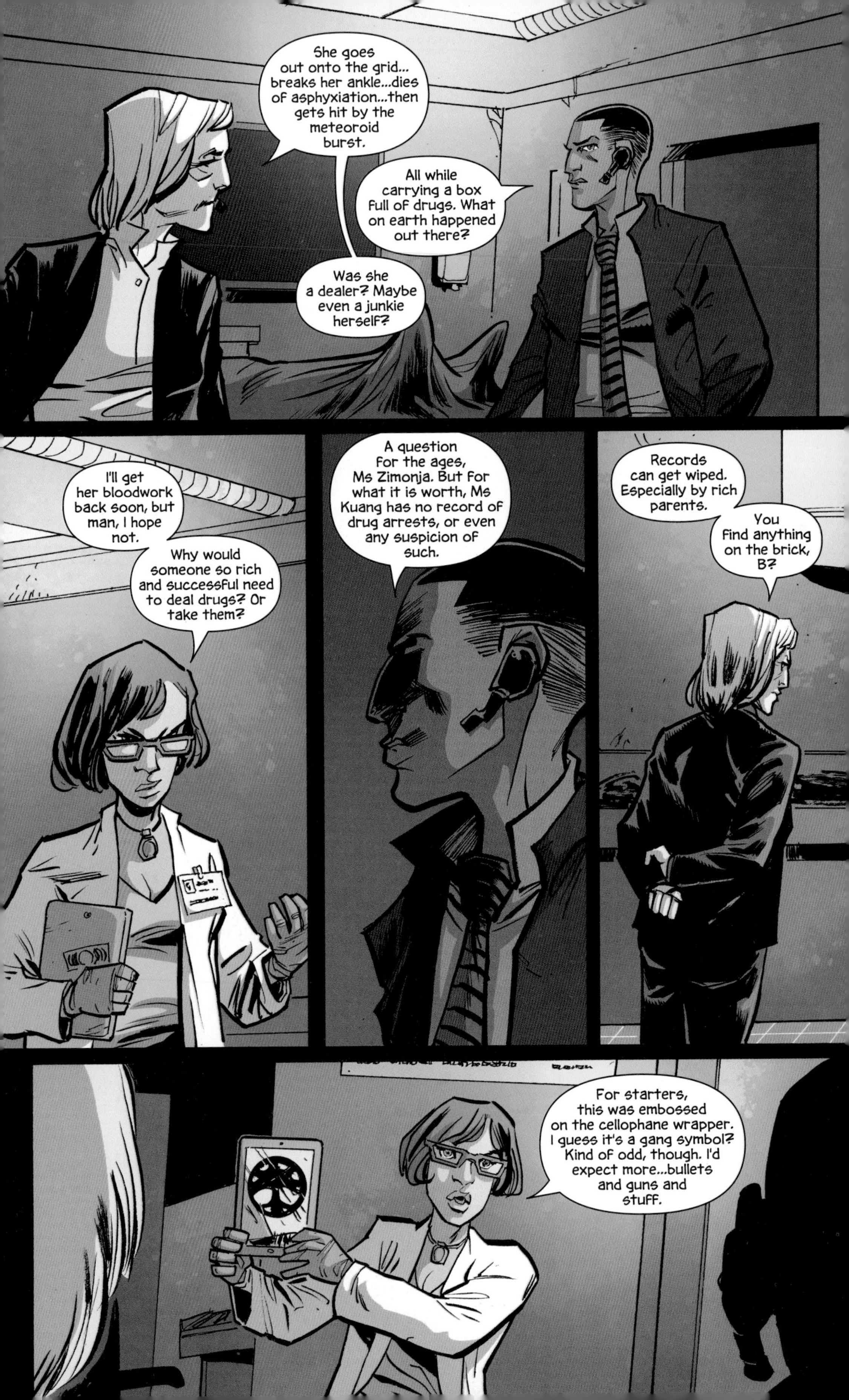
She goes out onto the grid... breaks her ankle...dies of asphyxiation...then gets hit by the meteoroid burst.
All while carrying a box full of drugs. What on earth happened out there?
Was she a dealer? Maybe even a junkie herself?
I'll get her bloodwork back soon, but man, I hope not.
Why would someone so rich and successful need to deal drugs? Or take them?
A question for the ages, Ms Zimonja. But for what it is worth, Ms Kuang has no record of drug arrests, or even any suspicion of such.
Records can get wiped. Especially by rich parents.
You find anything on the brick, B?
For starters, this was embossed on the cellophane wrapper. I guess it's a gang symbol? Kind of odd, though. I'd expect more...bullets and guns and stuff.

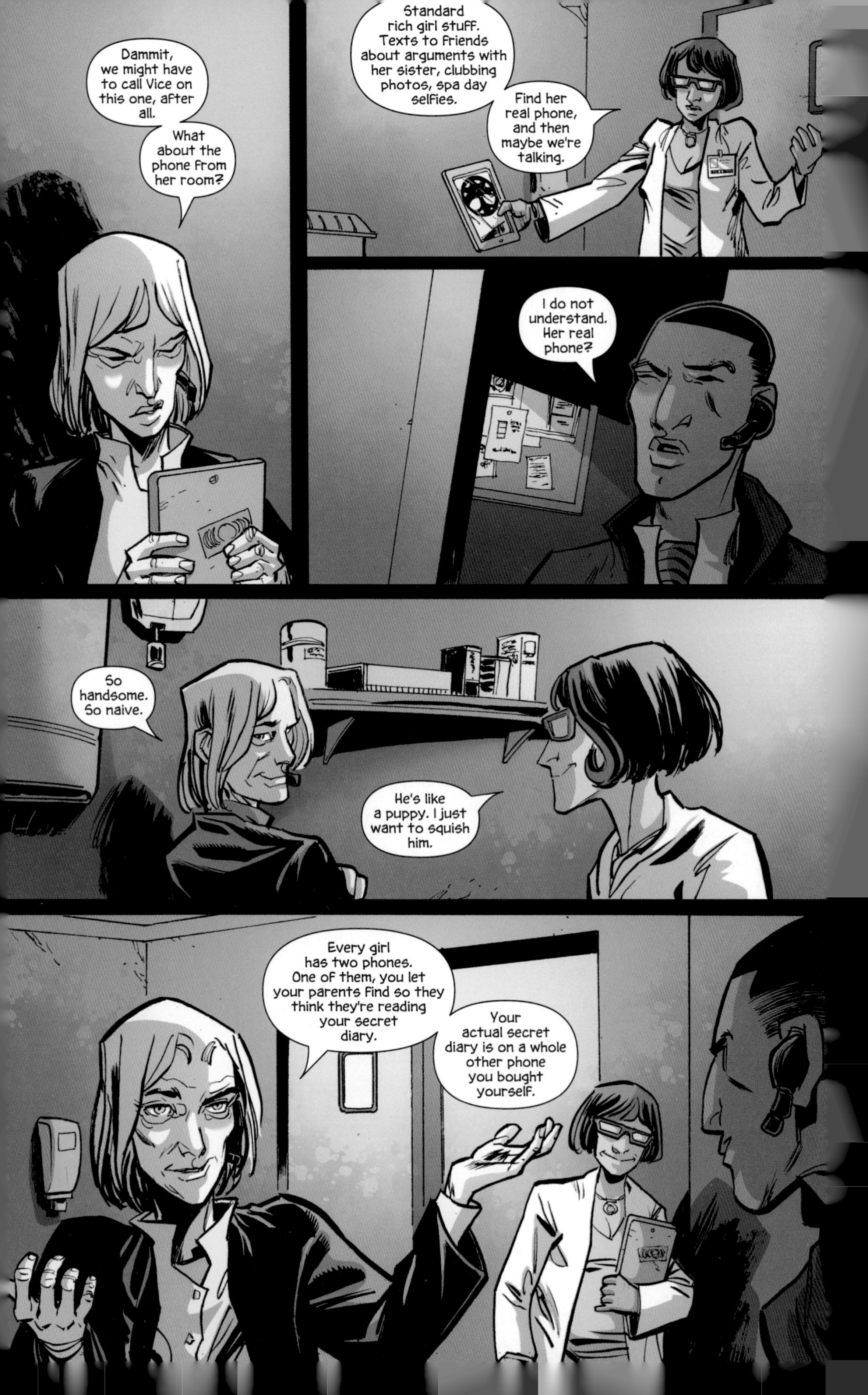

Dammit, we might have to call Vice on this one, after all.
What about the phone from her room?
Standard rich girl stuff. Texts to friends about arguments with her sister, clubbing photos, spa day selfies.
Find her real phone, and then maybe we're talking.
I do not understand. Her real phone?
So handsome. So naive.
He's like a puppy. I just want to squish him.
Every girl has two phones. One of them, you let your parents find so they think they're reading your secret diary.
Your actual secret diary is on a whole other phone you bought yourself.

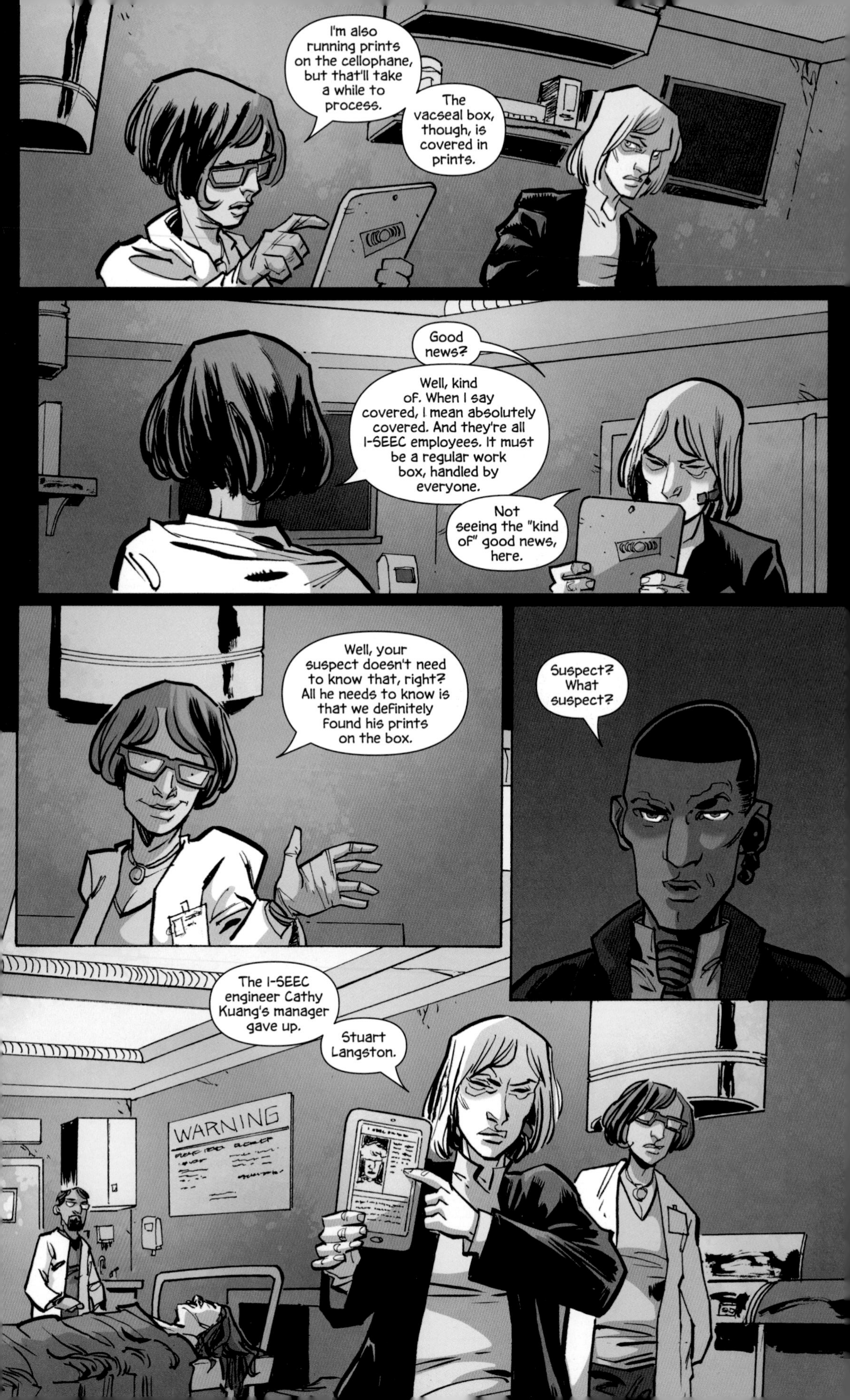
I'm also running prints on the cellophane, but that'll take a while to process.
The vacseal box, though, is covered in prints.
Good news?
Well, kind of. When I say covered, I mean absolutely covered. And they're all I-SEEC employees. It must be a regular work box, handled by everyone.
Not seeing the "kind of" good news, here.
Well, your suspect doesn't need to know that, right? All he needs to know is that we definitely found his prints on the box.
Suspect? What suspect?
The I-SEEC engineer Cathy Kuang's manager gave up.
Stuart Langston.
WARNING

I-SEEC CHECKPOINT 0-1 · REID & 1ST · LEVEL ZERO

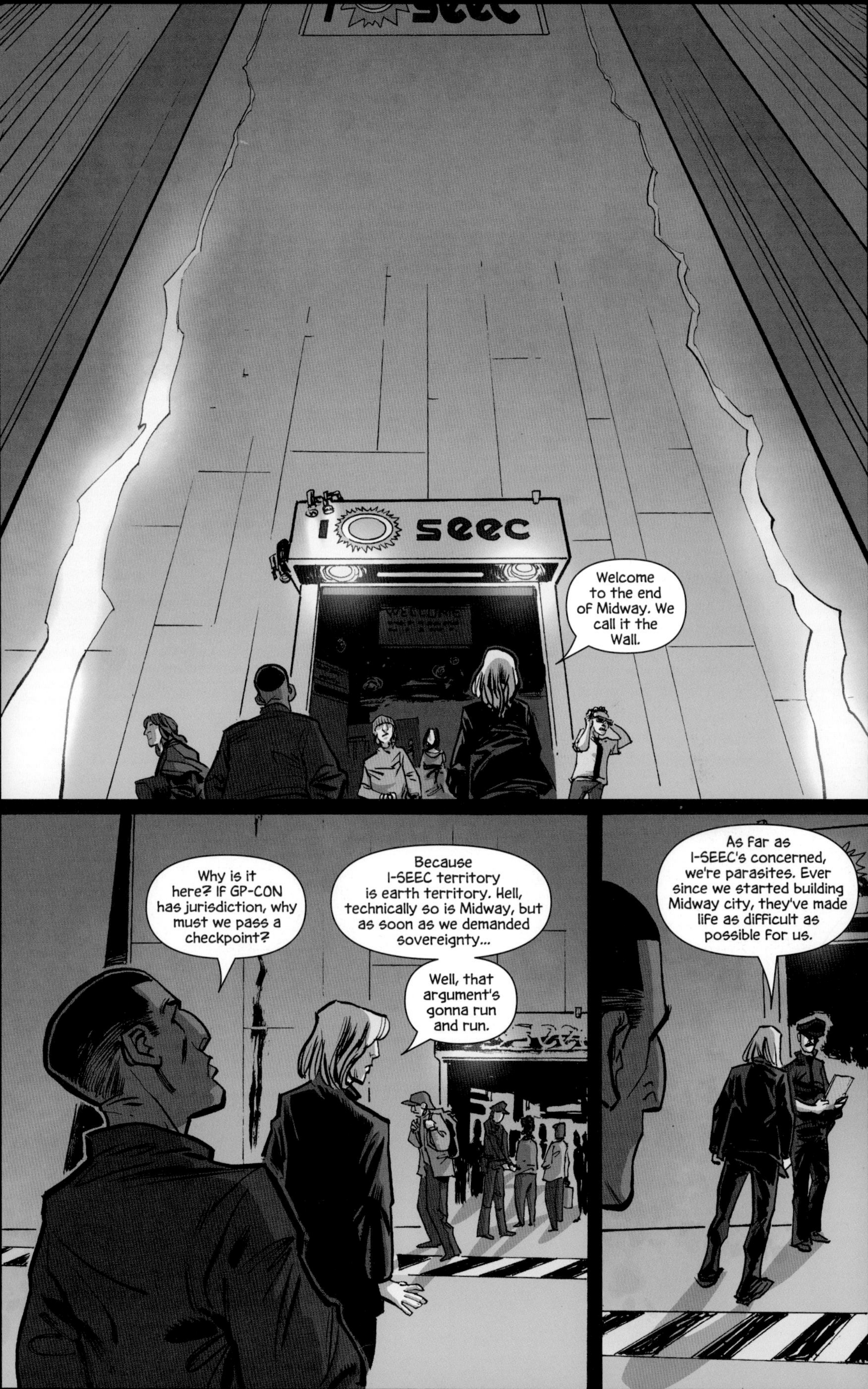
I SEEC
Welcome to the end of Midway. We call it the Wall.
Why is it here? If GP-CON has jurisdiction, why must we pass a checkpoint?
Because I-SEEC territory is earth territory. Hell, technically so is Midway, but as soon as we demanded sovereignty...
Well, that argument's gonna run and run.
As far as I-SEEC's concerned, we're parasites. Ever since we started building Midway city, they've made life as difficult as possible for us.

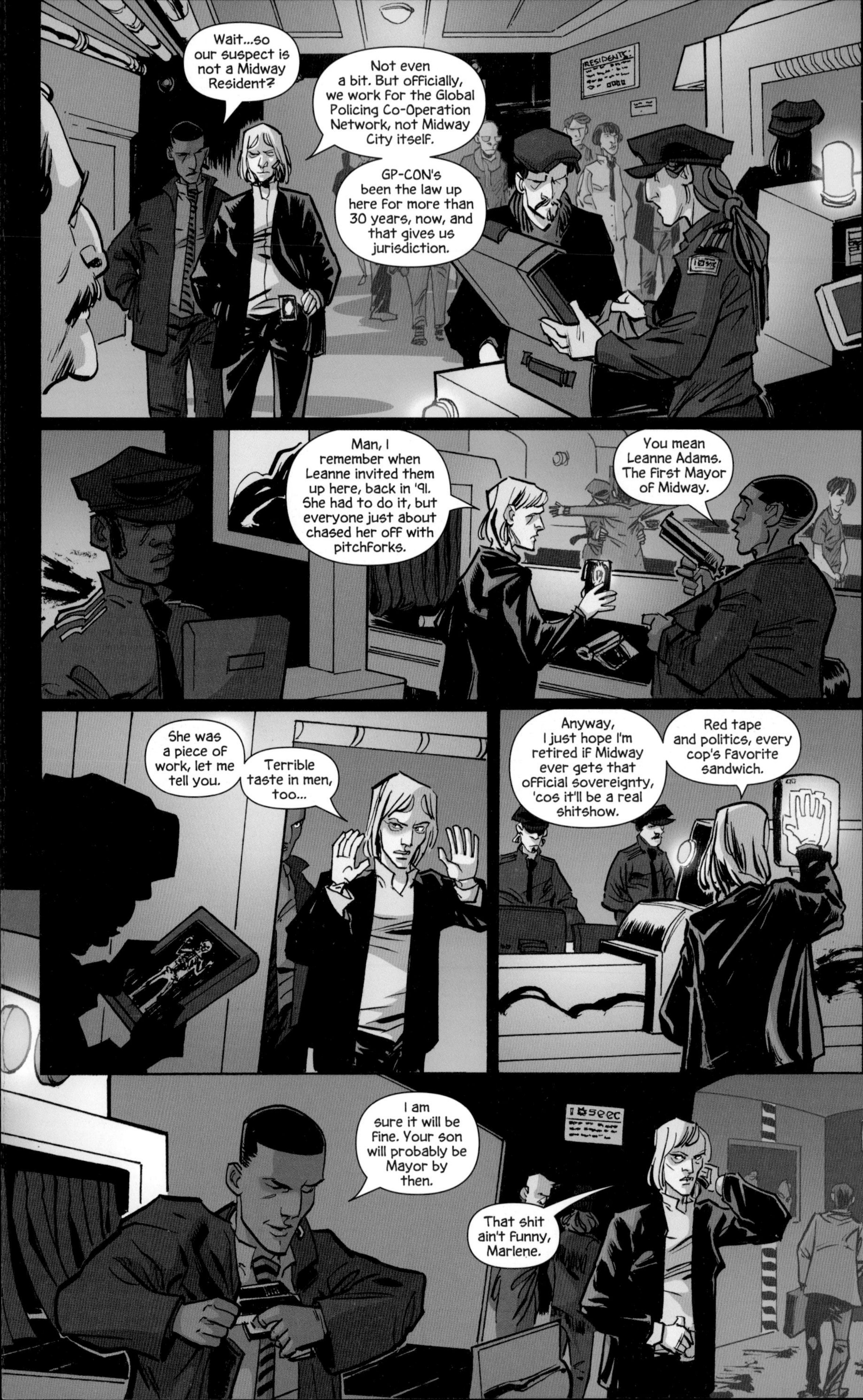

Wait...so our suspect is not a Midway Resident?
Not even a bit. But officially, we work for the Global Policing Co-Operation Network, not Midway City itself.
GP-CON's been the law up here for more than 30 years, now, and that gives us jurisdiction.
Man, I remember when Leanne invited them up here, back in '91. She had to do it, but everyone just about chased her off with pitchforks.
You mean Leanne Adams. The First Mayor of Midway.
She was a piece of work, let me tell you.
Terrible taste in men, too...
Anyway, I just hope I'm retired if Midway ever gets that official sovereignty, 'cos it'll be a real shitshow.
Red tape and politics, every cop's favorite sandwich.
I am sure it will be fine. Your son will probably be Mayor by then.
That shit ain't funny, Marlene.

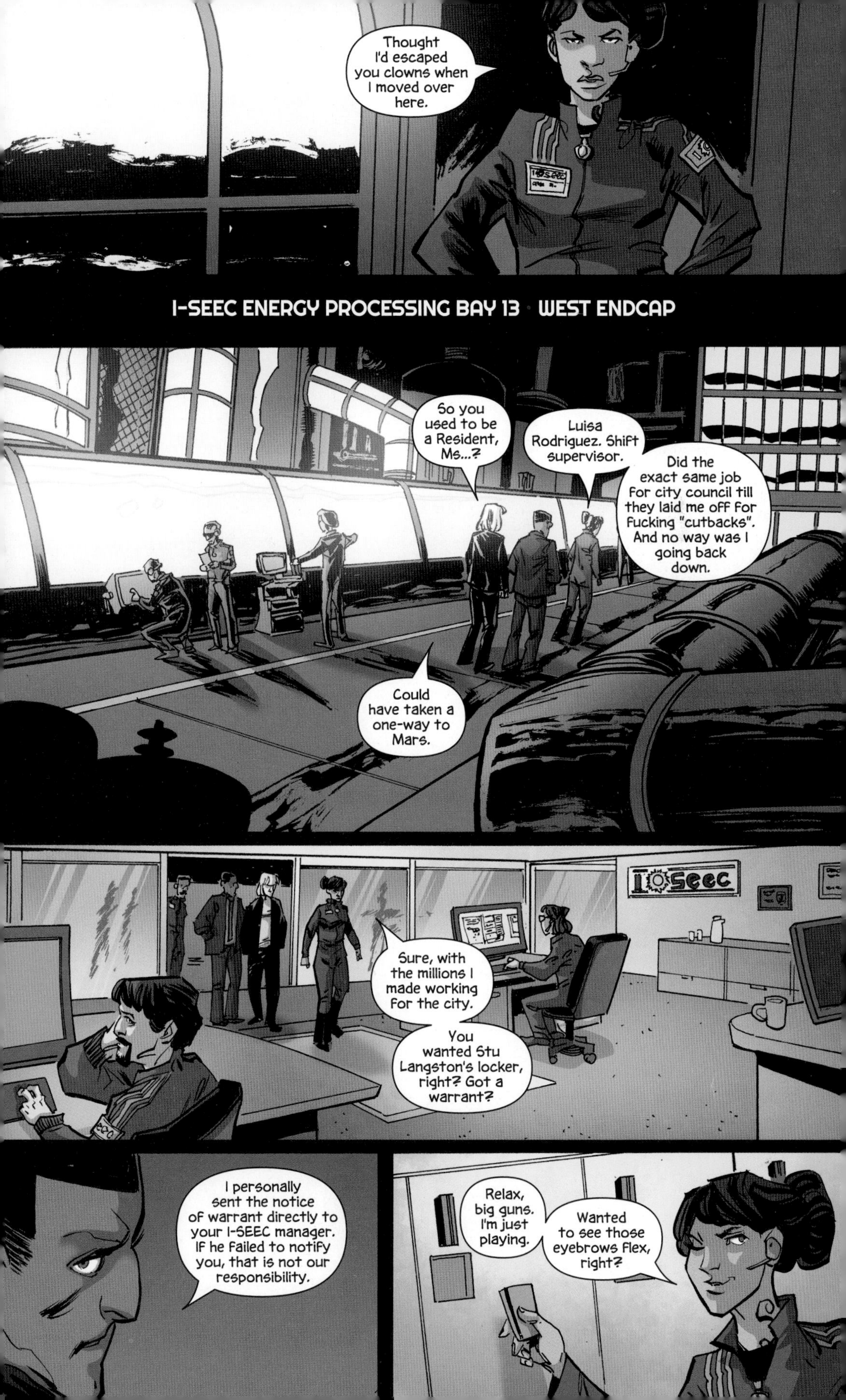

Thought I'd escaped you clowns when I moved over here.
I-SEEC ENERGY PROCESSING BAY 13 • WEST ENDCAP
So you used to be a Resident, Ms...?
Luisa Rodriguez. Shift supervisor.
Did the exact same job for city council till they laid me off for fucking "cutbacks". And no way was I going back down.
Could have taken a one-way to Mars.
Sure, with the millions I made working for the city.
You wanted Stu Langston's locker, right? Got a warrant?
I personally sent the notice of warrant directly to your I-SEEC manager. If he failed to notify you, that is not our responsibility.
Relax, big guns. I'm just playing.
Wanted to see those eyebrows flex, right?

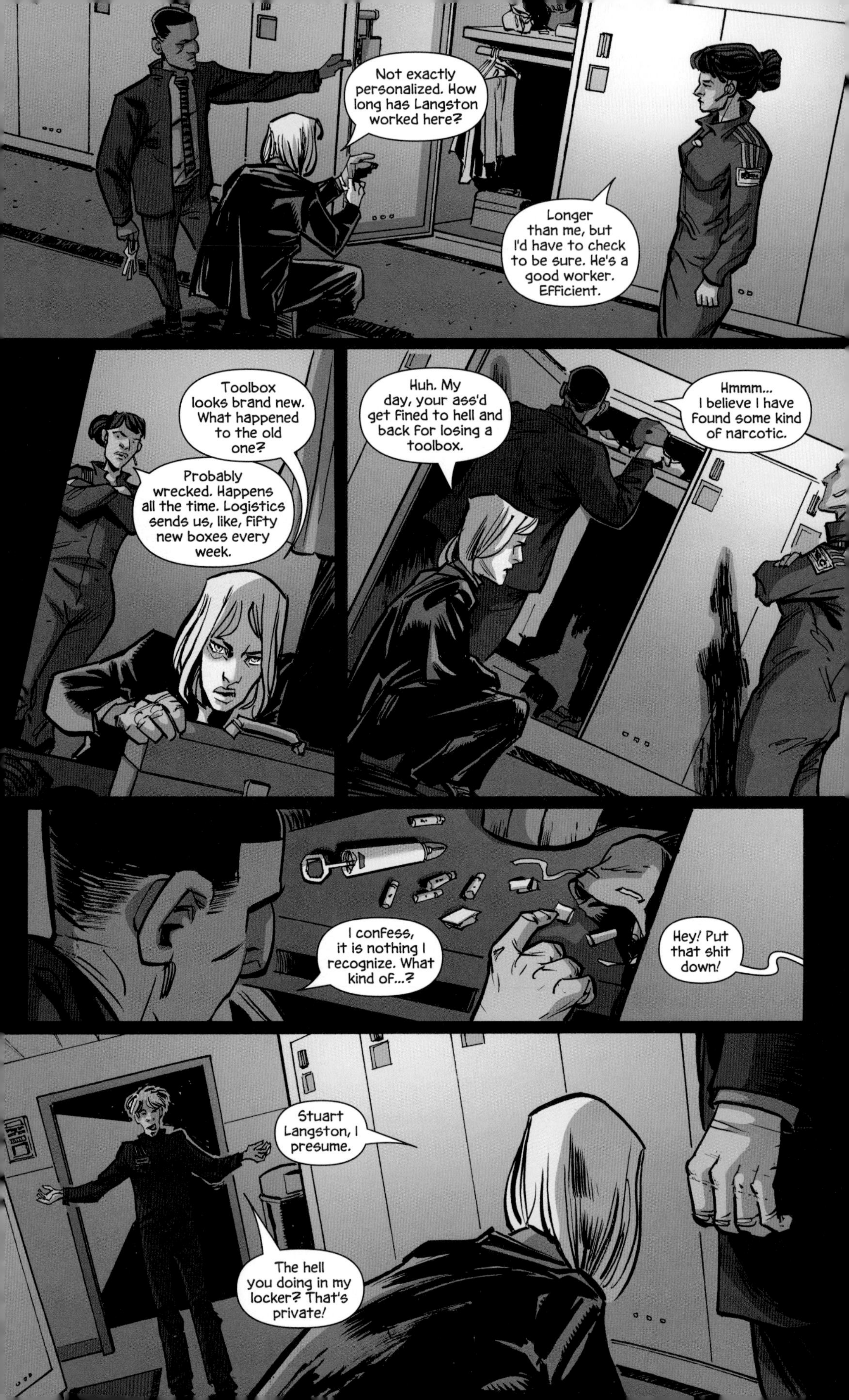
Not exactly personalized. How long has Langston worked here?
Longer than me, but I'd have to check to be sure. He's a good worker. Efficient.
Toolbox looks brand new. What happened to the old one?
Probably wrecked. Happens all the time. Logistics sends us, like, fifty new boxes every week.
Huh. My day, your ass'd get fined to hell and back for losing a toolbox.
Hmmm... I believe I have found some kind of narcotic.
I confess, it is nothing I recognize. What kind of...?
Hey! Put that shit down!
Stuart Langston, I presume.
The hell you doing in my locker? That's private!

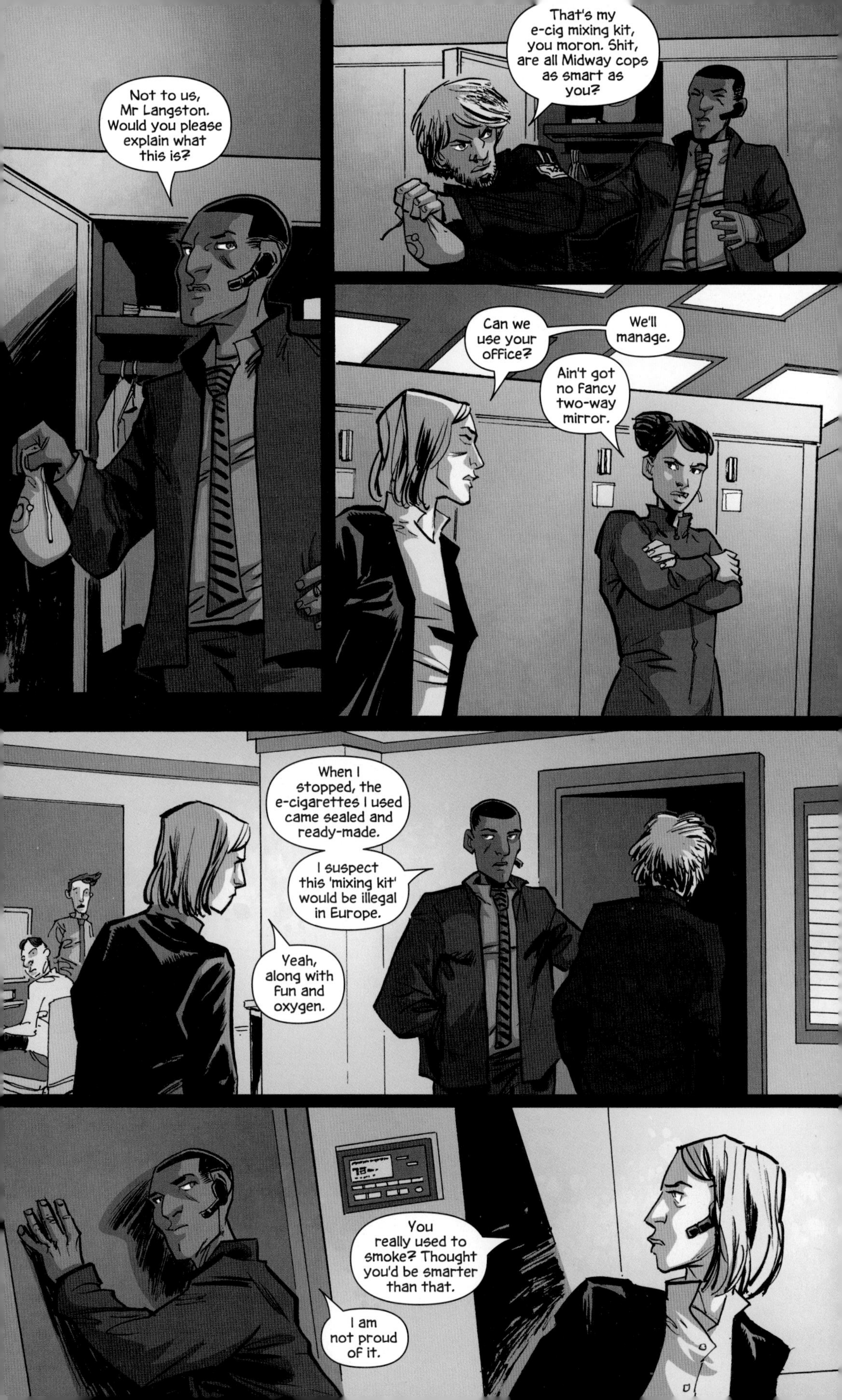
Not to us, Mr Langston. Would you please explain what this is?
That's my e-cig mixing kit, you moron. Shit, are all Midway cops as smart as you?
Can we use your office?
We'll manage.
Ain't got no fancy two-way mirror.
When I stopped, the e-cigarettes I used came sealed and ready-made.
I suspect this 'mixing kit' would be illegal in Europe.
Yeah, along with fun and oxygen.
You really used to smoke? Thought you'd be smarter than that.
I am not proud of it.

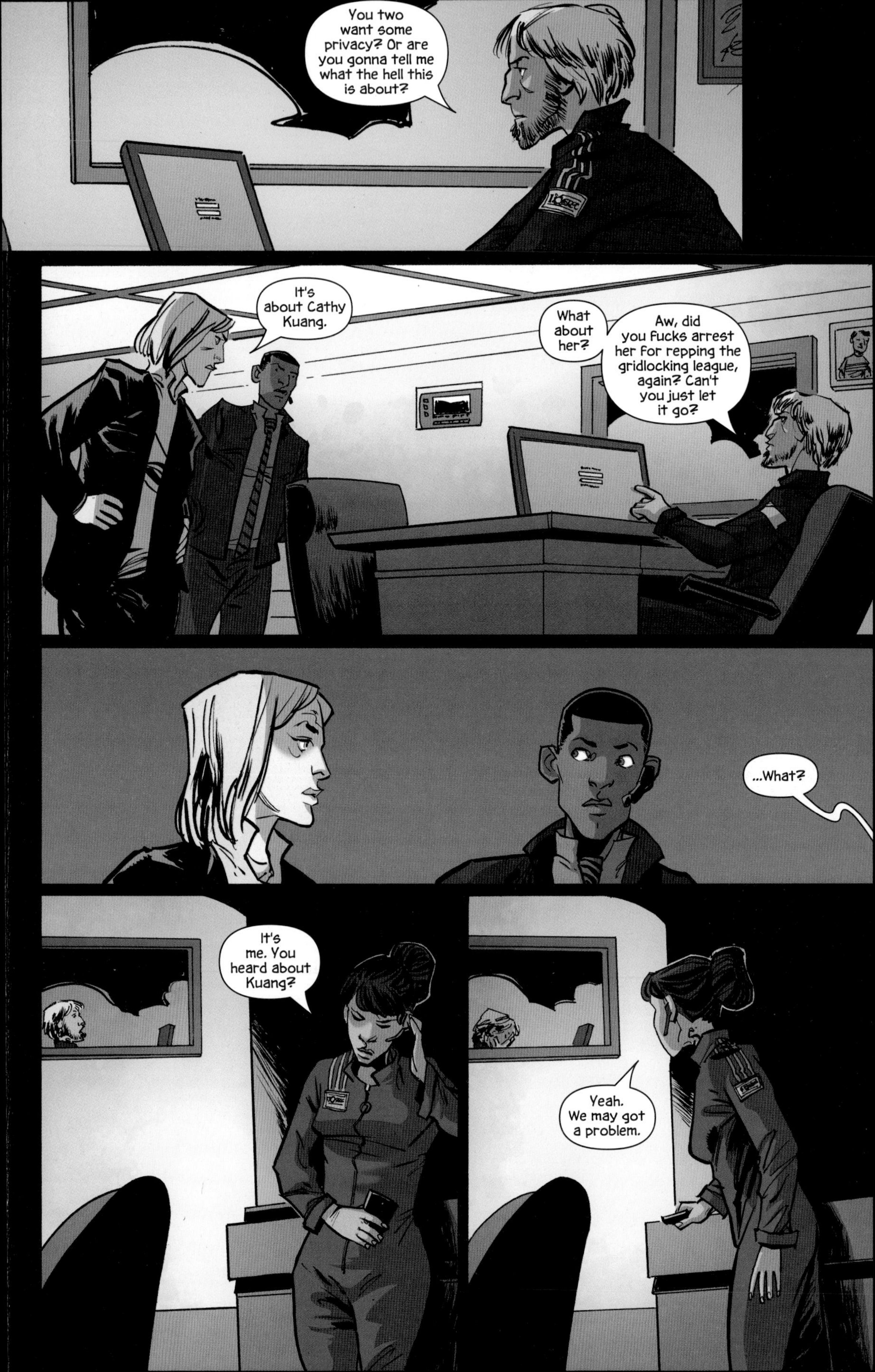
You two want some privacy? Or are you gonna tell me what the hell this is about?
It's about Cathy Kuang.
What about her?
Aw, did you fucks arrest her for repping the gridlocking league, again? Can't you just let it go?
...What?
It's me. You heard about Kuang?
Yeah. We may got a problem.

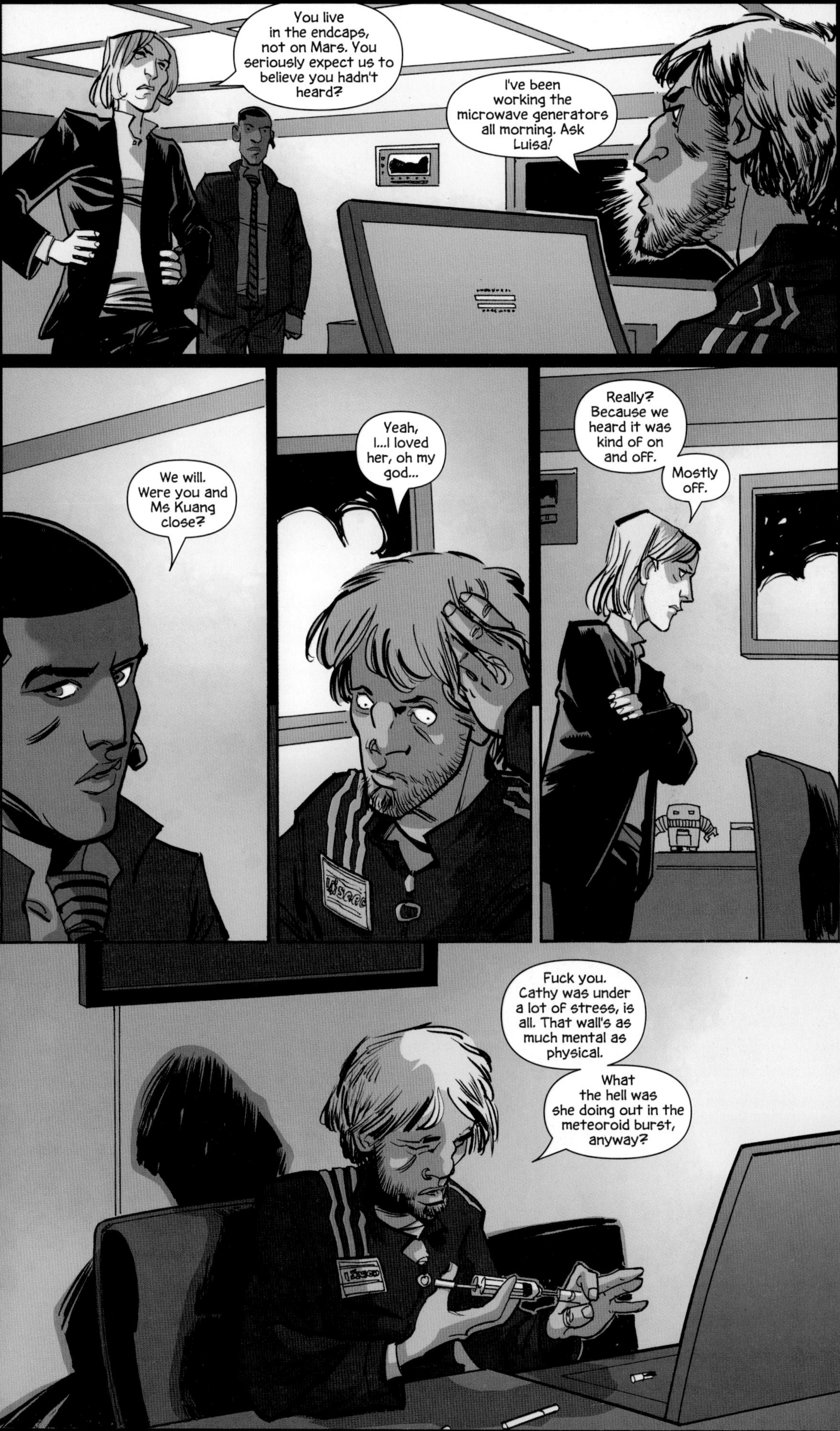
You live in the endcaps, not on Mars. You seriously expect us to believe you hadn't heard?
I've been working the microwave generators all morning. Ask Luisa!
We will. Were you and Ms Kuang close?
Yeah, I...I loved her, oh my god...
Really? Because we heard it was kind of on and off.
Mostly off.
Fuck you. Cathy was under a lot of stress, is all. That wall's as much mental as physical.
What the hell was she doing out in the meteoroid burst, anyway?

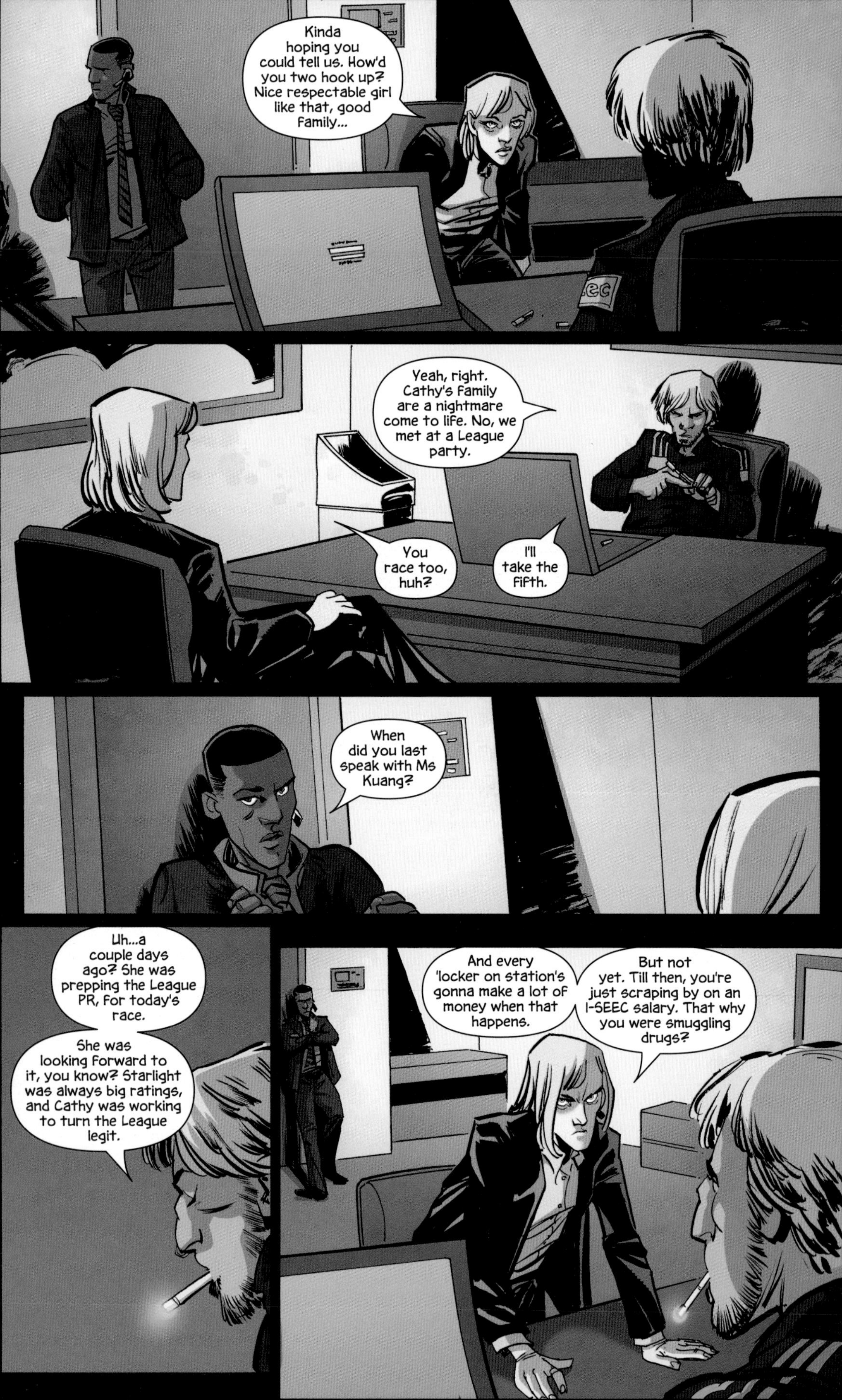
Kinda hoping you could tell us. How'd you two hook up? Nice respectable girl like that, good family...
Yeah, right. Cathy's family are a nightmare come to life. No, we met at a League party.
You race too, huh?
I'll take the fifth.
When did you last speak with Ms Kuang?
Uh...a couple days ago? She was prepping the League PR, for today's race.
She was looking forward to it, you know? Starlight was always big ratings, and Cathy was working to turn the League legit.
And every 'locker on station's gonna make a lot of money when that happens.
But not yet. Till then, you're just scraping by on an I-SEEC salary. That why you were smuggling drugs?

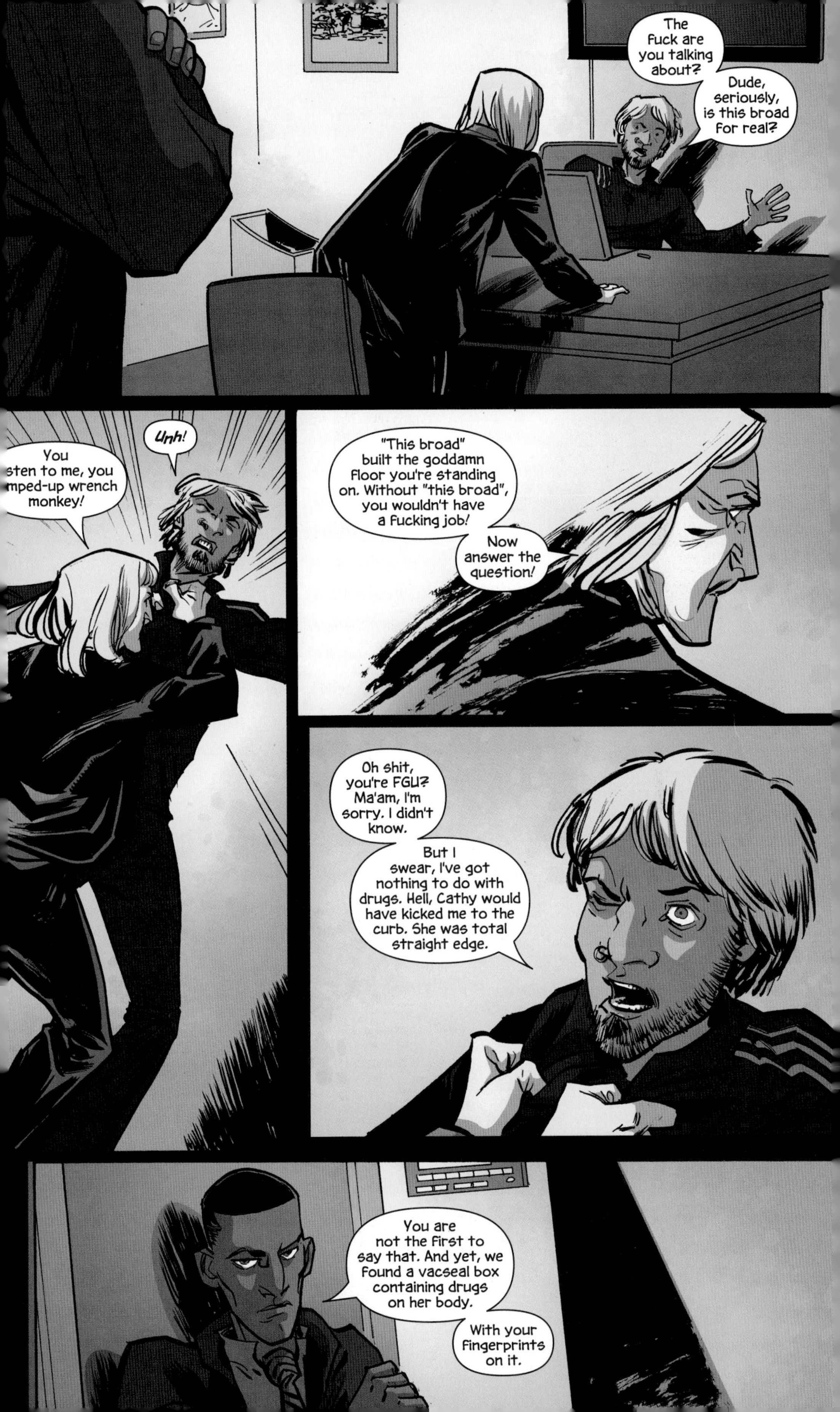
The fuck are you talking about?
Dude, seriously, is this broad for real?
Unh!
You sten to me, you mped-up wrench monkey!
"This broad" built the goddamn floor you're standing on. Without "this broad", you wouldn't have a fucking job!
Now answer the question!
Oh shit, you're FGU? Ma'am, I'm sorry. I didn't know.
But I swear, I've got nothing to do with drugs. Hell, Cathy would have kicked me to the curb. She was total straight edge.
You are not the first to say that. And yet, we found a vacseal box containing drugs on her body.
With your fingerprints on it.

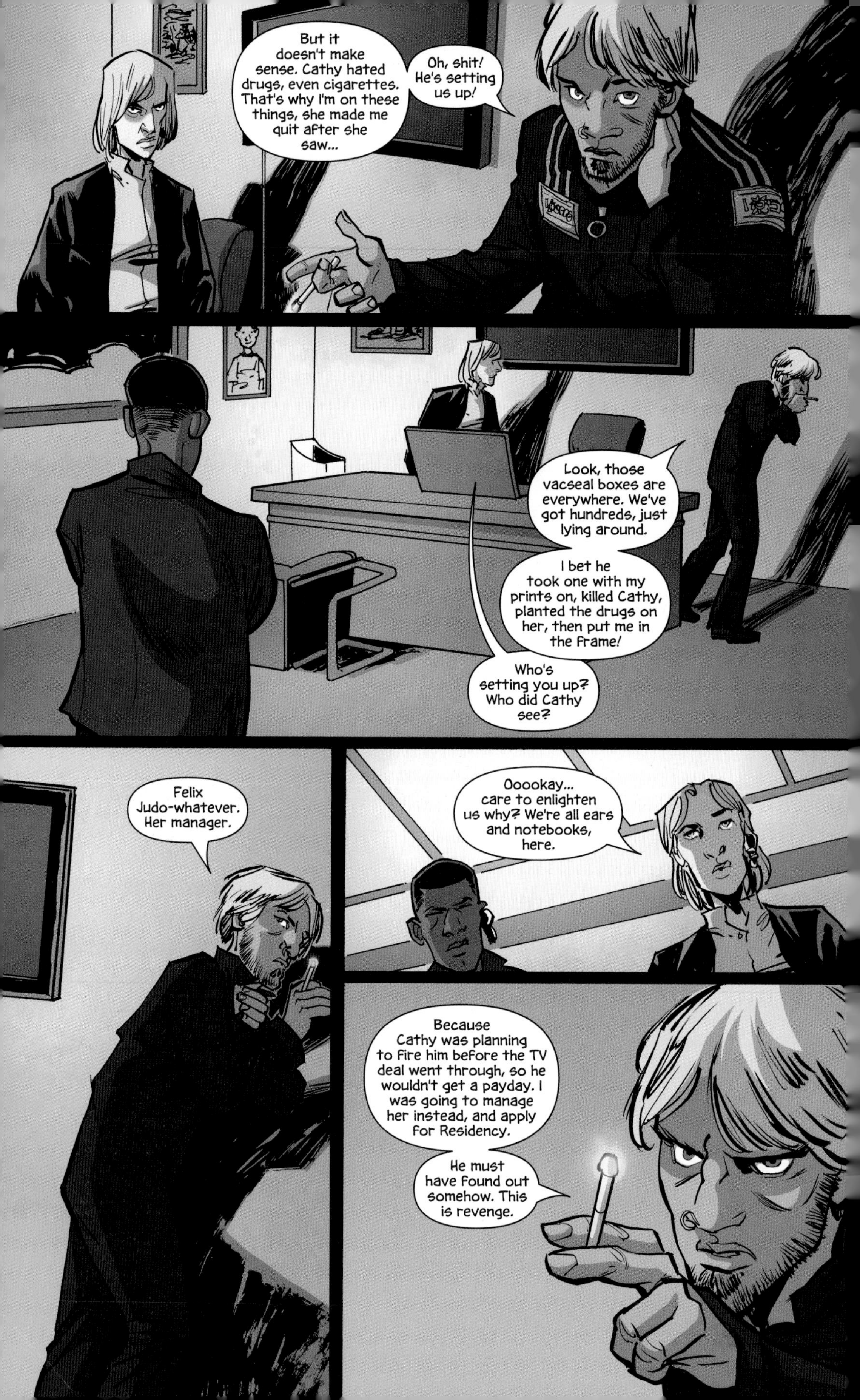
But it doesn't make sense. Cathy hated drugs, even cigarettes. That's why I'm on these things, she made me quit after she saw...
Oh, shit! He's setting us up!
Look, those vacseal boxes are everywhere. We've got hundreds, just lying around.
I bet he took one with my prints on, killed Cathy, planted the drugs on her, then put me in the frame!
Who's setting you up? Who did Cathy see?
Felix Judo-whatever. Her manager.
Ooookay... care to enlighten us why? We're all ears and notebooks, here.
Because Cathy was planning to fire him before the TV deal went through, so he wouldn't get a payday. I was going to manage her instead, and apply for Residency.
He must have found out somehow. This is revenge.

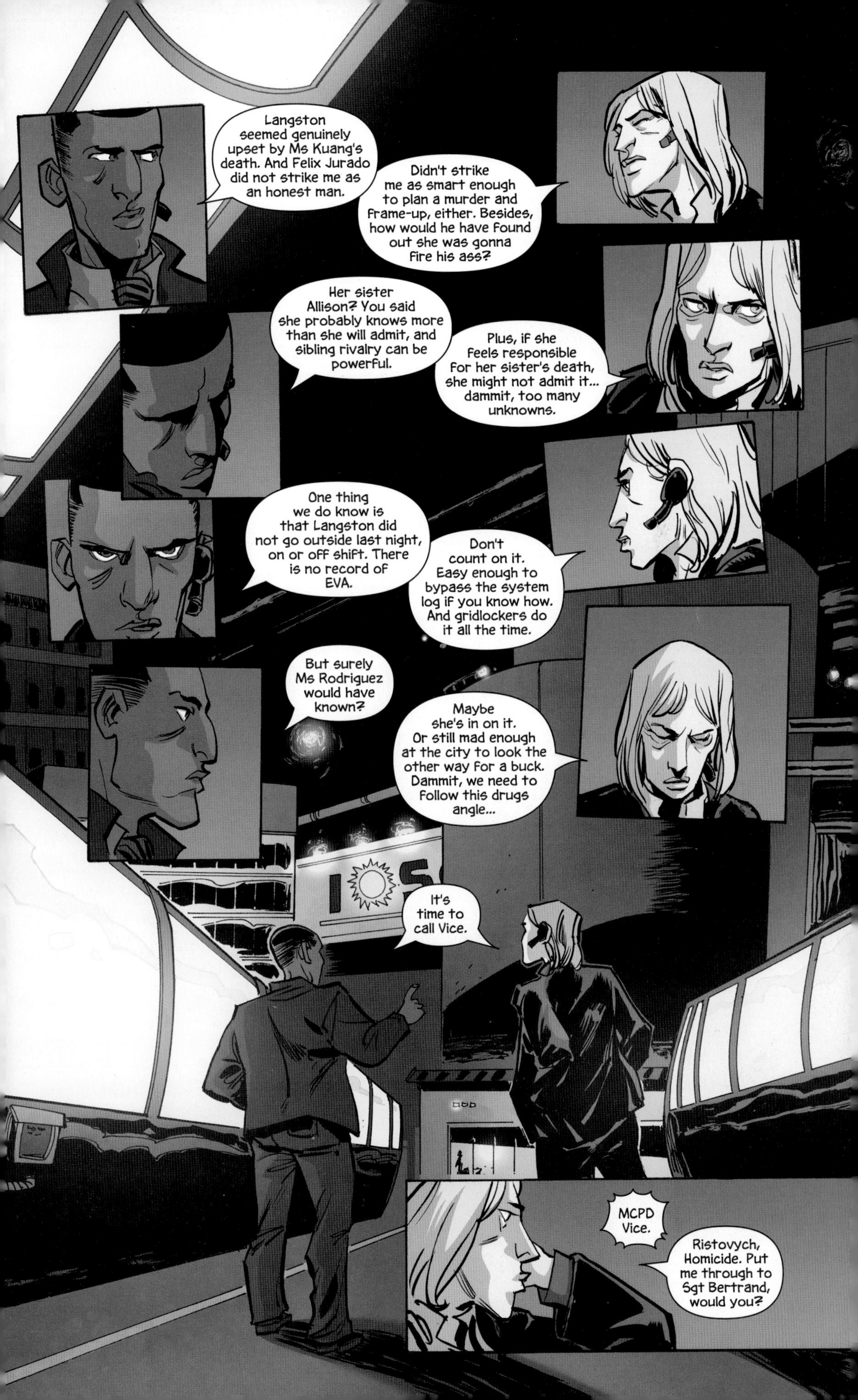
Langston seemed genuinely upset by Ms Kuang's death. And Felix Jurado did not strike me as an honest man.
Didn't strike me as smart enough to plan a murder and frame-up, either. Besides, how would he have found out she was gonna fire his ass?
Her sister Allison? You said she probably knows more than she will admit, and sibling rivalry can be powerful.
Plus, if she feels responsible for her sister's death, she might not admit it... dammit, too many unknowns.
One thing we do know is that Langston did not go outside last night, on or off shift. There is no record of EVA.
Don't count on it. Easy enough to bypass the system log if you know how. And gridlockers do it all the time.
But surely Ms Rodriguez would have known?
Maybe she's in on it. Or still mad enough at the city to look the other way for a buck. Dammit, we need to follow this drugs angle...
It's time to call Vice.
MCPD Vice.
Ristovych, Homicide. Put me through to Sgt Bertrand, would you?

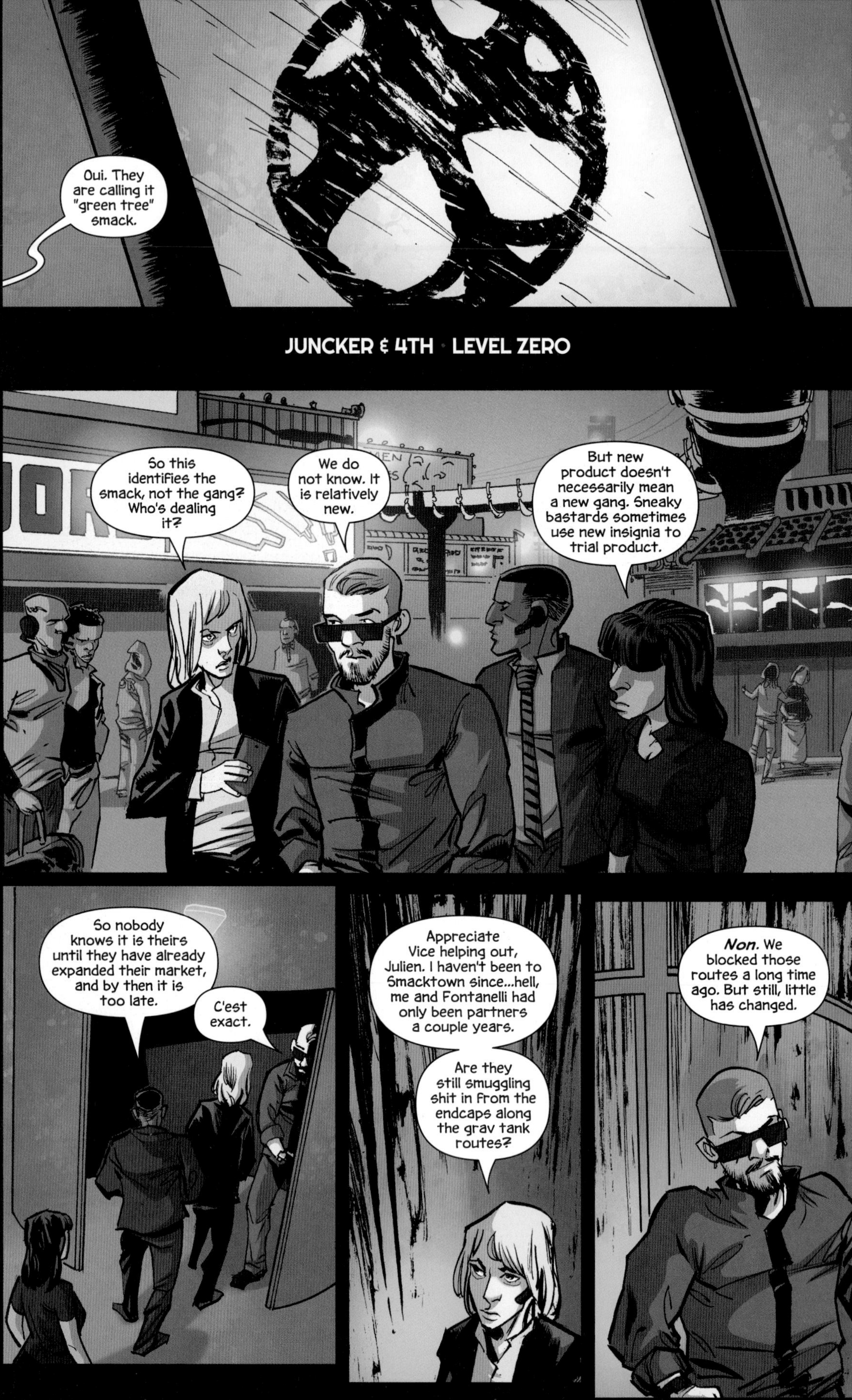

Oui. They are calling it "green tree" smack.
JUNCKER & 4TH · LEVEL ZERO
So this identifies the smack, not the gang? Who's dealing it?
We do not know. It is relatively new.
But new product doesn't necessarily mean a new gang. Sneaky bastards sometimes use new insignia to trial product.
So nobody knows it is theirs until they have already expanded their market, and by then it is too late.
C'est exact.
Appreciate Vice helping out, Julien. I haven't been to Smacktown since...hell, me and Fontanelli had only been partners a couple years.
Are they still smuggling shit in from the endcaps along the grav tank routes?
Non. We blocked those routes a long time ago. But still, little has changed.

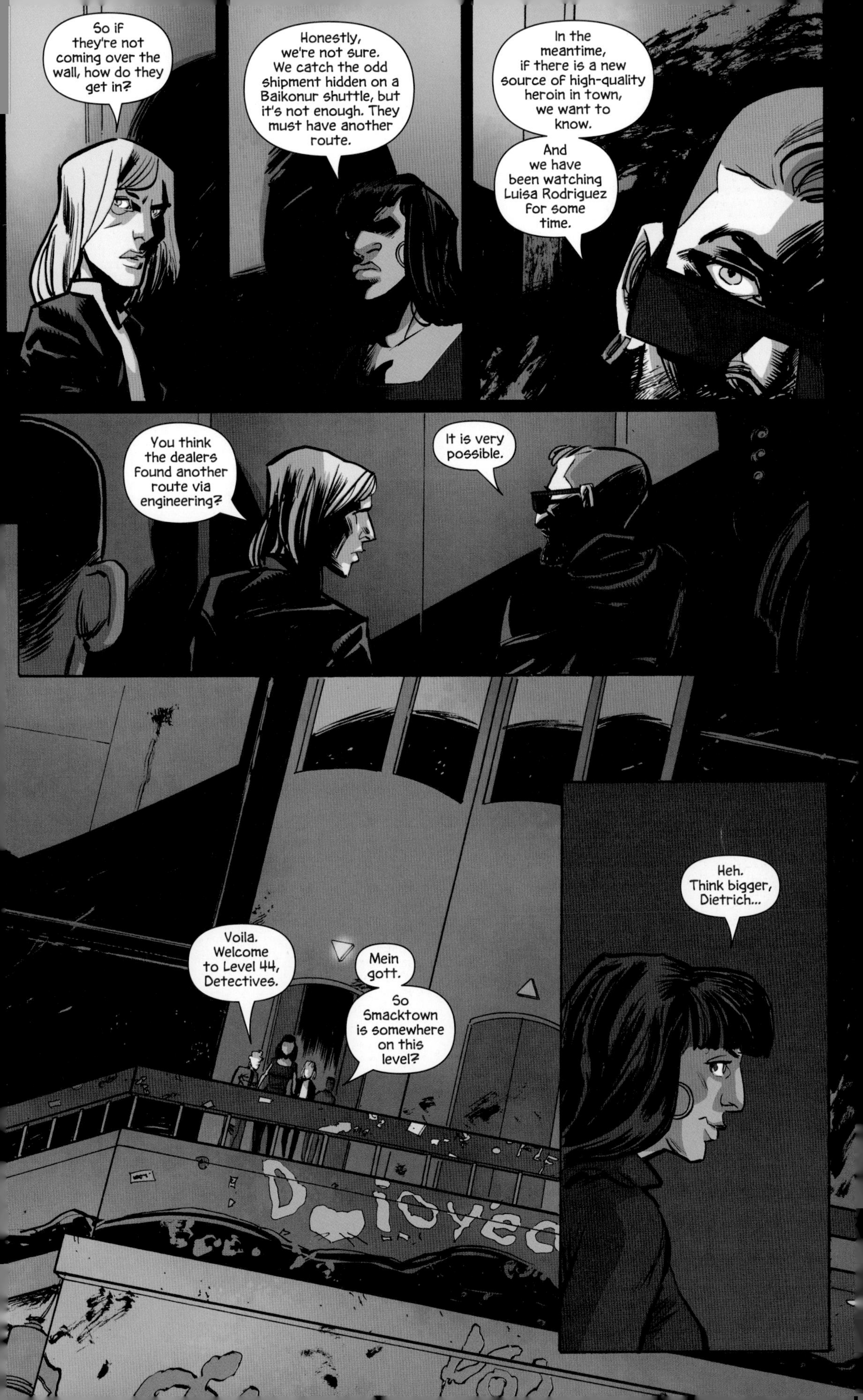
So if they're not coming over the wall, how do they get in?
Honestly, we're not sure. We catch the odd shipment hidden on a Baikonur shuttle, but it's not enough. They must have another route.
In the meantime, if there is a new source of high-quality heroin in town, we want to know.
And we have been watching Luisa Rodriguez for some time.
You think the dealers found another route via engineering?
It is very possible.
Voila. Welcome to Level 44, Detectives.
Mein gott.
So Smacktown is somewhere on this level?
Heh. Think bigger, Dietrich...

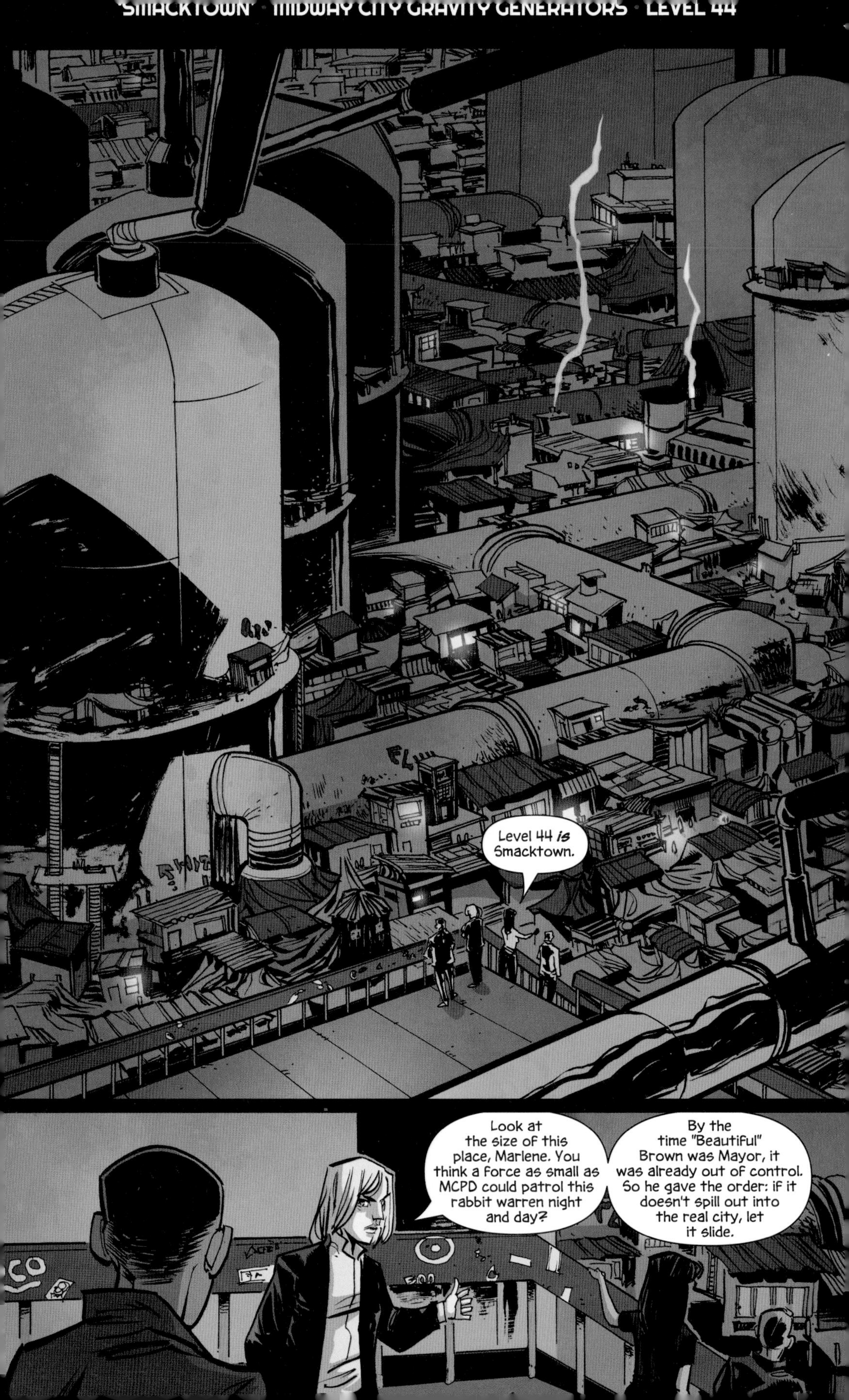
"SMACKTOWN" · MIDWAY CITY GRAVITY GENERATORS · LEVEL 44
Level 44 *is* Smacktown.
Look at the size of this place, Marlene. You think a force as small as MCPD could patrol this rabbit warren night and day?
By the time "Beautiful" Brown was Mayor, it was already out of control. So he gave the order: if it doesn't spill out into the real city, let it slide.

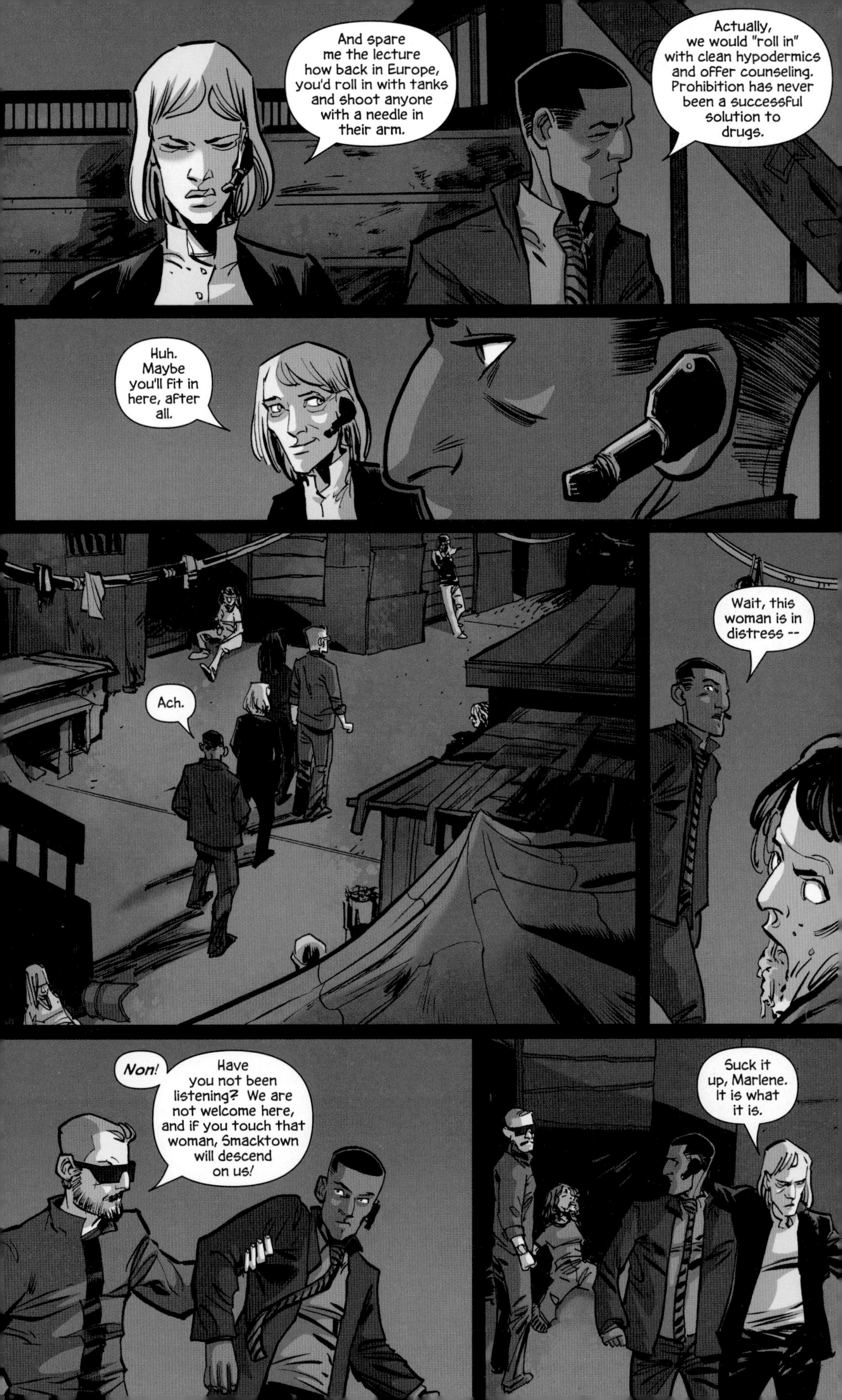

And spare me the lecture how back in Europe, you'd roll in with tanks and shoot anyone with a needle in their arm.
Actually, we would "roll in" with clean hypodermics and offer counseling. Prohibition has never been a successful solution to drugs.
Huh. Maybe you'll fit in here, after all.
Ach.
Wait, this woman is in distress --
Non!
Have you not been listening? We are not welcome here, and if you touch that woman, Smacktown will descend on us!
Suck it up, Marlene. It is what it is.

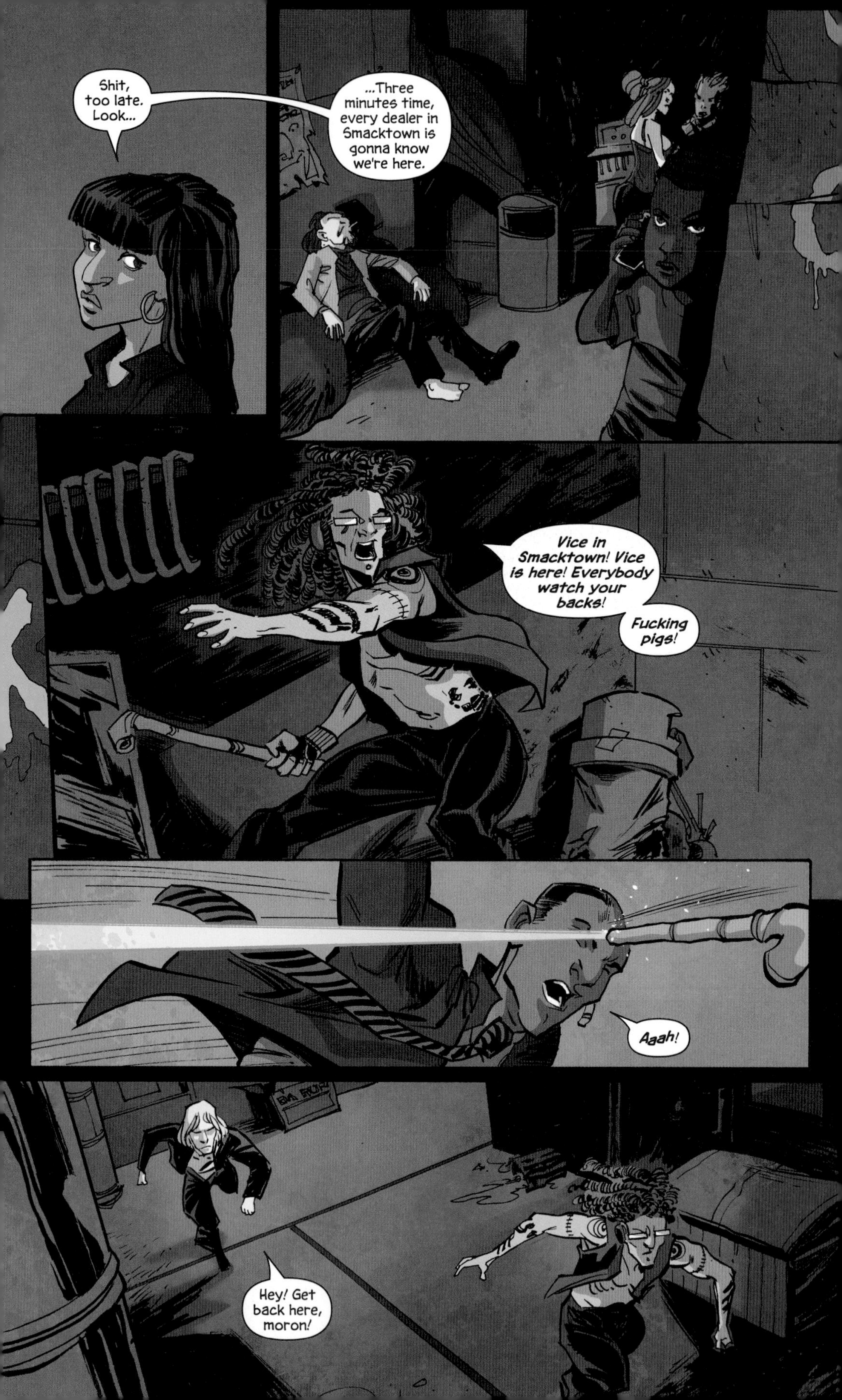
Shit, too late. Look...
...Three minutes time, every dealer in Smacktown is gonna know we're here.
Vice in Smacktown! Vice is here! Everybody watch your backs!
Fucking pigs!
Aaah!
Hey! Get back here, moron!

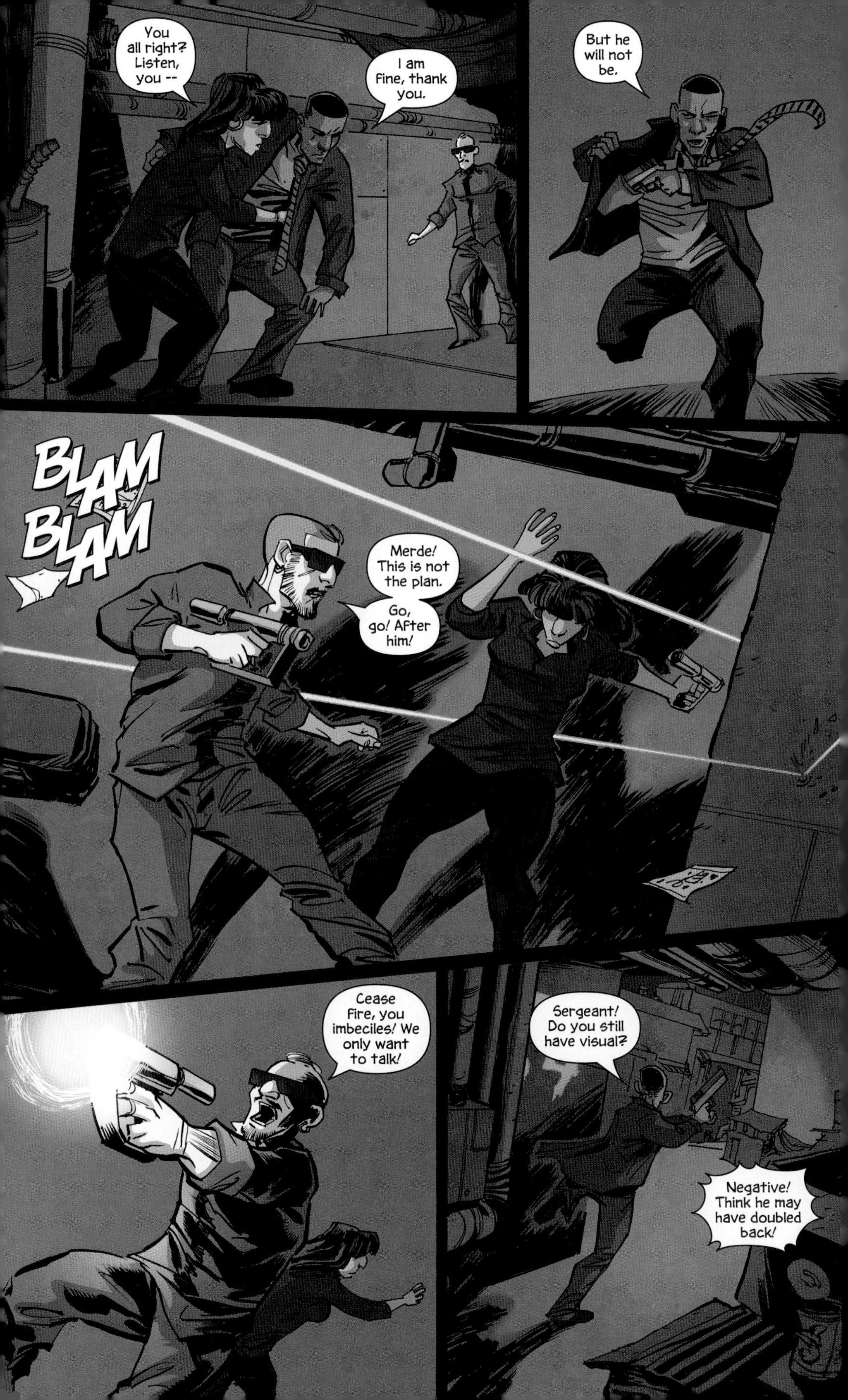
You all right? Listen, you --
I am fine, thank you.
But he will not be.
BLAM BLAM
Merde! This is not the plan.
Go, go! After him!
Cease fire, you imbeciles! We only want to talk!
Sergeant! Do you still have visual?
Negative! Think he may have doubled back!

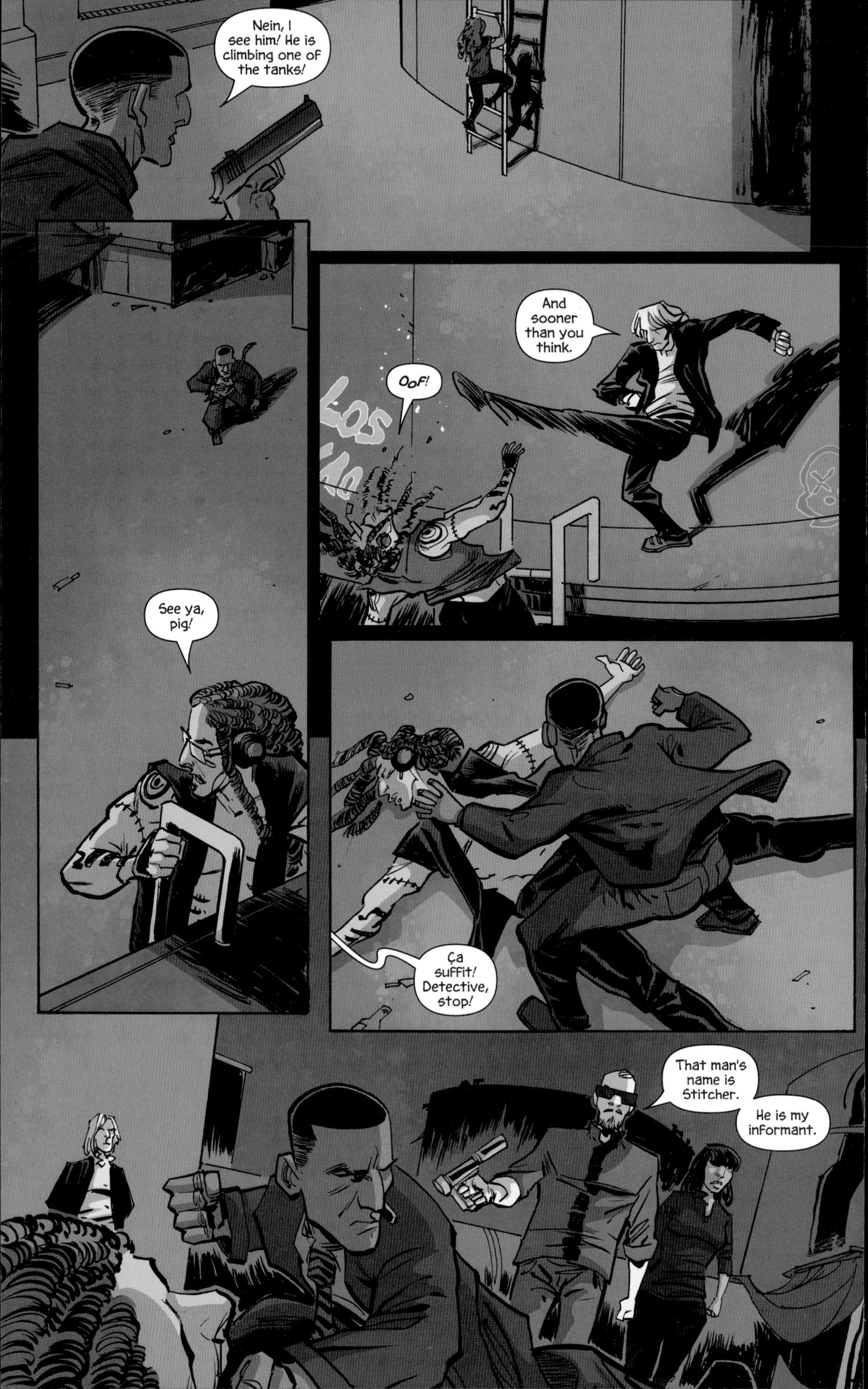

Nein, I see him! He is climbing one of the tanks!
And sooner than you think.
Oof!
See ya, pig!
Ça suffit! Detective, stop!
That man's name is Stitcher.
He is my informant.

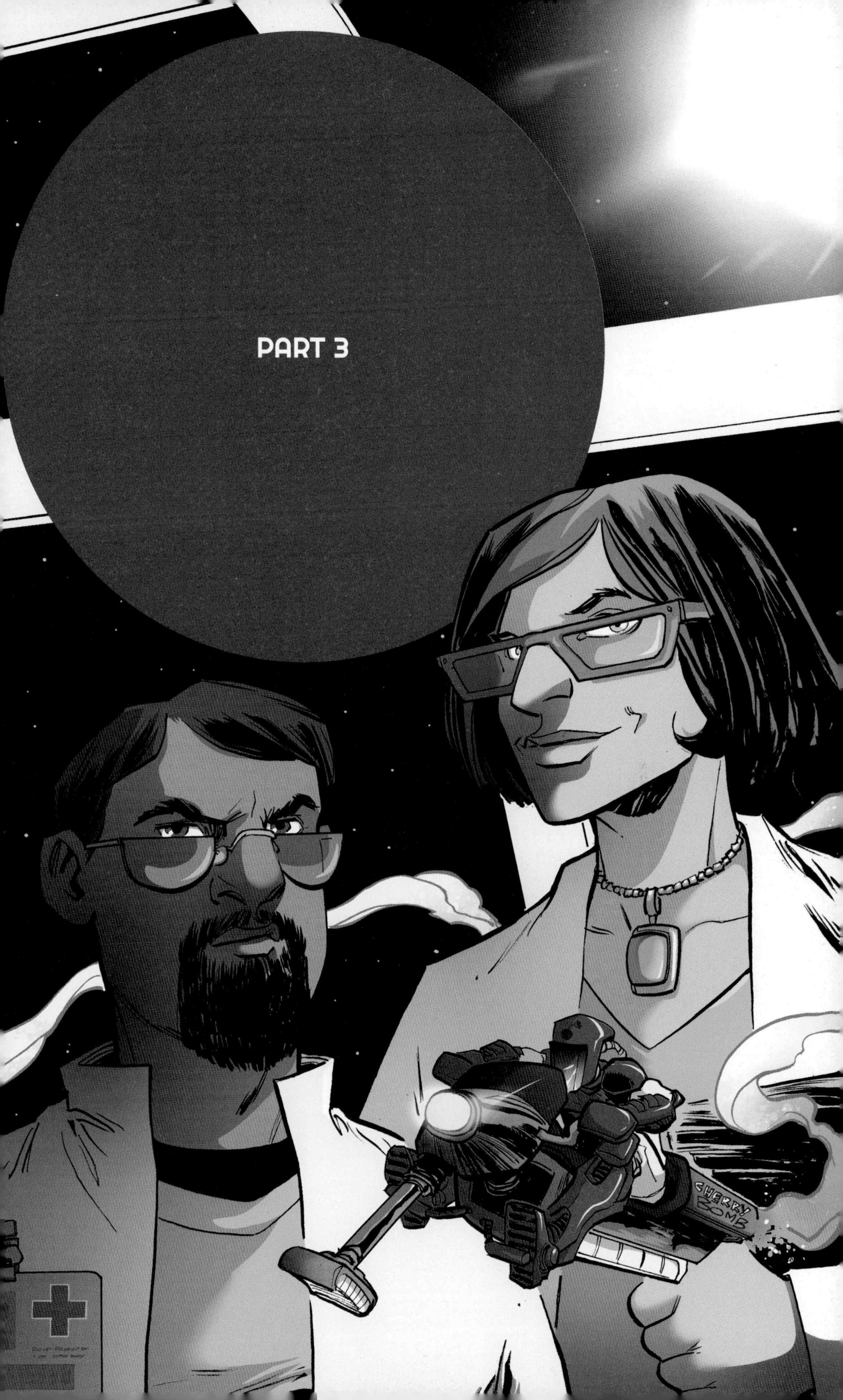
PART 3
CHERRY BOMB

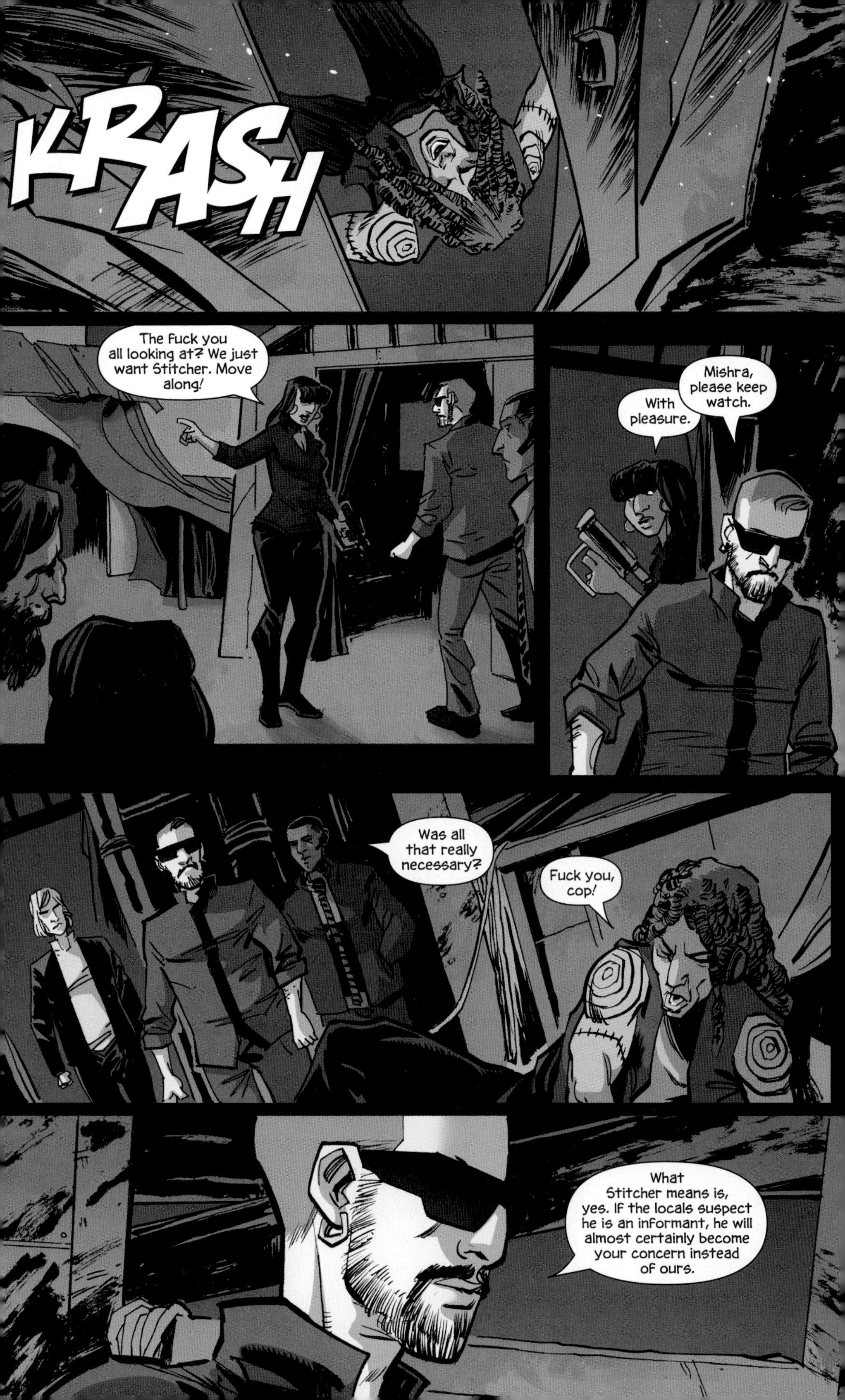
KRASH
The fuck you all looking at? We just want Stitcher. Move along!
With pleasure.
Mishra, please keep watch.
Was all that really necessary?
Fuck you, cop!
What Stitcher means is, yes. If the locals suspect he is an informant, he will almost certainly become your concern instead of ours.

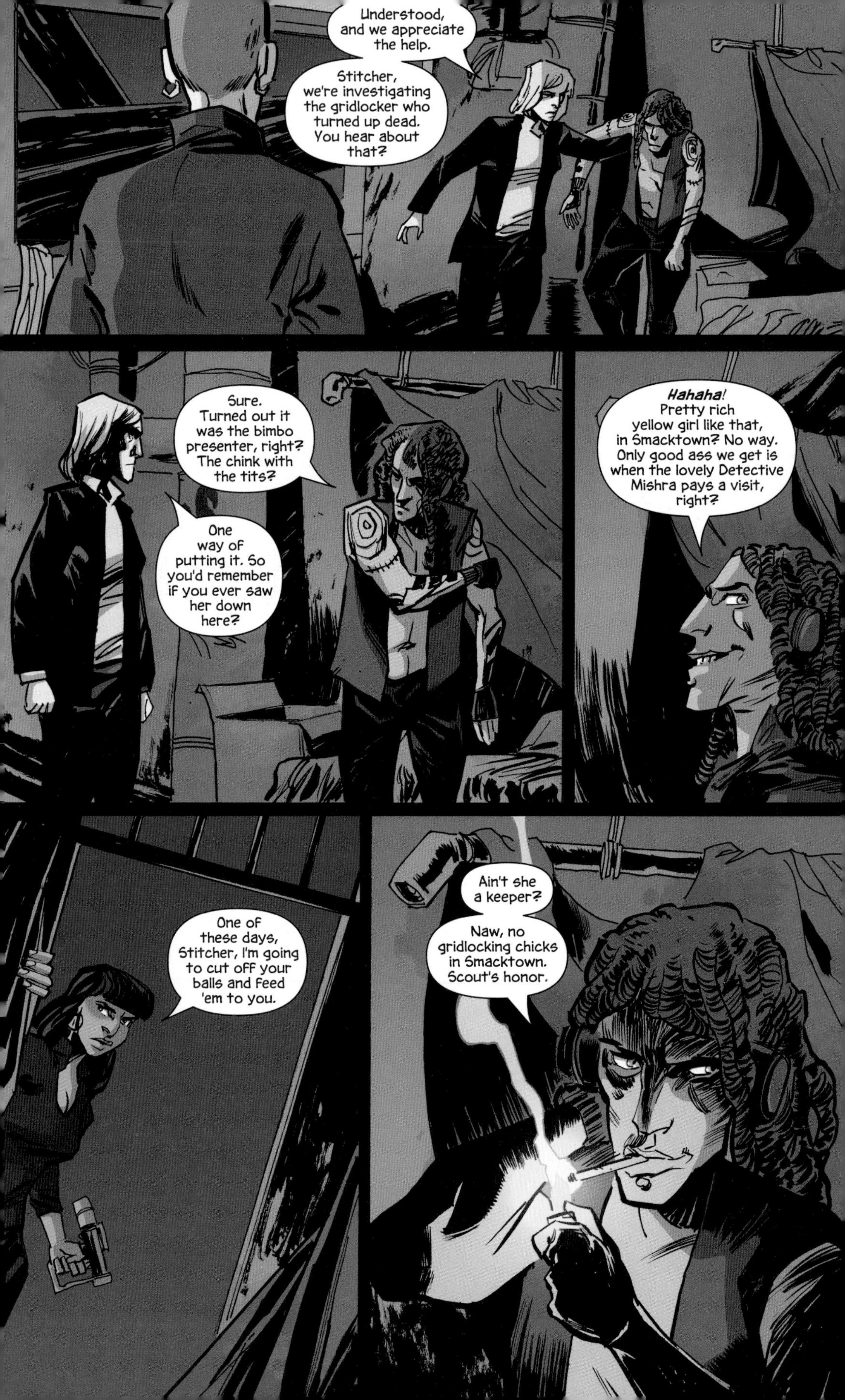
Understood, and we appreciate the help.
Stitcher, we're investigating the gridlocker who turned up dead. You hear about that?
Sure. Turned out it was the bimbo presenter, right? The chink with the tits?
One way of putting it. So you'd remember if you ever saw her down here?
Hahaha! Pretty rich yellow girl like that, in Smacktown? No way. Only good ass we get is when the lovely Detective Mishra pays a visit, right?
One of these days, Stitcher, I'm going to cut off your balls and feed 'em to you.
Ain't she a keeper?
Naw, no gridlocking chicks in Smacktown. Scout's honor.

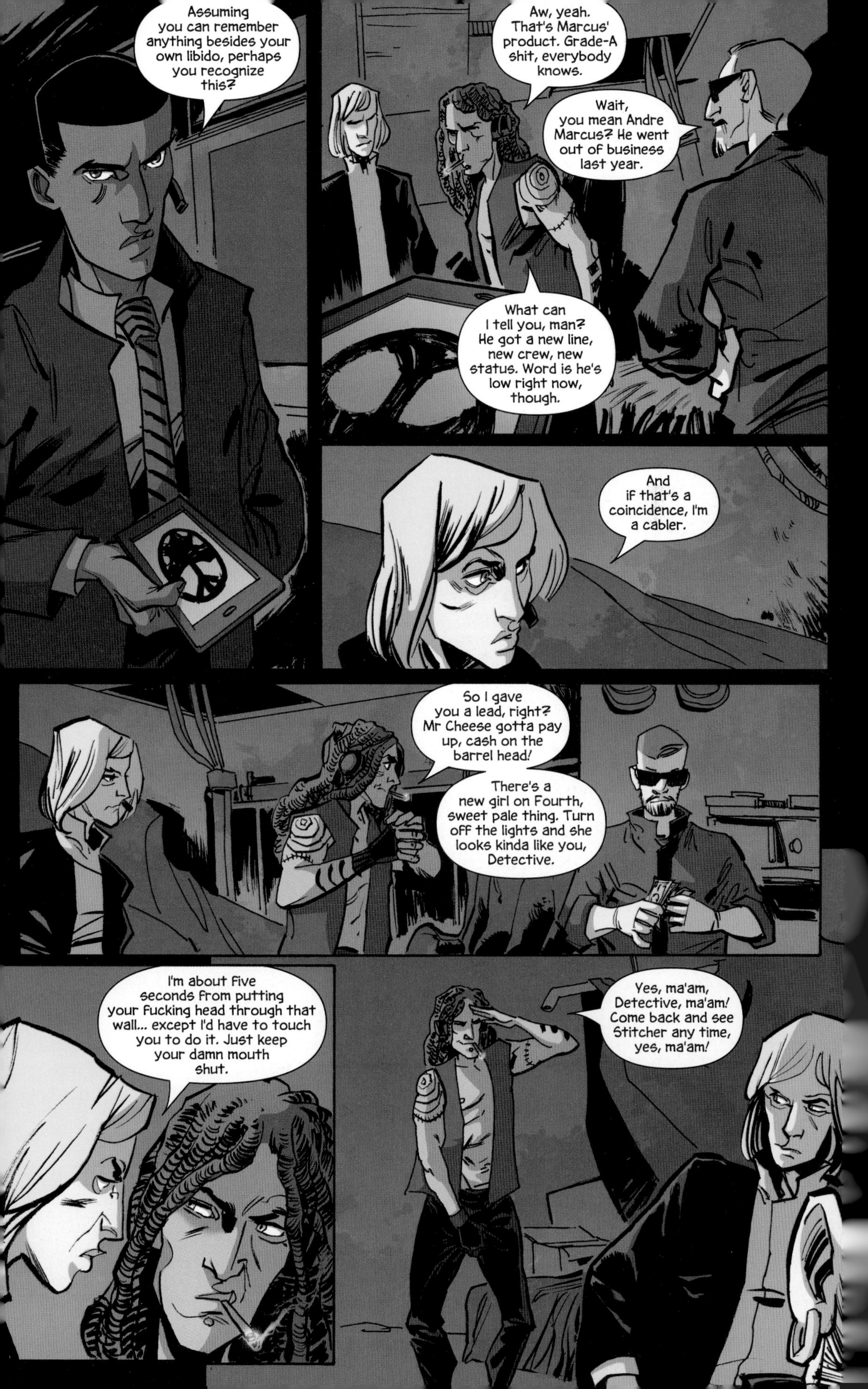
Assuming you can remember anything besides your own libido, perhaps you recognize this?
Aw, yeah. That's Marcus' product. Grade-A shit, everybody knows.
Wait, you mean Andre Marcus? He went out of business last year.
What can I tell you, man? He got a new line, new crew, new status. Word is he's low right now, though.
And if that's a coincidence, I'm a cabler.
So I gave you a lead, right? Mr Cheese gotta pay up, cash on the barrel head!
There's a new girl on Fourth, sweet pale thing. Turn off the lights and she looks kinda like you, Detective.
I'm about five seconds from putting your fucking head through that wall... except I'd have to touch you to do it. Just keep your damn mouth shut.
Yes, ma'am, Detective, ma'am! Come back and see Stitcher any time, yes, ma'am!

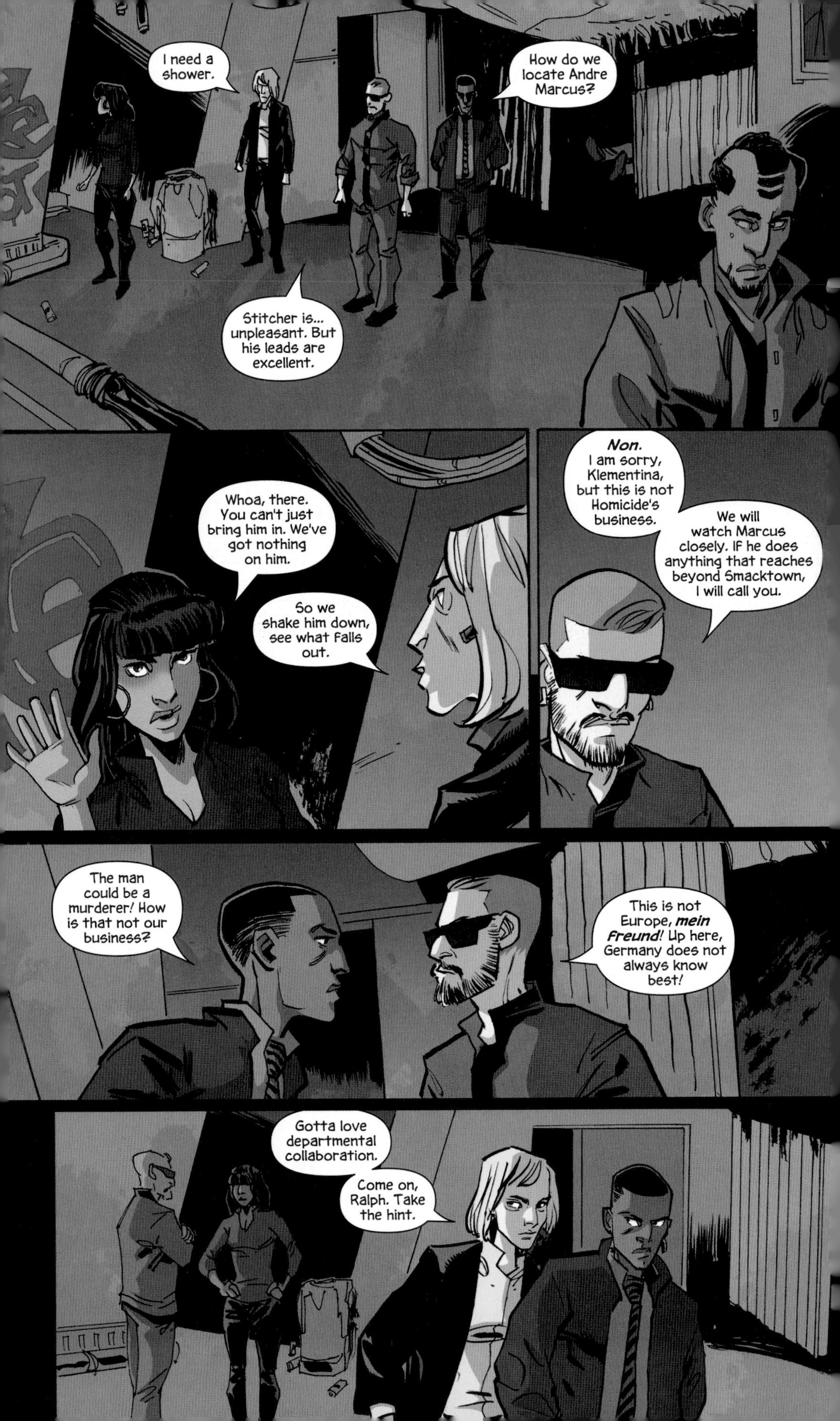
I need a shower.
How do we locate Andre Marcus?
Stitcher is... unpleasant. But his leads are excellent.
Whoa, there. You can't just bring him in. We've got nothing on him.
So we shake him down, see what falls out.
Non. I am sorry, Klementina, but this is not Homicide's business.
We will watch Marcus closely. If he does anything that reaches beyond Smacktown, I will call you.
The man could be a murderer! How is that not our business?
This is not Europe, *mein Freund*! Up here, Germany does not always know best!
Gotta love departmental collaboration.
Come on, Ralph. Take the hint.

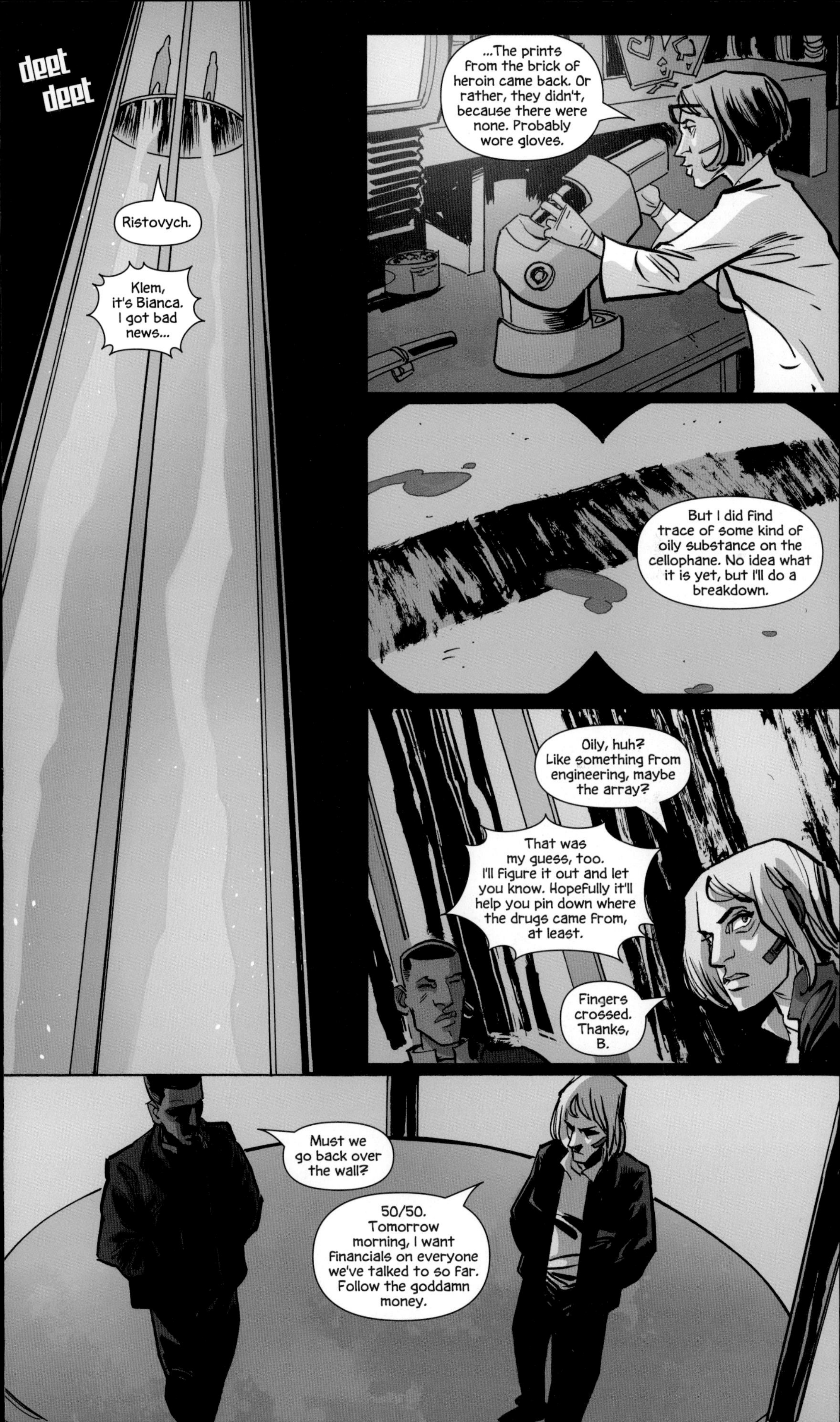
deet deet
Ristovych.
Klem, it's Bianca. I got bad news...
...The prints from the brick of heroin came back. Or rather, they didn't, because there were none. Probably wore gloves.
But I did find trace of some kind of oily substance on the cellophane. No idea what it is yet, but I'll do a breakdown.
Oily, huh? Like something from engineering, maybe the array?
That was my guess, too. I'll figure it out and let you know. Hopefully it'll help you pin down where the drugs came from, at least.
Fingers crossed. Thanks, B.
Must we go back over the wall?
50/50. Tomorrow morning, I want financials on everyone we've talked to so far. Follow the goddamn money.

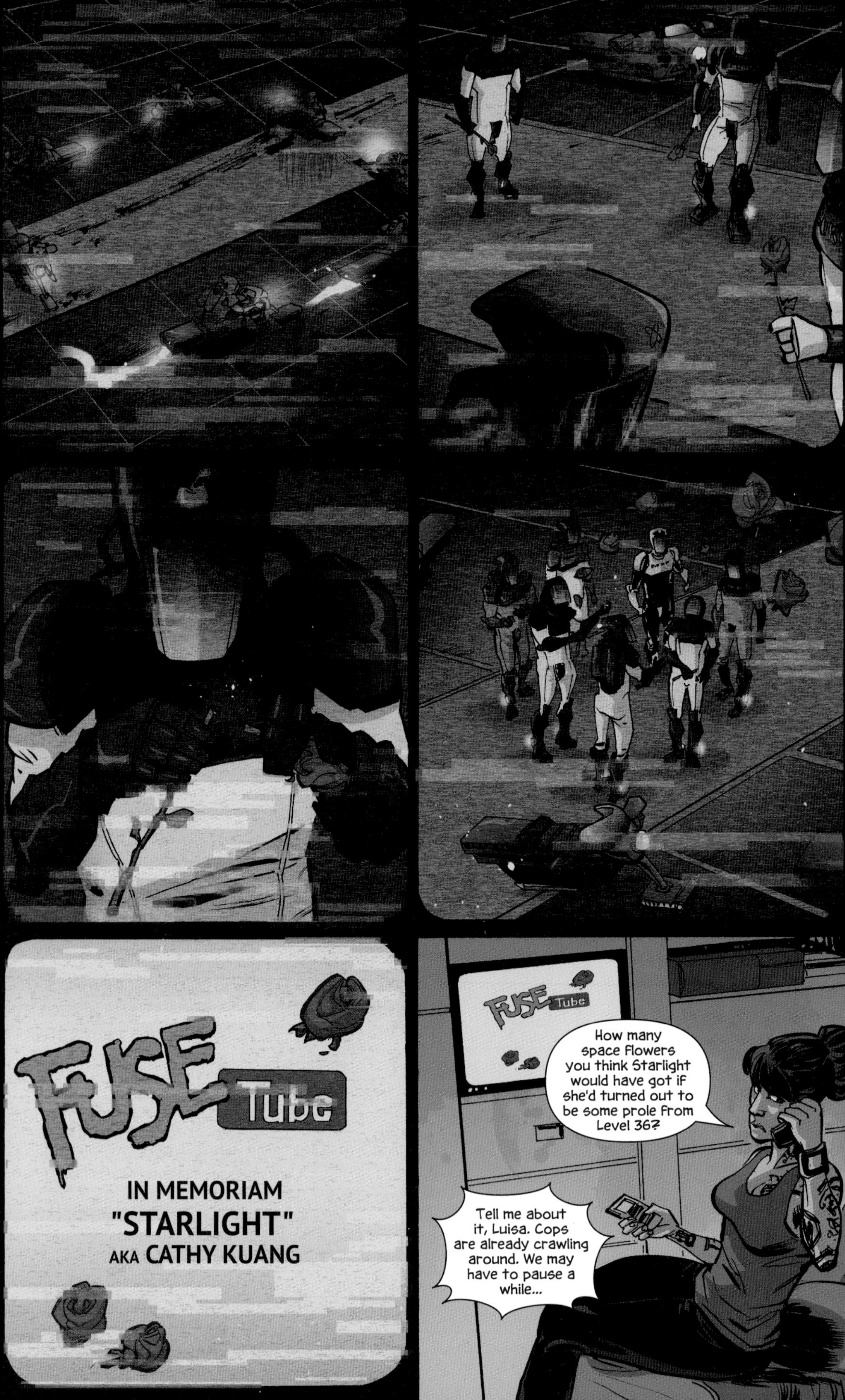
FUSE Tube
IN MEMORIAM
"STARLIGHT"
AKA CATHY KUANG
FUSE Tube
How many space flowers you think Starlight would have got if she'd turned out to be some prole from Level 36?
Tell me about it, Luisa. Cops are already crawling around. We may have to pause a while...

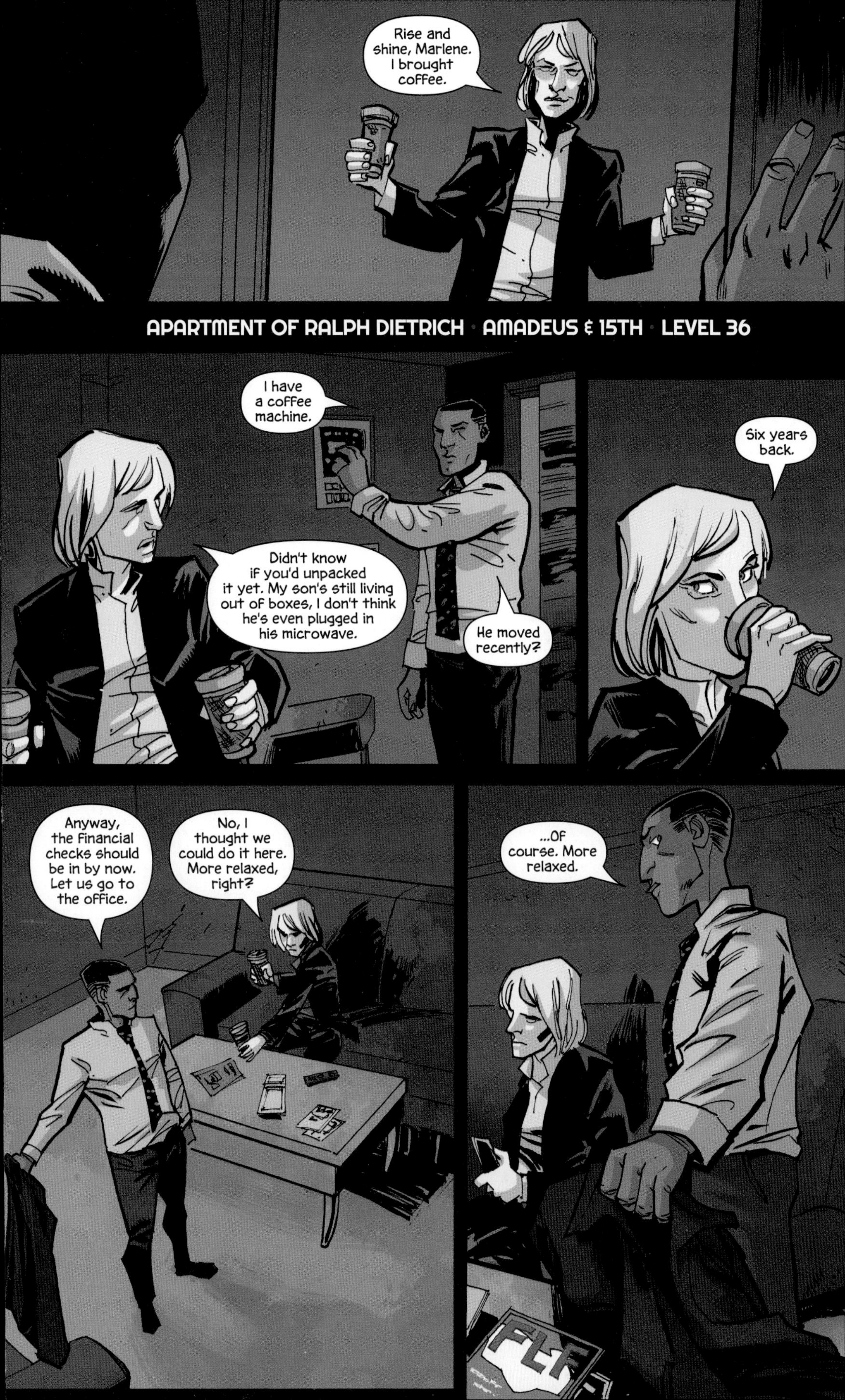
Rise and shine, Marlene. I brought coffee.
APARTMENT OF RALPH DIETRICH · AMADEUS & 15TH · LEVEL 36
I have a coffee machine.
Didn't know if you'd unpacked it yet. My son's still living out of boxes, I don't think he's even plugged in his microwave.
He moved recently?
Six years back.
Anyway, the financial checks should be in by now. Let us go to the office.
No, I thought we could do it here. More relaxed, right?
...Of course. More relaxed.
FLF

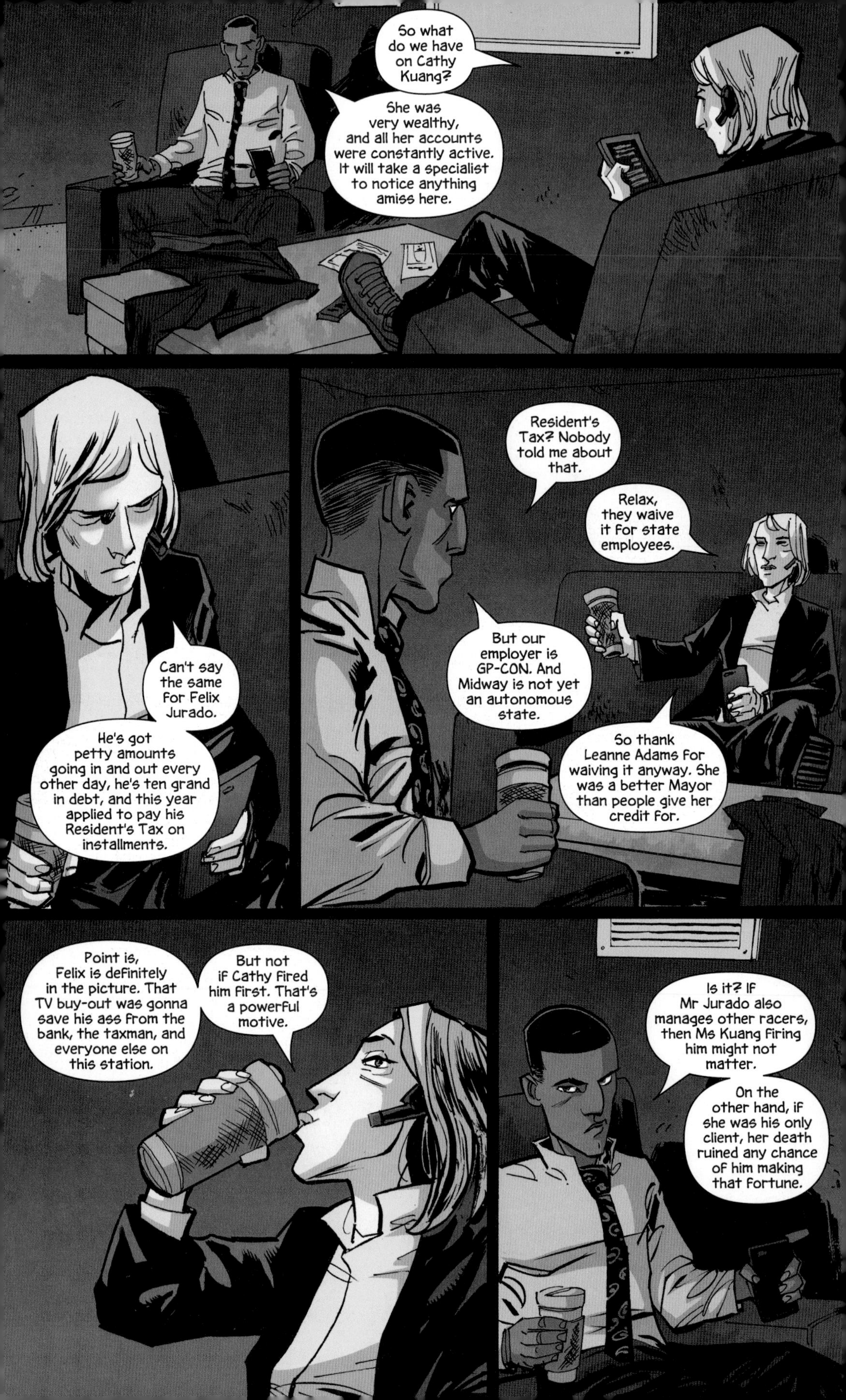
So what do we have on Cathy Kuang?
She was very wealthy, and all her accounts were constantly active. It will take a specialist to notice anything amiss here.
Can't say the same for Felix Jurado.
He's got petty amounts going in and out every other day, he's ten grand in debt, and this year applied to pay his Resident's Tax on installments.
Resident's Tax? Nobody told me about that.
Relax, they waive it for state employees.
But our employer is GP-CON. And Midway is not yet an autonomous state.
So thank Leanne Adams for waiving it anyway. She was a better Mayor than people give her credit for.
Point is, Felix is definitely in the picture. That TV buy-out was gonna save his ass from the bank, the taxman, and everyone else on this station.
But not if Cathy fired him first. That's a powerful motive.
Is it? If Mr Jurado also manages other racers, then Ms Kuang firing him might not matter.
On the other hand, if she was his only client, her death ruined any chance of him making that fortune.

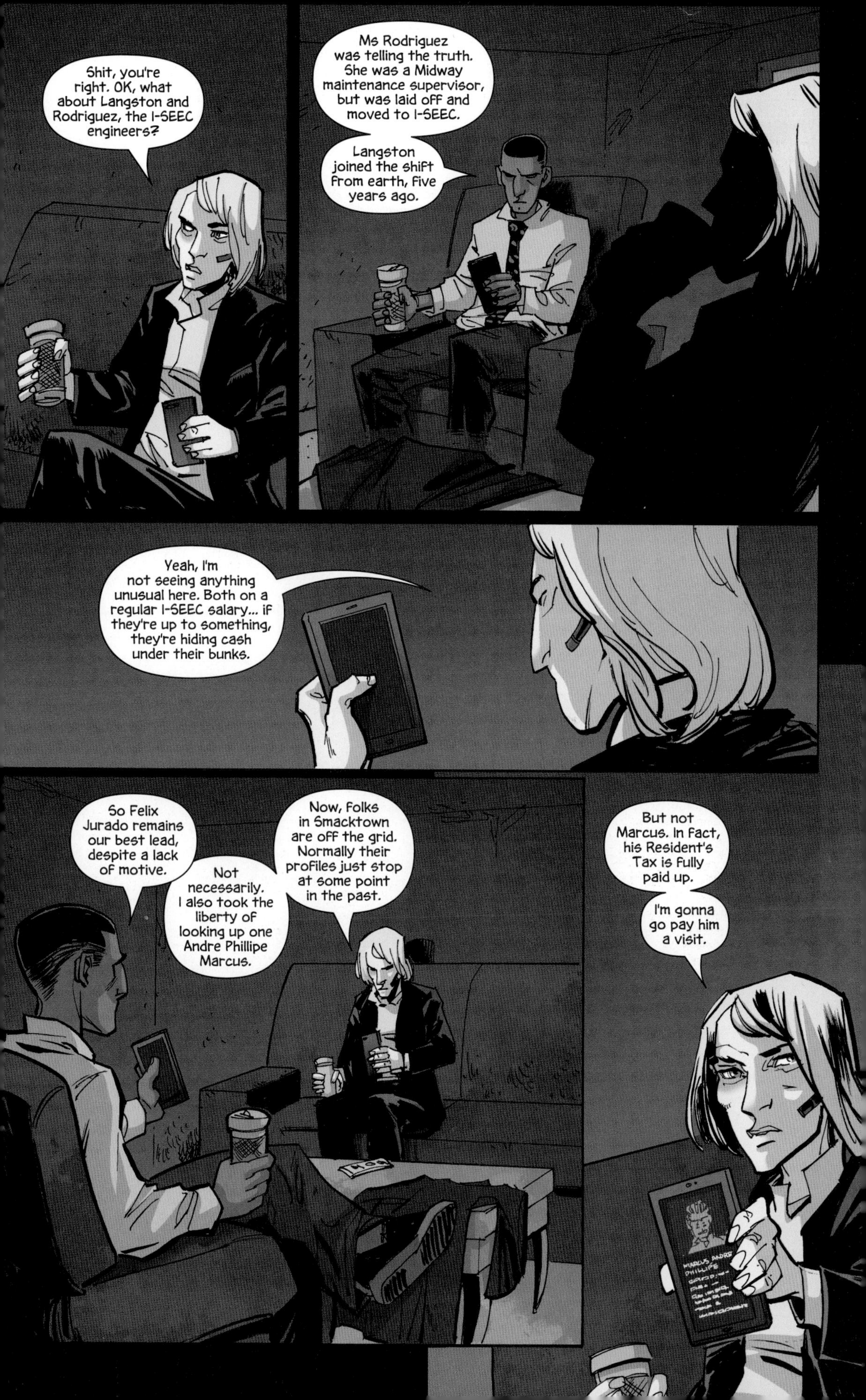
Shit, you're right. OK, what about Langston and Rodriguez, the I-SEEC engineers?
Ms Rodriguez was telling the truth. She was a Midway maintenance supervisor, but was laid off and moved to I-SEEC.
Langston joined the shift from earth, five years ago.
Yeah, I'm not seeing anything unusual here. Both on a regular I-SEEC salary... if they're up to something, they're hiding cash under their bunks.
So Felix Jurado remains our best lead, despite a lack of motive.
Not necessarily. I also took the liberty of looking up one Andre Phillipe Marcus.
Now, folks in Smacktown are off the grid. Normally their profiles just stop at some point in the past.
But not Marcus. In fact, his Resident's Tax is fully paid up.
I'm gonna go pay him a visit.

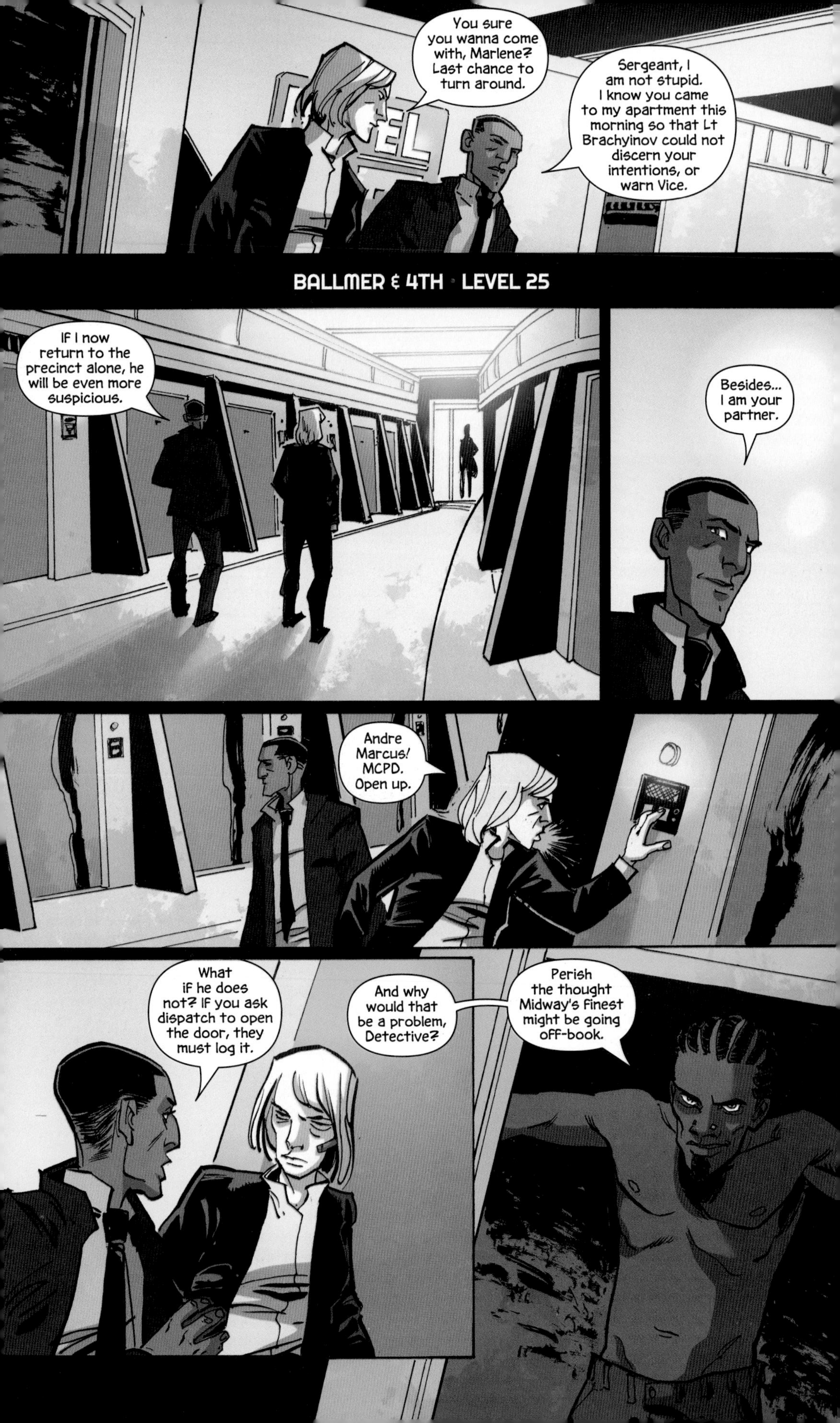
You sure you wanna come with, Marlene? Last chance to turn around.
Sergeant, I am not stupid. I know you came to my apartment this morning so that Lt Brachyinov could not discern your intentions, or warn Vice.
BALLMER & 4TH • LEVEL 25
If I now return to the precinct alone, he will be even more suspicious.
Besides... I am your partner.
Andre Marcus! MCPD. Open up.
What if he does not? If you ask dispatch to open the door, they must log it.
And why would that be a problem, Detective?
Perish the thought Midway's Finest might be going off-book.

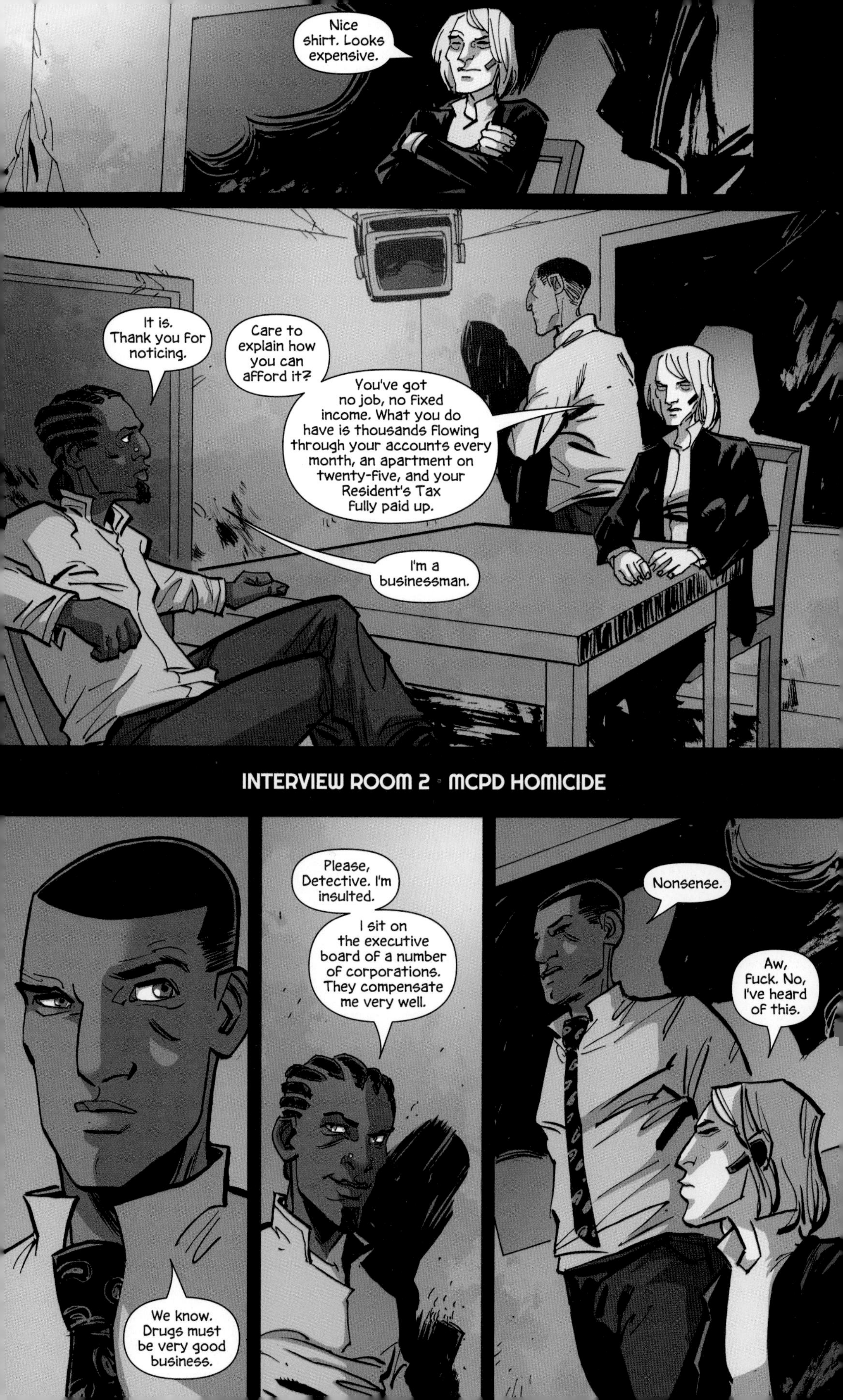
Nice shirt. Looks expensive.
It is. Thank you for noticing.
Care to explain how you can afford it?
You've got no job, no fixed income. What you do have is thousands flowing through your accounts every month, an apartment on twenty-five, and your Resident's Tax fully paid up.
I'm a businessman.
INTERVIEW ROOM 2 · MCPD HOMICIDE
We know. Drugs must be very good business.
Please, Detective. I'm insulted.
I sit on the executive board of a number of corporations. They compensate me very well.
Nonsense.
Aw, fuck. No, I've heard of this.

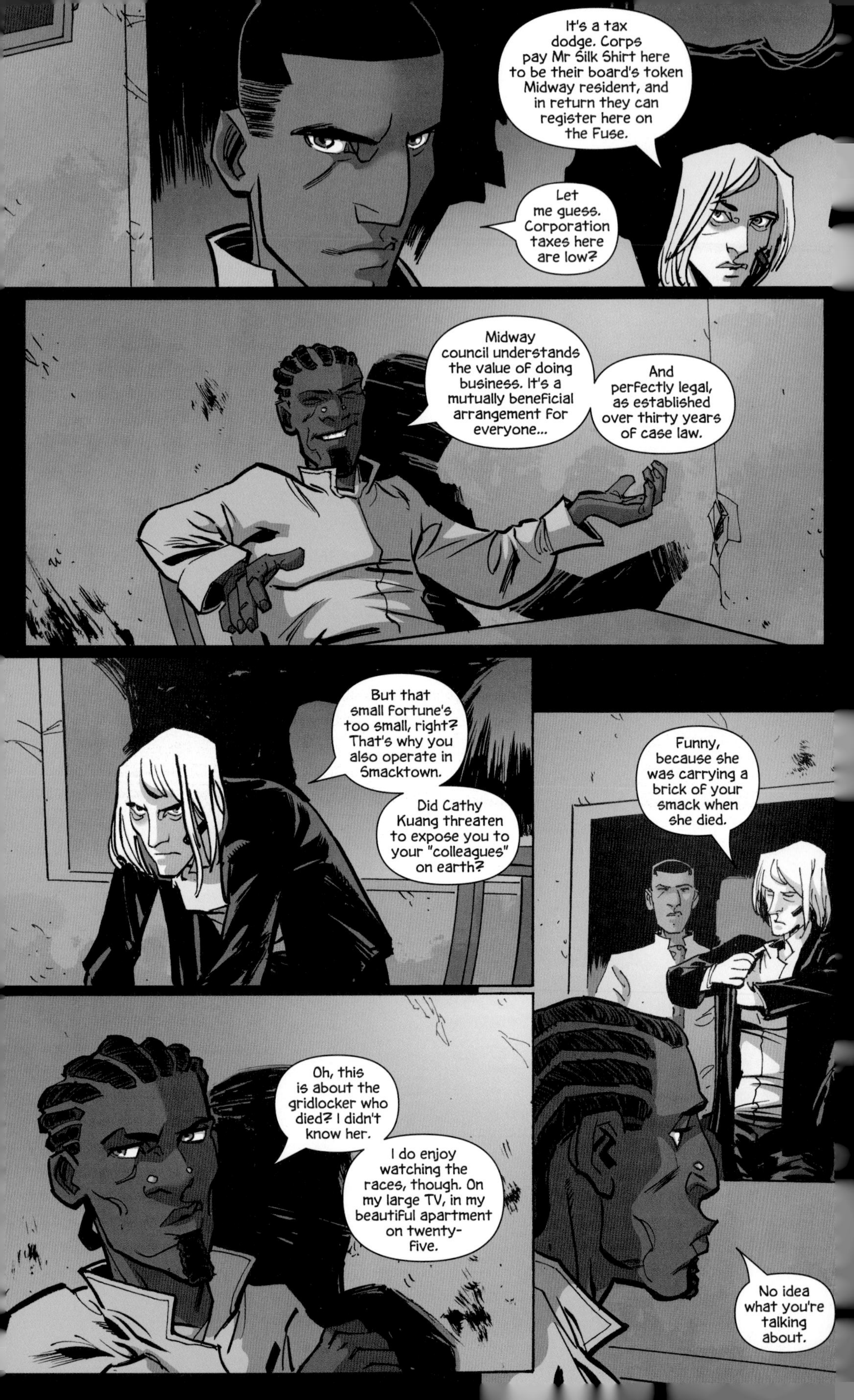
It's a tax dodge. Corps pay Mr Silk Shirt here to be their board's token Midway resident, and in return they can register here on the Fuse.
Let me guess. Corporation taxes here are low?
Midway council understands the value of doing business. It's a mutually beneficial arrangement for everyone...
And perfectly legal, as established over thirty years of case law.
But that small fortune's too small, right? That's why you also operate in Smacktown.
Did Cathy Kuang threaten to expose you to your "colleagues" on earth?
Oh, this is about the gridlocker who died? I didn't know her.
I do enjoy watching the races, though. On my large TV, in my beautiful apartment on twenty-five.
Funny, because she was carrying a brick of your smack when she died.
No idea what you're talking about.

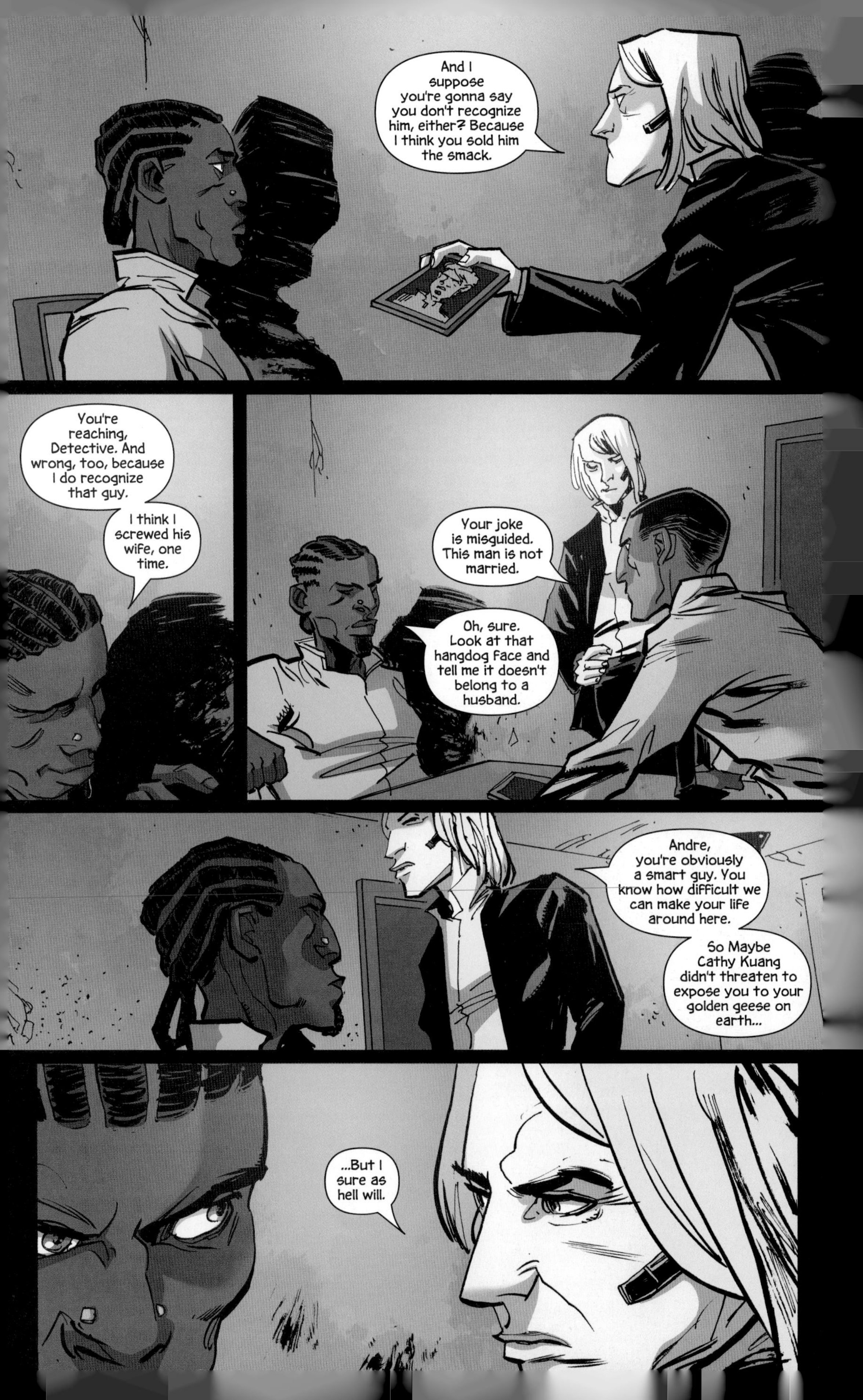
And I suppose you're gonna say you don't recognize him, either? Because I think you sold him the smack.
You're reaching, Detective. And wrong, too, because I do recognize that guy.
I think I screwed his wife, one time.
Your joke is misguided. This man is not married.
Oh, sure. Look at that hangdog face and tell me it doesn't belong to a husband.
Andre, you're obviously a smart guy. You know how difficult we can make your life around here.
So Maybe Cathy Kuang didn't threaten to expose you to your golden geese on earth...
...But I sure as hell will.

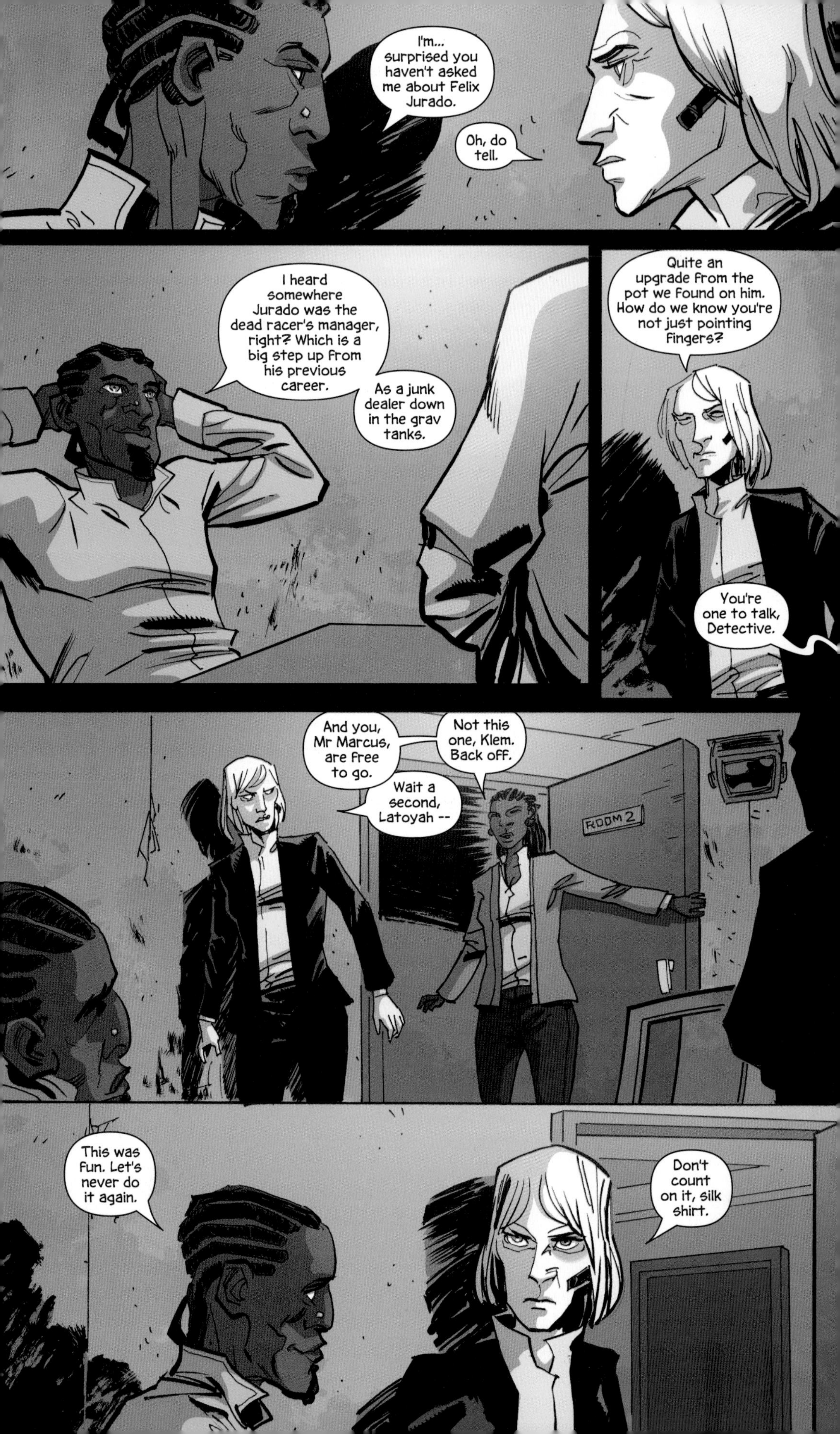
I'm... surprised you haven't asked me about Felix Jurado.
Oh, do tell.
I heard somewhere Jurado was the dead racer's manager, right? Which is a big step up from his previous career.
As a junk dealer down in the grav tanks.
Quite an upgrade from the pot we found on him. How do we know you're not just pointing fingers?
You're one to talk, Detective.
And you, Mr Marcus, are free to go.
Not this one, Klem. Back off.
Wait a second, Latoyah --
ROOM 2
This was fun. Let's never do it again.
Don't count on it, silk shirt.

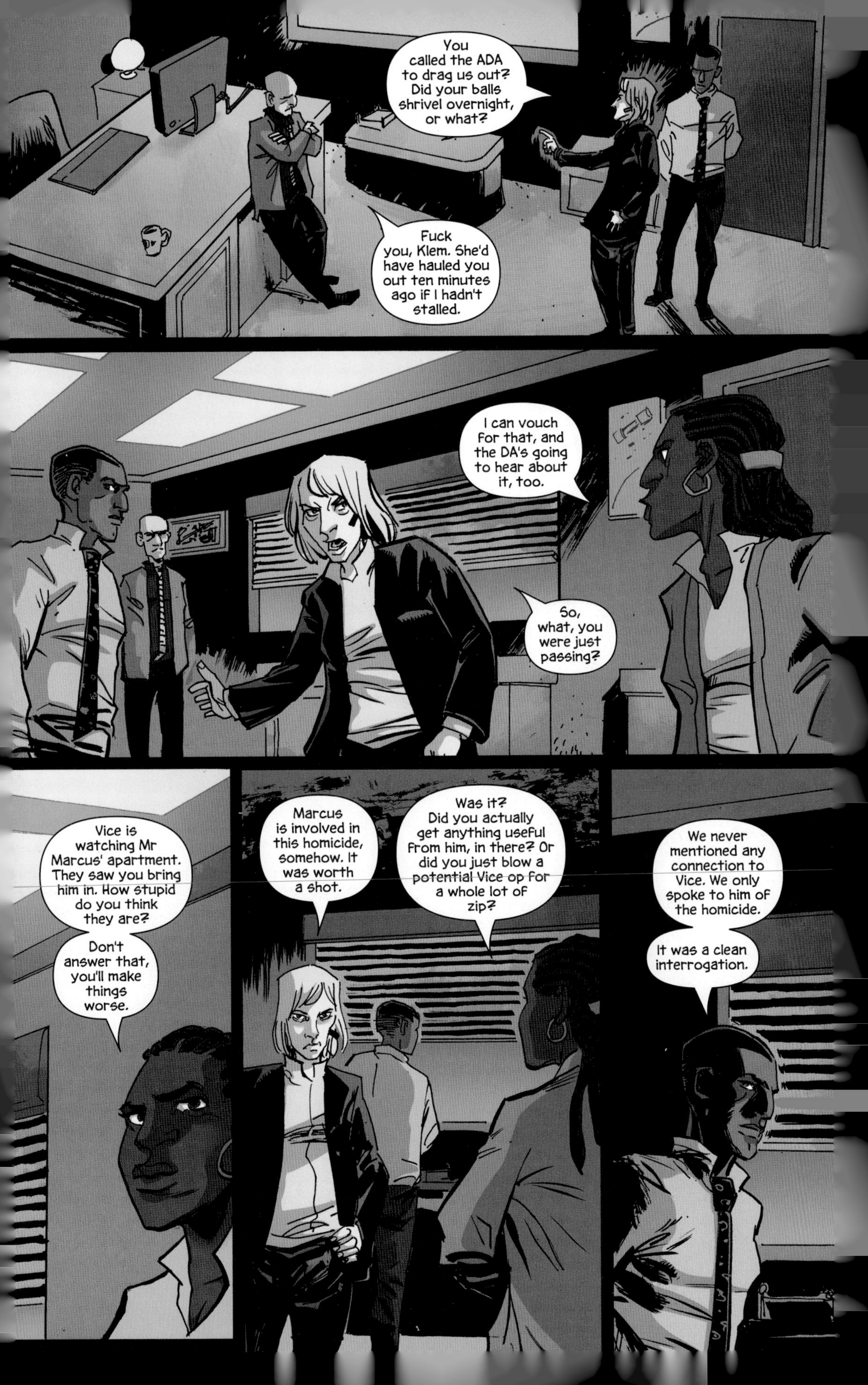
You called the ADA to drag us out? Did your balls shrivel overnight, or what?
Fuck you, Klem. She'd have hauled you out ten minutes ago if I hadn't stalled.
I can vouch for that, and the DA's going to hear about it, too.
So, what, you were just passing?
Vice is watching Mr Marcus' apartment. They saw you bring him in. How stupid do you think they are?
Don't answer that, you'll make things worse.
Marcus is involved in this homicide, somehow. It was worth a shot.
Was it? Did you actually get anything useful from him, in there? Or did you just blow a potential Vice op for a whole lot of zip?
We never mentioned any connection to Vice. We only spoke to him of the homicide.
It was a clean interrogation.

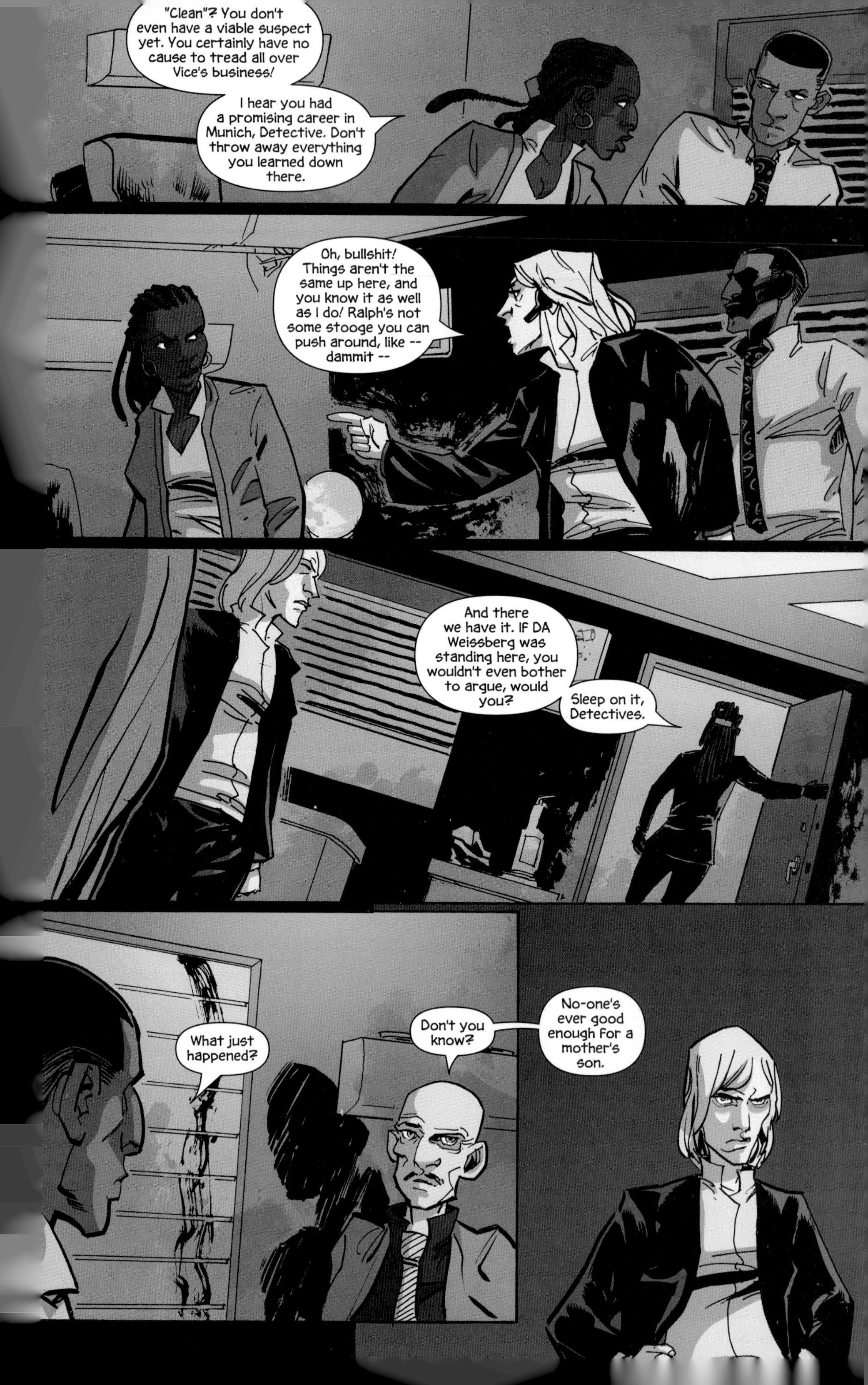
"Clean"? You don't even have a viable suspect yet. You certainly have no cause to tread all over Vice's business!
I hear you had a promising career in Munich, Detective. Don't throw away everything you learned down there.
Oh, bullshit! Things aren't the same up here, and you know it as well as I do! Ralph's not some stooge you can push around, like -- dammit --
And there we have it. If DA Weissberg was standing here, you wouldn't even bother to argue, would you?
Sleep on it, Detectives.
What just happened?
Don't you know?
No-one's ever good enough for a mother's son.

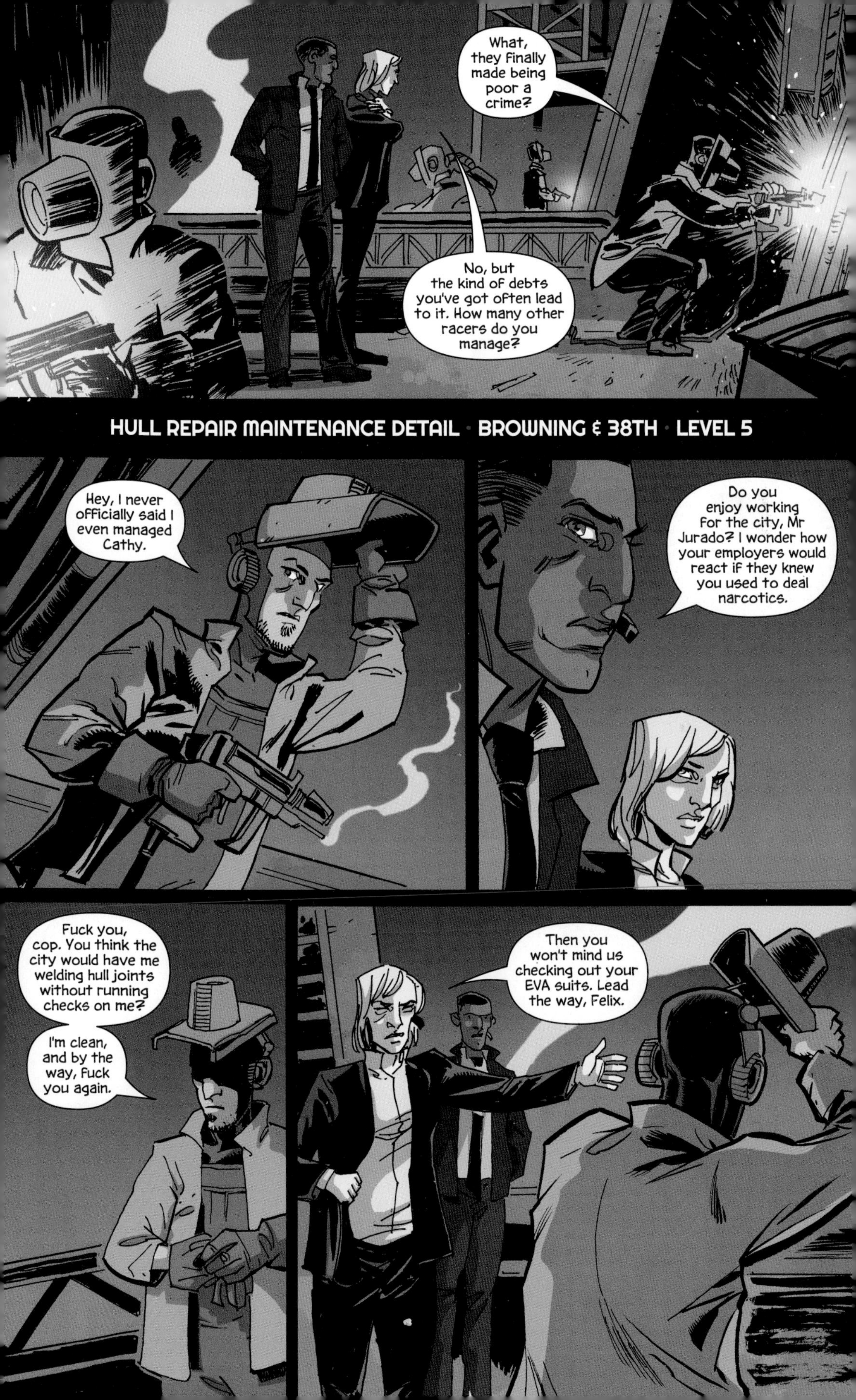
What, they finally made being poor a crime?
No, but the kind of debts you've got often lead to it. How many other racers do you manage?
HULL REPAIR MAINTENANCE DETAIL · BROWNING & 38TH · LEVEL 5
Hey, I never officially said I even managed Cathy.
Do you enjoy working for the city, Mr Jurado? I wonder how your employers would react if they knew you used to deal narcotics.
Fuck you, cop. You think the city would have me welding hull joints without running checks on me?
I'm clean, and by the way, fuck you again.
Then you won't mind us checking out your EVA suits. Lead the way, Felix.

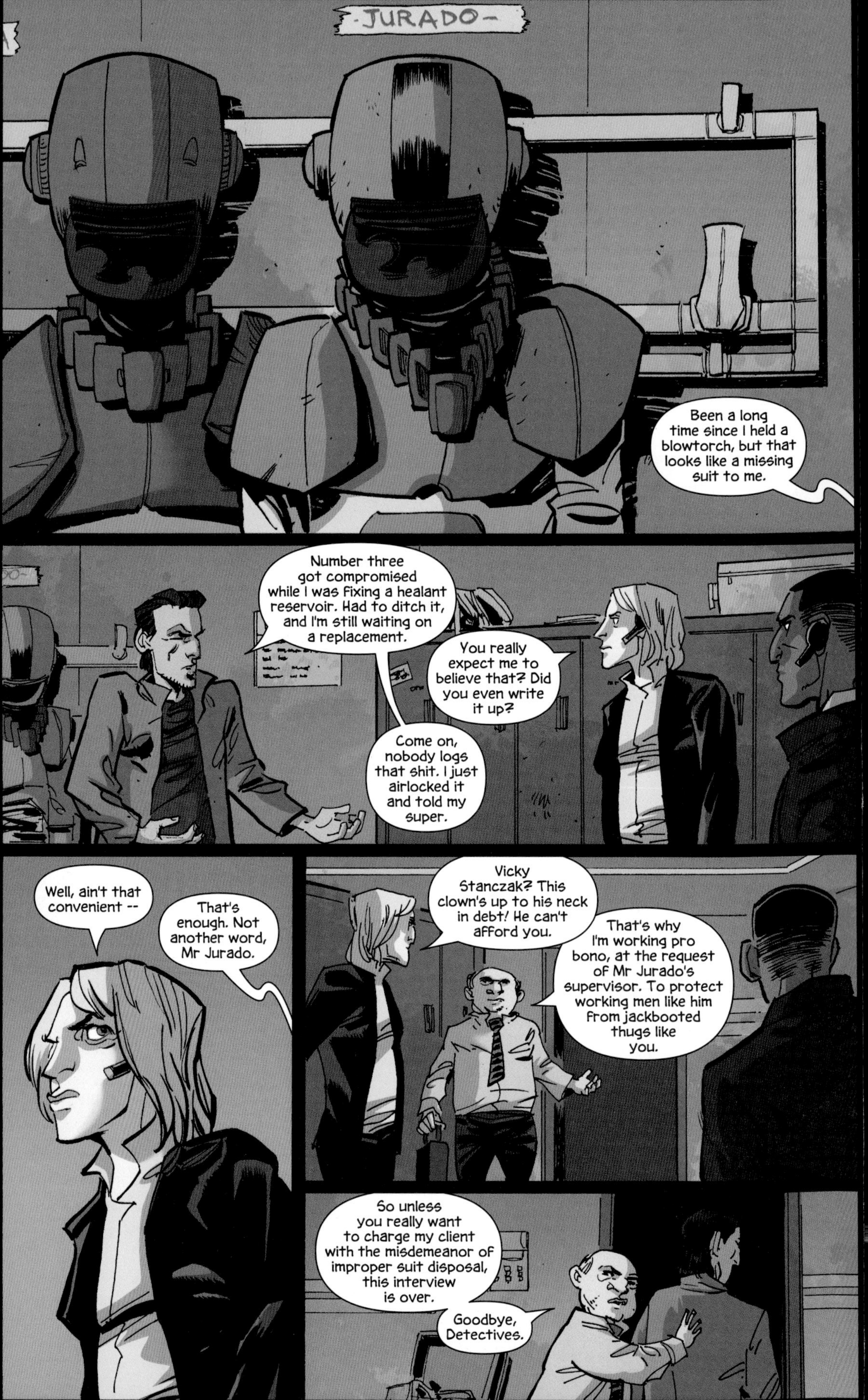
-JURADO-
Been a long time since I held a blowtorch, but that looks like a missing suit to me.
Number three got compromised while I was fixing a healant reservoir. Had to ditch it, and I'm still waiting on a replacement.
You really expect me to believe that? Did you even write it up?
Come on, nobody logs that shit. I just airlocked it and told my super.
Well, ain't that convenient --
That's enough. Not another word, Mr Jurado.
Vicky Stanczak? This clown's up to his neck in debt! He can't afford you.
That's why I'm working pro bono, at the request of Mr Jurado's supervisor. To protect working men like him from jackbooted thugs like you.
So unless you really want to charge my client with the misdemeanor of improper suit disposal, this interview is over.
Goodbye, Detectives.

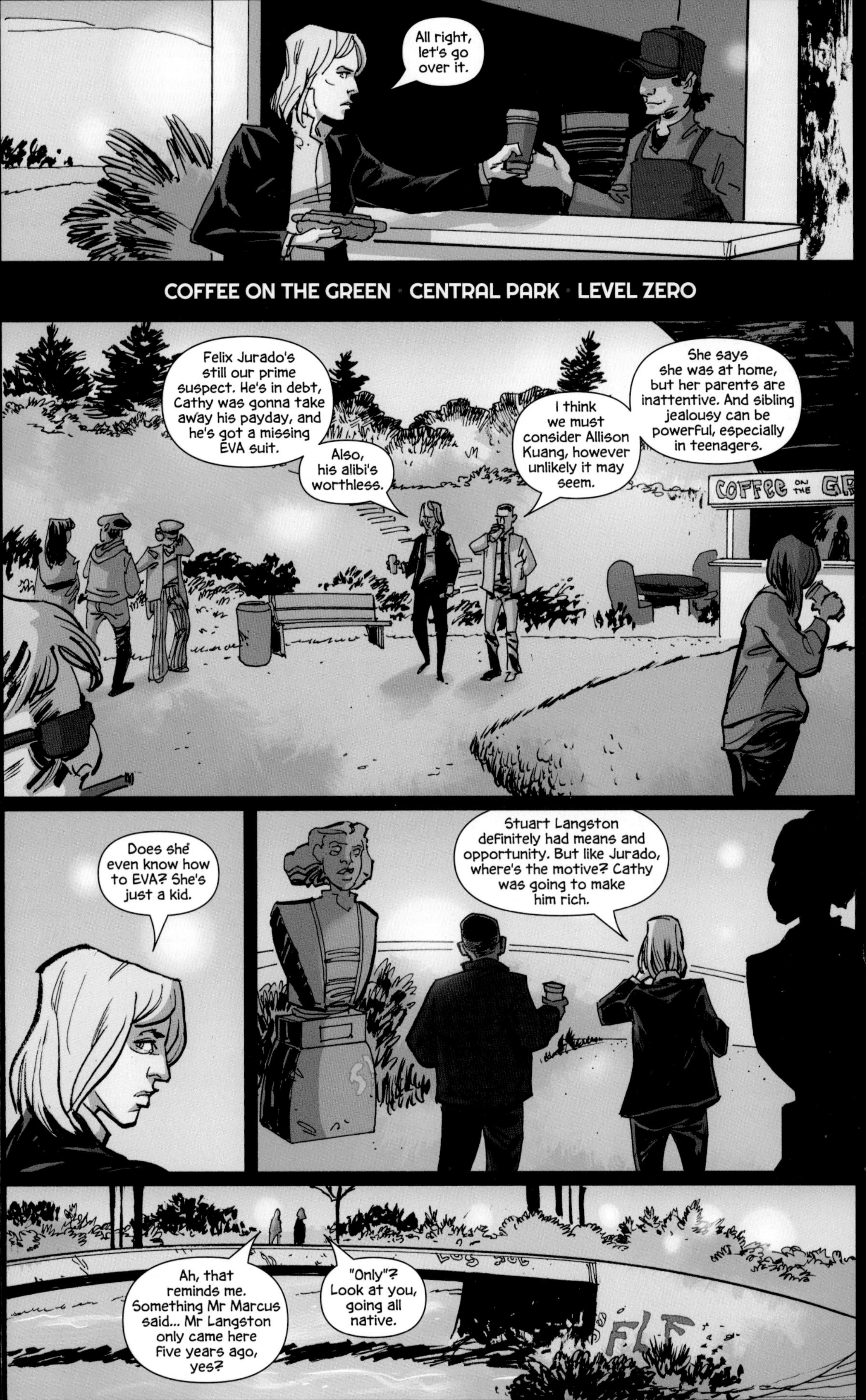

All right, let's go over it.
COFFEE ON THE GREEN • CENTRAL PARK • LEVEL ZERO
Felix Jurado's still our prime suspect. He's in debt, Cathy was gonna take away his payday, and he's got a missing EVA suit.
Also, his alibi's worthless.
I think we must consider Allison Kuang, however unlikely it may seem.
She says she was at home, but her parents are inattentive. And sibling jealousy can be powerful, especially in teenagers.
COFFEE ON THE GR
Does she even know how to EVA? She's just a kid.
Stuart Langston definitely had means and opportunity. But like Jurado, where's the motive? Cathy was going to make him rich.
Ah, that reminds me. Something Mr Marcus said... Mr Langston only came here five years ago, yes?
"Only"? Look at you, going all native.
FLF

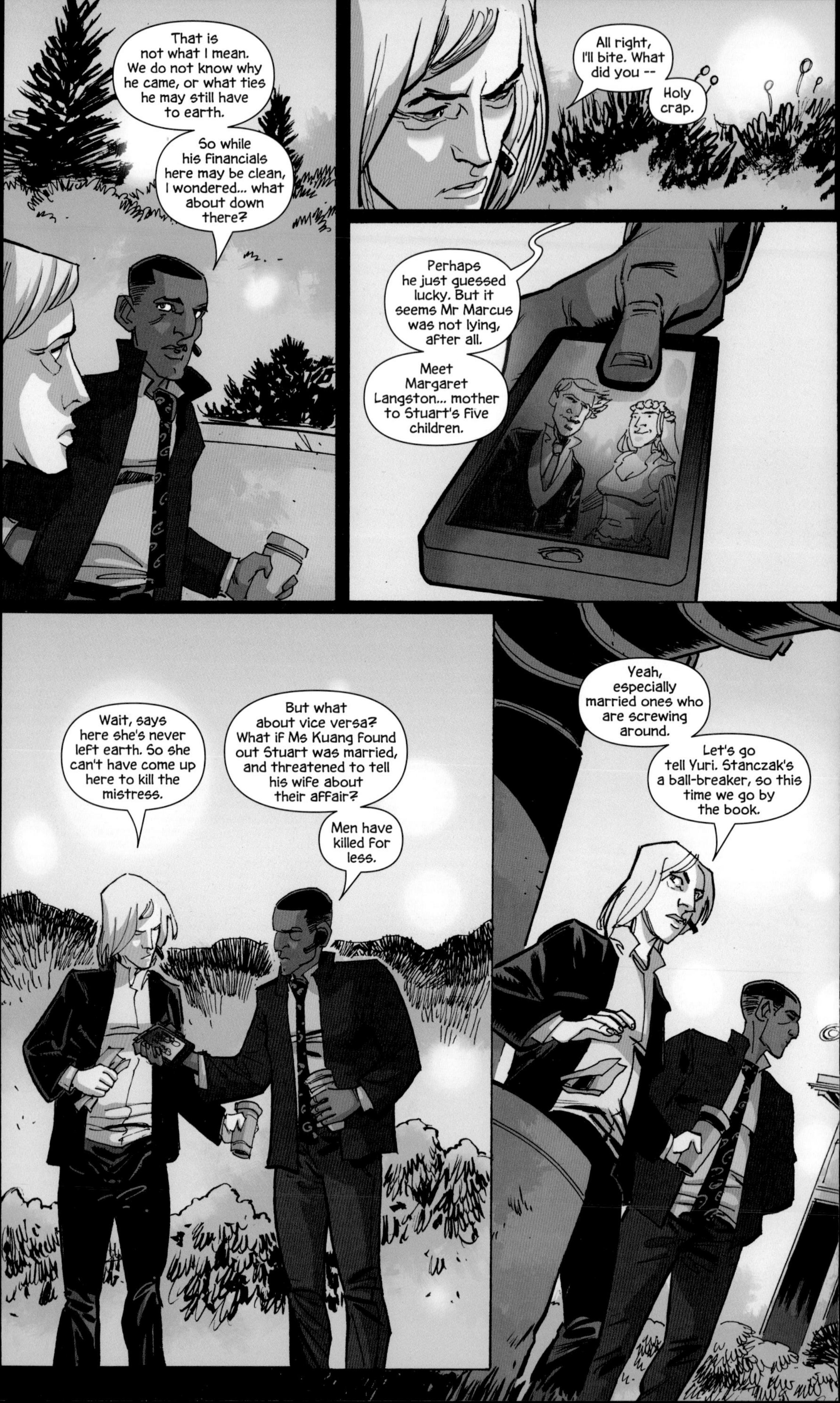

That is not what I mean. We do not know why he came, or what ties he may still have to earth.
So while his financials here may be clean, I wondered... what about down there?
All right, I'll bite. What did you --
Holy crap.
Perhaps he just guessed lucky. But it seems Mr Marcus was not lying, after all.
Meet Margaret Langston... mother to Stuart's five children.
Wait, says here she's never left earth. So she can't have come up here to kill the mistress.
But what about vice versa? What if Ms Kuang found out Stuart was married, and threatened to tell his wife about their affair?
Men have killed for less.
Yeah, especially married ones who are screwing around.
Let's go tell Yuri. Stanczak's a ball-breaker, so this time we go by the book.

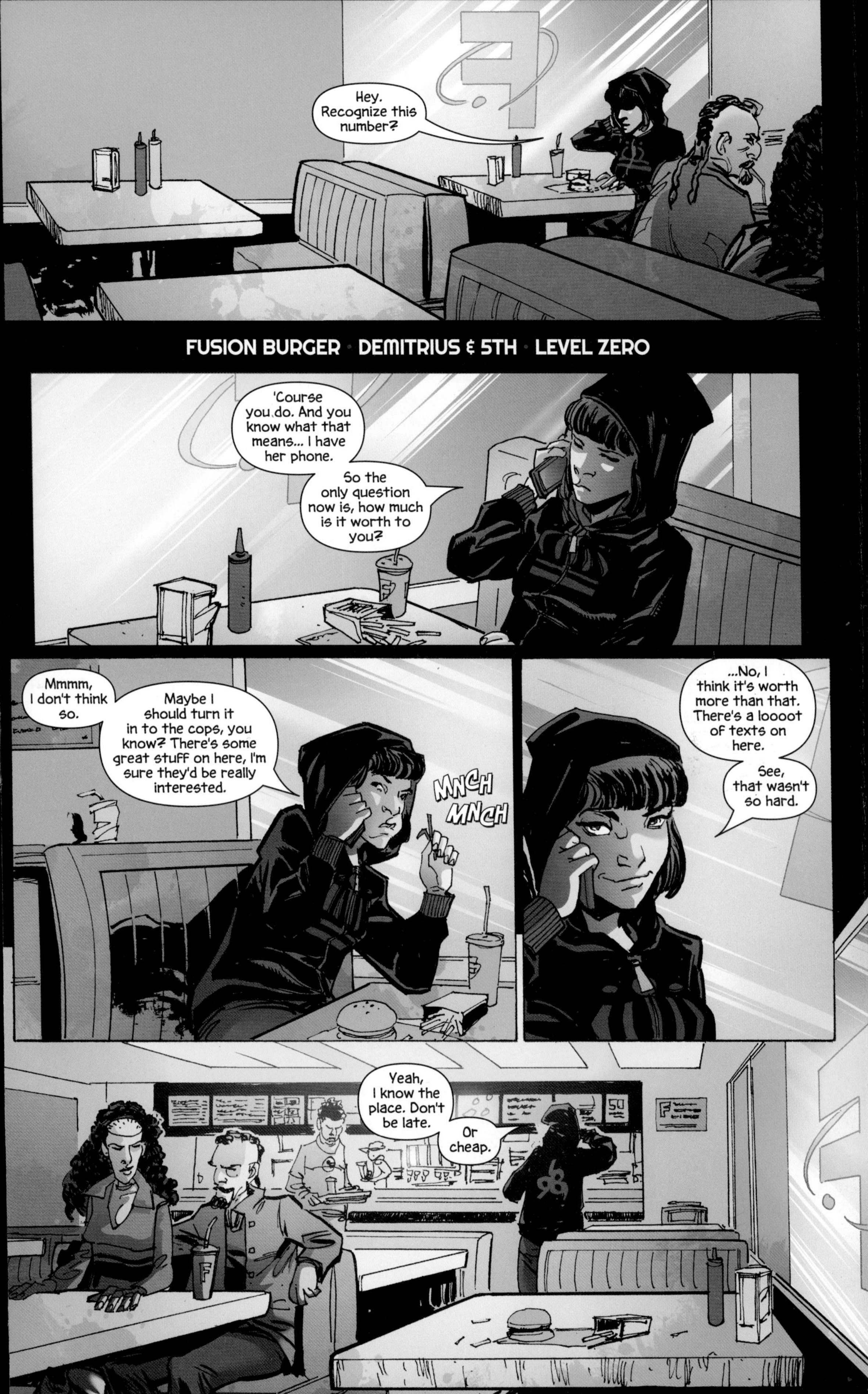
Hey. Recognize this number?
FUSION BURGER • DEMITRIUS & 5TH • LEVEL ZERO
'Course you do. And you know what that means... I have her phone.
So the only question now is, how much is it worth to you?
Mmmm, I don't think so.
Maybe I should turn it in to the cops, you know? There's some great stuff on here, I'm sure they'd be really interested.
MNCH MNCH
...No, I think it's worth more than that. There's a loooot of texts on here.
See, that wasn't so hard.
Yeah, I know the place. Don't be late.
Or cheap.

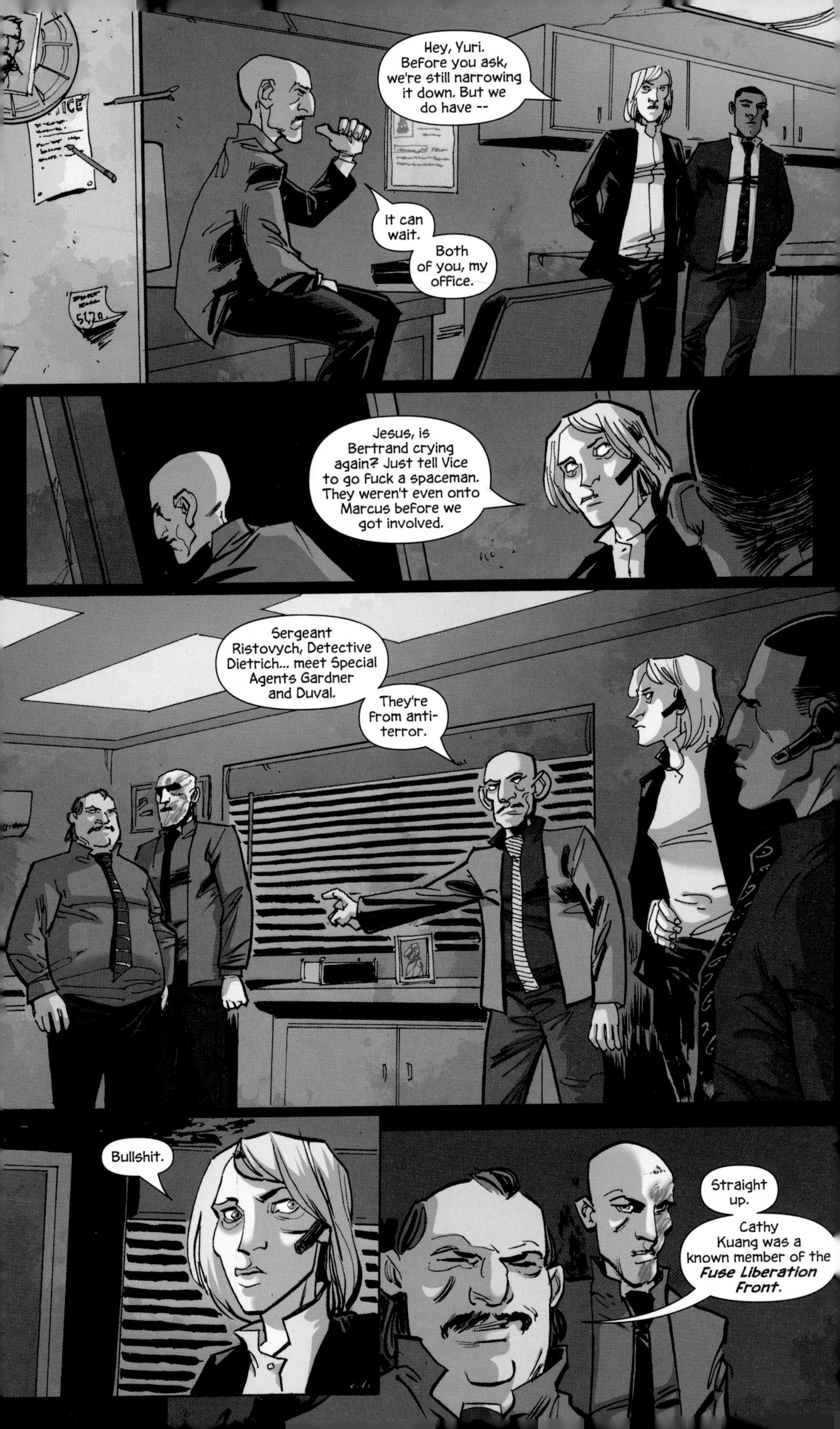
Hey, Yuri. Before you ask, we're still narrowing it down. But we do have --
It can wait.
Both of you, my office.
Jesus, is Bertrand crying again? Just tell Vice to go fuck a spaceman. They weren't even onto Marcus before we got involved.
Sergeant Ristovych, Detective Dietrich... meet Special Agents Gardner and Duval.
They're from anti-terror.
Bullshit.
Straight up.
Cathy Kuang was a known member of the *Fuse Liberation Front.*

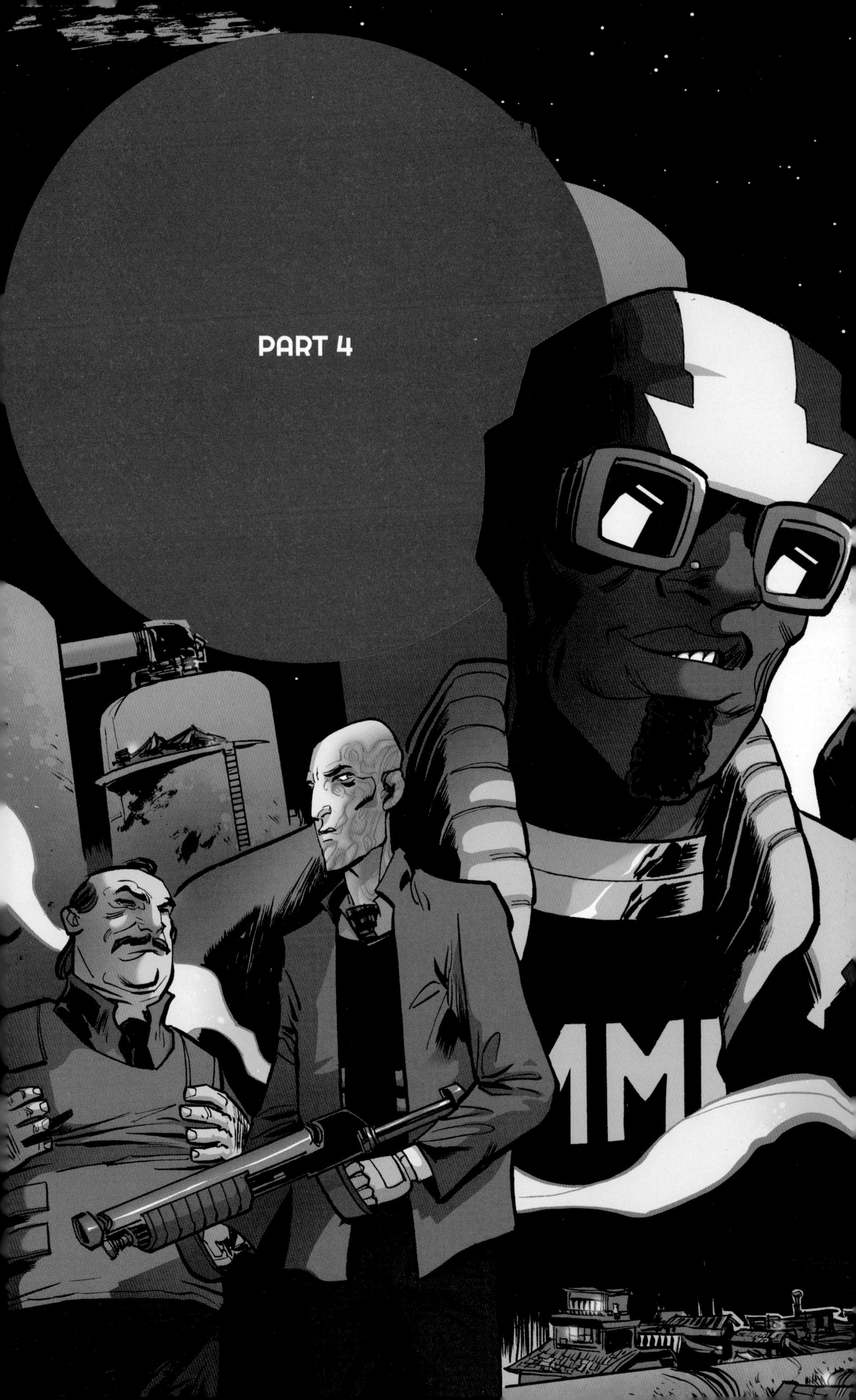
PART 4

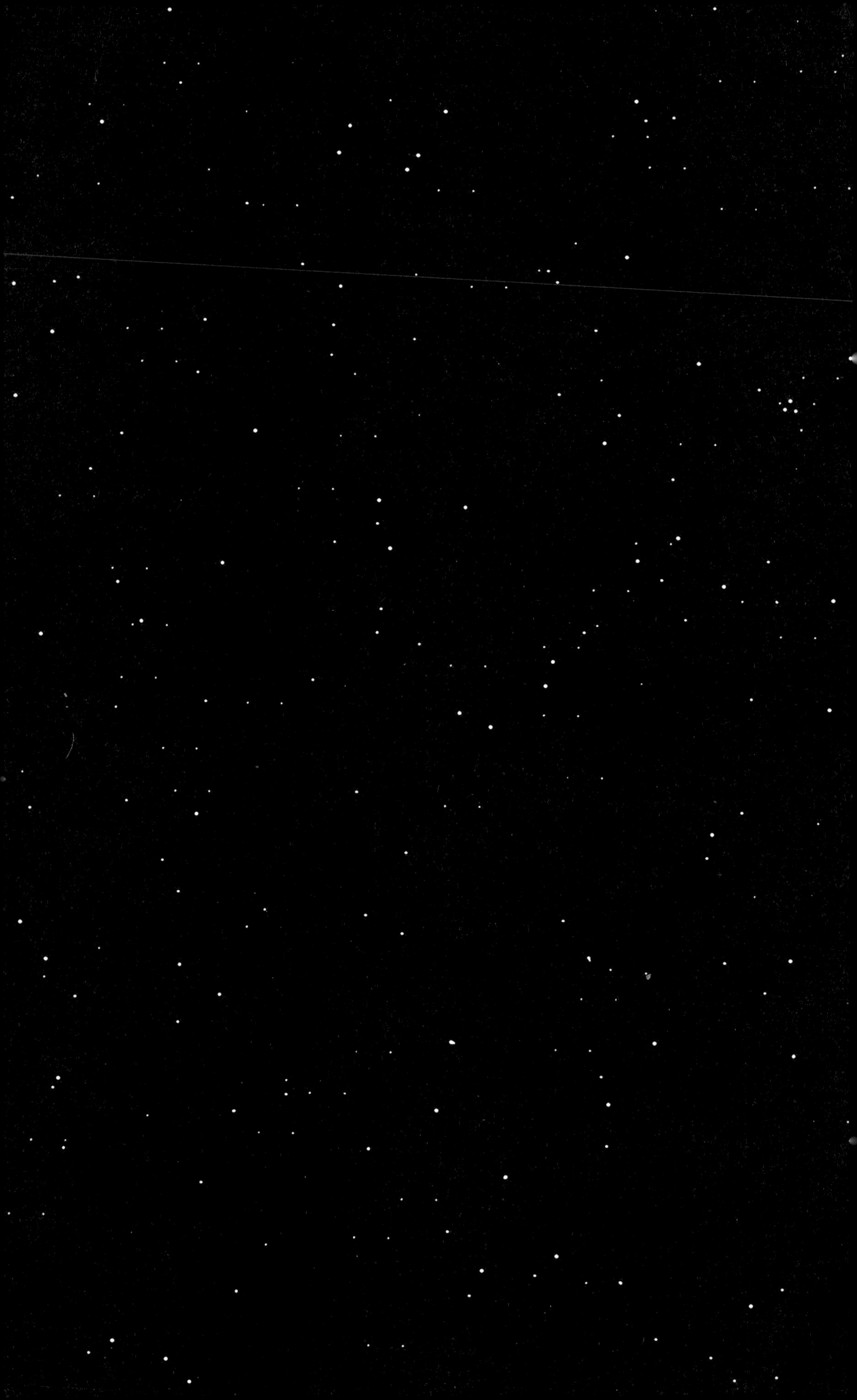

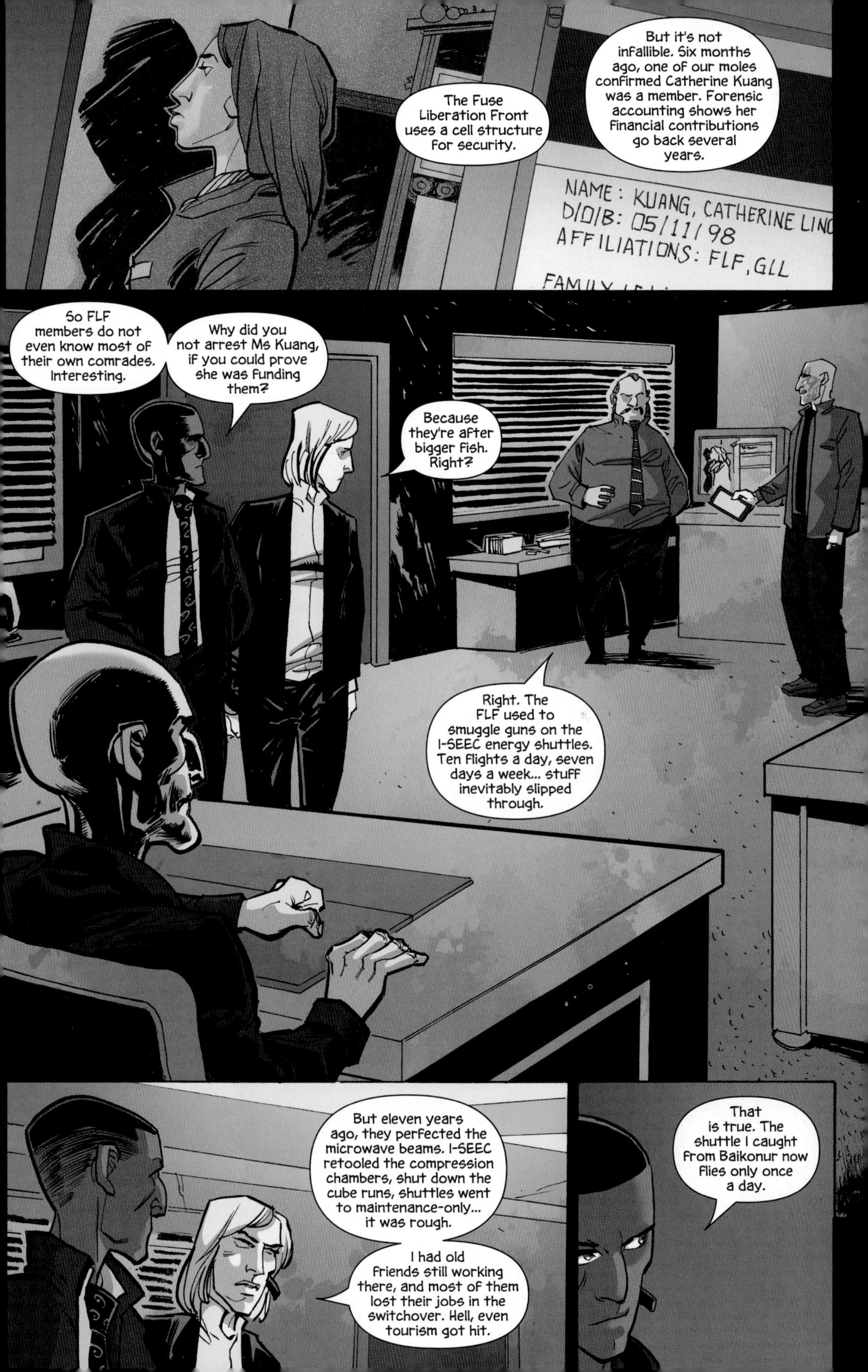
The Fuse Liberation Front uses a cell structure for security.
But it's not infallible. Six months ago, one of our moles confirmed Catherine Kuang was a member. Forensic accounting shows her financial contributions go back several years.
NAME : KUANG, CATHERINE LIN
D/O/B: 05/11/98
AFFILIATIONS: FLF, GLL
So FLF members do not even know most of their own comrades. Interesting.
Why did you not arrest Ms Kuang, if you could prove she was funding them?
Because they're after bigger fish. Right?
Right. The FLF used to smuggle guns on the I-SEEC energy shuttles. Ten flights a day, seven days a week... stuff inevitably slipped through.
But eleven years ago, they perfected the microwave beams. I-SEEC retooled the compression chambers, shut down the cube runs, shuttles went to maintenance-only... it was rough.
I had old friends still working there, and most of them lost their jobs in the switchover. Hell, even tourism got hit.
That is true. The shuttle I caught from Baikonur now flies only once a day.

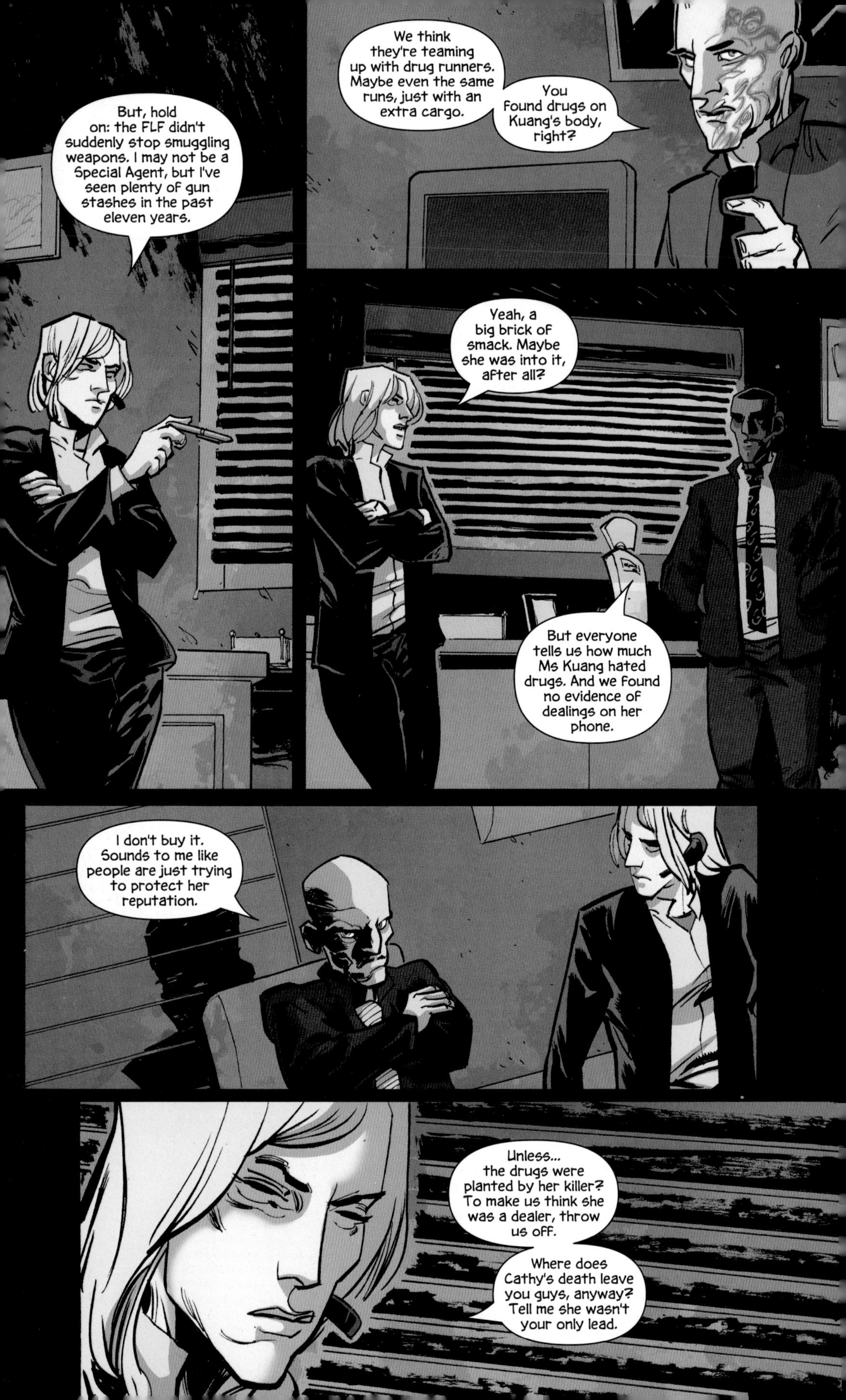
But, hold on: the FLF didn't suddenly stop smuggling weapons. I may not be a Special Agent, but I've seen plenty of gun stashes in the past eleven years.
We think they're teaming up with drug runners. Maybe even the same runs, just with an extra cargo.
You found drugs on Kuang's body, right?
Yeah, a big brick of smack. Maybe she was into it, after all?
But everyone tells us how much Ms Kuang hated drugs. And we found no evidence of dealings on her phone.
I don't buy it. Sounds to me like people are just trying to protect her reputation.
Unless... the drugs were planted by her killer? To make us think she was a dealer, throw us off.
Where does Cathy's death leave you guys, anyway? Tell me she wasn't your only lead.

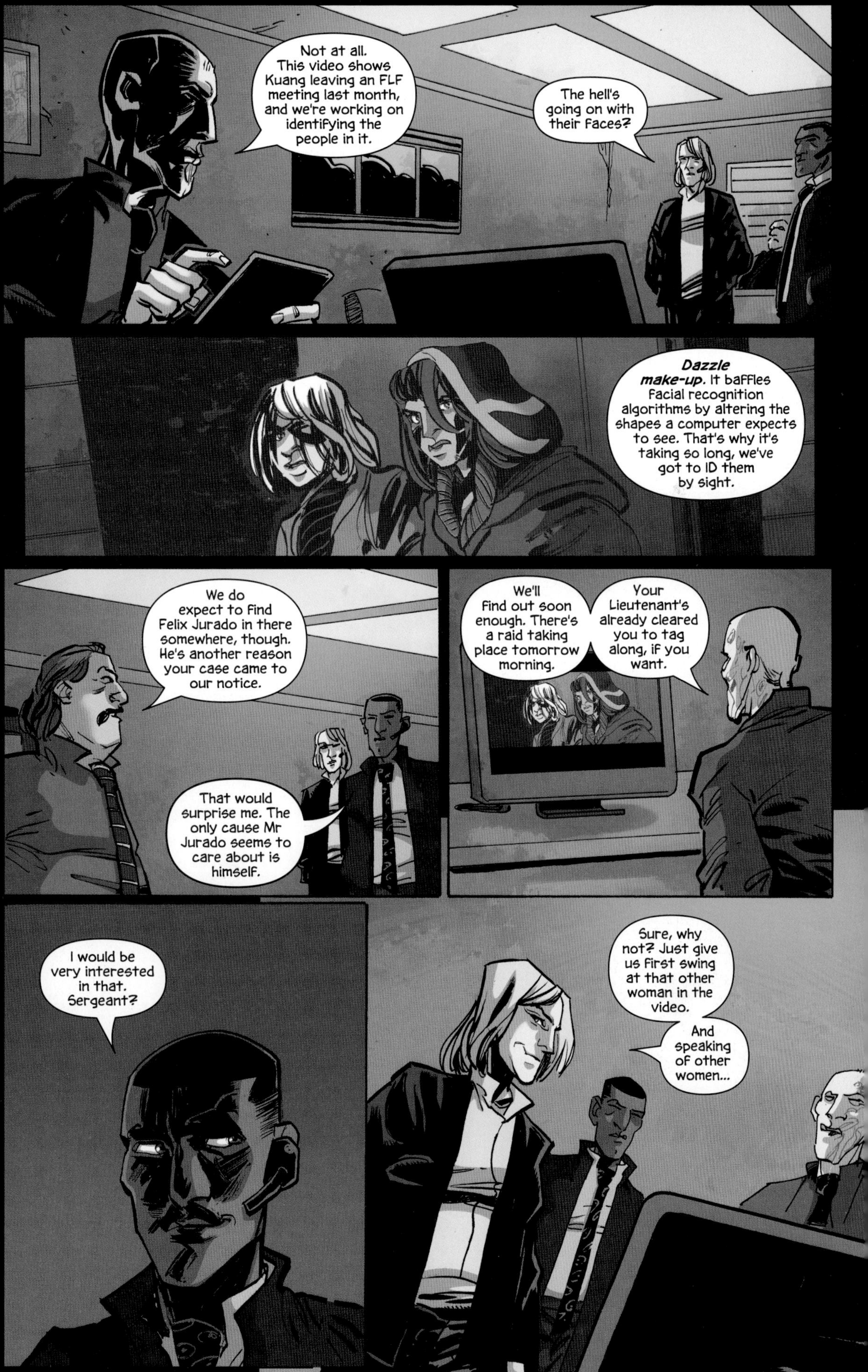
Not at all. This video shows Kuang leaving an FLF meeting last month, and we're working on identifying the people in it.
The hell's going on with their faces?
Dazzle make-up. It baffles facial recognition algorithms by altering the shapes a computer expects to see. That's why it's taking so long, we've got to ID them by sight.
We do expect to find Felix Jurado in there somewhere, though. He's another reason your case came to our notice.
That would surprise me. The only cause Mr Jurado seems to care about is himself.
We'll find out soon enough. There's a raid taking place tomorrow morning.
Your Lieutenant's already cleared you to tag along, if you want.
I would be very interested in that. Sergeant?
Sure, why not? Just give us first swing at that other woman in the video.
And speaking of other women...

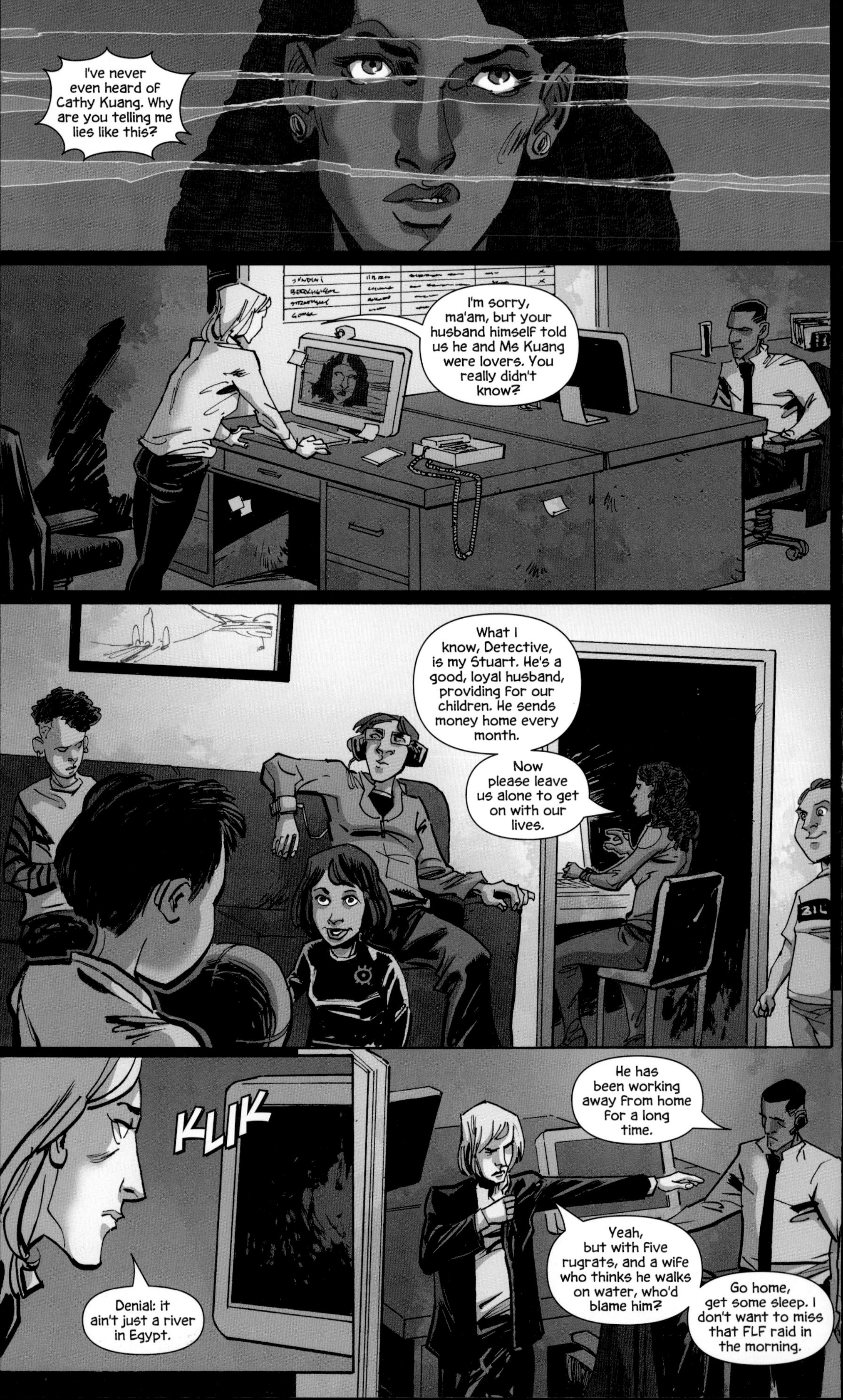

I've never even heard of Cathy Kuang. Why are you telling me lies like this?
I'm sorry, ma'am, but your husband himself told us he and Ms Kuang were lovers. You really didn't know?
What I know, Detective, is my Stuart. He's a good, loyal husband, providing for our children. He sends money home every month.
Now please leave us alone to get on with our lives.
KLIK
Denial: it ain't just a river in Egypt.
He has been working away from home for a long time.
Yeah, but with five rugrats, and a wife who thinks he walks on water, who'd blame him?
Go home, get some sleep. I don't want to miss that FLF raid in the morning.

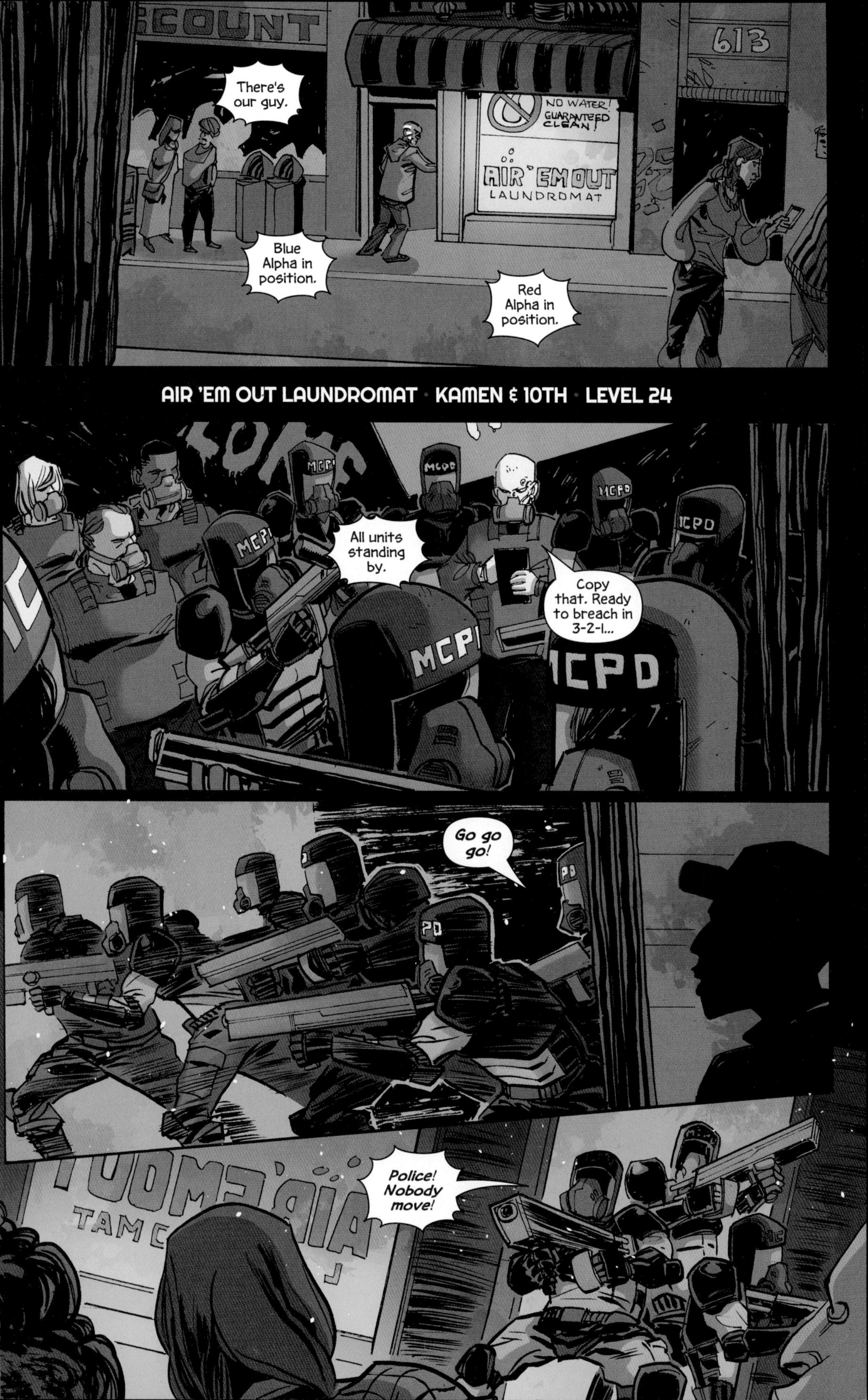

There's our guy.
Blue Alpha in position.
Red Alpha in position.
AIR 'EM OUT LAUNDROMAT • KAMEN & 10TH • LEVEL 24
All units standing by.
Copy that. Ready to breach in 3-2-1...
Go go go!
Police! Nobody move!

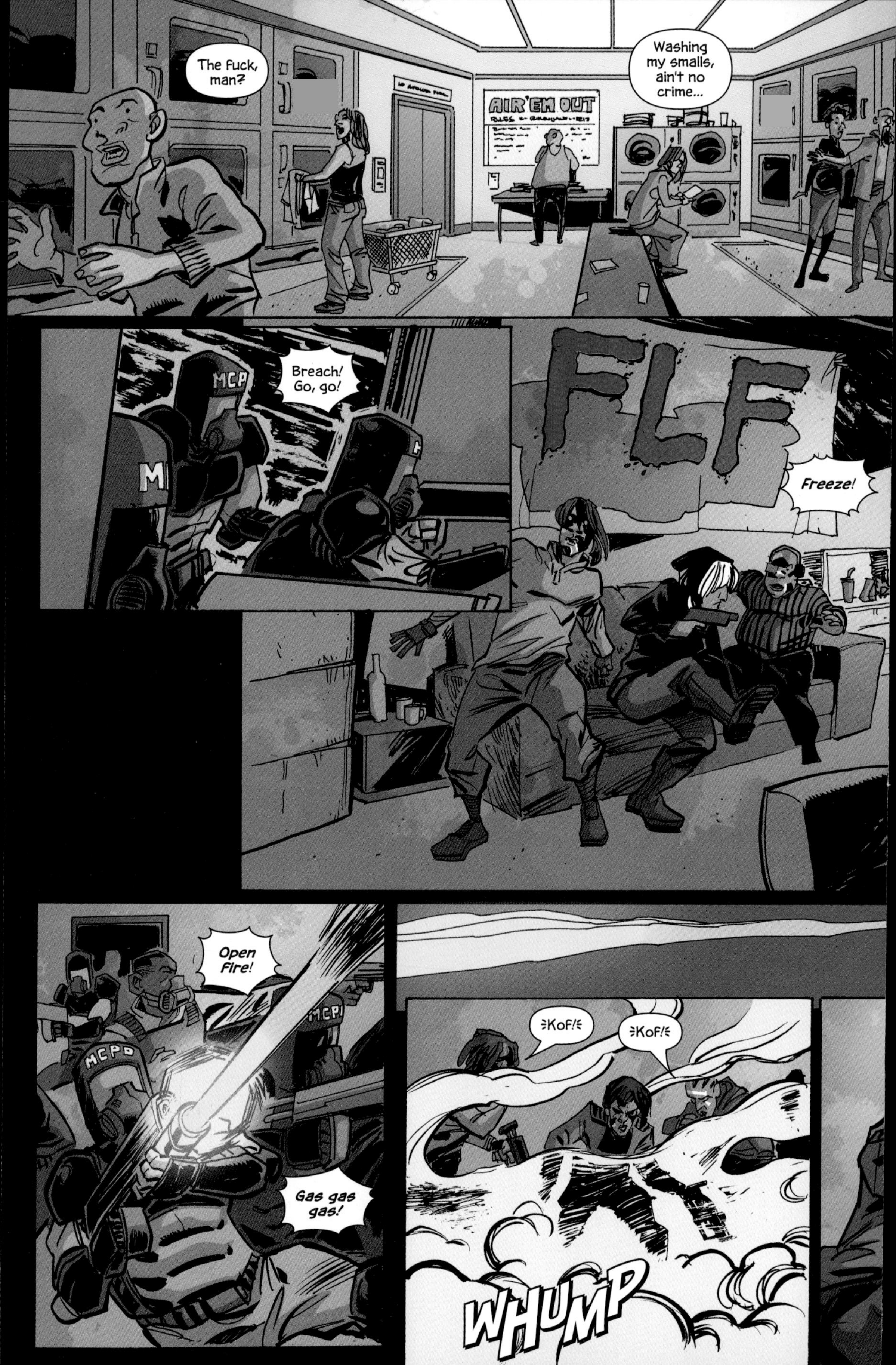

The fuck, man?
AIR'EM OUT
Washing my smalls, ain't no crime...
Breach! Go, go!
FLF
Freeze!
Open Fire!
MCPD
Gas gas gas!
Kof!
Kof!
WHUMP

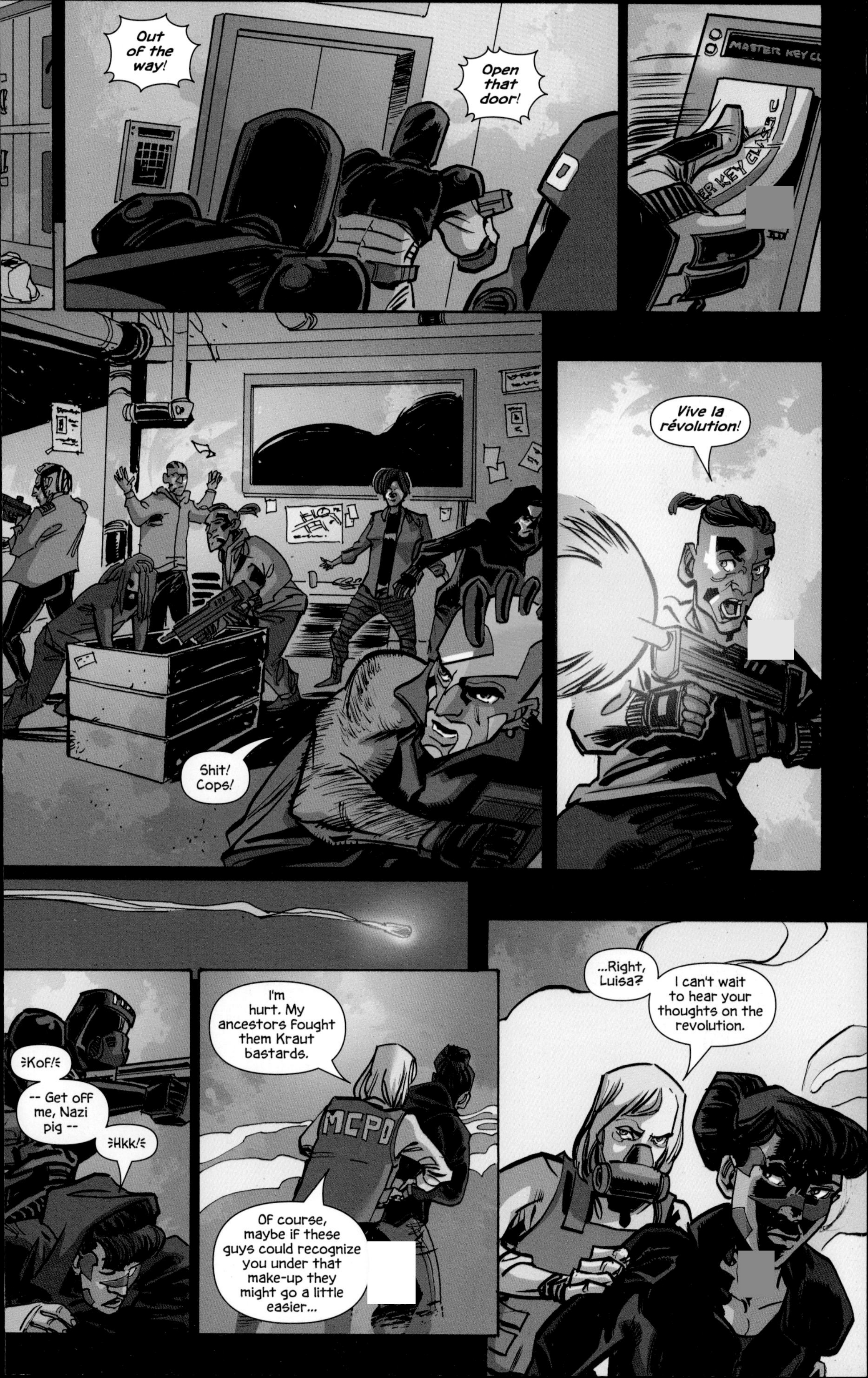
Out of the way!
Open that door!
MASTER KEY CL
Vive la révolution!
Shit! Cops!
...Right, Luisa?
I can't wait to hear your thoughts on the revolution.
Kof!
-- Get off me, Nazi pig --
Hkk!
I'm hurt. My ancestors fought them Kraut bastards.
MCPD
Of course, maybe if these guys could recognize you under that make-up they might go a little easier...

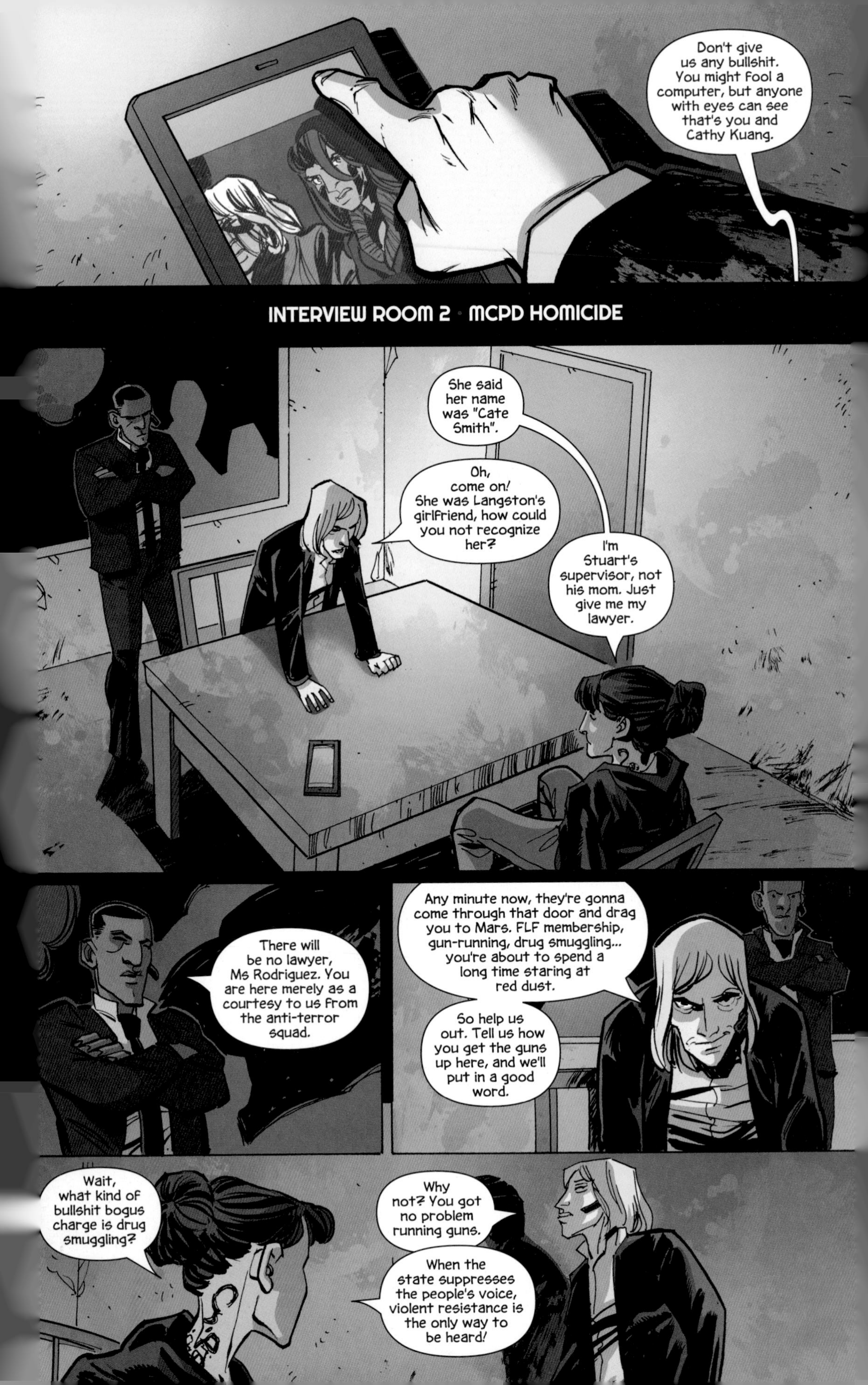
Don't give us any bullshit. You might fool a computer, but anyone with eyes can see that's you and Cathy Kuang.
INTERVIEW ROOM 2 · MCPD HOMICIDE
She said her name was "Cate Smith".
Oh, come on! She was Langston's girlfriend, how could you not recognize her?
I'm Stuart's supervisor, not his mom. Just give me my lawyer.
There will be no lawyer, Ms Rodriguez. You are here merely as a courtesy to us from the anti-terror squad.
Any minute now, they're gonna come through that door and drag you to Mars. FLF membership, gun-running, drug smuggling... you're about to spend a long time staring at red dust.
So help us out. Tell us how you get the guns up here, and we'll put in a good word.
Wait, what kind of bullshit bogus charge is drug smuggling?
Why not? You got no problem running guns.
When the state suppresses the people's voice, violent resistance is the only way to be heard!

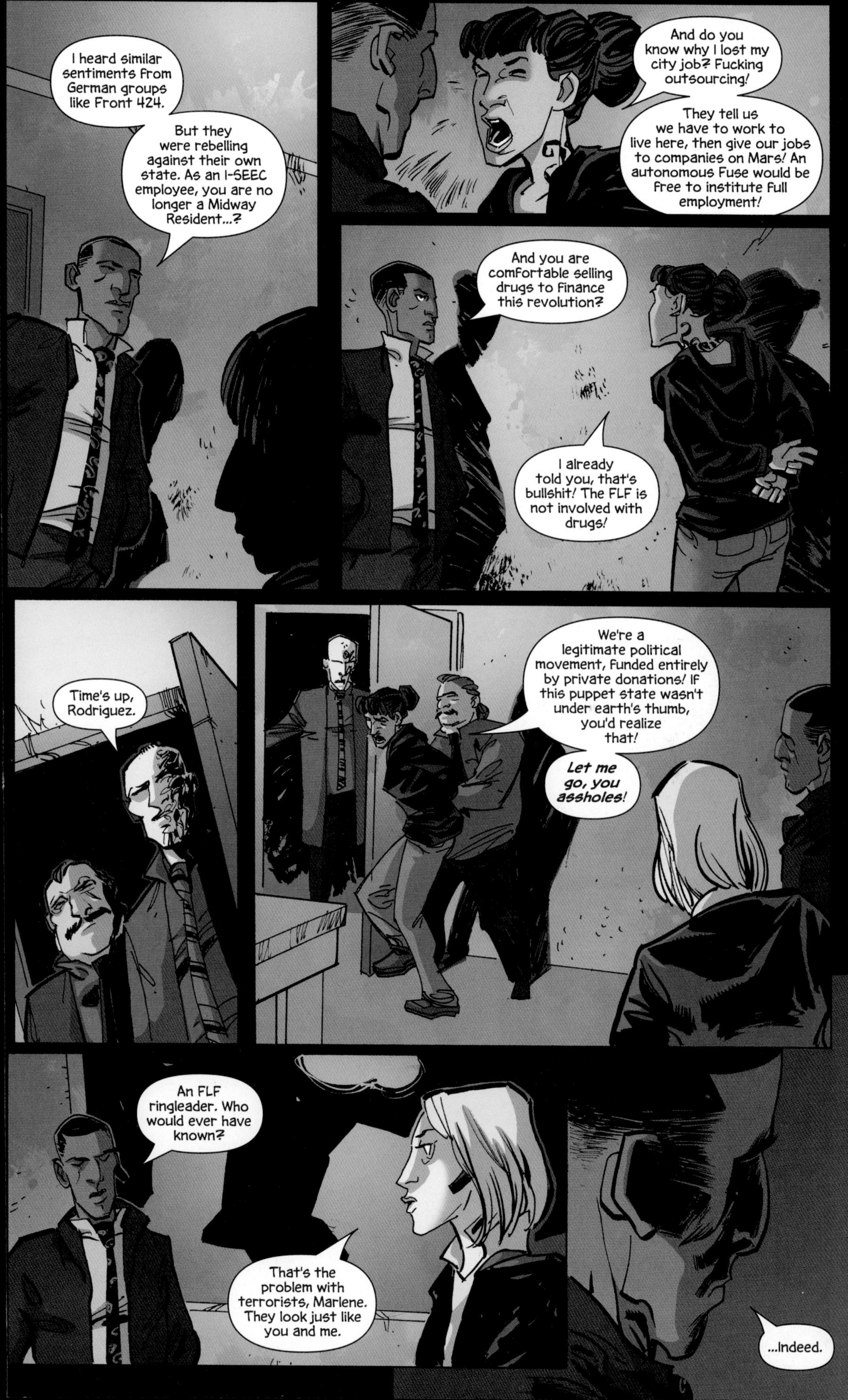
I heard similar sentiments from German groups like Front 424.
But they were rebelling against their own state. As an I-SEEC employee, you are no longer a Midway Resident...?
And do you know why I lost my city job? Fucking outsourcing!
They tell us we have to work to live here, then give our jobs to companies on Mars! An autonomous Fuse would be free to institute full employment!
And you are comfortable selling drugs to finance this revolution?
I already told you, that's bullshit! The FLF is not involved with drugs!
Time's up, Rodriguez.
We're a legitimate political movement, funded entirely by private donations! If this puppet state wasn't under earth's thumb, you'd realize that!
Let me go, you assholes!
An FLF ringleader. Who would ever have known?
That's the problem with terrorists, Marlene. They look just like you and me.
...Indeed.

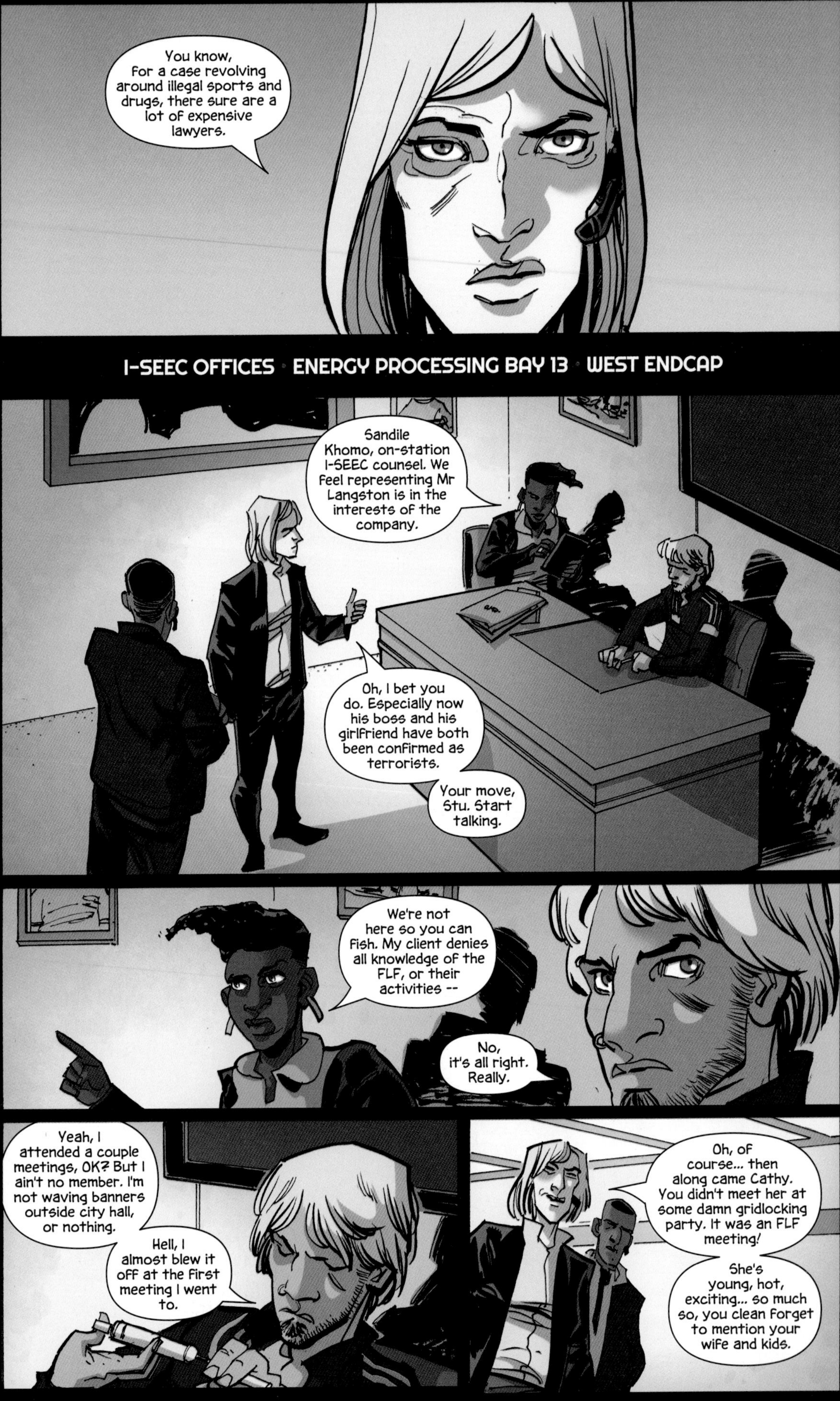

You know, for a case revolving around illegal sports and drugs, there sure are a lot of expensive lawyers.
I-SEEC OFFICES · ENERGY PROCESSING BAY 13 · WEST ENDCAP
Sandile Khomo, on-station I-SEEC counsel. We feel representing Mr Langston is in the interests of the company.
Oh, I bet you do. Especially now his boss and his girlfriend have both been confirmed as terrorists.
Your move, Stu. Start talking.
We're not here so you can fish. My client denies all knowledge of the FLF, or their activities --
No, it's all right. Really.
Yeah, I attended a couple meetings, OK? But I ain't no member. I'm not waving banners outside city hall, or nothing.
Hell, I almost blew it off at the first meeting I went to.
Oh, of course... then along came Cathy. You didn't meet her at some damn gridlocking party. It was an FLF meeting!
She's young, hot, exciting... so much so, you clean forget to mention your wife and kids.

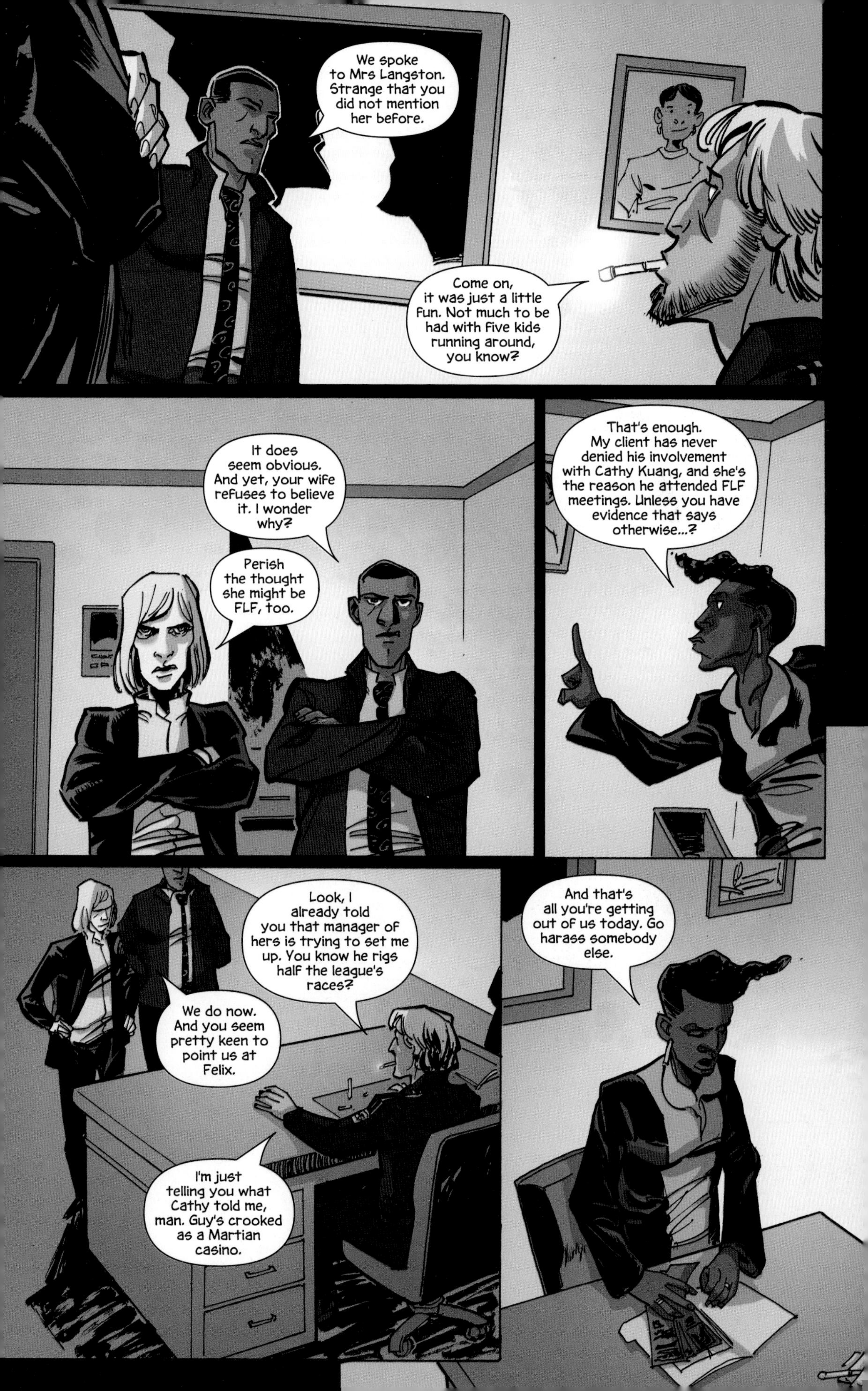
We spoke to Mrs Langston. Strange that you did not mention her before.
Come on, it was just a little fun. Not much to be had with five kids running around, you know?
It does seem obvious. And yet, your wife refuses to believe it. I wonder why?
Perish the thought she might be FLF, too.
That's enough. My client has never denied his involvement with Cathy Kuang, and she's the reason he attended FLF meetings. Unless you have evidence that says otherwise...?
Look, I already told you that manager of hers is trying to set me up. You know he rigs half the league's races?
We do now. And you seem pretty keen to point us at Felix.
I'm just telling you what Cathy told me, man. Guy's crooked as a Martian casino.
And that's all you're getting out of us today. Go harass somebody else.

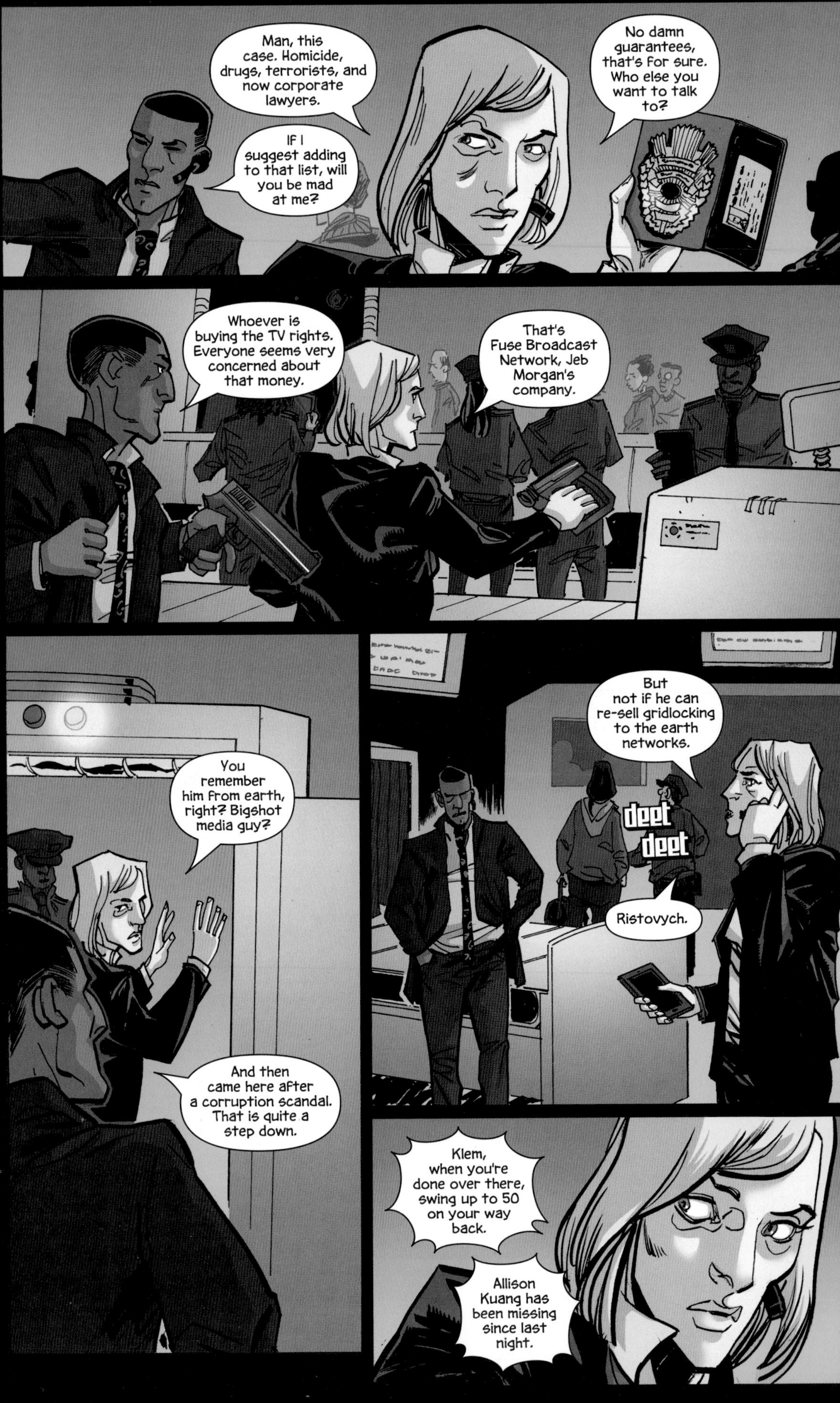

Man, this case. Homicide, drugs, terrorists, and now corporate lawyers.
If I suggest adding to that list, will you be mad at me?
No damn guarantees, that's for sure. Who else you want to talk to?
Whoever is buying the TV rights. Everyone seems very concerned about that money.
That's Fuse Broadcast Network, Jeb Morgan's company.
You remember him from earth, right? Bigshot media guy?
And then came here after a corruption scandal. That is quite a step down.
But not if he can re-sell gridlocking to the earth networks.
deet
deet
Ristovych.
Klem, when you're done over there, swing up to 50 on your way back.
Allison Kuang has been missing since last night.

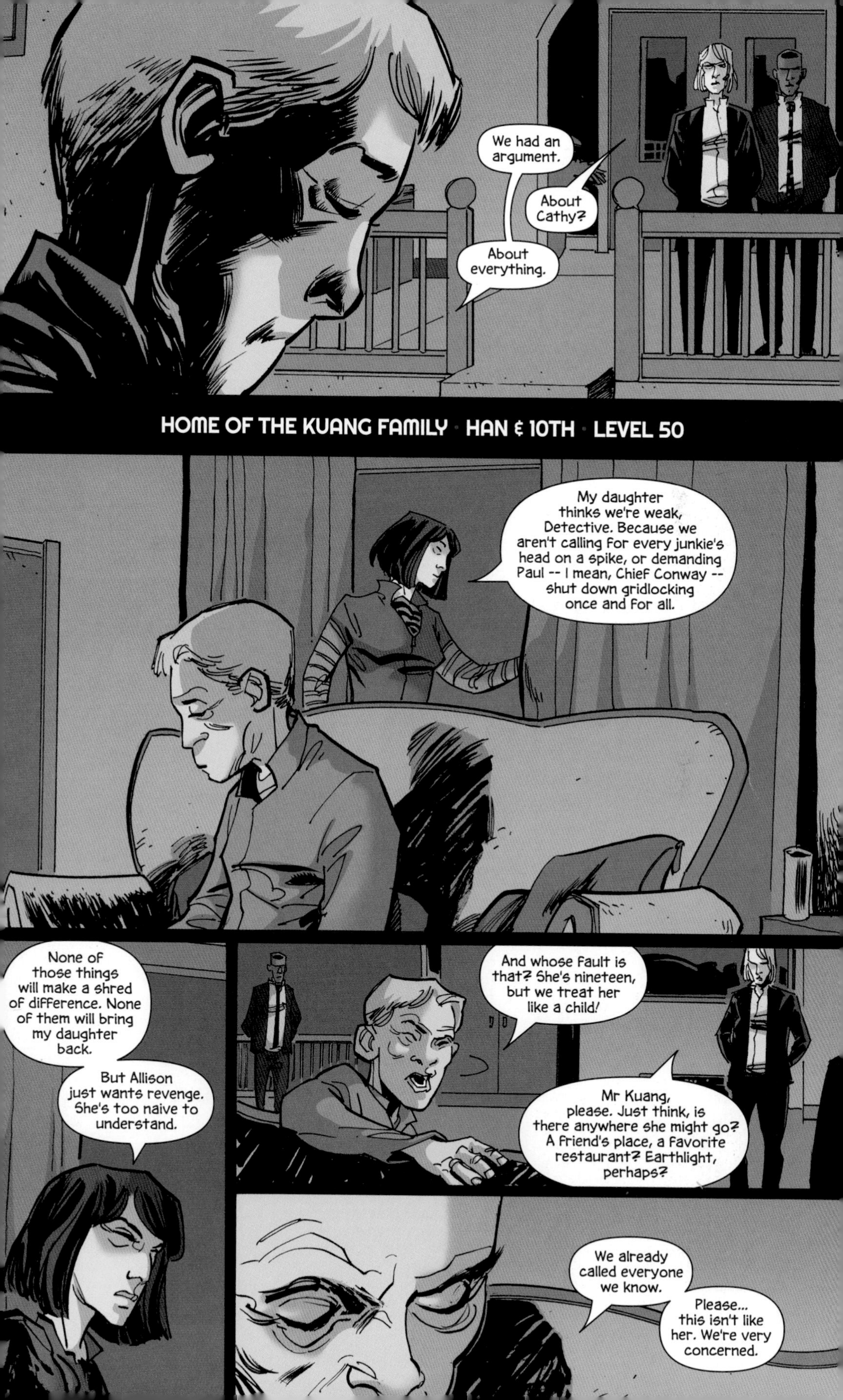
We had an argument.
About Cathy?
About everything.
HOME OF THE KUANG FAMILY · HAN & 10TH · LEVEL 50
My daughter thinks we're weak, Detective. Because we aren't calling for every junkie's head on a spike, or demanding Paul -- I mean, Chief Conway -- shut down gridlocking once and for all.
None of those things will make a shred of difference. None of them will bring my daughter back.
But Allison just wants revenge. She's too naive to understand.
And whose fault is that? She's nineteen, but we treat her like a child!
Mr Kuang, please. Just think, is there anywhere she might go? A friend's place, a favorite restaurant? Earthlight, perhaps?
We already called everyone we know.
Please... this isn't like her. We're very concerned.

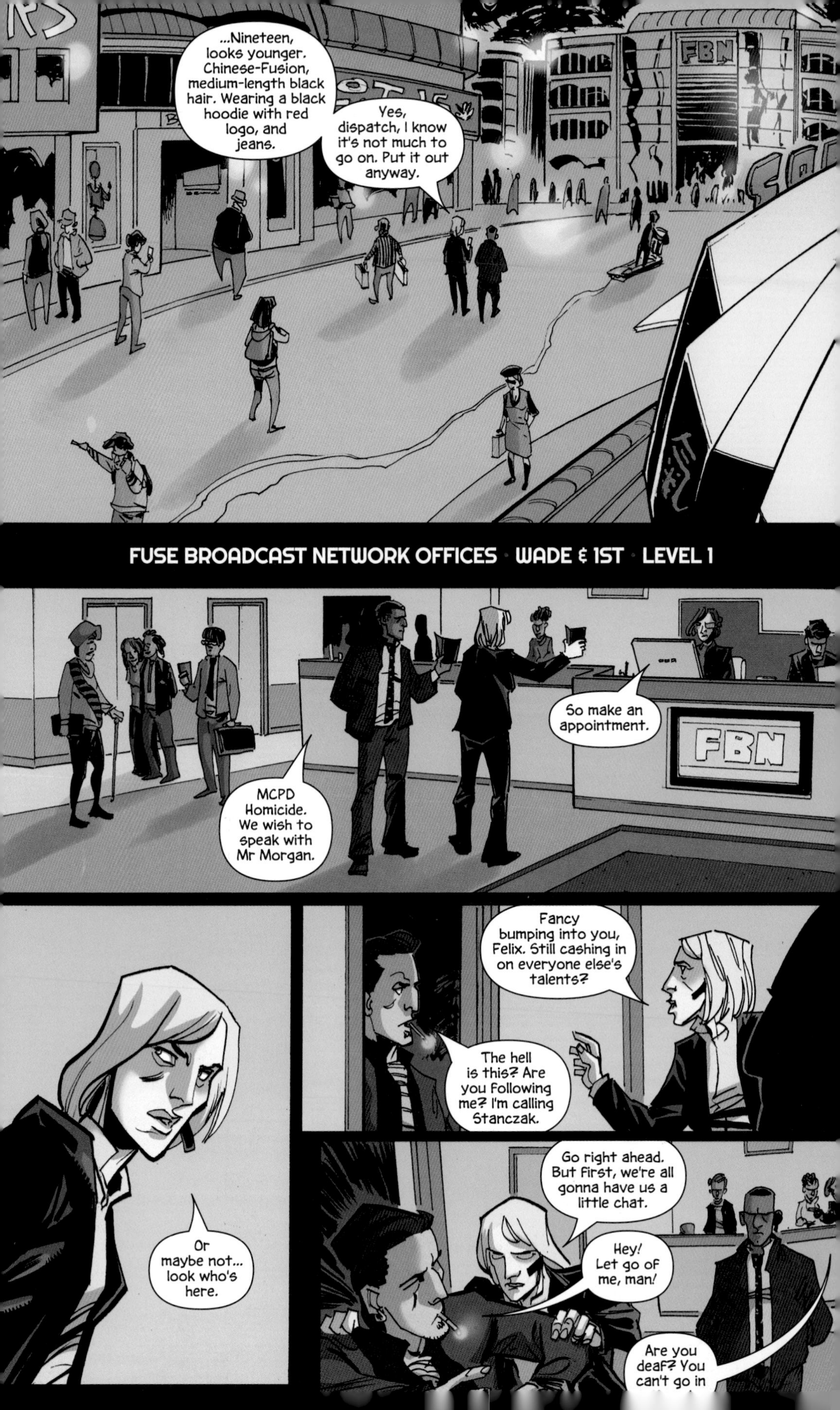
...Nineteen, looks younger. Chinese-Fusion, medium-length black hair. Wearing a black hoodie with red logo, and jeans.
Yes, dispatch, I know it's not much to go on. Put it out anyway.
FBN
FUSE BROADCAST NETWORK OFFICES · WADE & 1ST · LEVEL 1
So make an appointment.
MCPD Homicide. We wish to speak with Mr Morgan.
FBN
Or maybe not... look who's here.
Fancy bumping into you, Felix. Still cashing in on everyone else's talents?
The hell is this? Are you following me? I'm calling Stanczak.
Go right ahead. But first, we're all gonna have us a little chat.
Hey! Let go of me, man!
Are you deaf? You can't go in

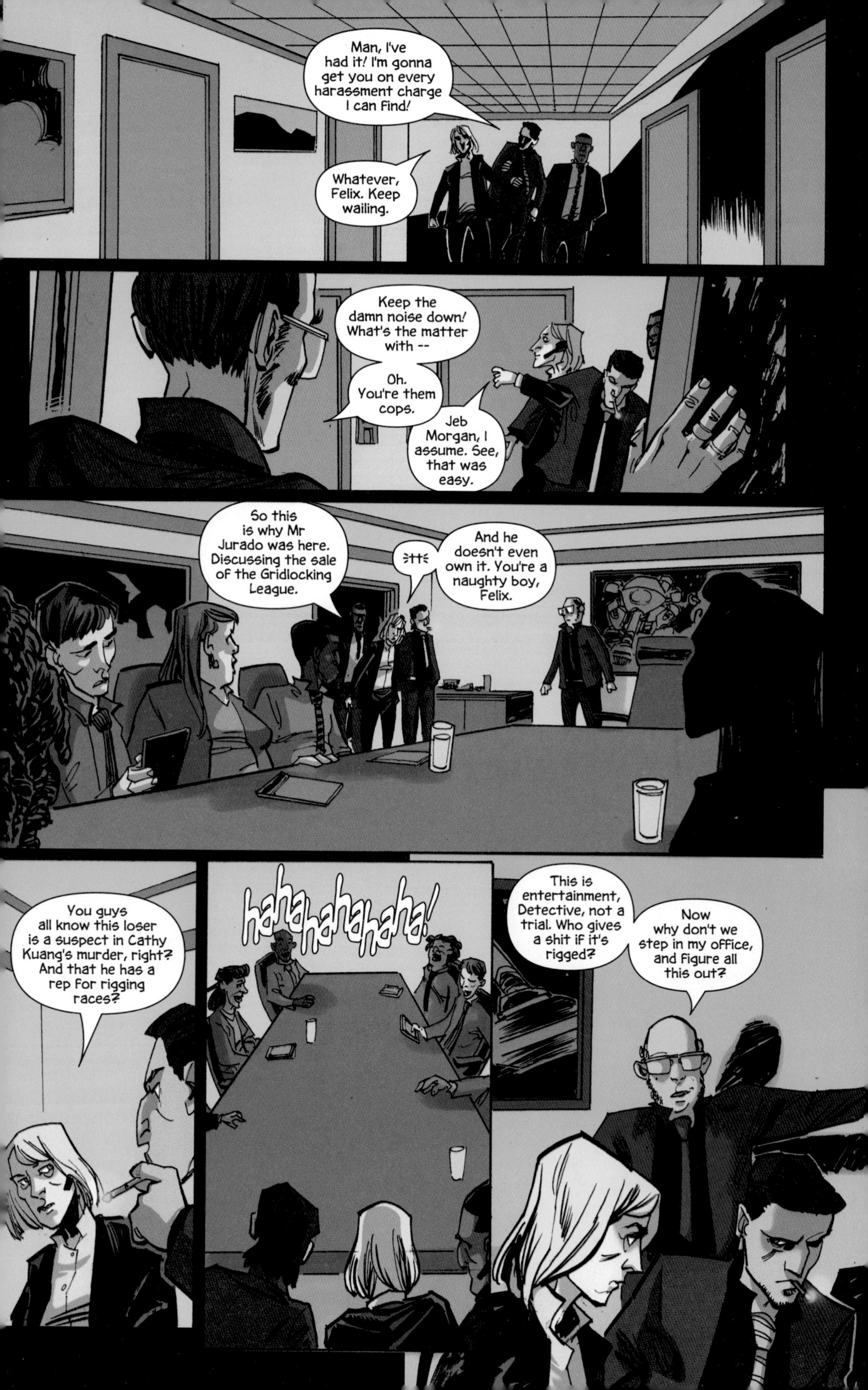
Man, I've had it! I'm gonna get you on every harassment charge I can find!
Whatever, Felix. Keep wailing.
Keep the damn noise down! What's the matter with --
Oh. You're them cops.
Jeb Morgan, I assume. See, that was easy.
So this is why Mr Jurado was here. Discussing the sale of the Gridlocking League.
!!!
And he doesn't even own it. You're a naughty boy, Felix.
You guys all know this loser is a suspect in Cathy Kuang's murder, right? And that he has a rep for rigging races?
hahahahahahaha!
This is entertainment, Detective, not a trial. Who gives a shit if it's rigged?
Now why don't we step in my office, and figure all this out?

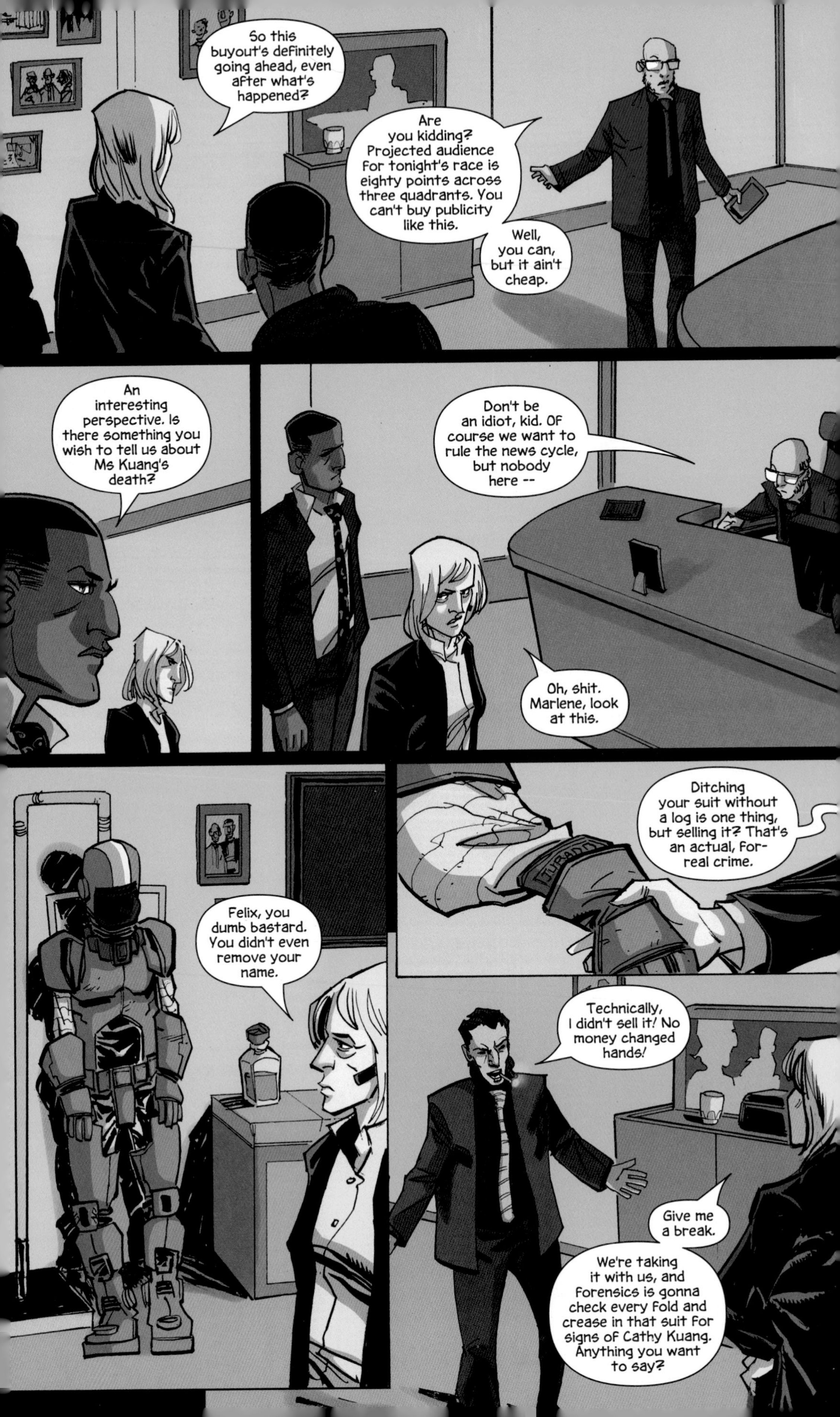
So this buyout's definitely going ahead, even after what's happened?
Are you kidding? Projected audience for tonight's race is eighty points across three quadrants. You can't buy publicity like this.
Well, you can, but it ain't cheap.
An interesting perspective. Is there something you wish to tell us about Ms Kuang's death?
Don't be an idiot, kid. Of course we want to rule the news cycle, but nobody here --
Oh, shit. Marlene, look at this.
Felix, you dumb bastard. You didn't even remove your name.
JURADO
Ditching your suit without a log is one thing, but selling it? That's an actual, for-real crime.
Technically, I didn't sell it! No money changed hands!
Give me a break.
We're taking it with us, and forensics is gonna check every fold and crease in that suit for signs of Cathy Kuang. Anything you want to say?

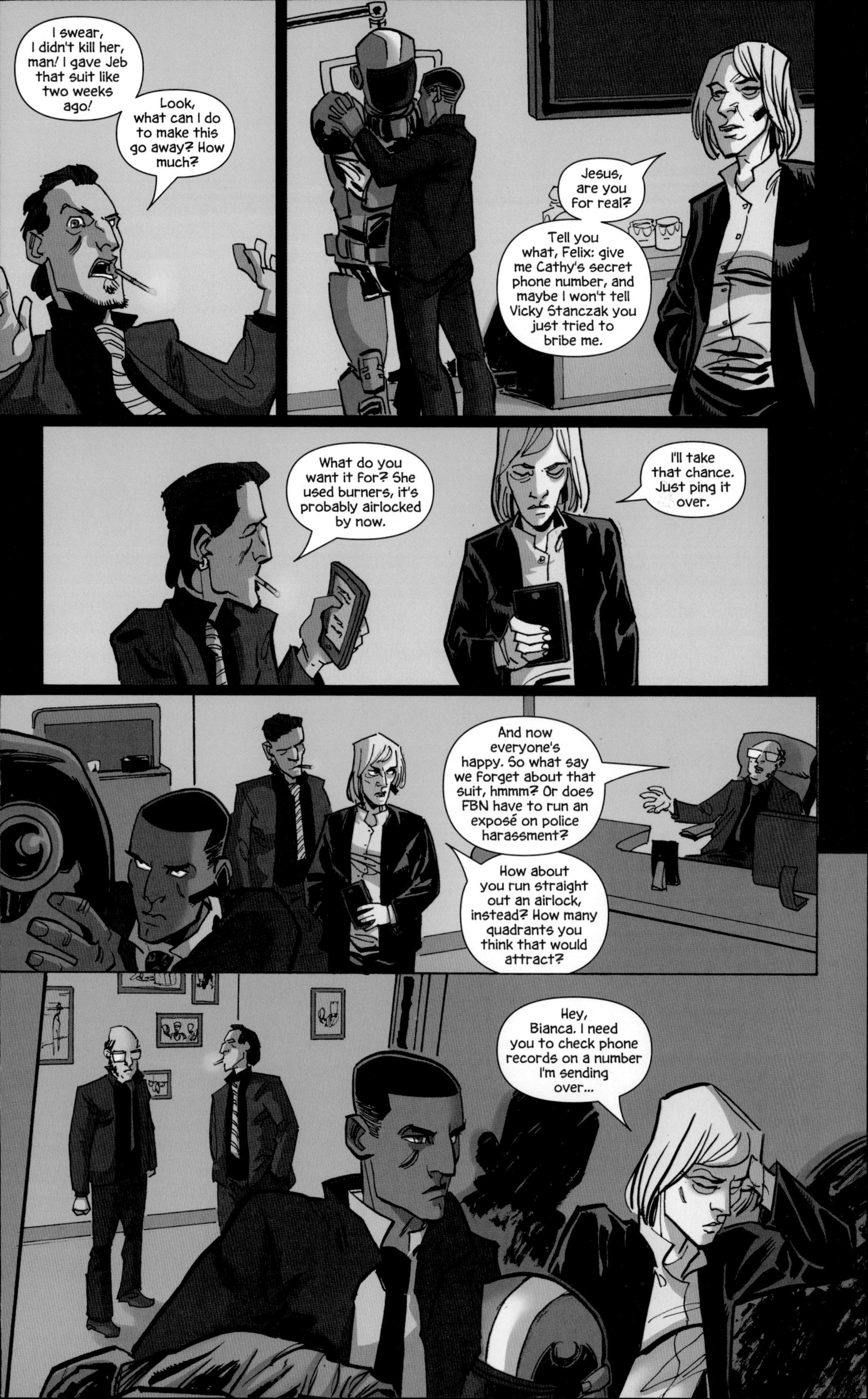

I swear, I didn't kill her, man! I gave Jeb that suit like two weeks ago!
Look, what can I do to make this go away? How much?
Jesus, are you for real?
Tell you what, Felix: give me Cathy's secret phone number, and maybe I won't tell Vicky Stanczak you just tried to bribe me.
What do you want it for? She used burners, it's probably airlocked by now.
I'll take that chance. Just ping it over.
And now everyone's happy. So what say we forget about that suit, hmmm? Or does FBN have to run an exposé on police harassment?
How about you run straight out an airlock, instead? How many quadrants you think that would attract?
Hey, Bianca. I need you to check phone records on a number I'm sending over...

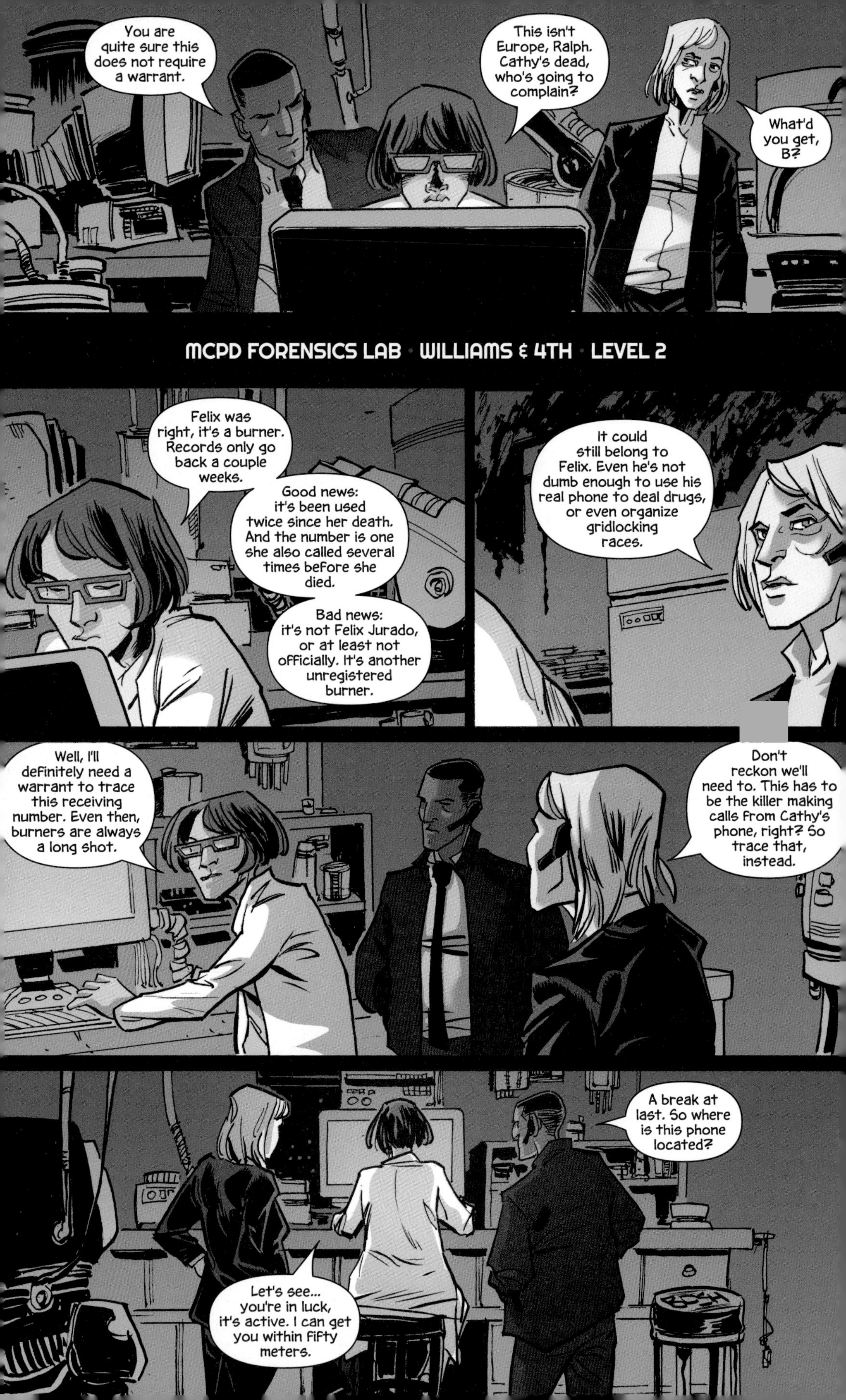

You are quite sure this does not require a warrant.
This isn't Europe, Ralph. Cathy's dead, who's going to complain?
What'd you get, B?
MCPD FORENSICS LAB · WILLIAMS & 4TH · LEVEL 2
Felix was right, it's a burner. Records only go back a couple weeks.
Good news: it's been used twice since her death. And the number is one she also called several times before she died.
Bad news: it's not Felix Jurado, or at least not officially. It's another unregistered burner.
It could still belong to Felix. Even he's not dumb enough to use his real phone to deal drugs, or even organize gridlocking races.
Well, I'll definitely need a warrant to trace this receiving number. Even then, burners are always a long shot.
Don't reckon we'll need to. This has to be the killer making calls from Cathy's phone, right? So trace that, instead.
A break at last. So where is this phone located?
Let's see... you're in luck, it's active. I can get you within fifty meters.

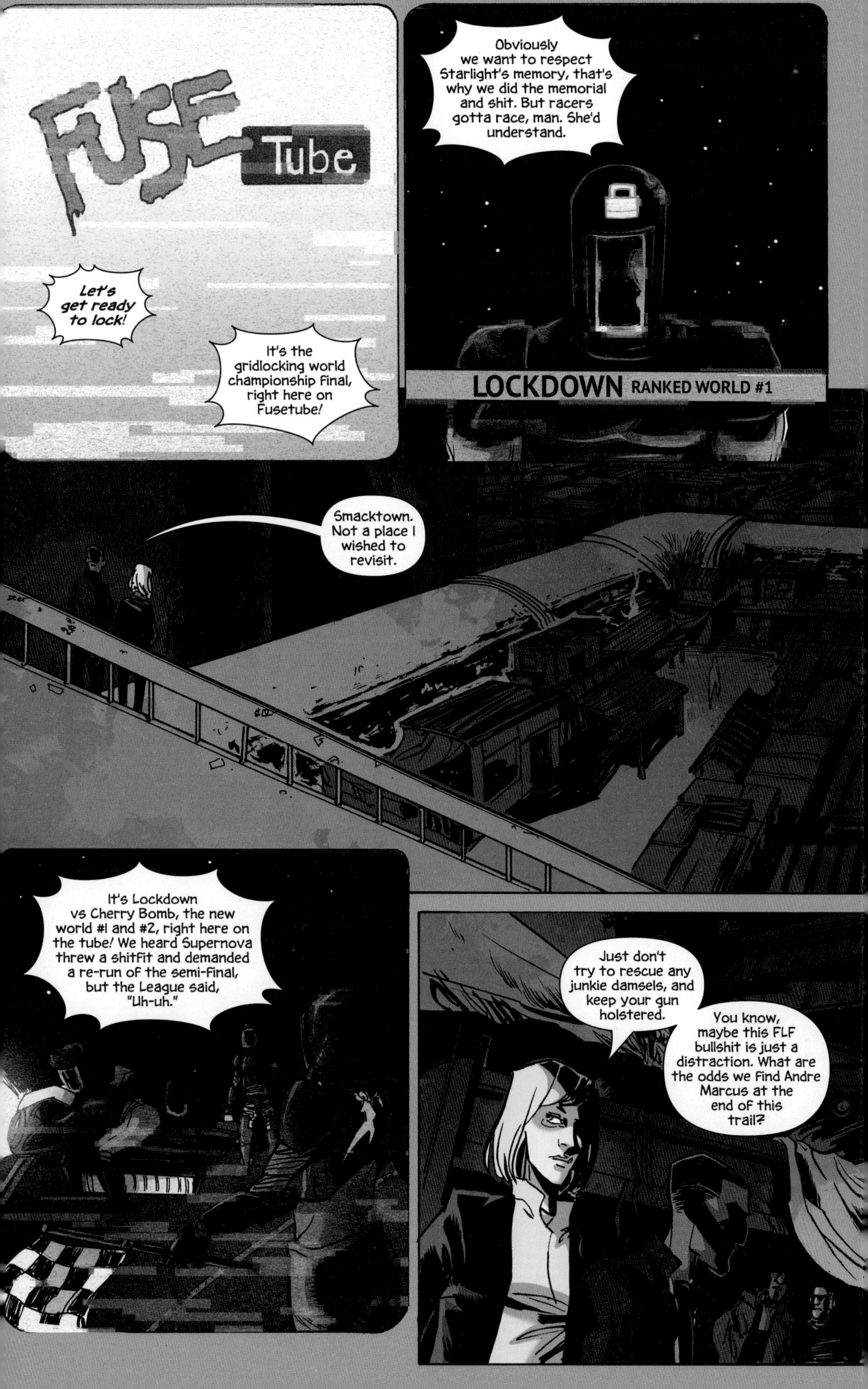

FUSE Tube
Let's get ready to lock!
It's the gridlocking world championship final, right here on Fusetube!
Obviously we want to respect Starlight's memory, that's why we did the memorial and shit. But racers gotta race, man. She'd understand.
LOCKDOWN RANKED WORLD #1
Smacktown. Not a place I wished to revisit.
It's Lockdown vs Cherry Bomb, the new world #1 and #2, right here on the tube! We heard Supernova threw a shitfit and demanded a re-run of the semi-final, but the League said, "Uh-uh."
Just don't try to rescue any junkie damsels, and keep your gun holstered.
You know, maybe this FLF bullshit is just a distraction. What are the odds we find Andre Marcus at the end of this trail?

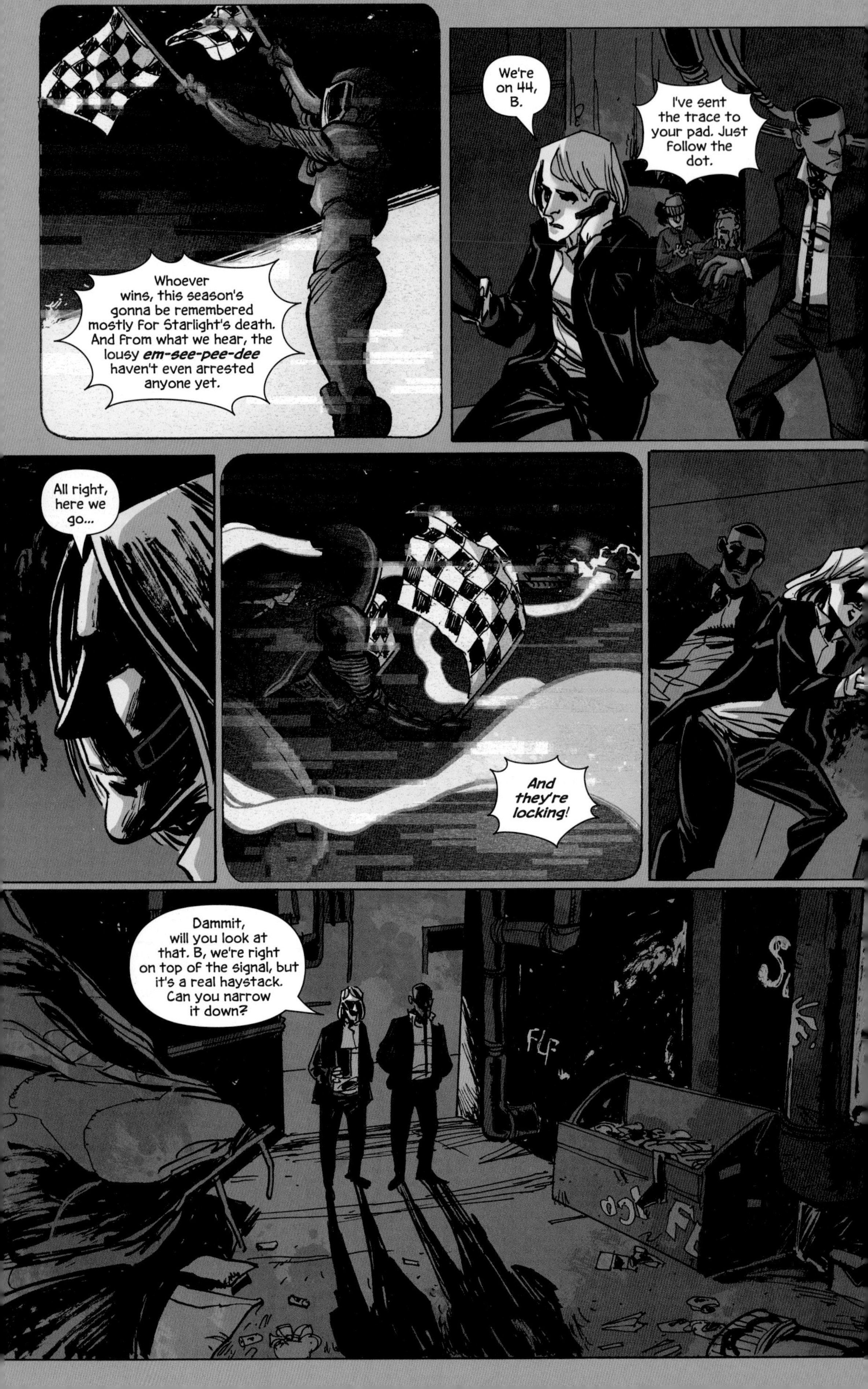
Whoever wins, this season's gonna be remembered mostly for Starlight's death. And from what we hear, the lousy *em-see-pee-dee* haven't even arrested anyone yet.
We're on 44, B.
I've sent the trace to your pad. Just follow the dot.
All right, here we go...
And they're locking!
Dammit, will you look at that. B, we're right on top of the signal, but it's a real haystack. Can you narrow it down?

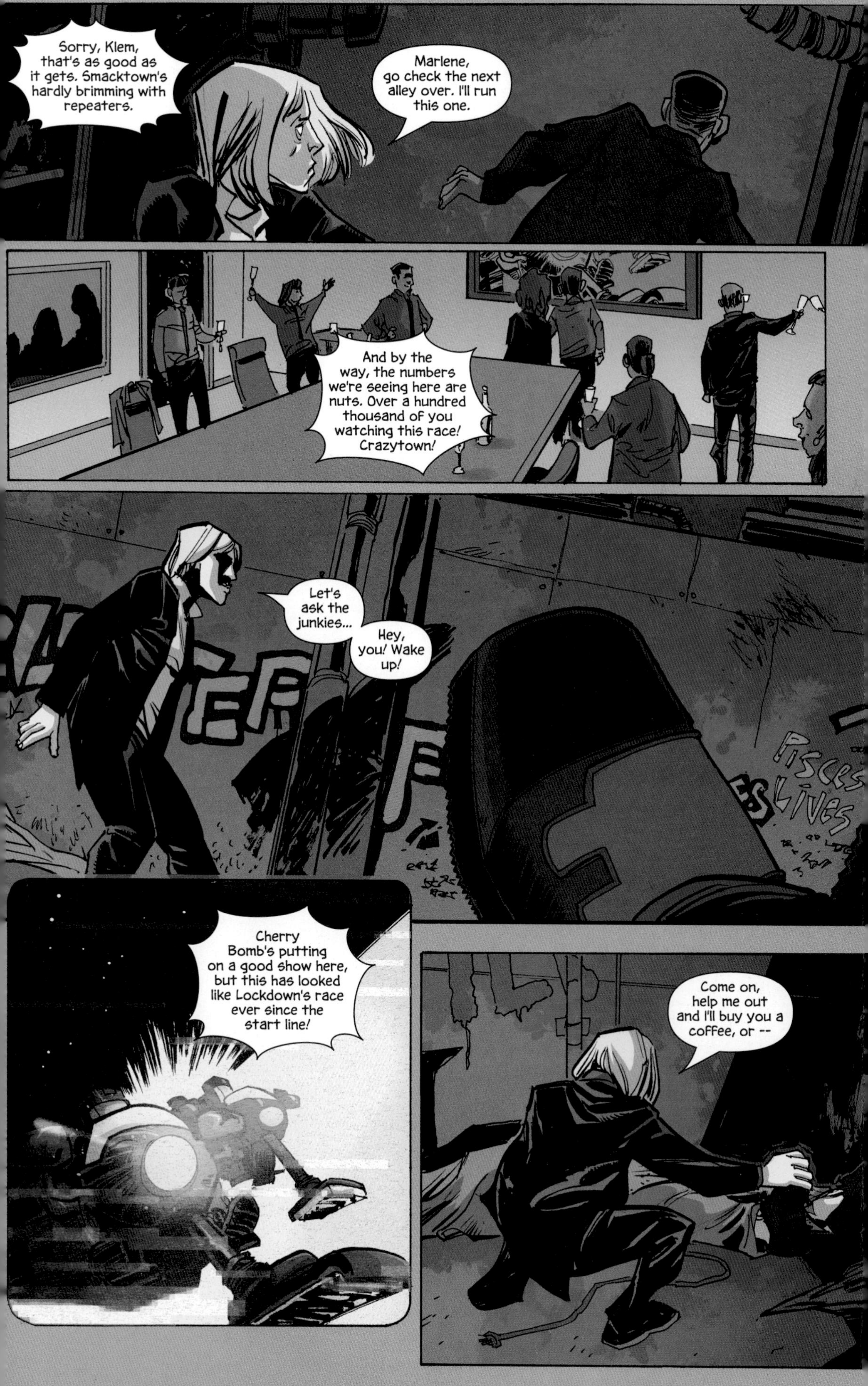
Sorry, Klem, that's as good as it gets. Smacktown's hardly brimming with repeaters.
Marlene, go check the next alley over. I'll run this one.
And by the way, the numbers we're seeing here are nuts. Over a hundred thousand of you watching this race! Crazytown!
Let's ask the junkies...
Hey, you! Wake up!
PISCES LIVES
Cherry Bomb's putting on a good show here, but this has looked like Lockdown's race ever since the start line!
Come on, help me out and I'll buy you a coffee, or --

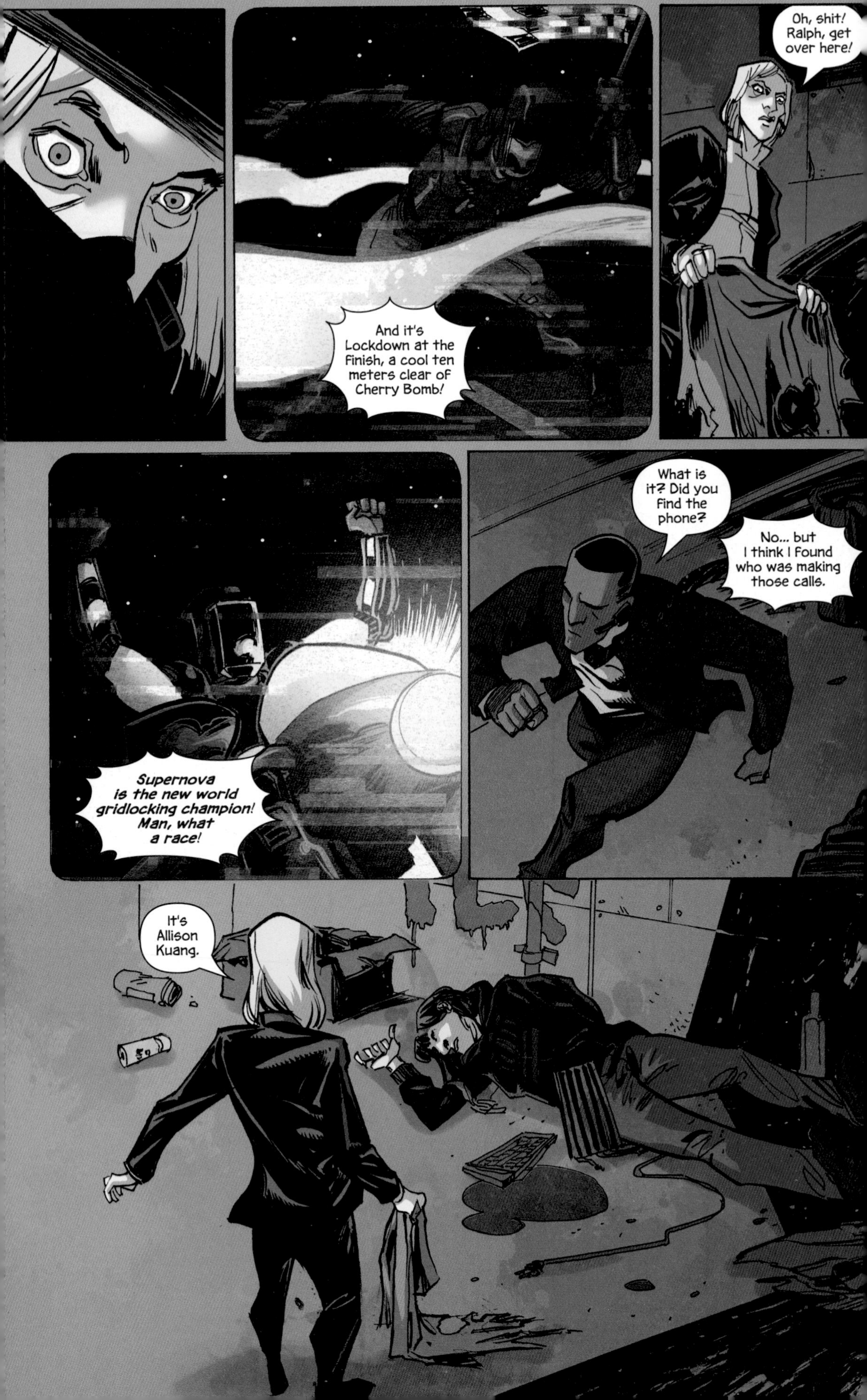
And it's Lockdown at the Finish, a cool ten meters clear of Cherry Bomb!
Oh, shit! Ralph, get over here!
Supernova is the new world gridlocking champion! Man, what a race!
What is it? Did you find the phone?
No... but I think I found who was making those calls.
It's Allison Kuang.

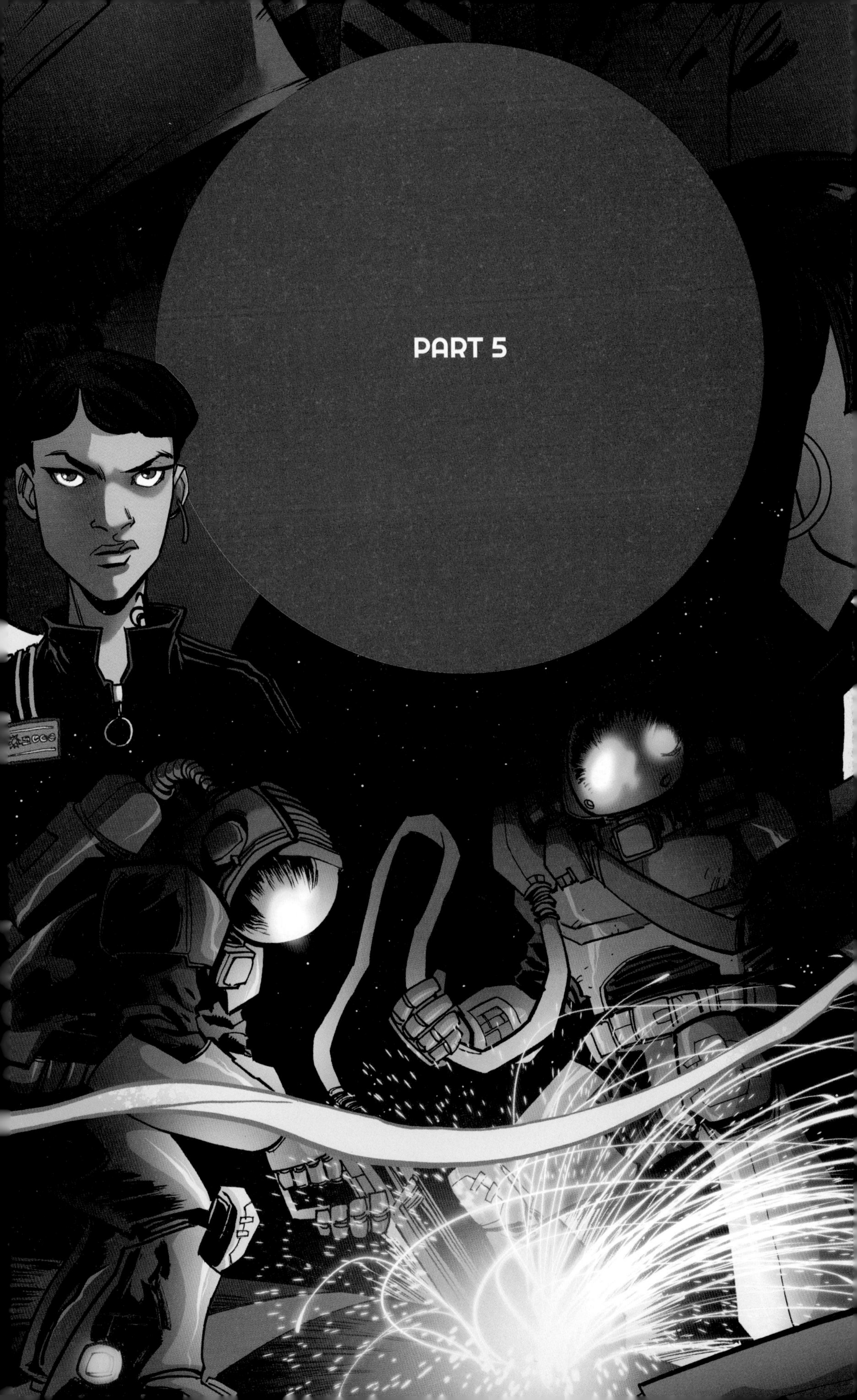
PART 5

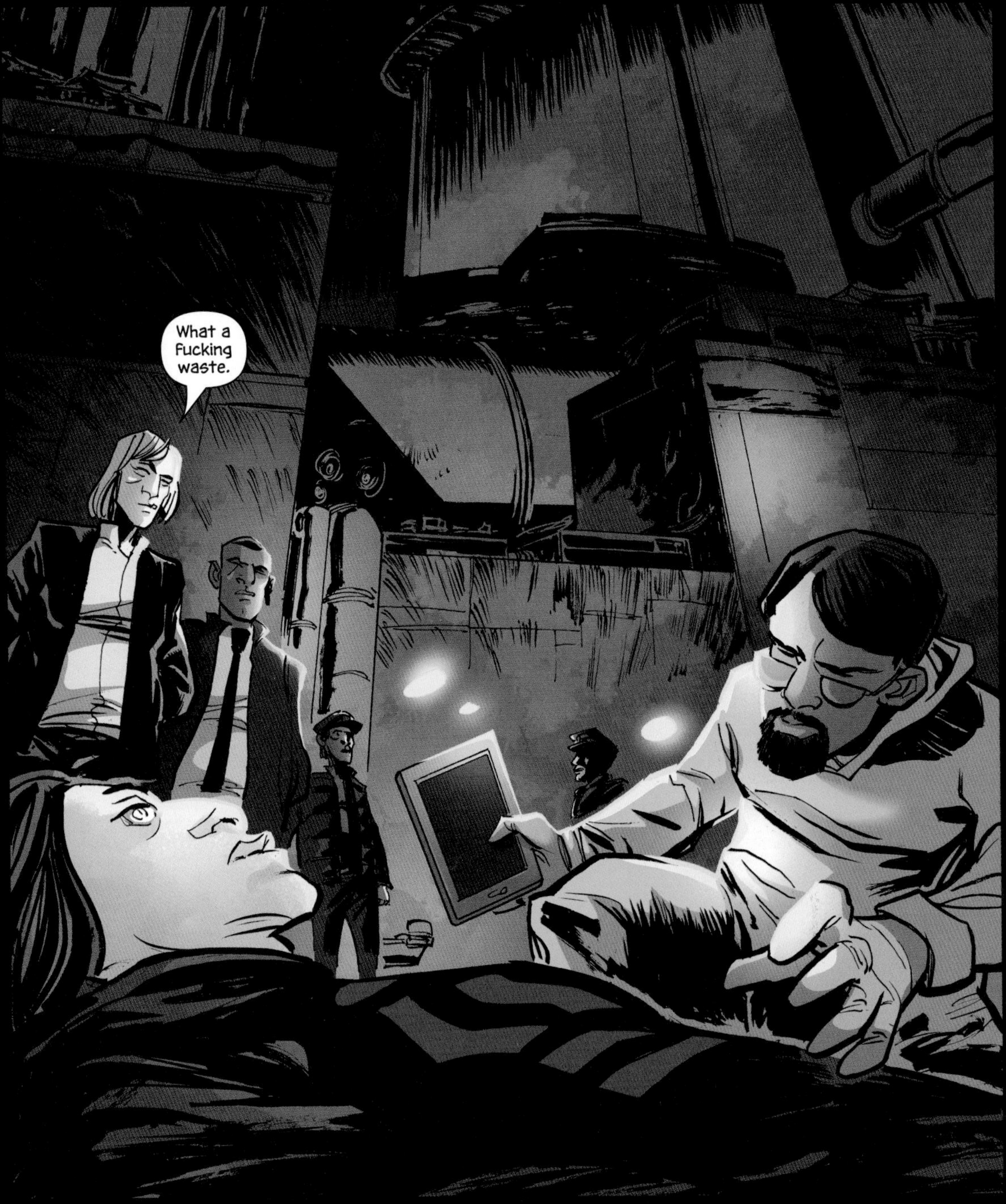
What a fucking waste.

'SMACKTOWN' · MIDWAY CITY GRAVITY GENERATORS · LEVEL 44

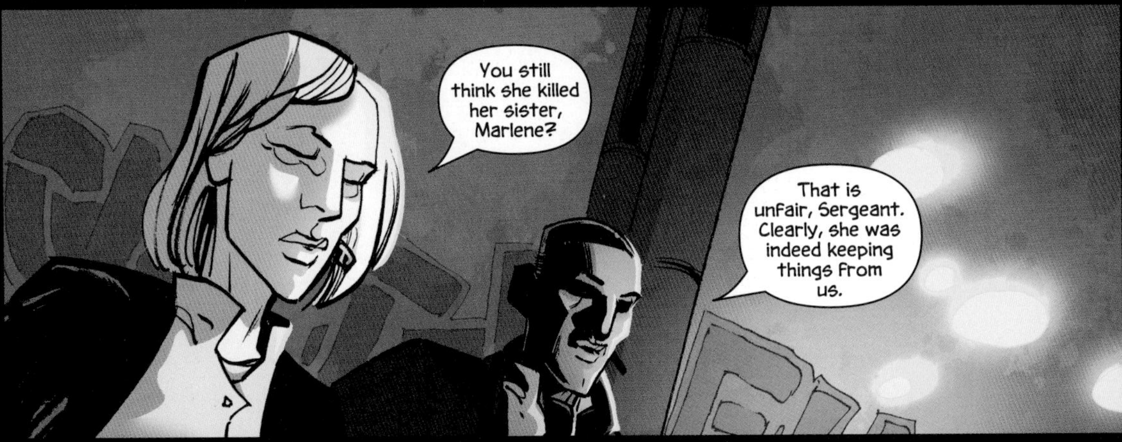
You still think she killed her sister, Marlene?
That is unfair, Sergeant. Clearly, she was indeed keeping things from us.

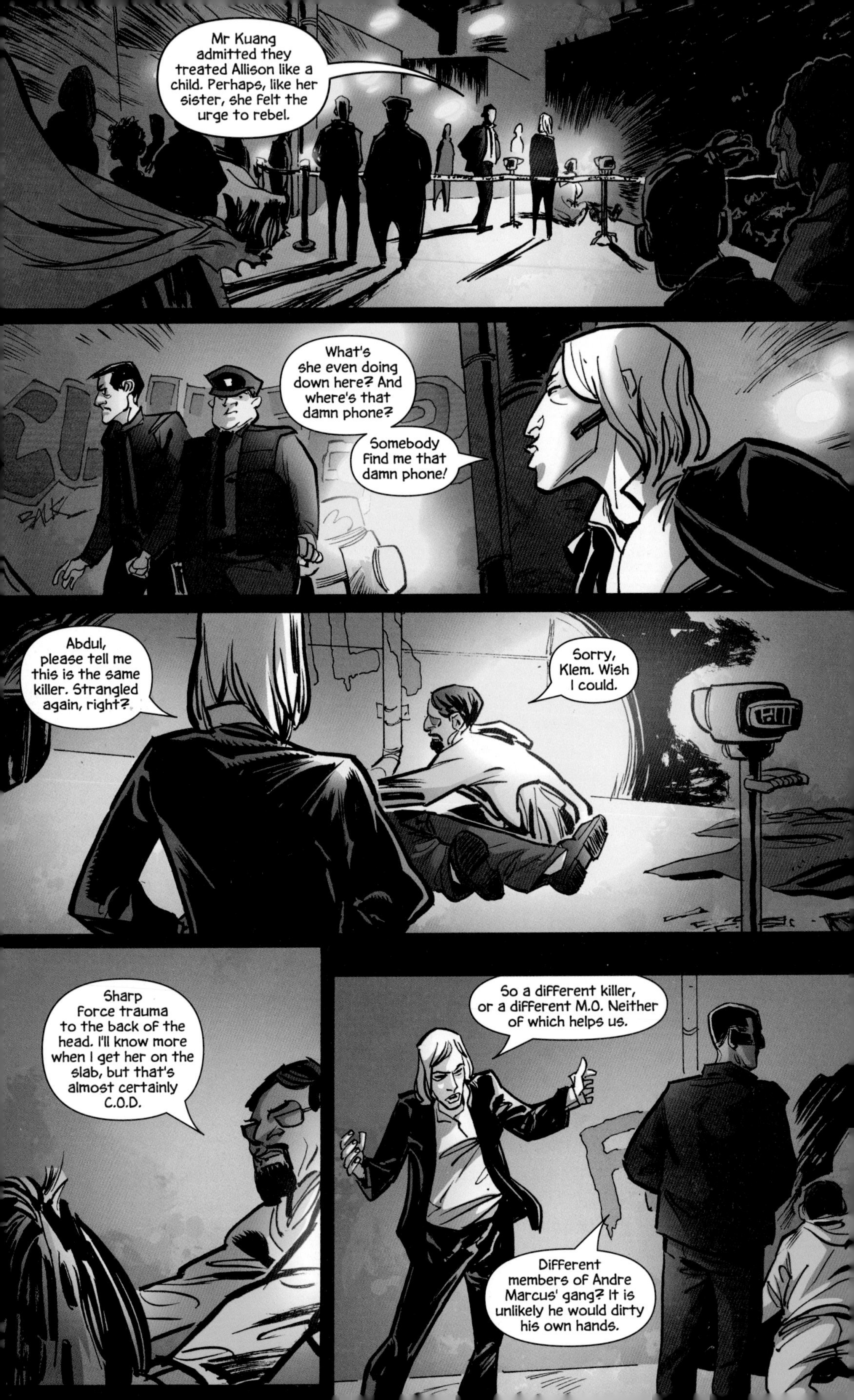

Mr Kuang admitted they treated Allison like a child. Perhaps, like her sister, she felt the urge to rebel.
What's she even doing down here? And where's that damn phone?
Somebody find me that damn phone!
Abdul, please tell me this is the same killer. Strangled again, right?
Sorry, Klem. Wish I could.
Sharp force trauma to the back of the head. I'll know more when I get her on the slab, but that's almost certainly C.O.D.
So a different killer, or a different M.O. Neither of which helps us.
Different members of Andre Marcus' gang? It is unlikely he would dirty his own hands.

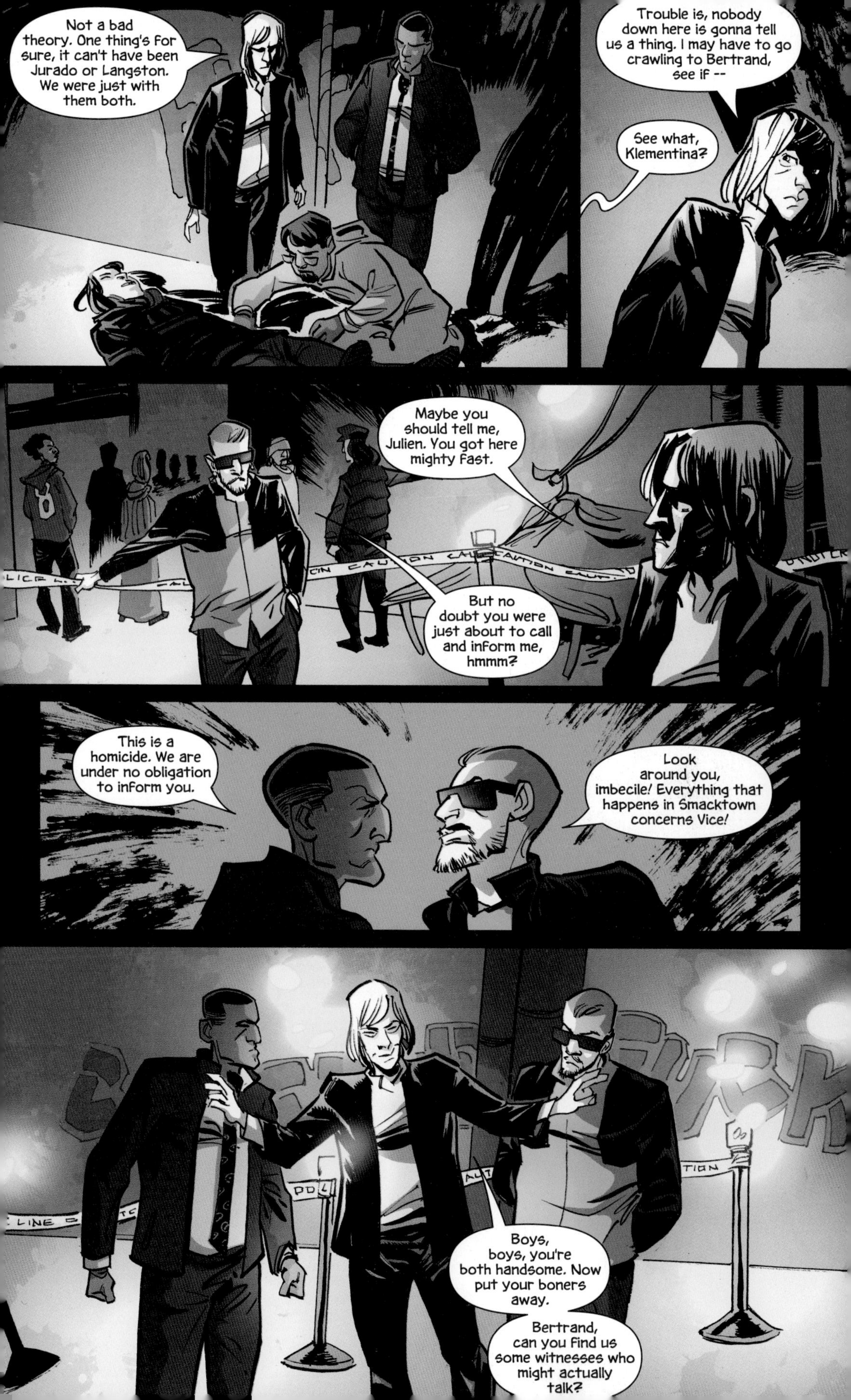
Not a bad theory. One thing's for sure, it can't have been Jurado or Langston. We were just with them both.
Trouble is, nobody down here is gonna tell us a thing. I may have to go crawling to Bertrand, see if --
See what, Klementina?
Maybe you should tell me, Julien. You got here mighty fast.
But no doubt you were just about to call and inform me, hmmm?
This is a homicide. We are under no obligation to inform you.
Look around you, imbecile! Everything that happens in Smacktown concerns Vice!
Boys, boys, you're both handsome. Now put your boners away.
Bertrand, can you find us some witnesses who might actually talk?

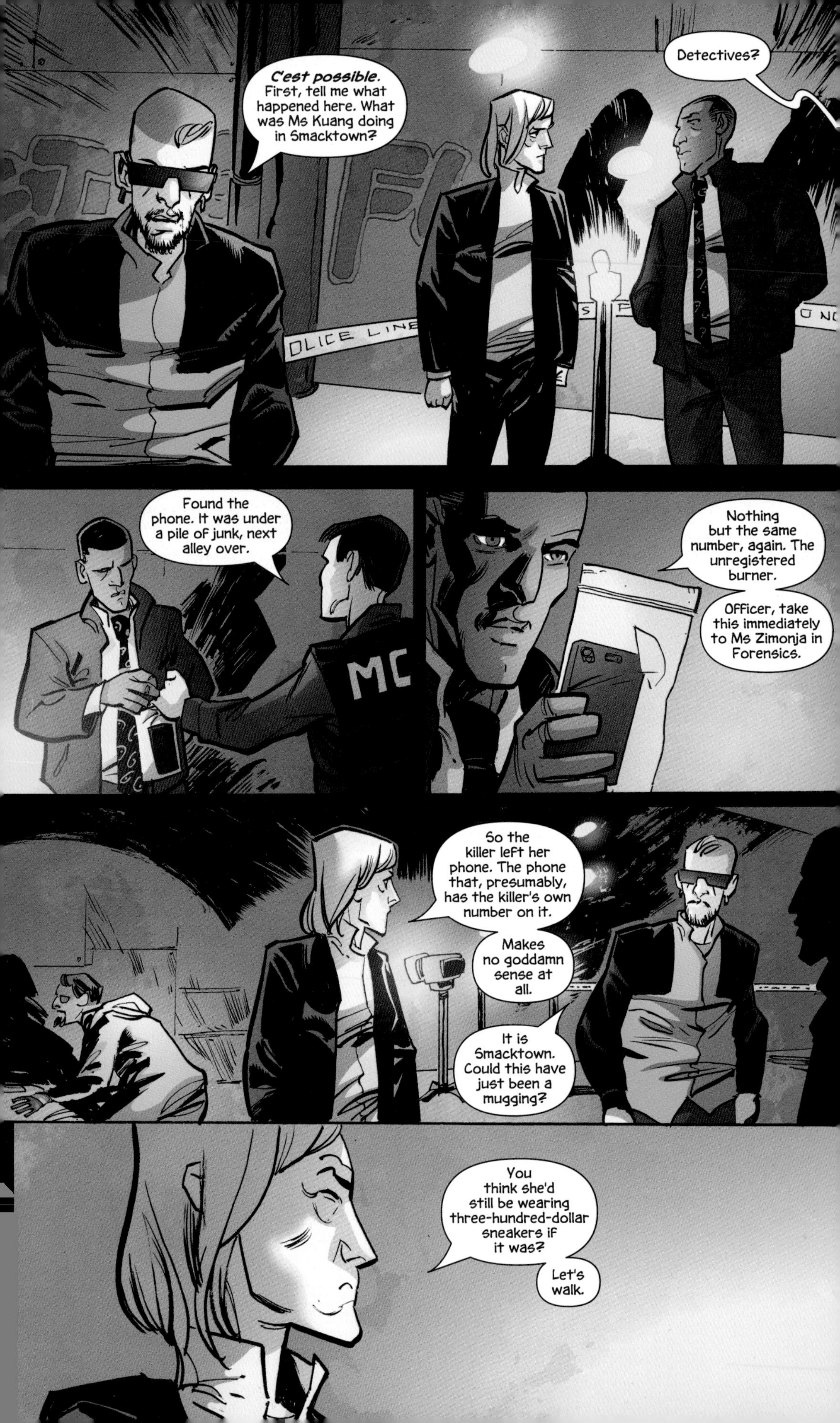
C'est possible. First, tell me what happened here. What was Ms Kuang doing in Smacktown?
Detectives?
OLICE LINE
Found the phone. It was under a pile of junk, next alley over.
MC
Nothing but the same number, again. The unregistered burner.
Officer, take this immediately to Ms Zimonja in Forensics.
So the killer left her phone. The phone that, presumably, has the killer's own number on it.
Makes no goddamn sense at all.
It is Smacktown. Could this have just been a mugging?
You think she'd still be wearing three-hundred-dollar sneakers if it was?
Let's walk.

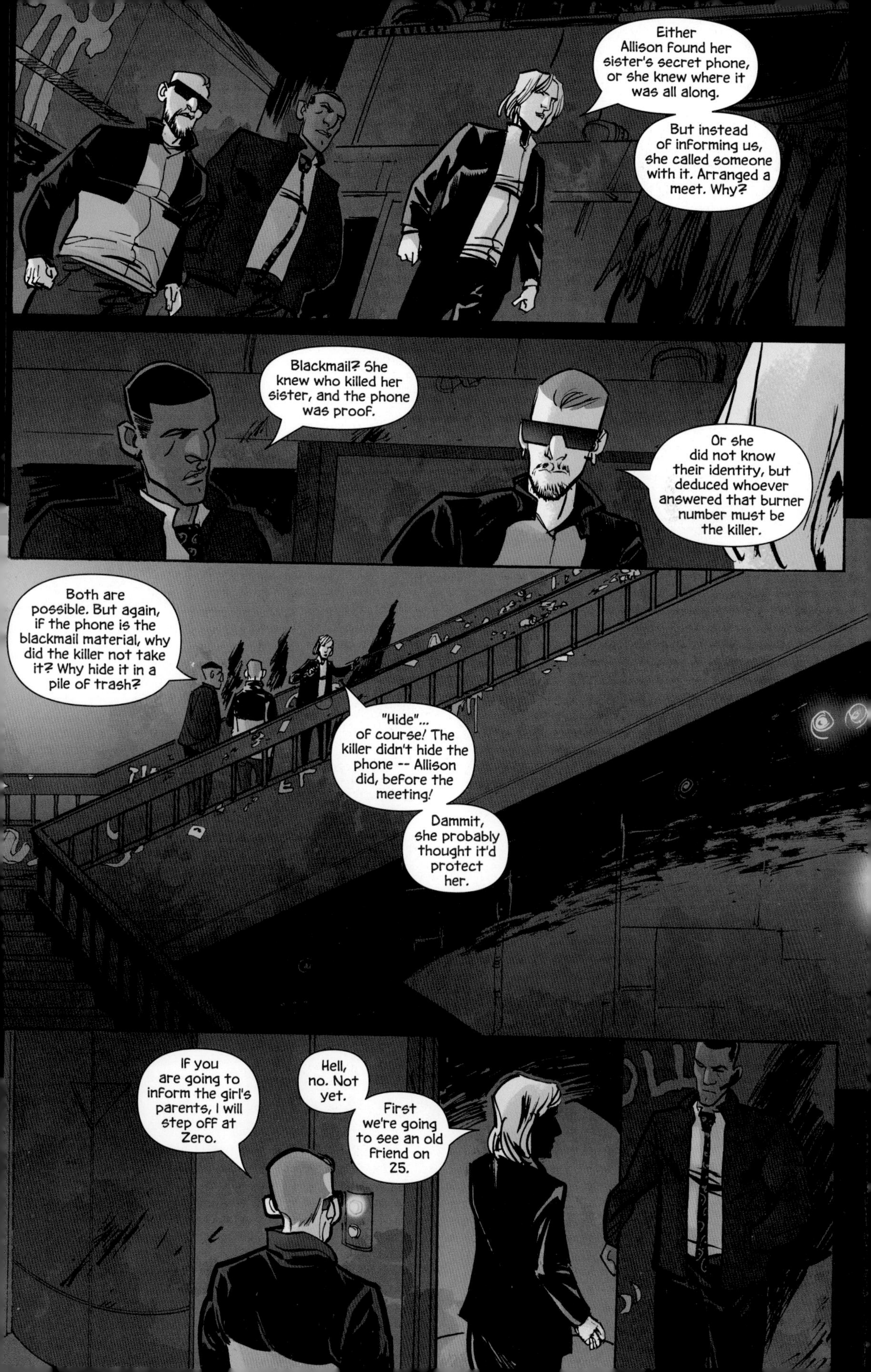
Either Allison found her sister's secret phone, or she knew where it was all along.
But instead of informing us, she called someone with it. Arranged a meet. Why?
Blackmail? She knew who killed her sister, and the phone was proof.
Or she did not know their identity, but deduced whoever answered that burner number must be the killer.
Both are possible. But again, if the phone is the blackmail material, why did the killer not take it? Why hide it in a pile of trash?
"Hide"... of course! The killer didn't hide the phone -- Allison did, before the meeting!
Dammit, she probably thought it'd protect her.
If you are going to inform the girl's parents, I will step off at Zero.
Hell, no. Not yet.
First we're going to see an old friend on 25.

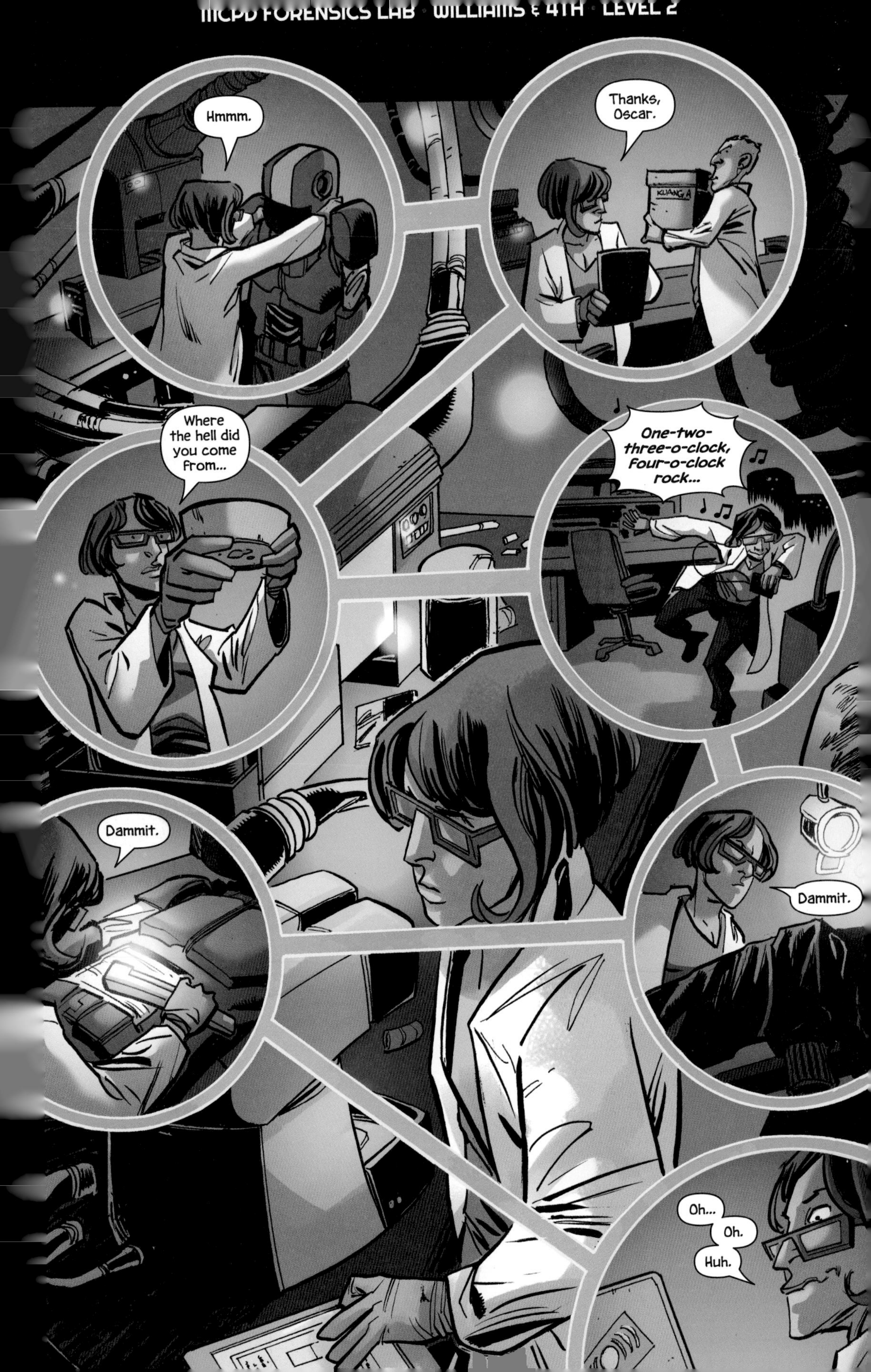
MCPD FORENSICS LAB • WILLIAMS & 4TH • LEVEL 2
Hmmm.
Thanks, Oscar.
KUANG, A
Where the hell did you come from...
One-two-three-o-clock, four-o-clock rock...
Dammit.
Dammit.
Oh...
Oh.
Huh.

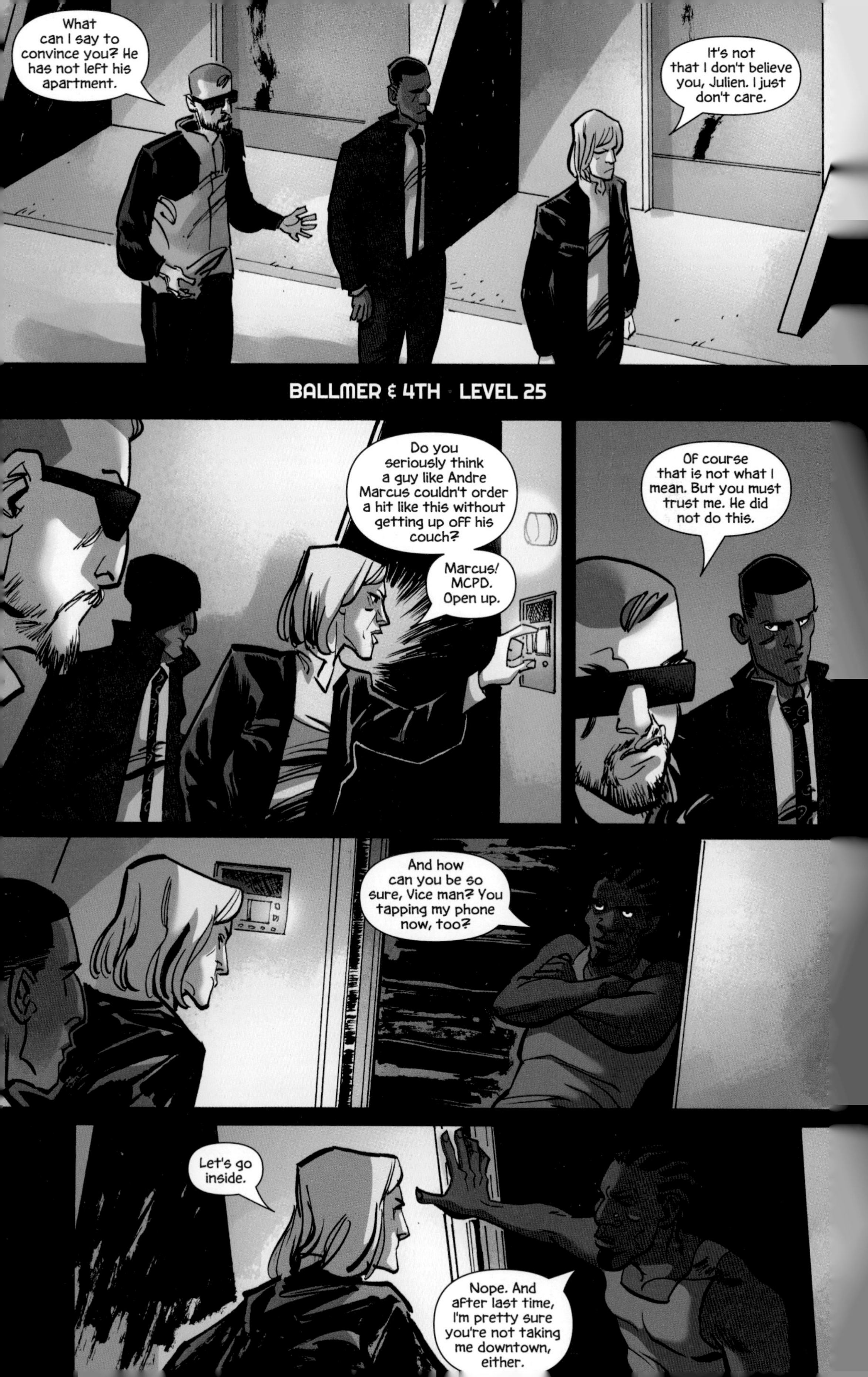
What can I say to convince you? He has not left his apartment.
It's not that I don't believe you, Julien. I just don't care.
BALLMER & 4TH · LEVEL 25
Do you seriously think a guy like Andre Marcus couldn't order a hit like this without getting up off his couch?
Marcus! MCPD. Open up.
Of course that is not what I mean. But you must trust me. He did not do this.
And how can you be so sure, Vice man? You tapping my phone now, too?
Let's go inside.
Nope. And after last time, I'm pretty sure you're not taking me downtown, either.

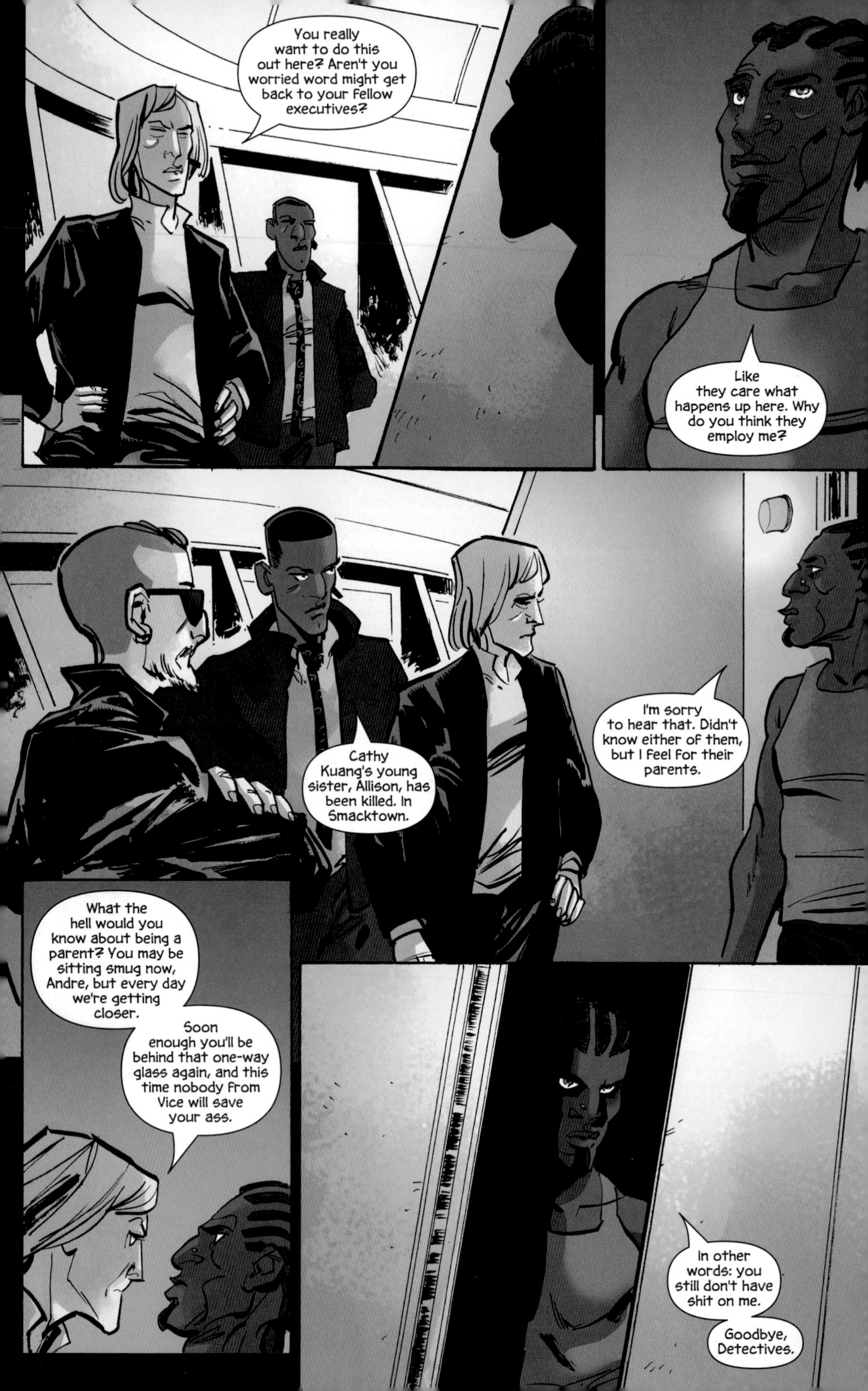
You really want to do this out here? Aren't you worried word might get back to your fellow executives?
Like they care what happens up here. Why do you think they employ me?
Cathy Kuang's young sister, Allison, has been killed. In Smacktown.
I'm sorry to hear that. Didn't know either of them, but I feel for their parents.
What the hell would you know about being a parent? You may be sitting smug now, Andre, but every day we're getting closer.
Soon enough you'll be behind that one-way glass again, and this time nobody from Vice will save your ass.
In other words: you still don't have shit on me.
Goodbye, Detectives.

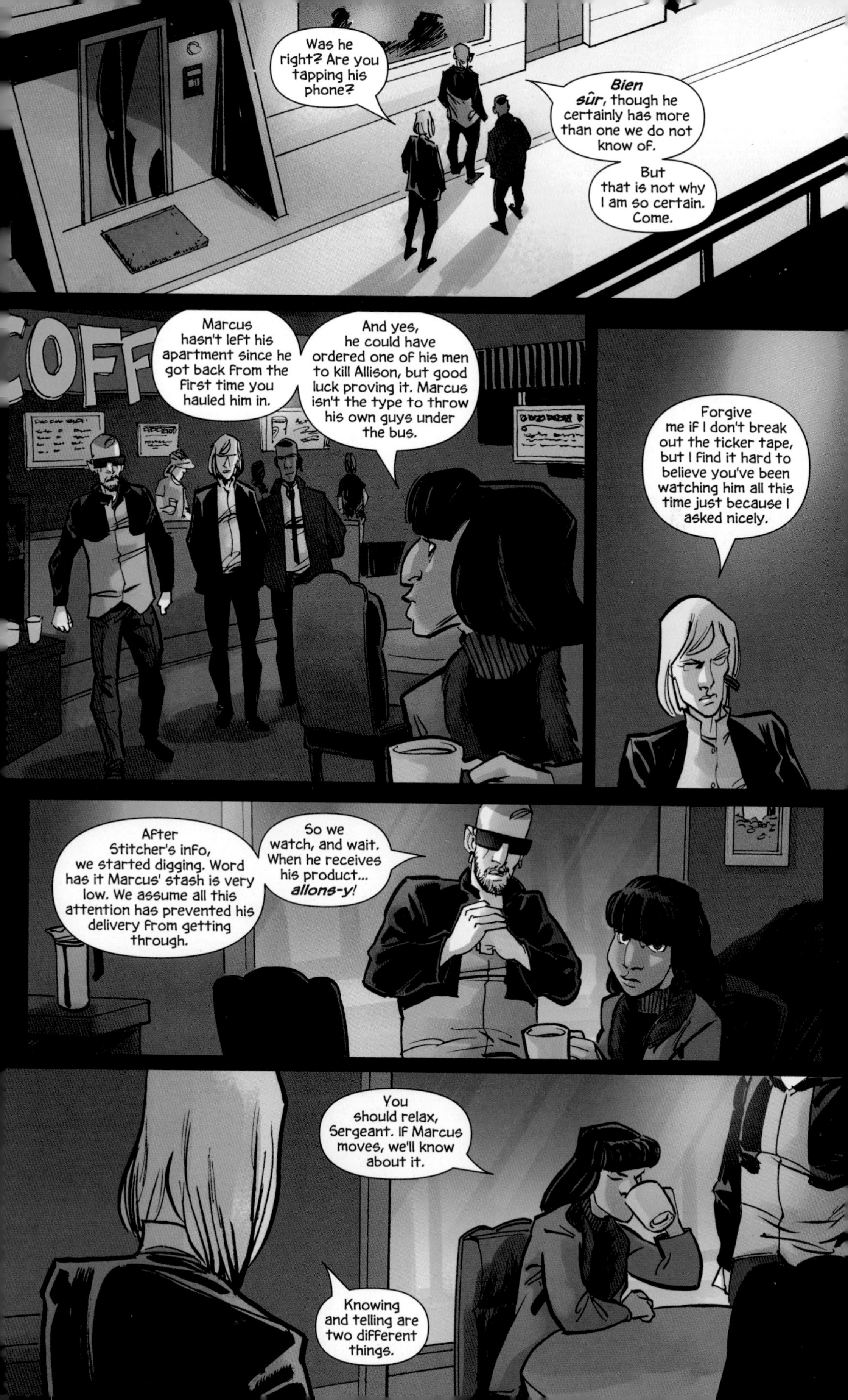

Was he right? Are you tapping his phone?
Bien sûr, though he certainly has more than one we do not know of.
But that is not why I am so certain. Come.
Marcus hasn't left his apartment since he got back from the first time you hauled him in.
And yes, he could have ordered one of his men to kill Allison, but good luck proving it. Marcus isn't the type to throw his own guys under the bus.
Forgive me if I don't break out the ticker tape, but I find it hard to believe you've been watching him all this time just because I asked nicely.
After Stitcher's info, we started digging. Word has it Marcus' stash is very low. We assume all this attention has prevented his delivery from getting through.
So we watch, and wait. When he receives his product... allons-y!
You should relax, Sergeant. If Marcus moves, we'll know about it.
Knowing and telling are two different things.

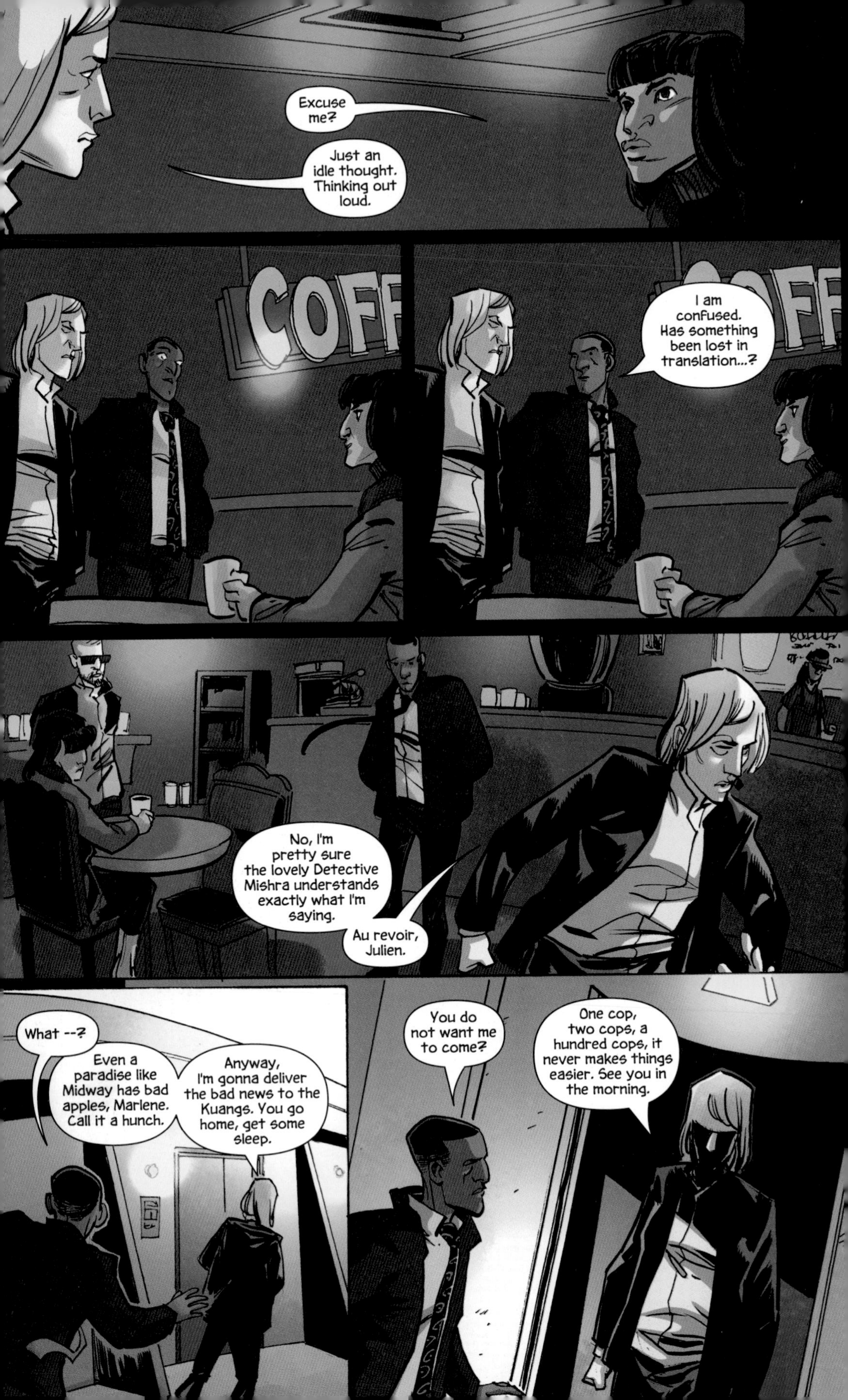
Excuse me?
Just an idle thought. Thinking out loud.
I am confused. Has something been lost in translation...?
No, I'm pretty sure the lovely Detective Mishra understands exactly what I'm saying.
Au revoir, Julien.
What --?
Even a paradise like Midway has bad apples, Marlene. Call it a hunch.
Anyway, I'm gonna deliver the bad news to the Kuangs. You go home, get some sleep.
You do not want me to come?
One cop, two cops, a hundred cops, it never makes things easier. See you in the morning.

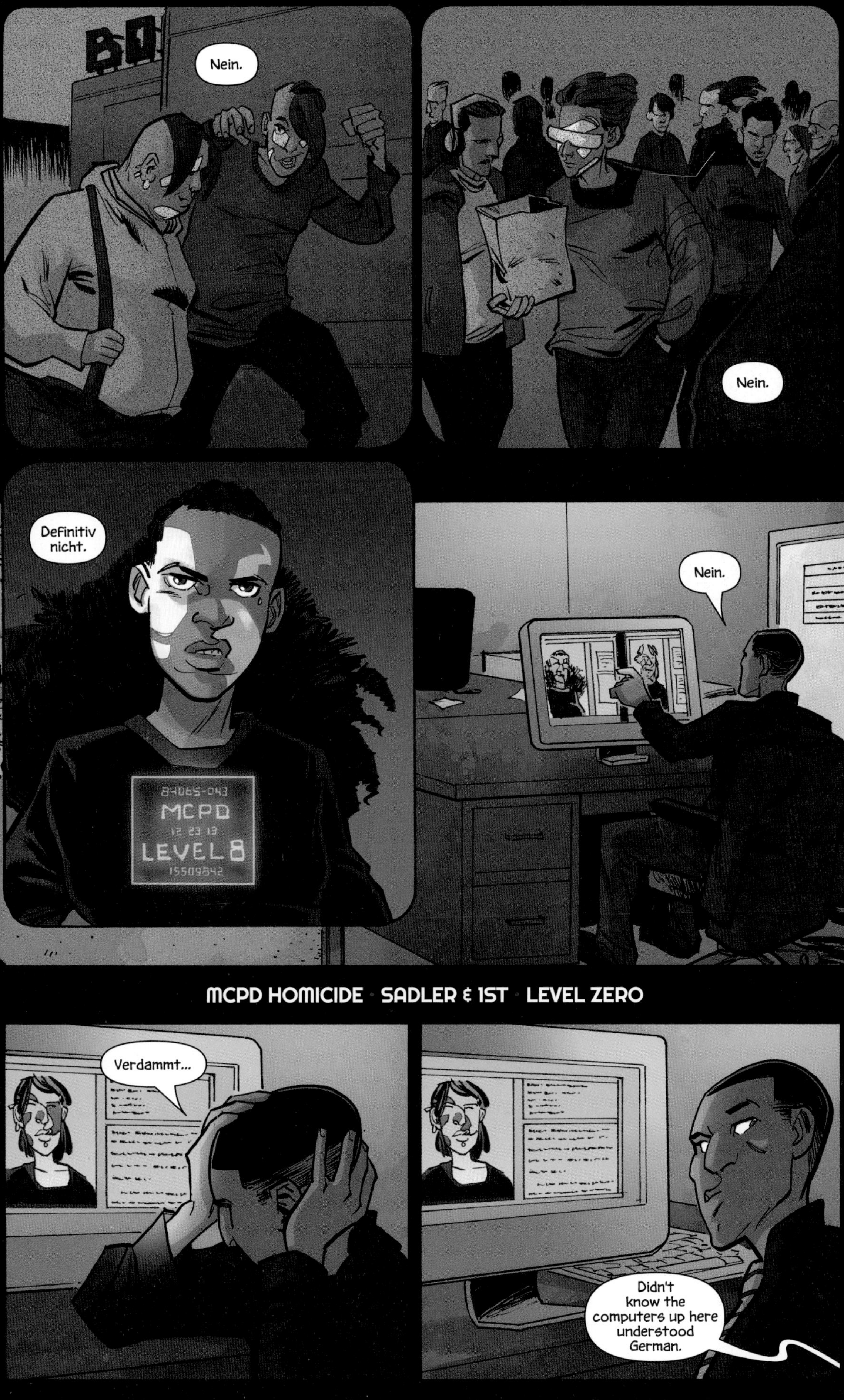
Nein.
Nein.
Definitiv nicht.
84065-043
MCPD
12 23 19
LEVEL 8
15509842
Nein.
MCPD HOMICIDE · SADLER & 1ST · LEVEL ZERO
Verdammt...
Didn't know the computers up here understood German.

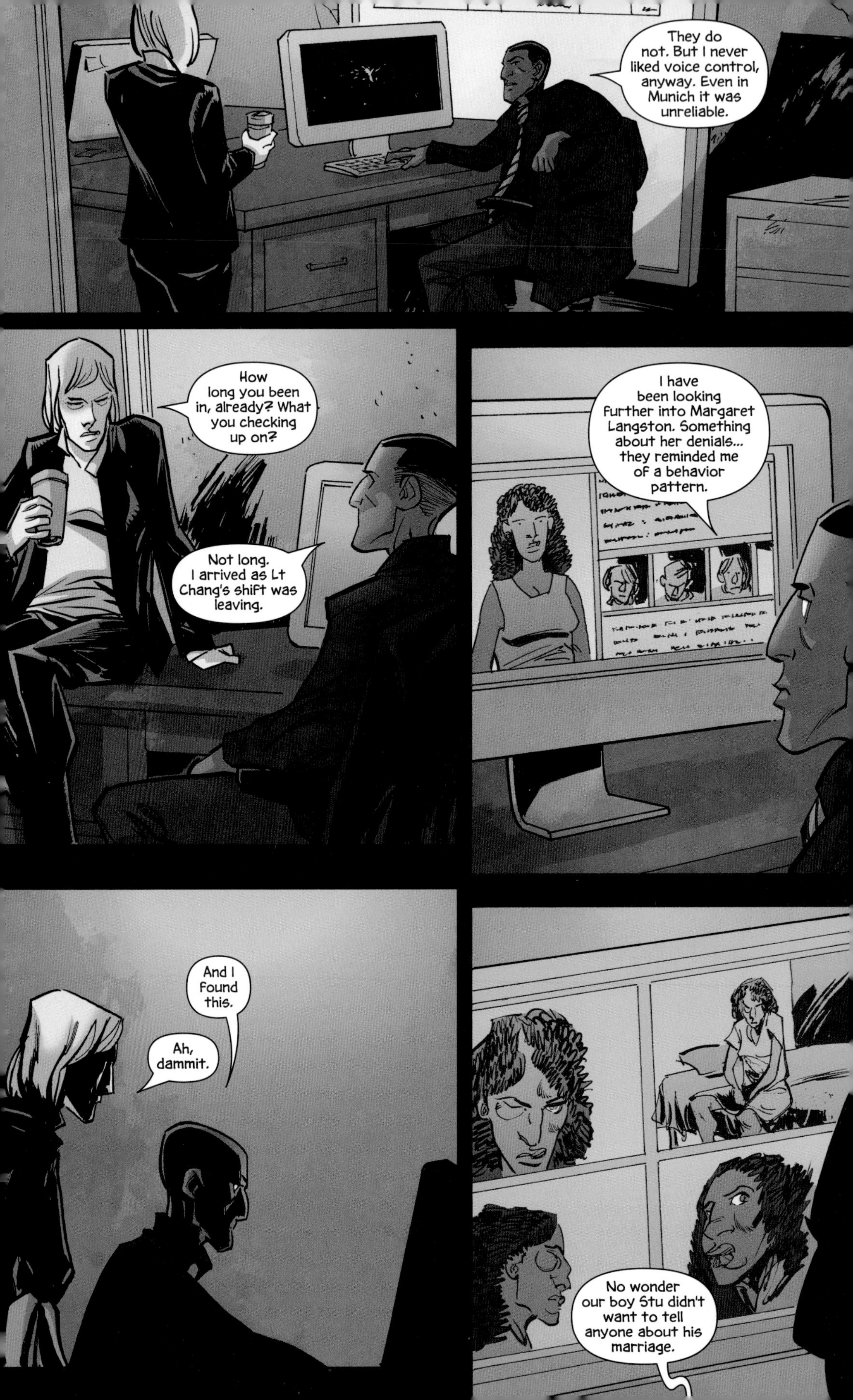
They do not. But I never liked voice control, anyway. Even in Munich it was unreliable.
How long you been in, already? What you checking up on?
Not long. I arrived as Lt Chang's shift was leaving.
I have been looking further into Margaret Langston. Something about her denials... they reminded me of a behavior pattern.
And I found this.
Ah, dammit.
No wonder our boy Stu didn't want to tell anyone about his marriage.

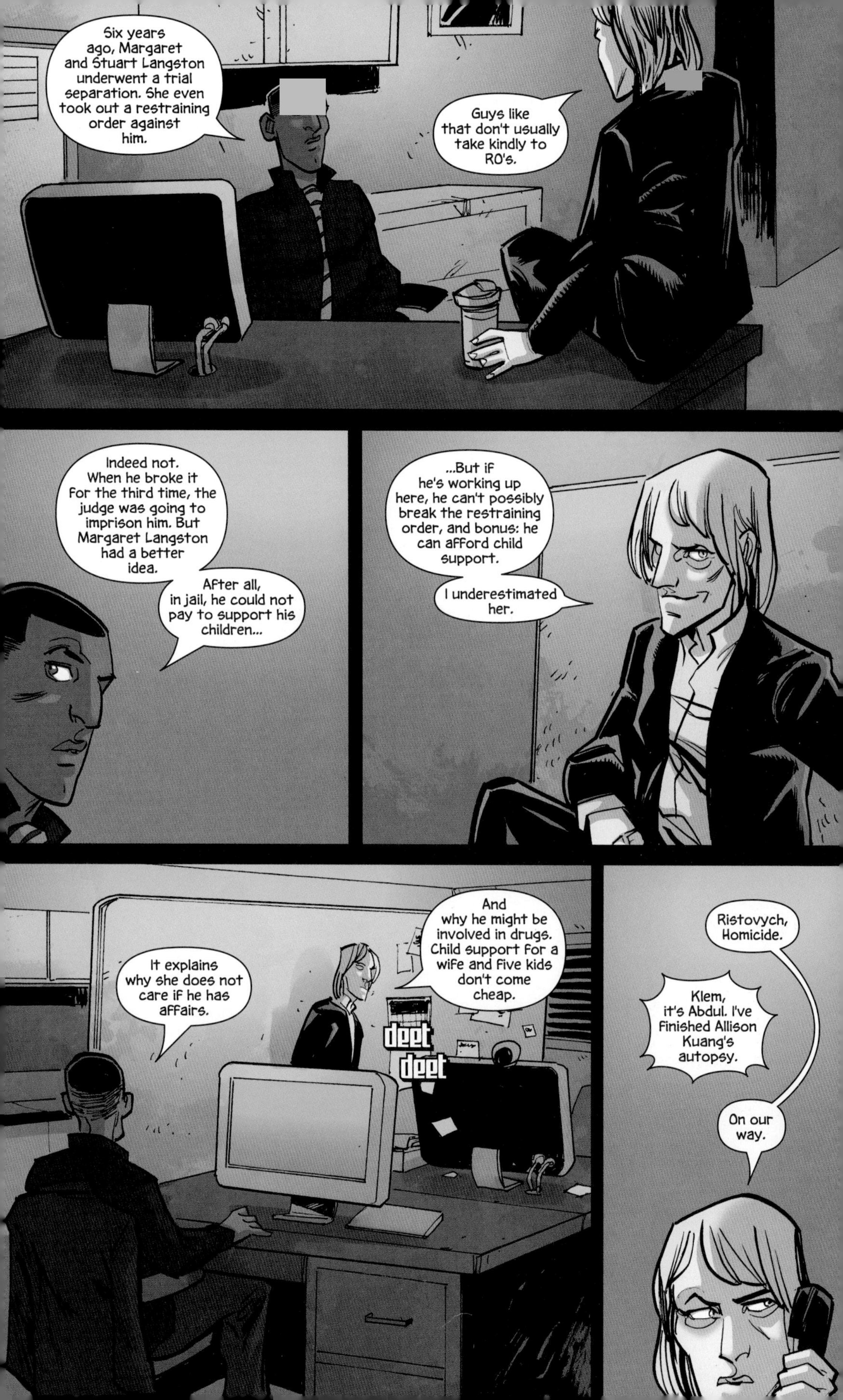
Six years ago, Margaret and Stuart Langston underwent a trial separation. She even took out a restraining order against him.
Guys like that don't usually take kindly to RO's.
Indeed not. When he broke it for the third time, the judge was going to imprison him. But Margaret Langston had a better idea.
After all, in jail, he could not pay to support his children...
...But if he's working up here, he can't possibly break the restraining order, and bonus: he can afford child support.
I underestimated her.
It explains why she does not care if he has affairs.
And why he might be involved in drugs. Child support for a wife and five kids don't come cheap.
deet
deet
Ristovych, Homicide.
Klem, it's Abdul. I've finished Allison Kuang's autopsy.
On our way.

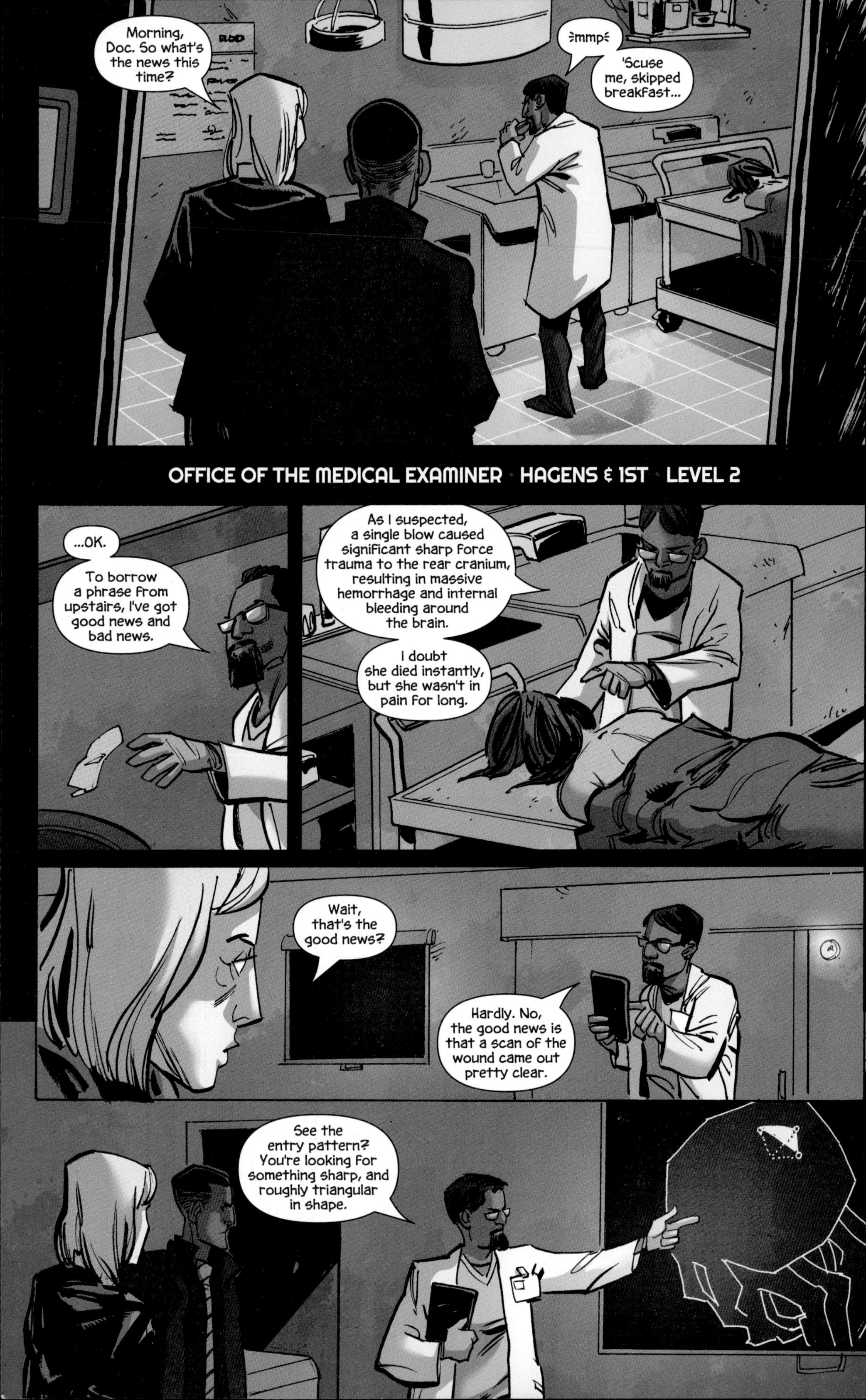
Morning, Doc. So what's the news this time?
mmp
'Scuse me, skipped breakfast...
OFFICE OF THE MEDICAL EXAMINER · HAGENS & 1ST · LEVEL 2
...OK.
To borrow a phrase from upstairs, I've got good news and bad news.
As I suspected, a single blow caused significant sharp force trauma to the rear cranium, resulting in massive hemorrhage and internal bleeding around the brain.
I doubt she died instantly, but she wasn't in pain for long.
Wait, that's the good news?
Hardly. No, the good news is that a scan of the wound came out pretty clear.
See the entry pattern? You're looking for something sharp, and roughly triangular in shape.

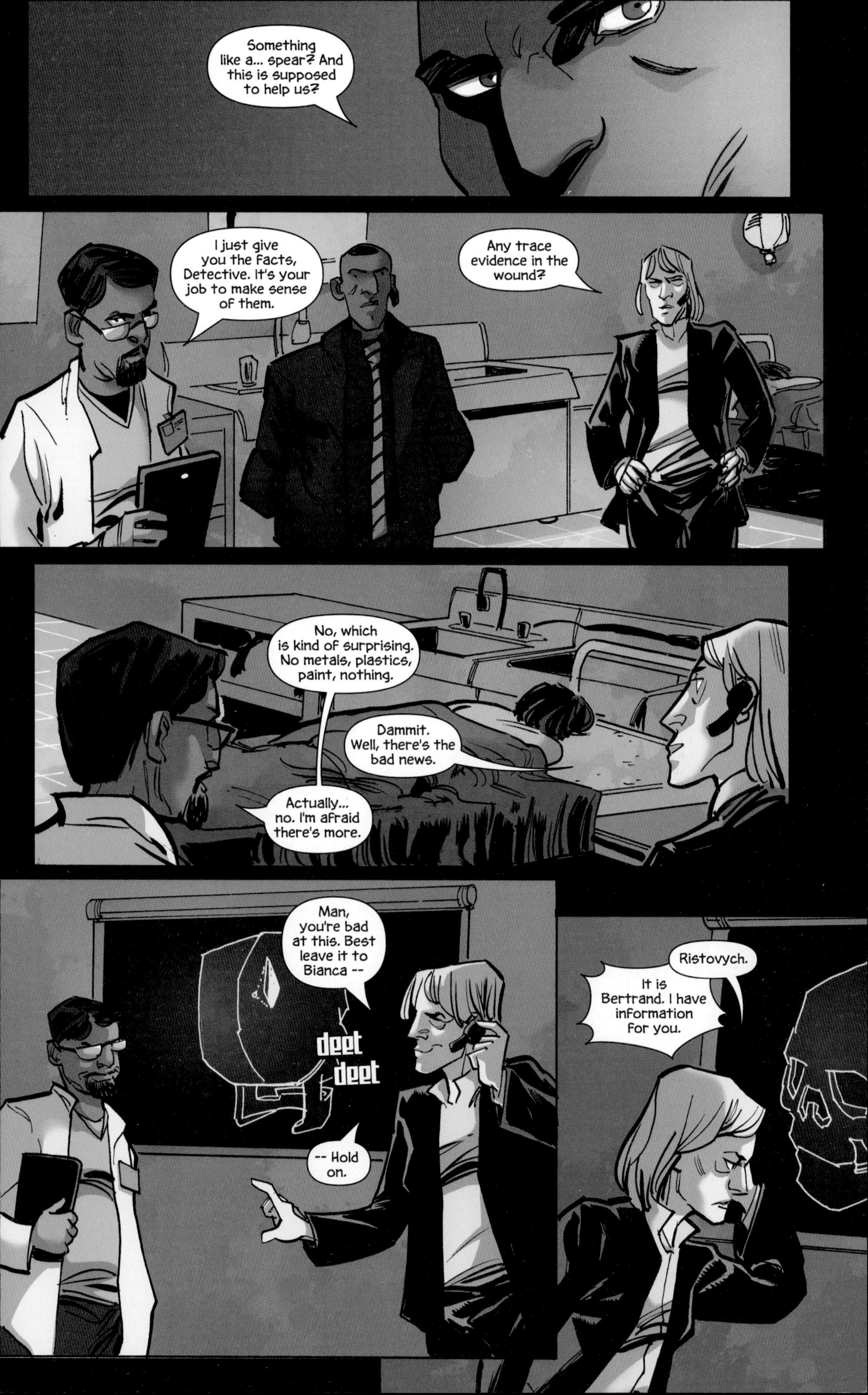
Something like a... spear? And this is supposed to help us?
I just give you the facts, Detective. It's your job to make sense of them.
Any trace evidence in the wound?
No, which is kind of surprising. No metals, plastics, paint, nothing.
Dammit. Well, there's the bad news.
Actually... no. I'm afraid there's more.
Man, you're bad at this. Best leave it to Bianca --
deet deet
-- Hold on.
Ristovych.
It is Bertrand. I have information for you.

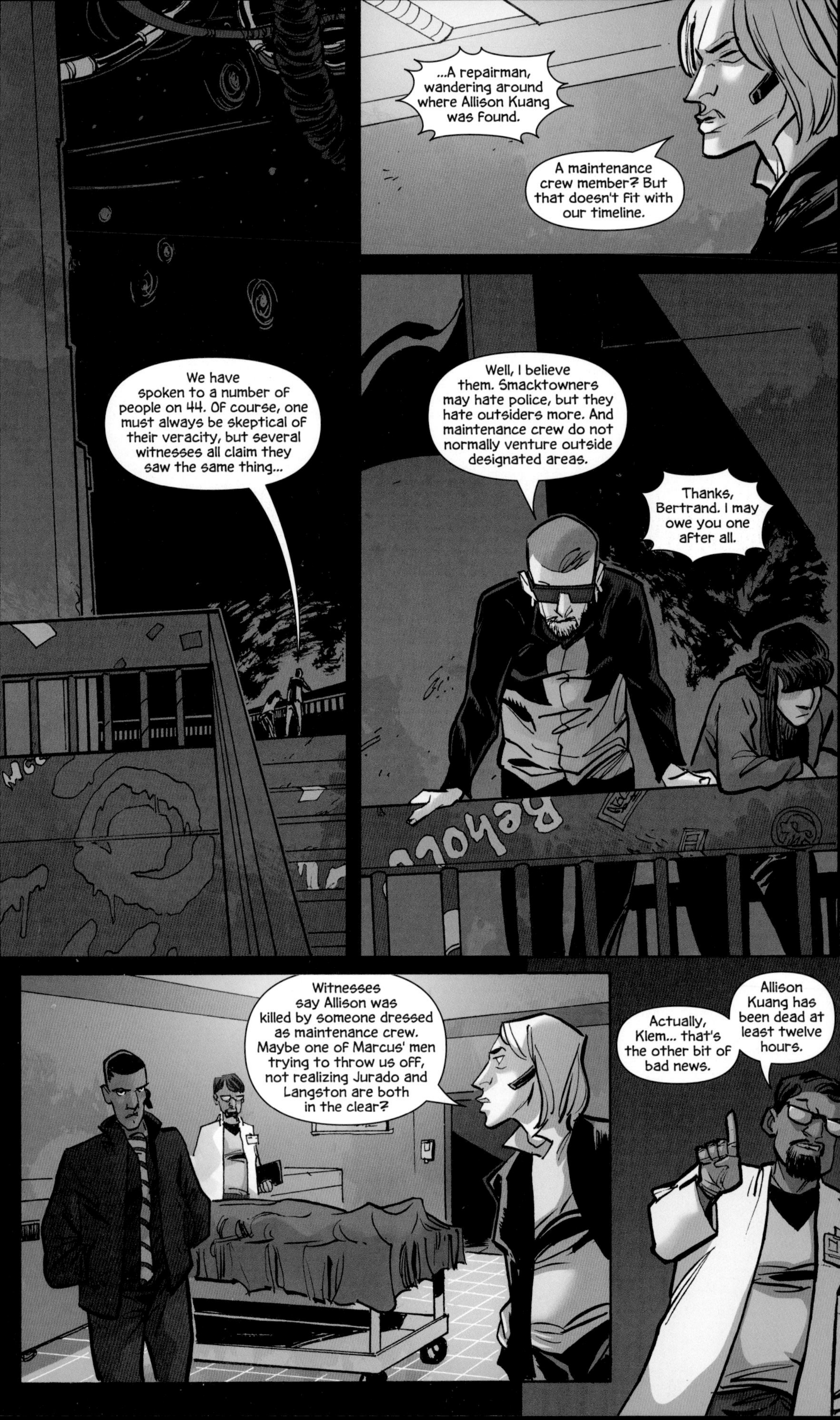

...A repairman, wandering around where Allison Kuang was found.
A maintenance crew member? But that doesn't fit with our timeline.
We have spoken to a number of people on 44. Of course, one must always be skeptical of their veracity, but several witnesses all claim they saw the same thing...
Well, I believe them. Smacktowners may hate police, but they hate outsiders more. And maintenance crew do not normally venture outside designated areas.
Thanks, Bertrand. I may owe you one after all.
Witnesses say Allison was killed by someone dressed as maintenance crew. Maybe one of Marcus' men trying to throw us off, not realizing Jurado and Langston are both in the clear?
Actually, Klem... that's the other bit of bad news.
Allison Kuang has been dead at least twelve hours.

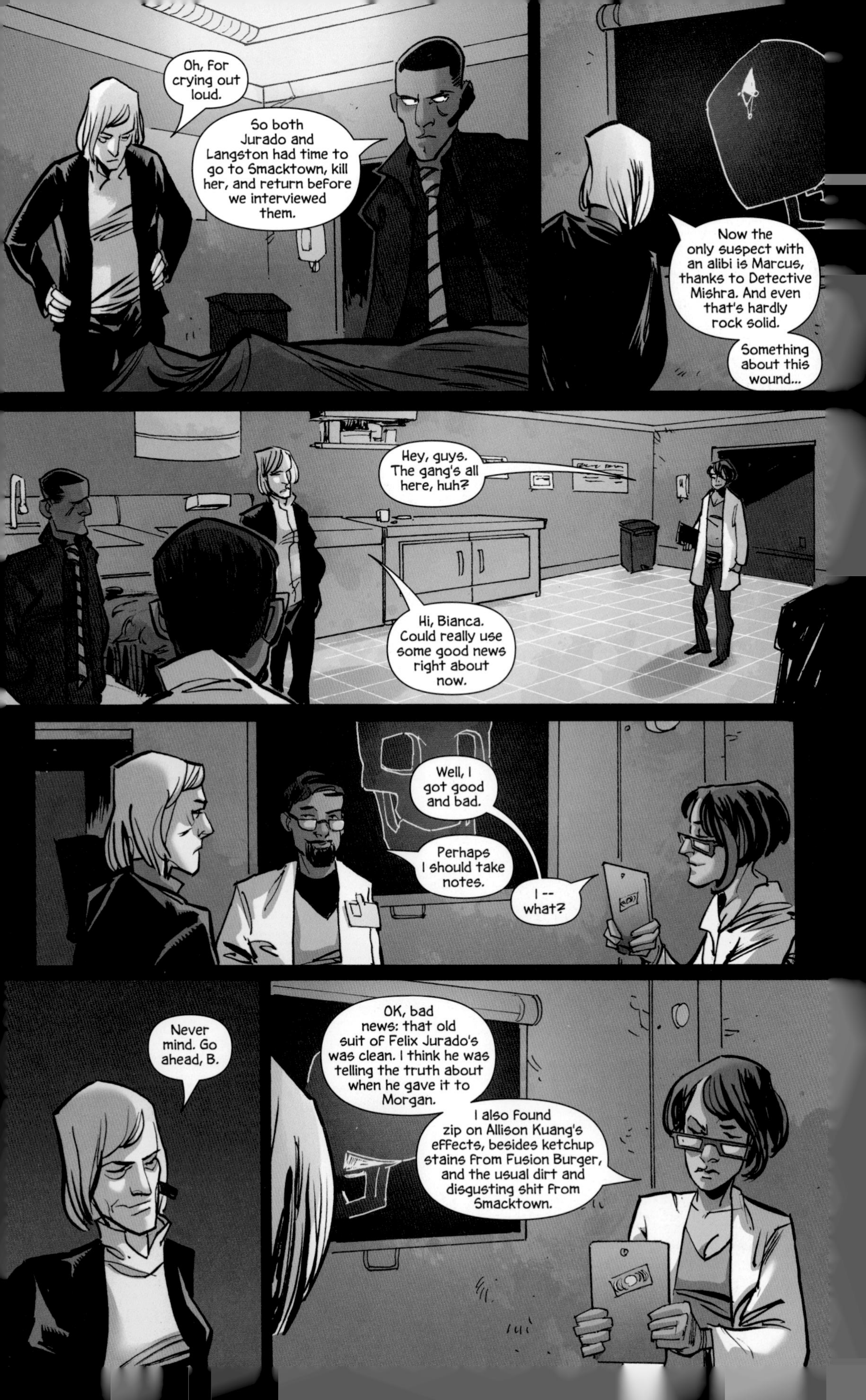

Oh, for crying out loud.
So both Jurado and Langston had time to go to Smacktown, kill her, and return before we interviewed them.
Now the only suspect with an alibi is Marcus, thanks to Detective Mishra. And even that's hardly rock solid.
Something about this wound...
Hey, guys. The gang's all here, huh?
Hi, Bianca. Could really use some good news right about now.
Well, I got good and bad.
Perhaps I should take notes.
I -- what?
Never mind. Go ahead, B.
OK, bad news: that old suit of Felix Jurado's was clean. I think he was telling the truth about when he gave it to Morgan.
I also found zip on Allison Kuang's effects, besides ketchup stains from Fusion Burger, and the usual dirt and disgusting shit from Smacktown.

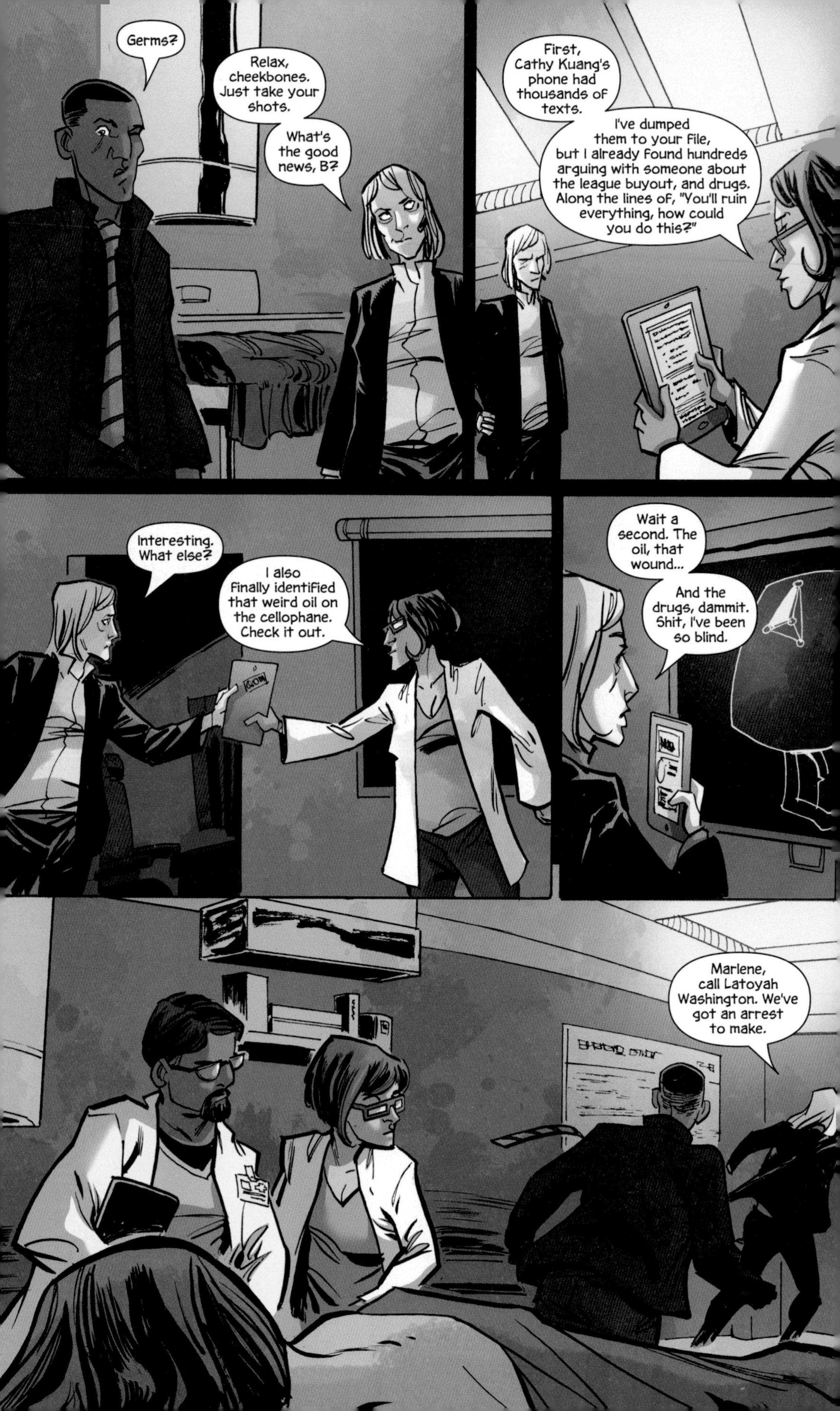
Germs?
Relax, cheekbones. Just take your shots.
What's the good news, B?
First, Cathy Kuang's phone had thousands of texts.
I've dumped them to your file, but I already found hundreds arguing with someone about the league buyout, and drugs. Along the lines of, "You'll ruin everything, how could you do this?"
Interesting. What else?
I also finally identified that weird oil on the cellophane. Check it out.
Wait a second. The oil, that wound...
And the drugs, dammit. Shit, I've been so blind.
Marlene, call Latoyah Washington. We've got an arrest to make.

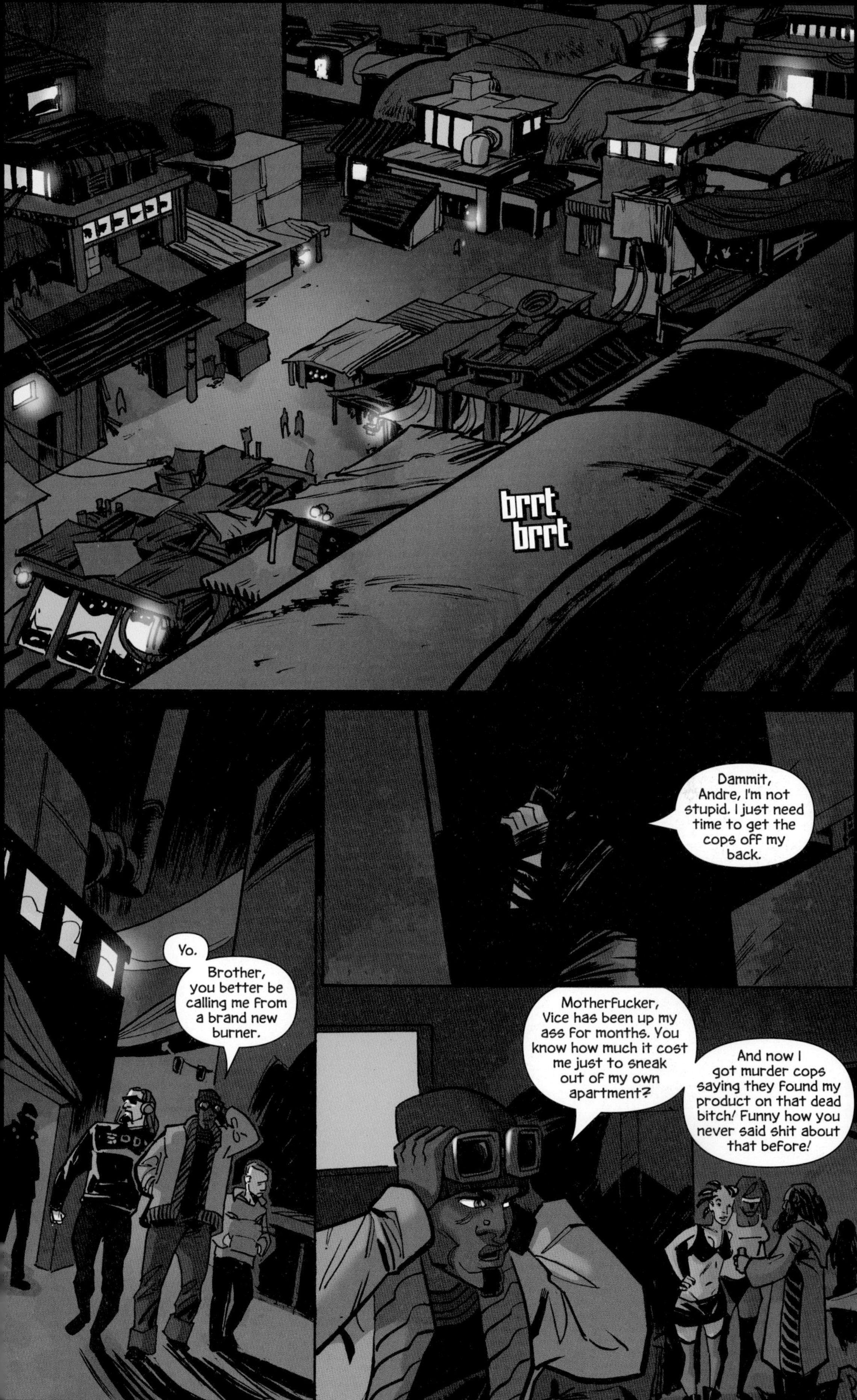
brrt
brrt
Dammit, Andre, I'm not stupid. I just need time to get the cops off my back.
Yo.
Brother, you better be calling me from a brand new burner.
Motherfucker, Vice has been up my ass for months. You know how much it cost me just to sneak out of my own apartment?
And now I got murder cops saying they found my product on that dead bitch! Funny how you never said shit about that before!

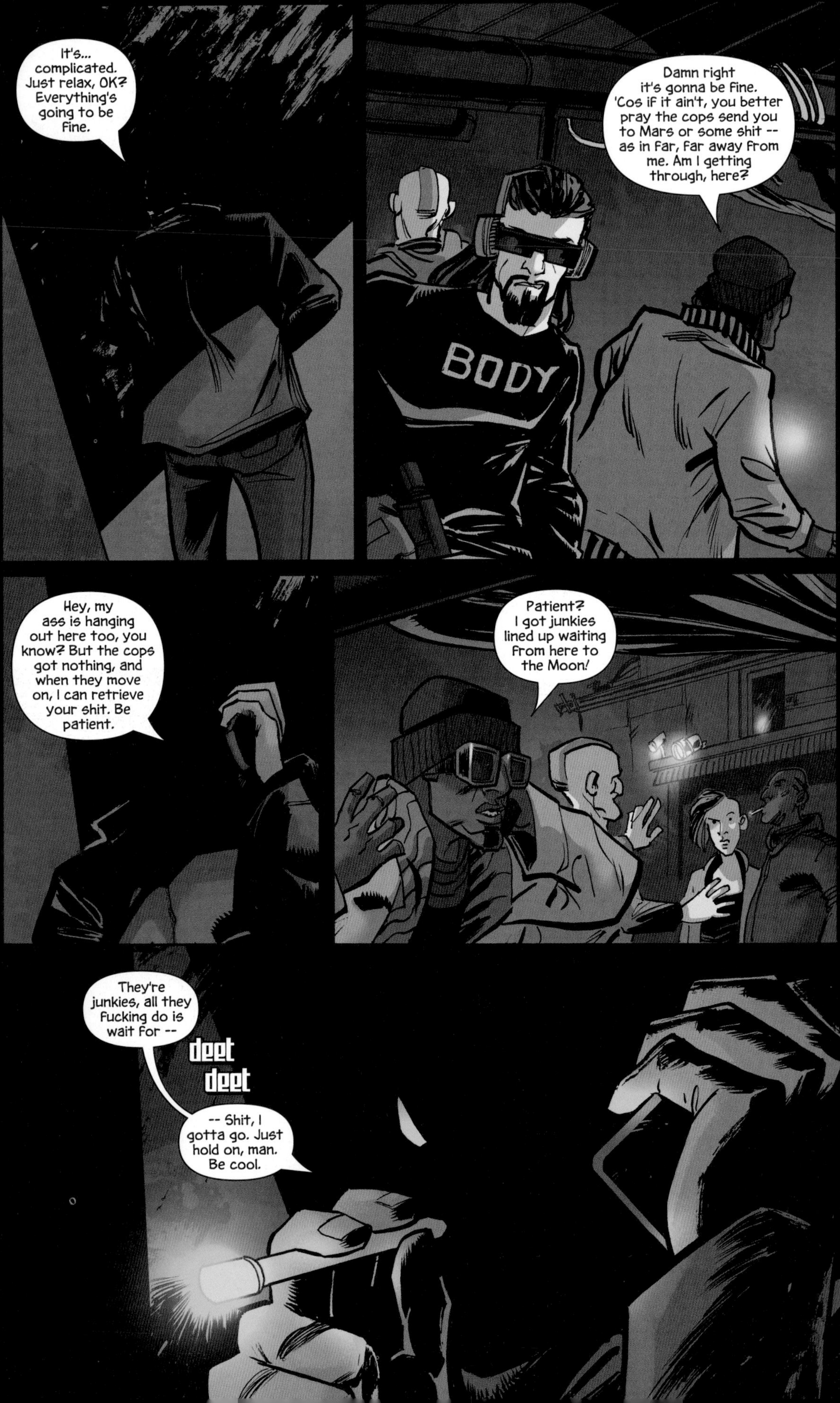
It's... complicated. Just relax, OK? Everything's going to be fine.
Damn right it's gonna be fine. 'Cos if it ain't, you better pray the cops send you to Mars or some shit -- as in far, far away from me. Am I getting through, here?
BODY
Hey, my ass is hanging out here too, you know? But the cops got nothing, and when they move on, I can retrieve your shit. Be patient.
Patient? I got junkies lined up waiting from here to the Moon!
They're junkies, all they fucking do is wait for --
deet
deet
-- Shit, I gotta go. Just hold on, man. Be cool.

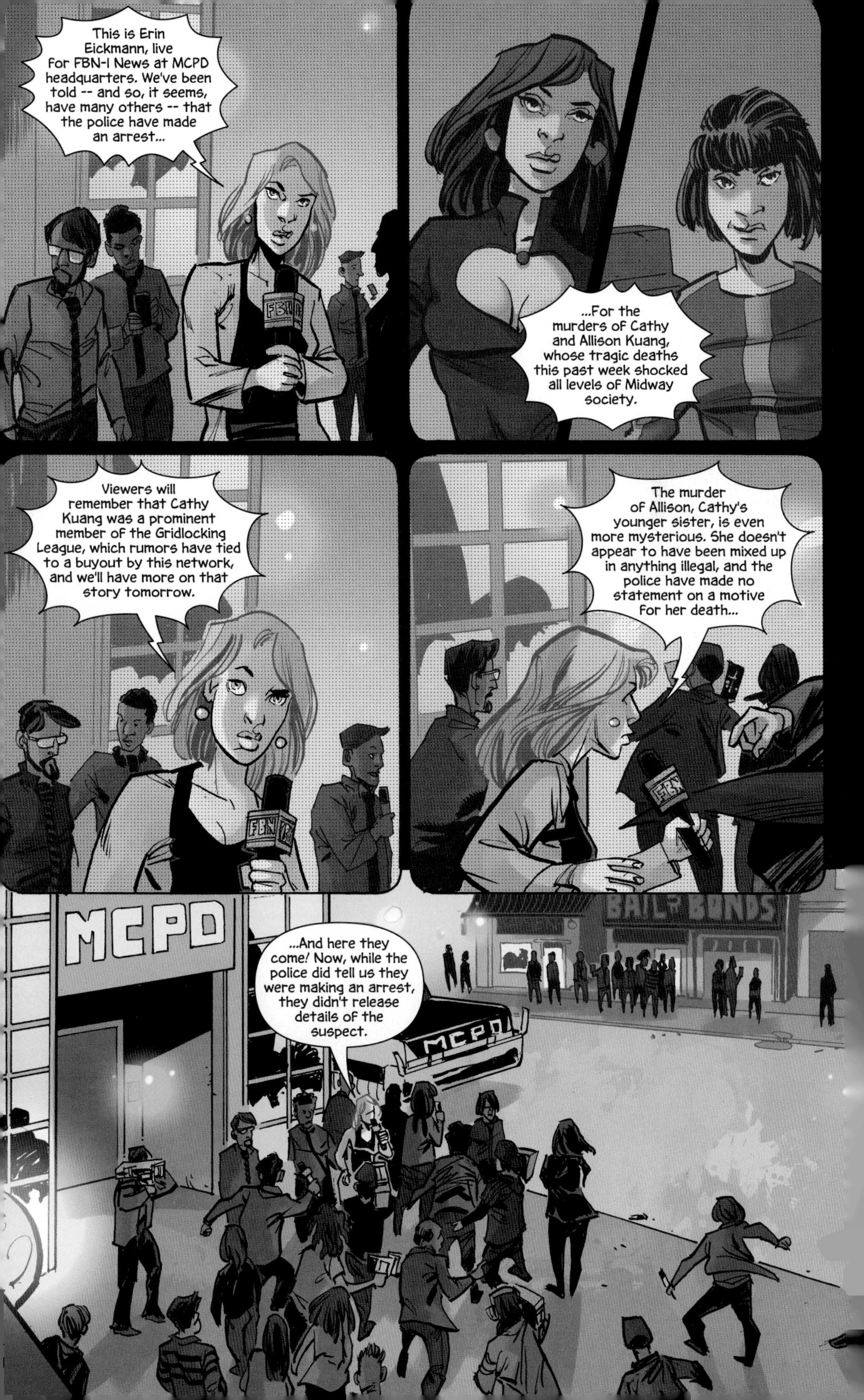
This is Erin Eickmann, live for FBN-1 News at MCPD headquarters. We've been told -- and so, it seems, have many others -- that the police have made an arrest...
FBN
...For the murders of Cathy and Allison Kuang, whose tragic deaths this past week shocked all levels of Midway society.
Viewers will remember that Cathy Kuang was a prominent member of the Gridlocking League, which rumors have tied to a buyout by this network, and we'll have more on that story tomorrow.
FBN
The murder of Allison, Cathy's younger sister, is even more mysterious. She doesn't appear to have been mixed up in anything illegal, and the police have made no statement on a motive for her death...
FBN
MCPD
BAIL BONDS
...And here they come! Now, while the police did tell us they were making an arrest, they didn't release details of the suspect.
MCPD

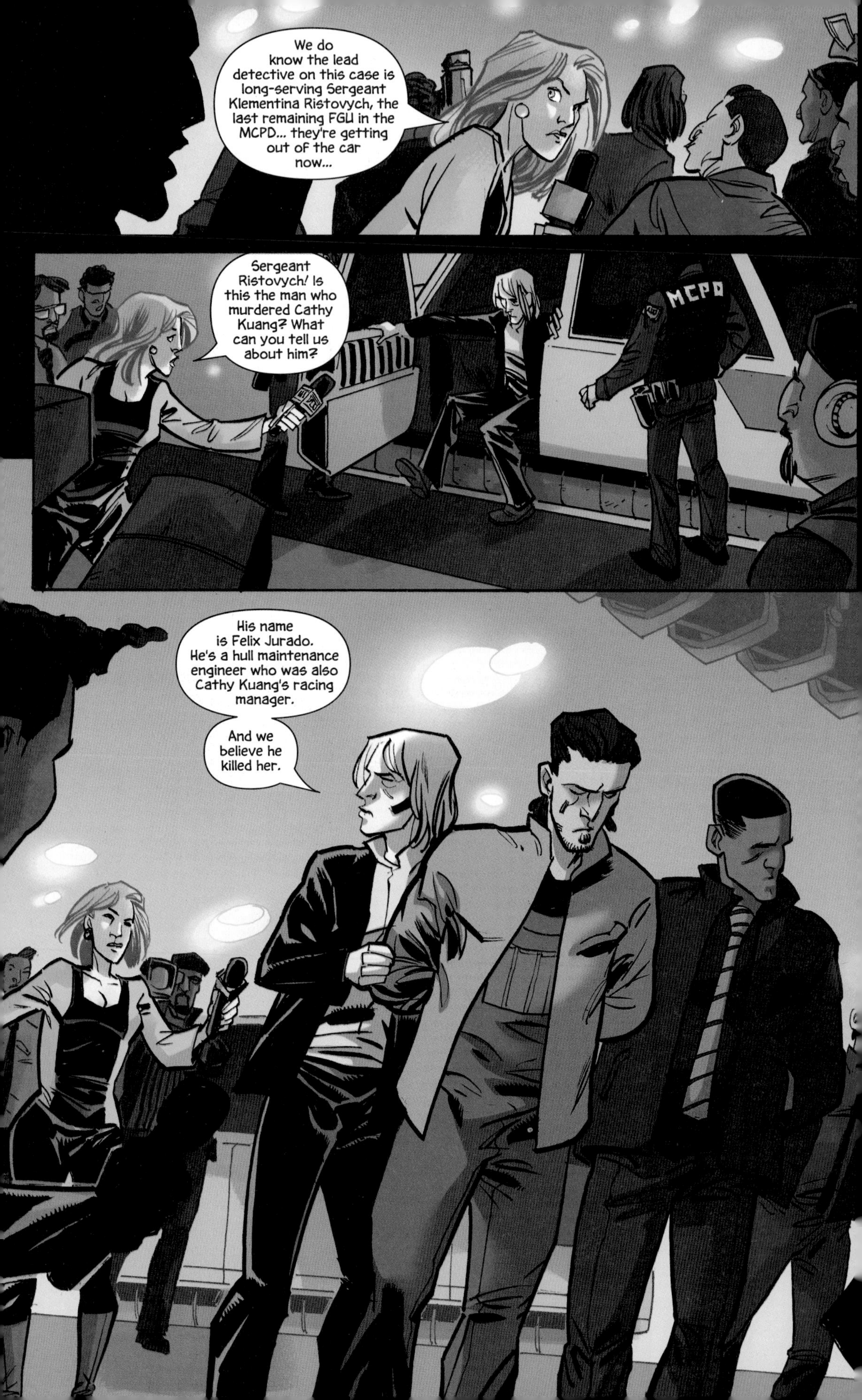
We do know the lead detective on this case is long-serving Sergeant Klementina Ristovych, the last remaining FGU in the MCPD... they're getting out of the car now...
Sergeant Ristovych! Is this the man who murdered Cathy Kuang? What can you tell us about him?
MCPD
His name is Felix Jurado. He's a hull maintenance engineer who was also Cathy Kuang's racing manager.
And we believe he killed her.

PART 6

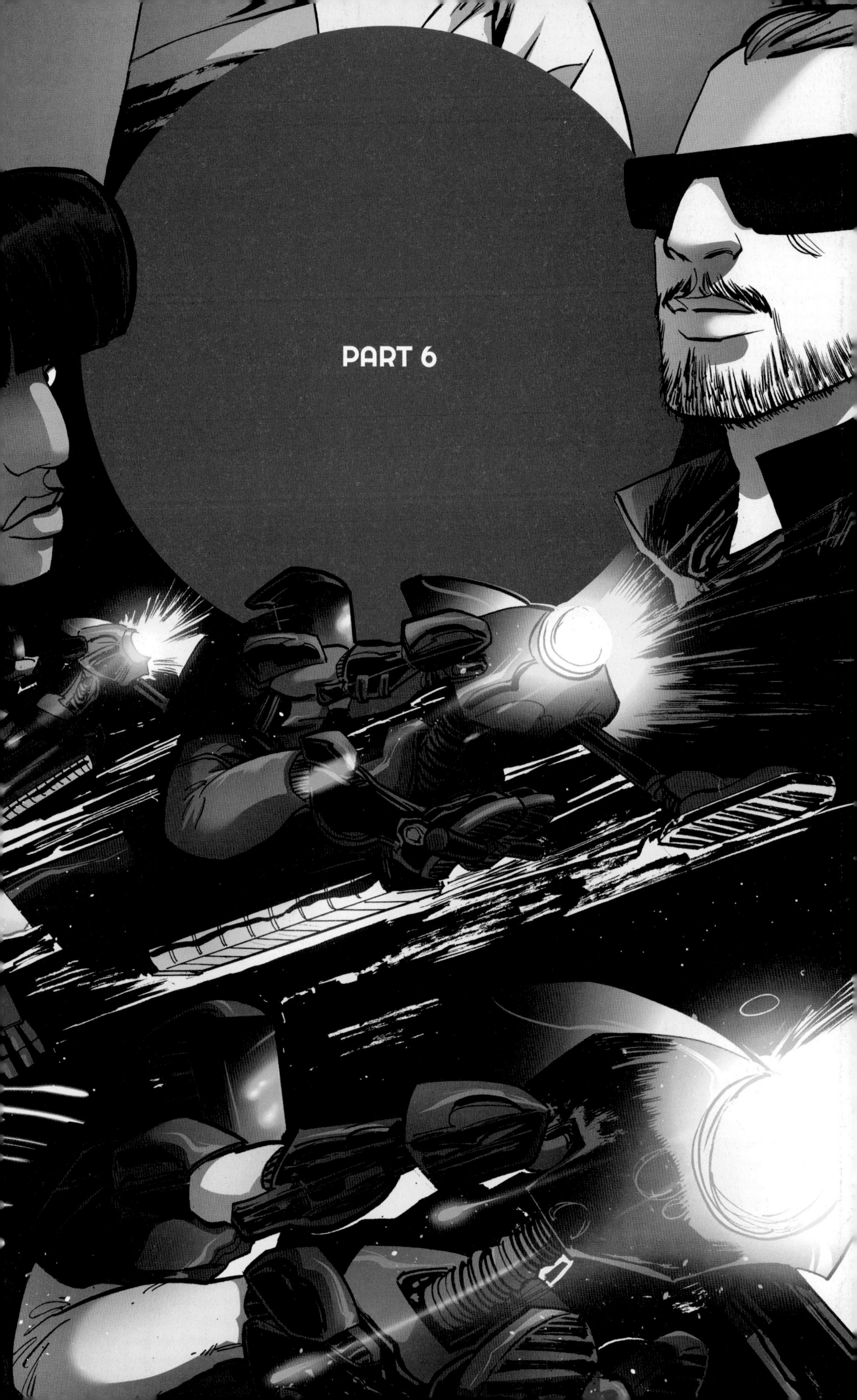

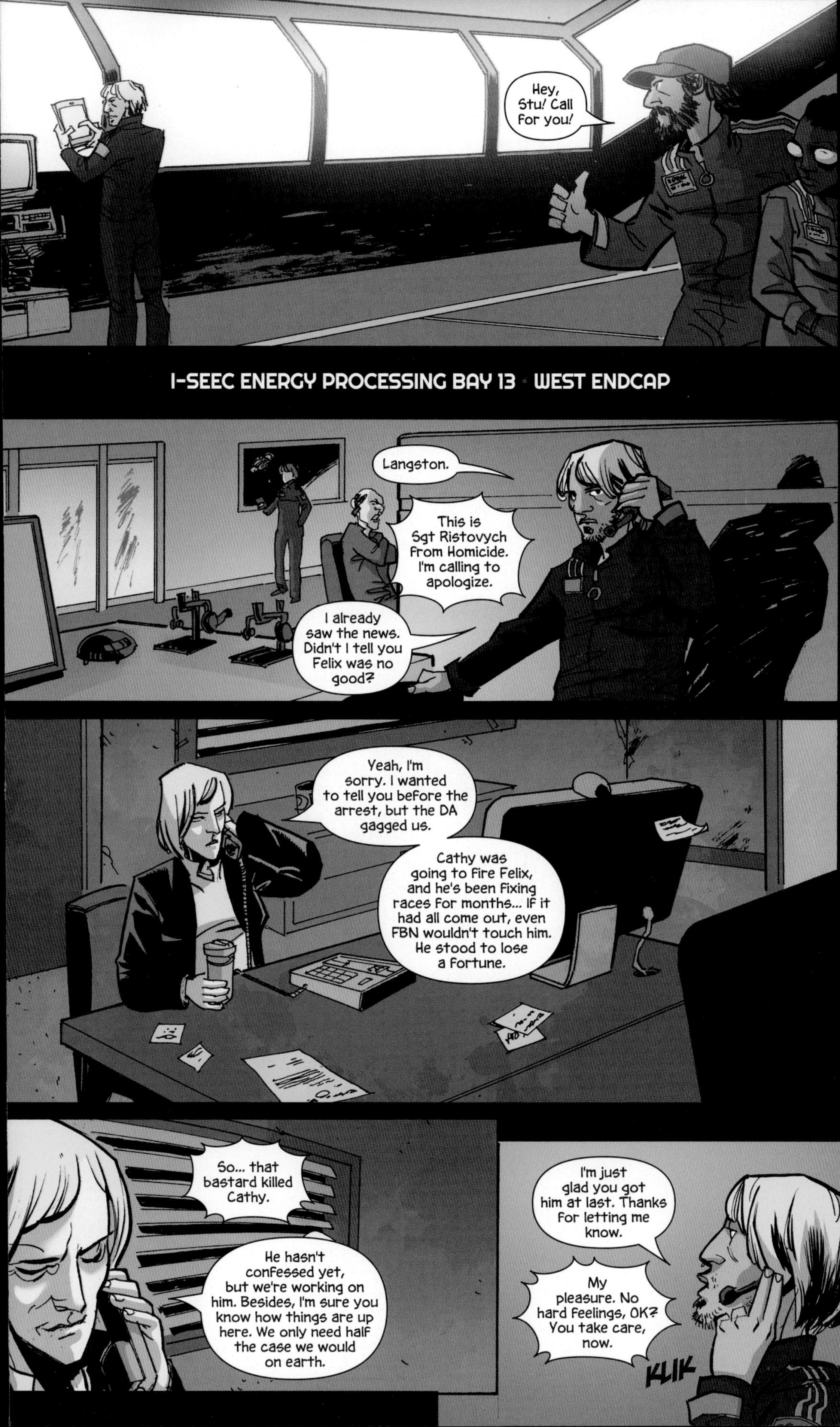
Hey, Stu! Call for you!
I-SEEC ENERGY PROCESSING BAY 13 • WEST ENDCAP
Langston.
This is Sgt Ristovych from Homicide. I'm calling to apologize.
I already saw the news. Didn't I tell you Felix was no good?
Yeah, I'm sorry. I wanted to tell you before the arrest, but the DA gagged us.
Cathy was going to fire Felix, and he's been fixing races for months... If it had all come out, even FBN wouldn't touch him. He stood to lose a fortune.
So... that bastard killed Cathy.
He hasn't confessed yet, but we're working on him. Besides, I'm sure you know how things are up here. We only need half the case we would on earth.
I'm just glad you got him at last. Thanks for letting me know.
My pleasure. No hard feelings, OK? You take care, now.
KLIK

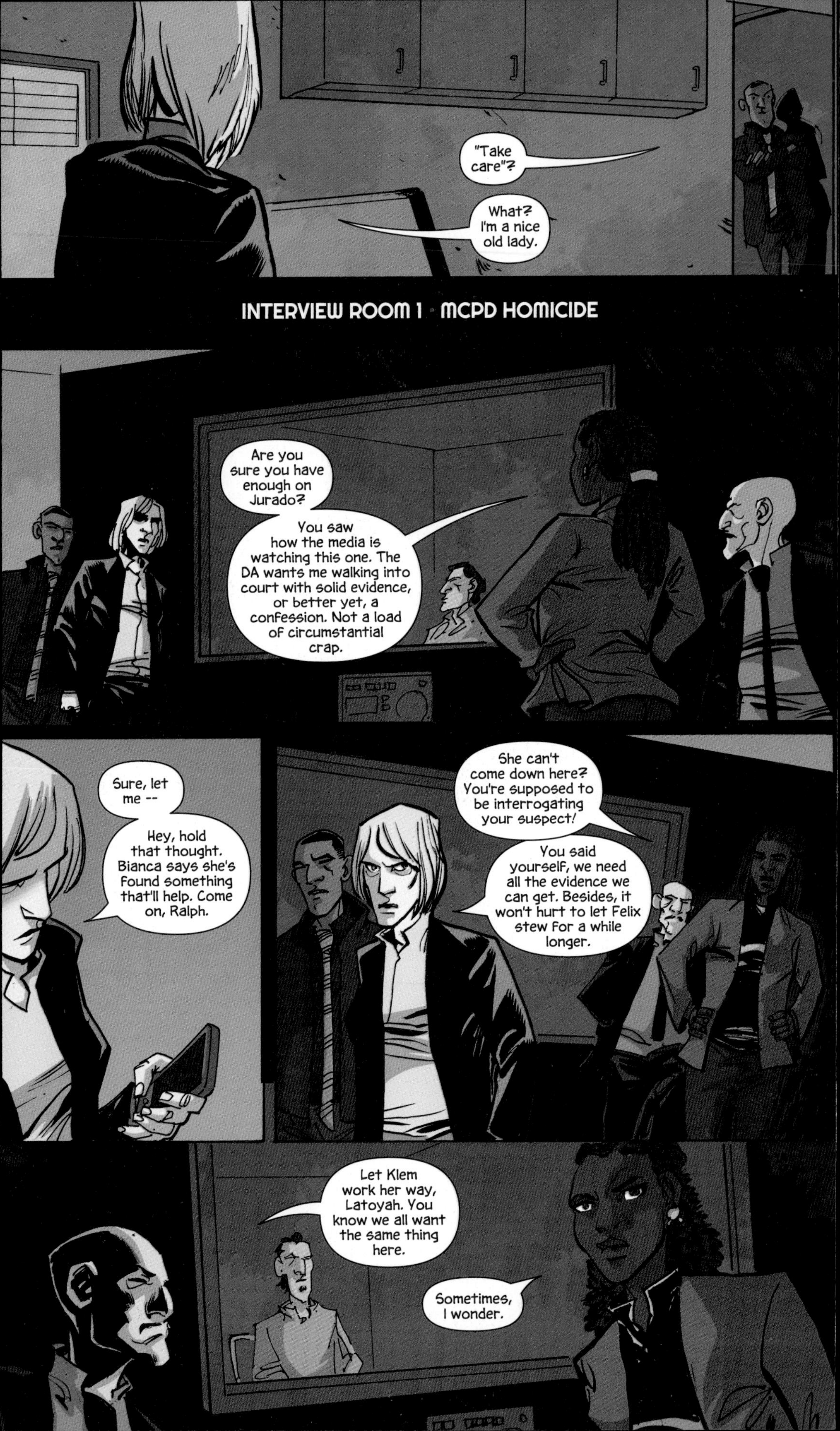
"Take care"?
What? I'm a nice old lady.
INTERVIEW ROOM 1 · MCPD HOMICIDE
Are you sure you have enough on Jurado?
You saw how the media is watching this one. The DA wants me walking into court with solid evidence, or better yet, a confession. Not a load of circumstantial crap.
Sure, let me --
Hey, hold that thought. Bianca says she's found something that'll help. Come on, Ralph.
She can't come down here? You're supposed to be interrogating your suspect!
You said yourself, we need all the evidence we can get. Besides, it won't hurt to let Felix stew for a while longer.
Let Klem work her way, Latoyah. You know we all want the same thing here.
Sometimes, I wonder.

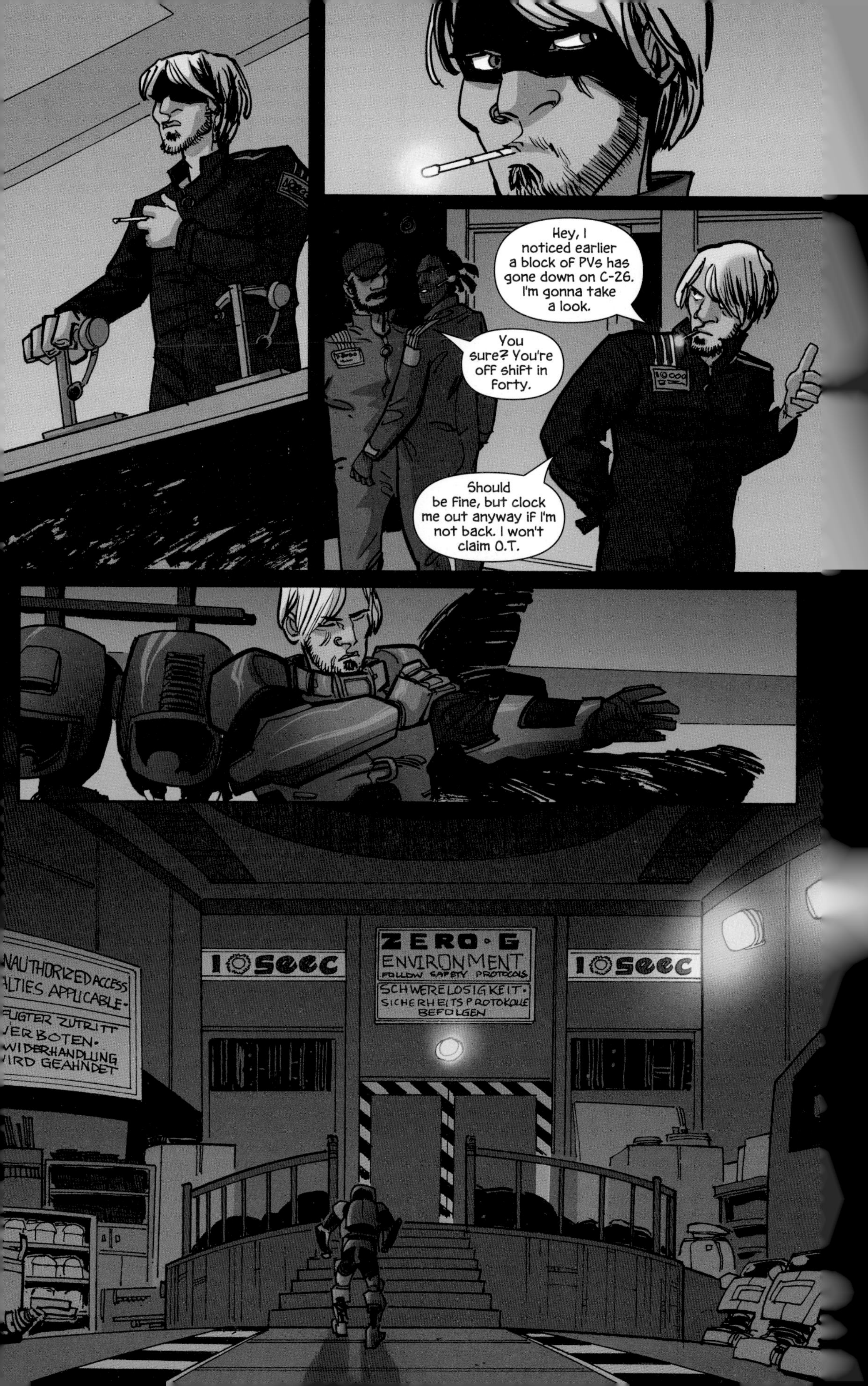
Hey, I noticed earlier a block of PVs has gone down on C-26. I'm gonna take a look.
You sure? You're off shift in forty.
Should be fine, but clock me out anyway if I'm not back. I won't claim O.T.
NAUTHORIZED ACCESS
ALTIES APPLICABLE-
FLIGTER ZUTRITT
VERBOTEN.
WIDERHANDLUNG
VIRD GEAHNDET
ZERO-G
ENVIRONMENT
FOLLOW SAFETY PROTOCOLS
SCHWERELOSIGKEIT.
SICHERHEITSPROTOKOLLE
BEFOLGEN

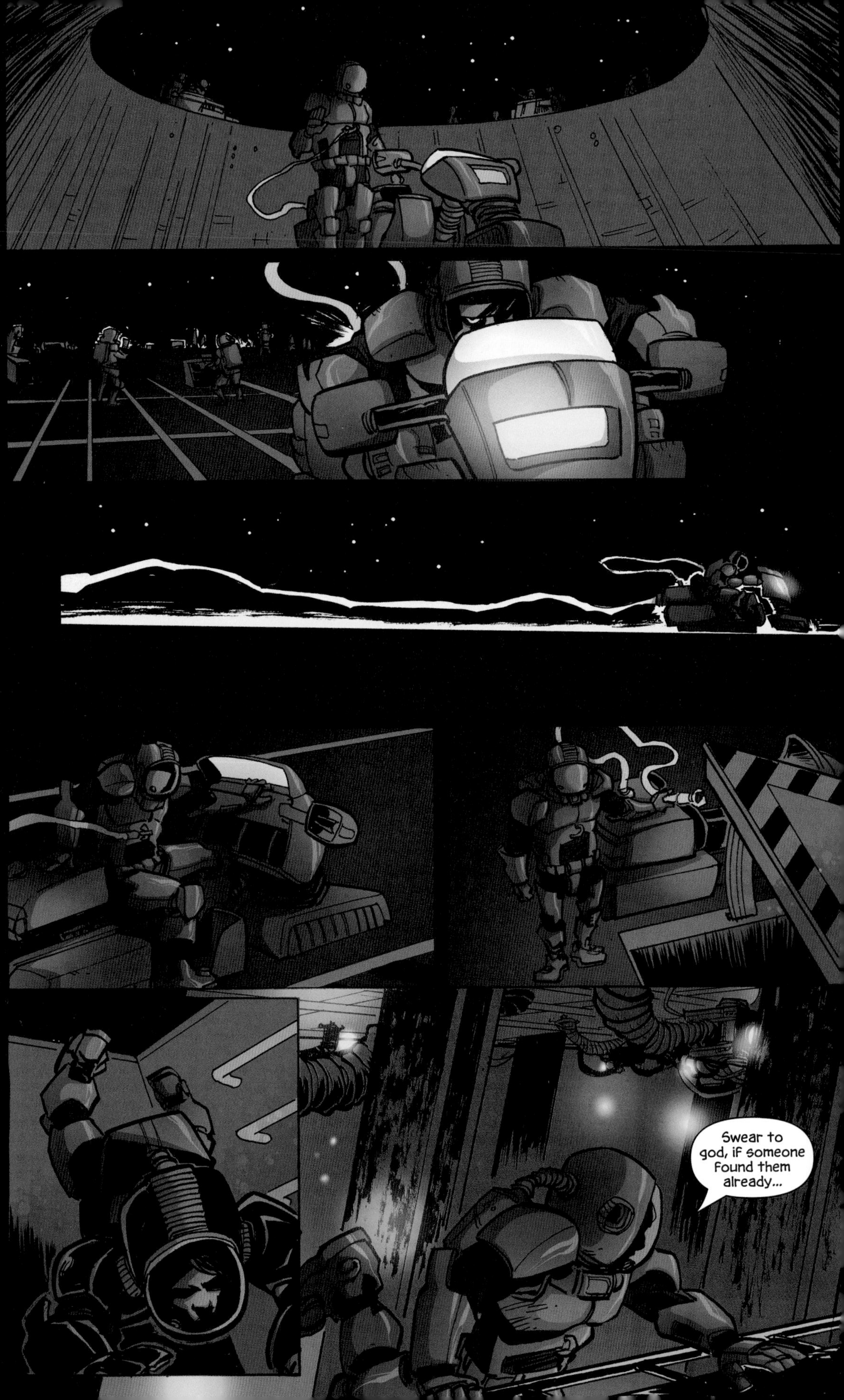
Swear to god, if someone found them already...

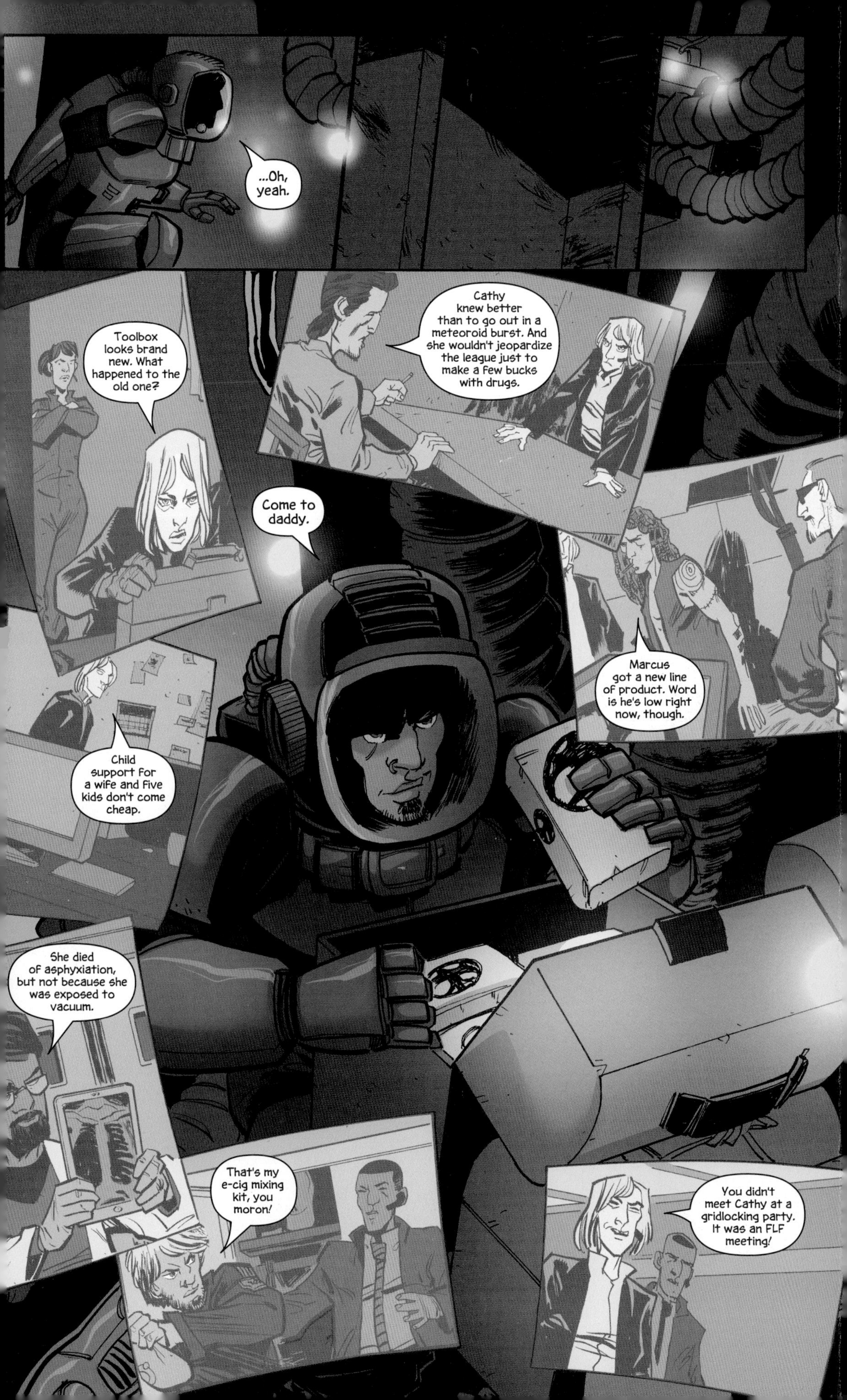
...Oh, yeah.
Toolbox looks brand new. What happened to the old one?
Cathy knew better than to go out in a meteoroid burst. And she wouldn't jeopardize the league just to make a few bucks with drugs.
Come to daddy.
Marcus got a new line of product. Word is he's low right now, though.
Child support for a wife and five kids don't come cheap.
She died of asphyxiation, but not because she was exposed to vacuum.
That's my e-cig mixing kit, you moron!
You didn't meet Cathy at a gridlocking party. It was an FLF meeting!

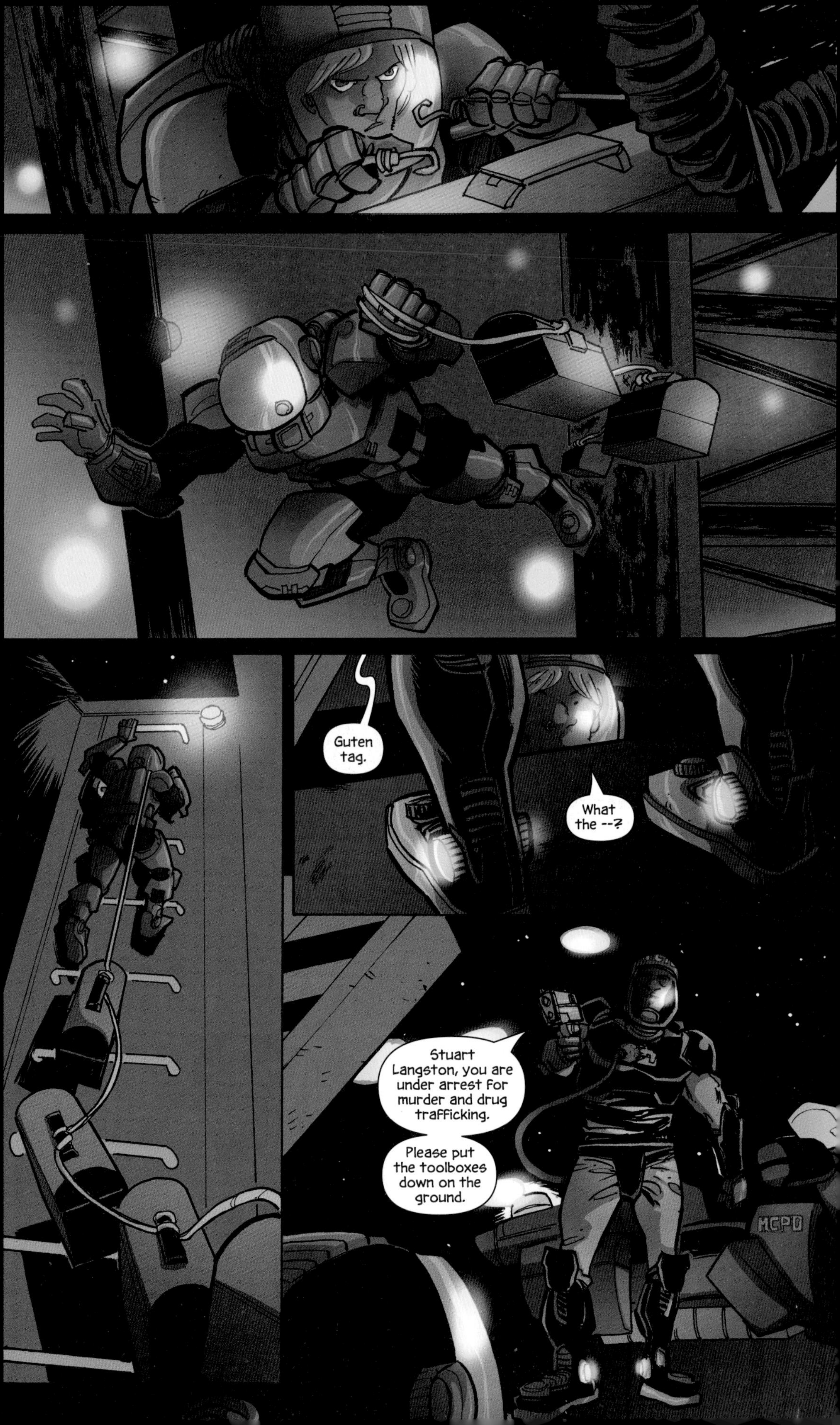
Guten tag.
What the --?
Stuart Langston, you are under arrest for murder and drug trafficking.
Please put the toolboxes down on the ground.
MCPD

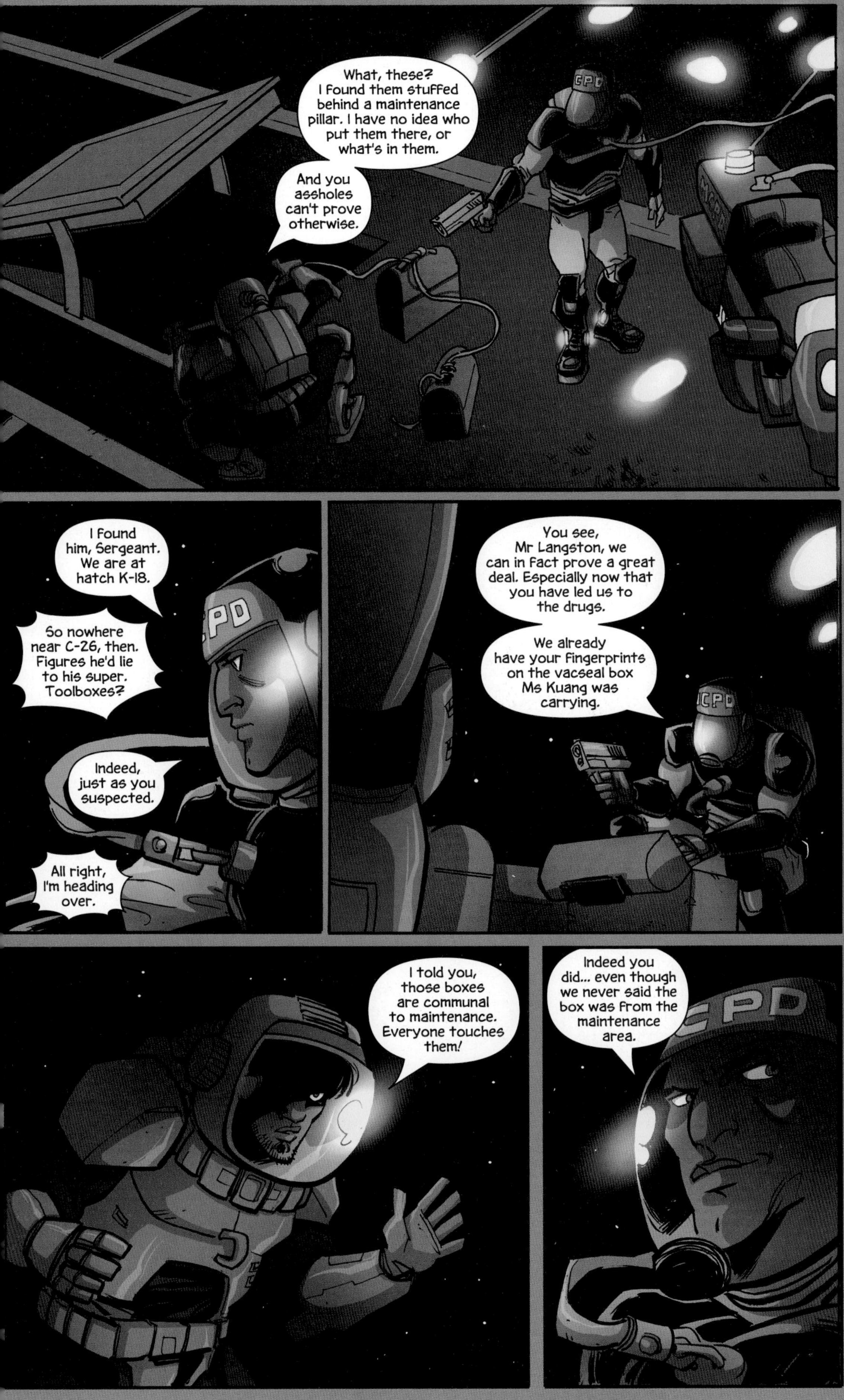
What, these? I found them stuffed behind a maintenance pillar. I have no idea who put them there, or what's in them.
And you assholes can't prove otherwise.
I found him, Sergeant. We are at hatch K-18.
So nowhere near C-26, then. Figures he'd lie to his super. Toolboxes?
Indeed, just as you suspected.
All right, I'm heading over.
You see, Mr Langston, we can in fact prove a great deal. Especially now that you have led us to the drugs.
We already have your fingerprints on the vacseal box Ms Kuang was carrying.
I told you, those boxes are communal to maintenance. Everyone touches them!
Indeed you did... even though we never said the box was from the maintenance area.

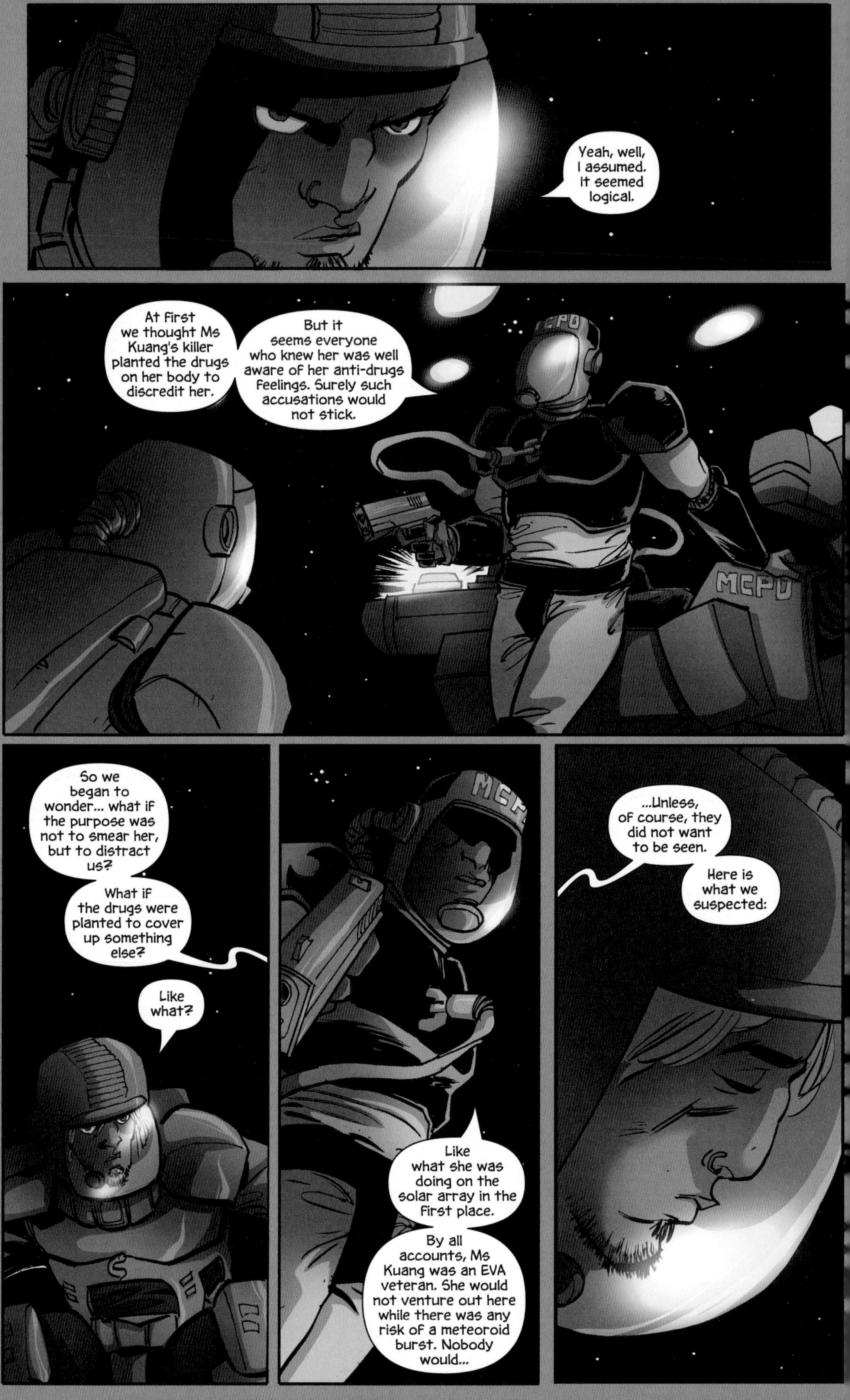
Yeah, well, I assumed. It seemed logical.
At first we thought Ms Kuang's killer planted the drugs on her body to discredit her.
But it seems everyone who knew her was well aware of her anti-drugs feelings. Surely such accusations would not stick.
MCPU
MCPU
So we began to wonder... what if the purpose was not to smear her, but to distract us?
What if the drugs were planted to cover up something else?
Like what?
MCPU
Like what she was doing on the solar array in the first place.
By all accounts, Ms Kuang was an EVA veteran. She would not venture out here while there was any risk of a meteoroid burst. Nobody would...
...Unless, of course, they did not want to be seen.
Here is what we suspected:

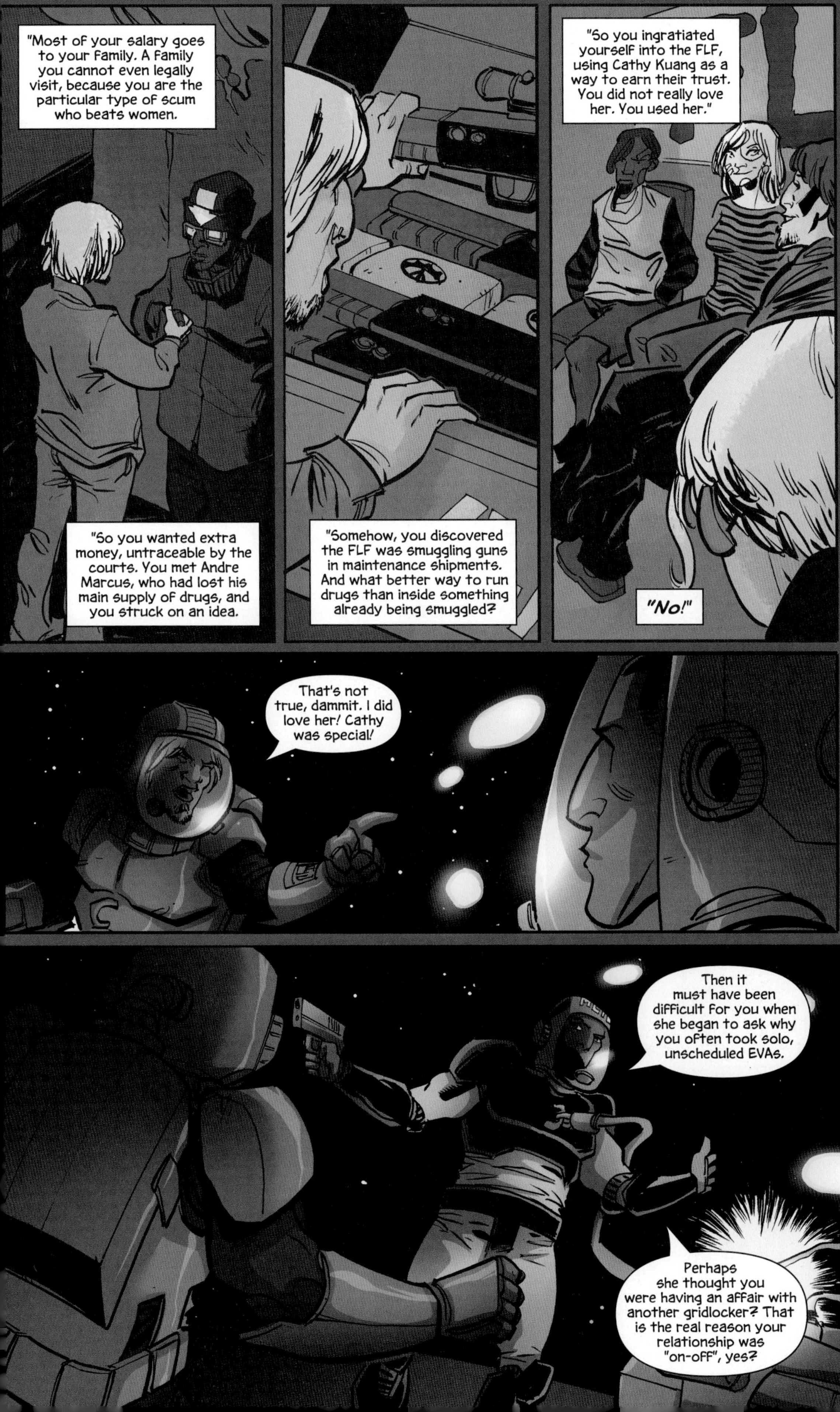
"Most of your salary goes to your family. A family you cannot even legally visit, because you are the particular type of scum who beats women.
"So you wanted extra money, untraceable by the courts. You met Andre Marcus, who had lost his main supply of drugs, and you struck on an idea.
"Somehow, you discovered the FLF was smuggling guns in maintenance shipments. And what better way to run drugs than inside something already being smuggled?
"So you ingratiated yourself into the FLF, using Cathy Kuang as a way to earn their trust. You did not really love her. You used her."
"No!"
That's not true, dammit. I did love her! Cathy was special!
Then it must have been difficult for you when she began to ask why you often took solo, unscheduled EVAs.
Perhaps she thought you were having an affair with another gridlocker? That is the real reason your relationship was "on-off", yes?

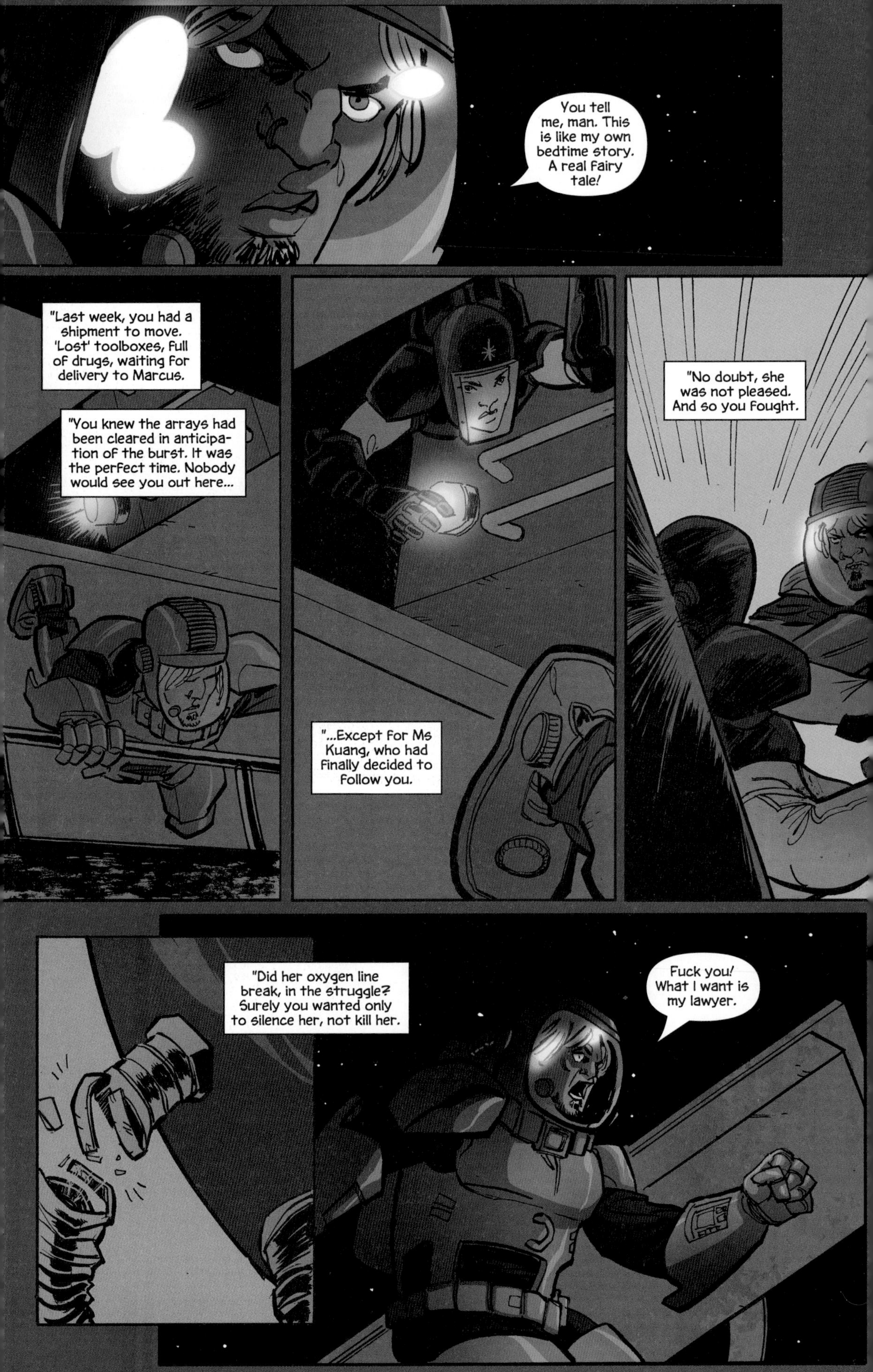
You tell me, man. This is like my own bedtime story. A real fairy tale!
"Last week, you had a shipment to move. 'Lost' toolboxes, full of drugs, waiting for delivery to Marcus.
"You knew the arrays had been cleared in anticipation of the burst. It was the perfect time. Nobody would see you out here...
"...Except for Ms Kuang, who had finally decided to follow you.
"No doubt, she was not pleased. And so you fought.
"Did her oxygen line break, in the struggle? Surely you wanted only to silence her, not kill her.
Fuck you! What I want is my lawyer.

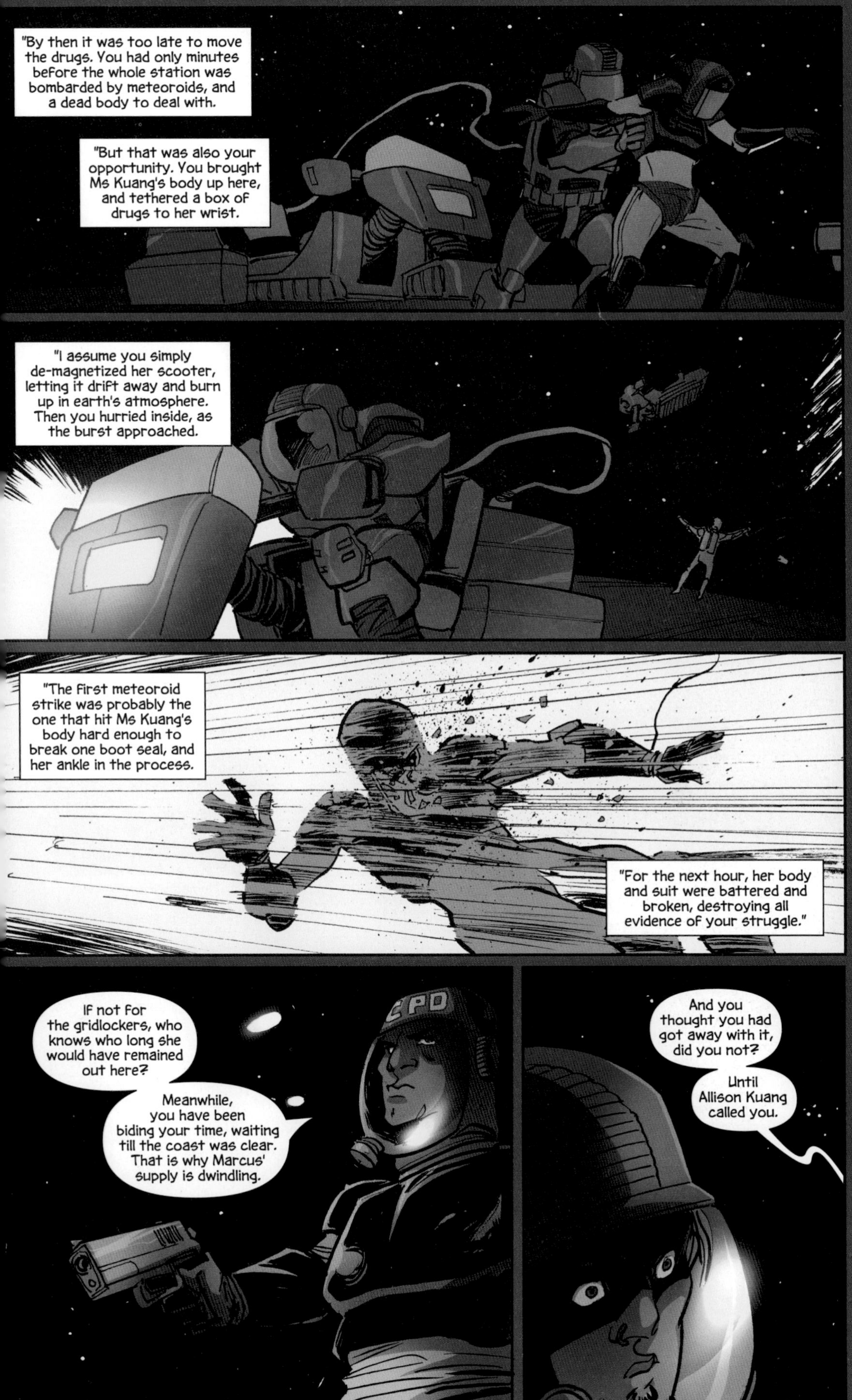
"By then it was too late to move the drugs. You had only minutes before the whole station was bombarded by meteoroids, and a dead body to deal with.
"But that was also your opportunity. You brought Ms Kuang's body up here, and tethered a box of drugs to her wrist.
"I assume you simply de-magnetized her scooter, letting it drift away and burn up in earth's atmosphere. Then you hurried inside, as the burst approached.
"The first meteoroid strike was probably the one that hit Ms Kuang's body hard enough to break one boot seal, and her ankle in the process.
"For the next hour, her body and suit were battered and broken, destroying all evidence of your struggle."
CPD
If not for the gridlockers, who knows who long she would have remained out here?
Meanwhile, you have been biding your time, waiting till the coast was clear. That is why Marcus' supply is dwindling.
And you thought you had got away with it, did you not?
Until Allison Kuang called you.

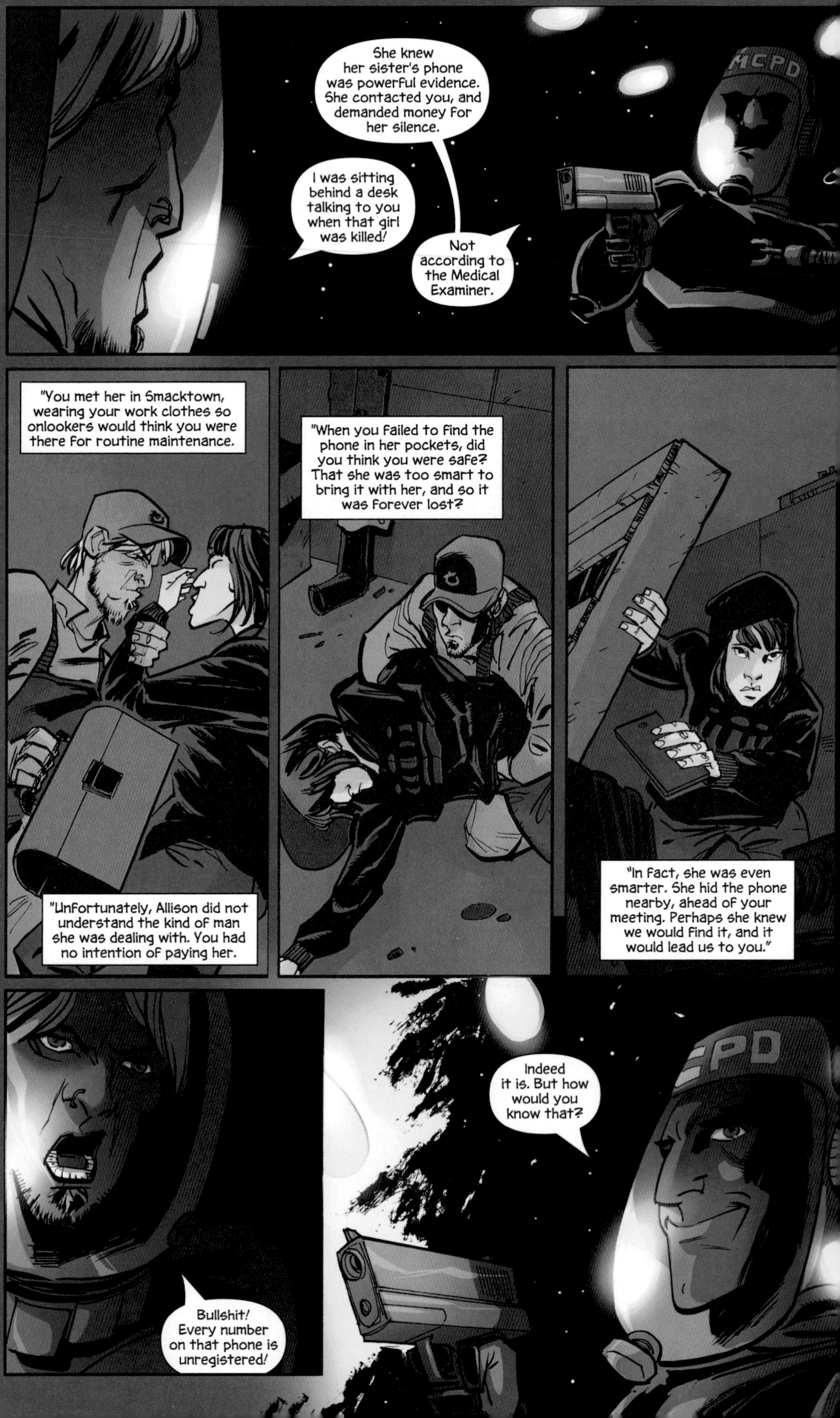
She knew her sister's phone was powerful evidence. She contacted you, and demanded money for her silence.
I was sitting behind a desk talking to you when that girl was killed!
Not according to the Medical Examiner.
MCPD
"You met her in Smacktown, wearing your work clothes so onlookers would think you were there for routine maintenance.
"Unfortunately, Allison did not understand the kind of man she was dealing with. You had no intention of paying her.
"When you failed to find the phone in her pockets, did you think you were safe? That she was too smart to bring it with her, and so it was forever lost?
"In fact, she was even smarter. She hid the phone nearby, ahead of your meeting. Perhaps she knew we would find it, and it would lead us to you."
Bullshit! Every number on that phone is unregistered!
Indeed it is. But how would you know that?

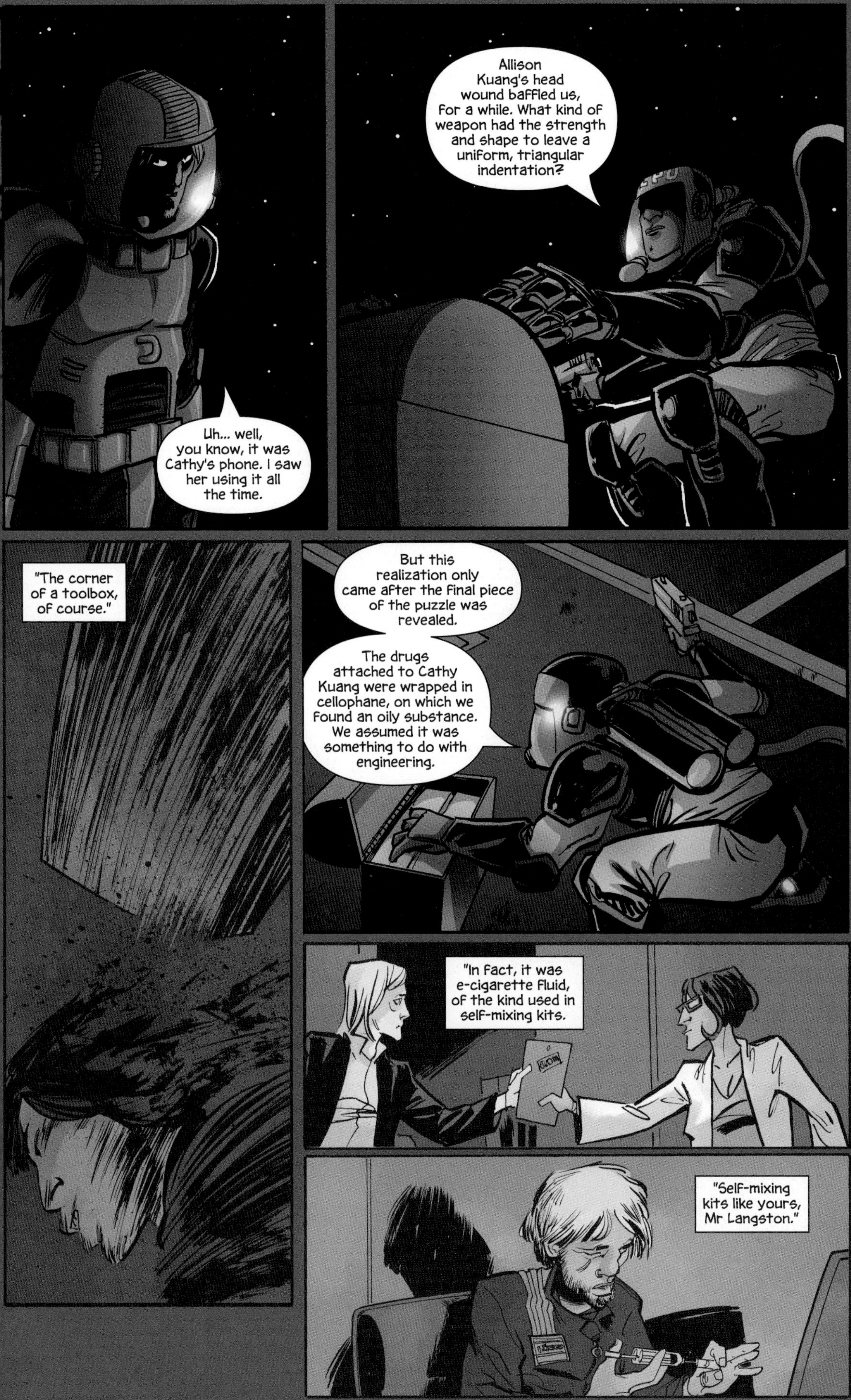
Uh... well, you know, it was Cathy's phone. I saw her using it all the time.
Allison Kuang's head wound baffled us, for a while. What kind of weapon had the strength and shape to leave a uniform, triangular indentation?
"The corner of a toolbox, of course."
But this realization only came after the final piece of the puzzle was revealed.
The drugs attached to Cathy Kuang were wrapped in cellophane, on which we found an oily substance. We assumed it was something to do with engineering.
"In fact, it was e-cigarette fluid, of the kind used in self-mixing kits.
"Self-mixing kits like yours, Mr Langston."

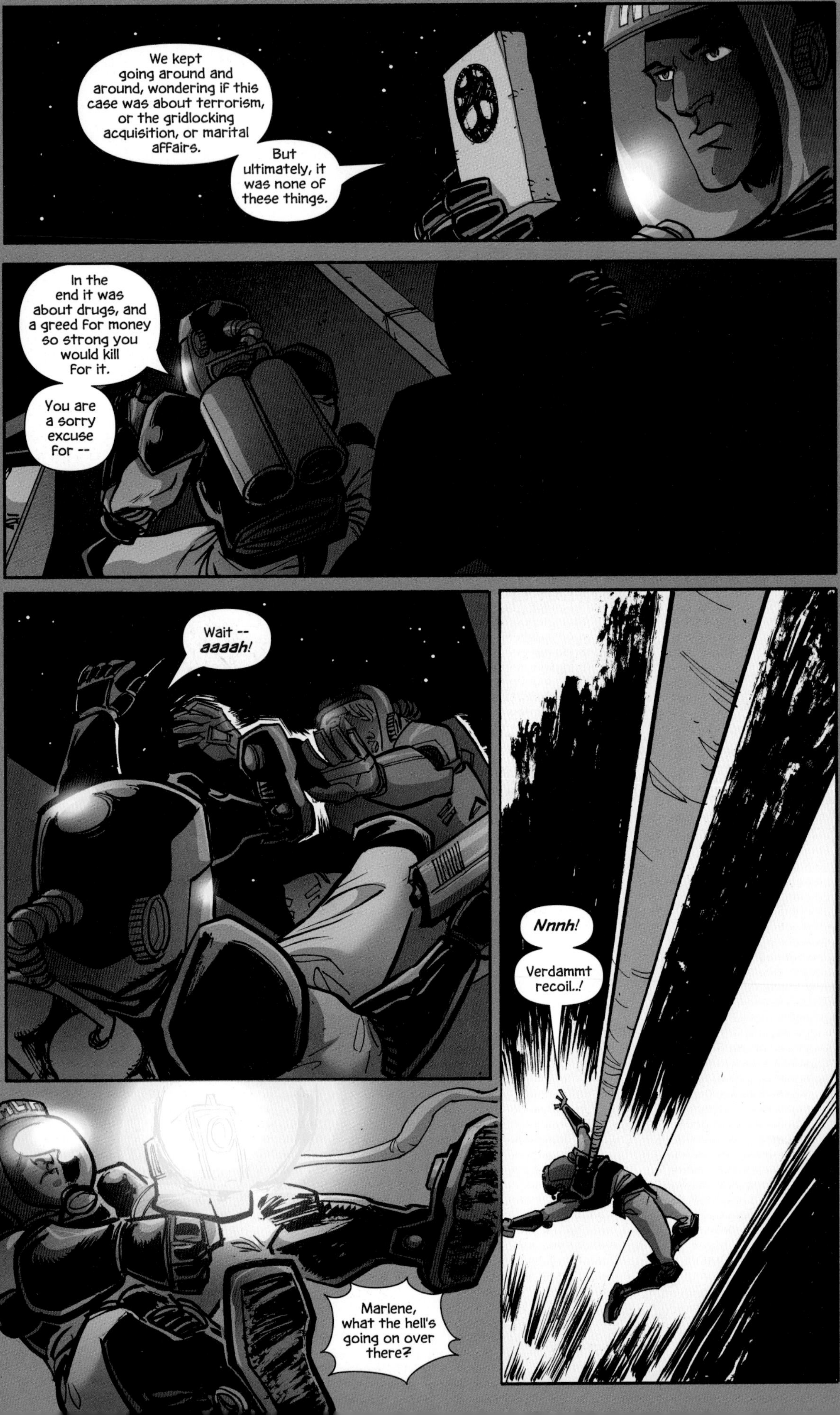
We kept going around and around, wondering if this case was about terrorism, or the gridlocking acquisition, or marital affairs.
But ultimately, it was none of these things.
In the end it was about drugs, and a greed for money so strong you would kill for it.
You are a sorry excuse for --
Wait -- *aaaah*!
Nnnh!
Verdammt recoil..!
Marlene, what the hell's going on over there?

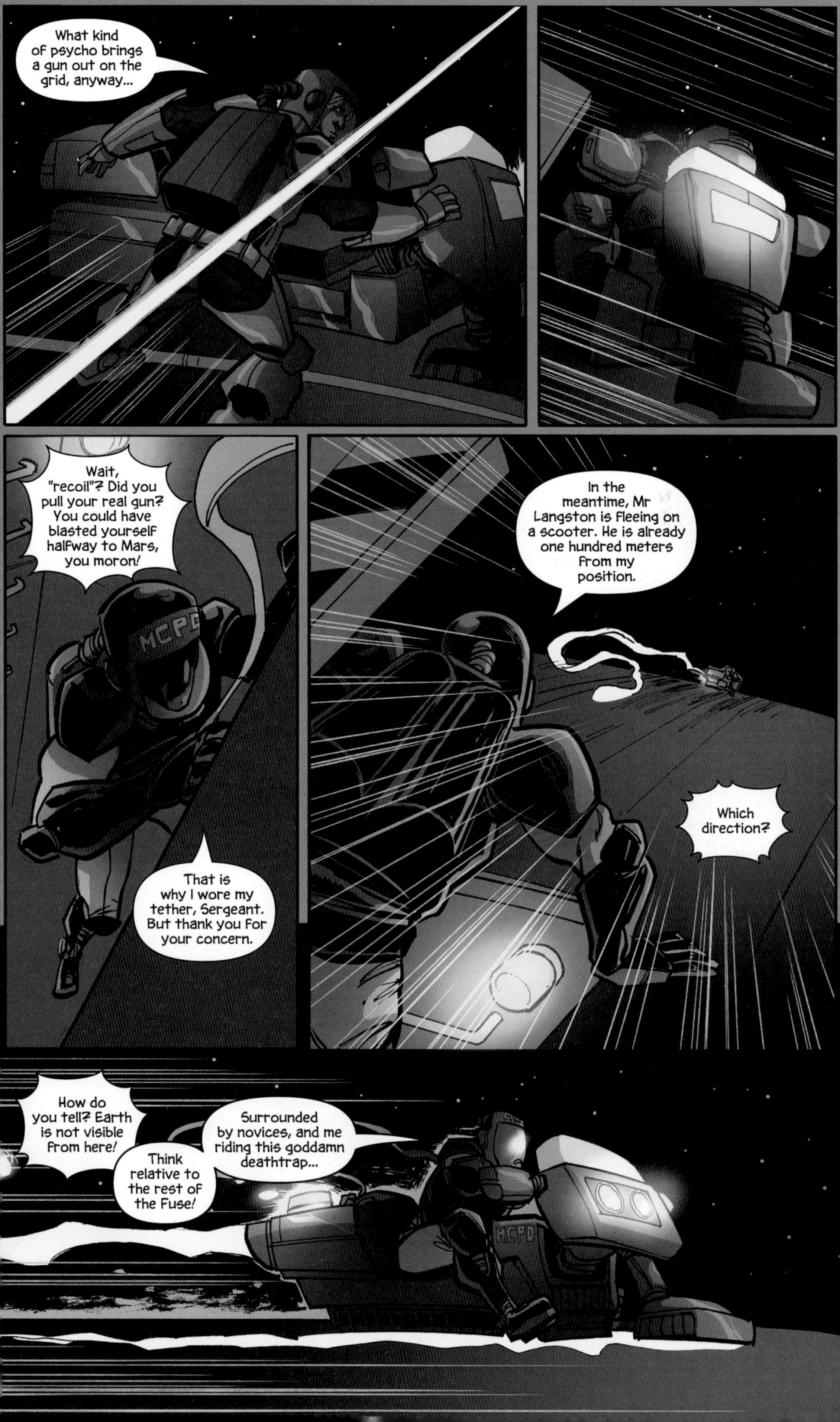
What kind of psycho brings a gun out on the grid, anyway...
Wait, "recoil"? Did you pull your real gun? You could have blasted yourself halfway to Mars, you moron!
That is why I wore my tether, Sergeant. But thank you for your concern.
In the meantime, Mr Langston is fleeing on a scooter. He is already one hundred meters from my position.
Which direction?
How do you tell? Earth is not visible from here!
Surrounded by novices, and me riding this goddamn deathtrap...
Think relative to the rest of the Fuse!

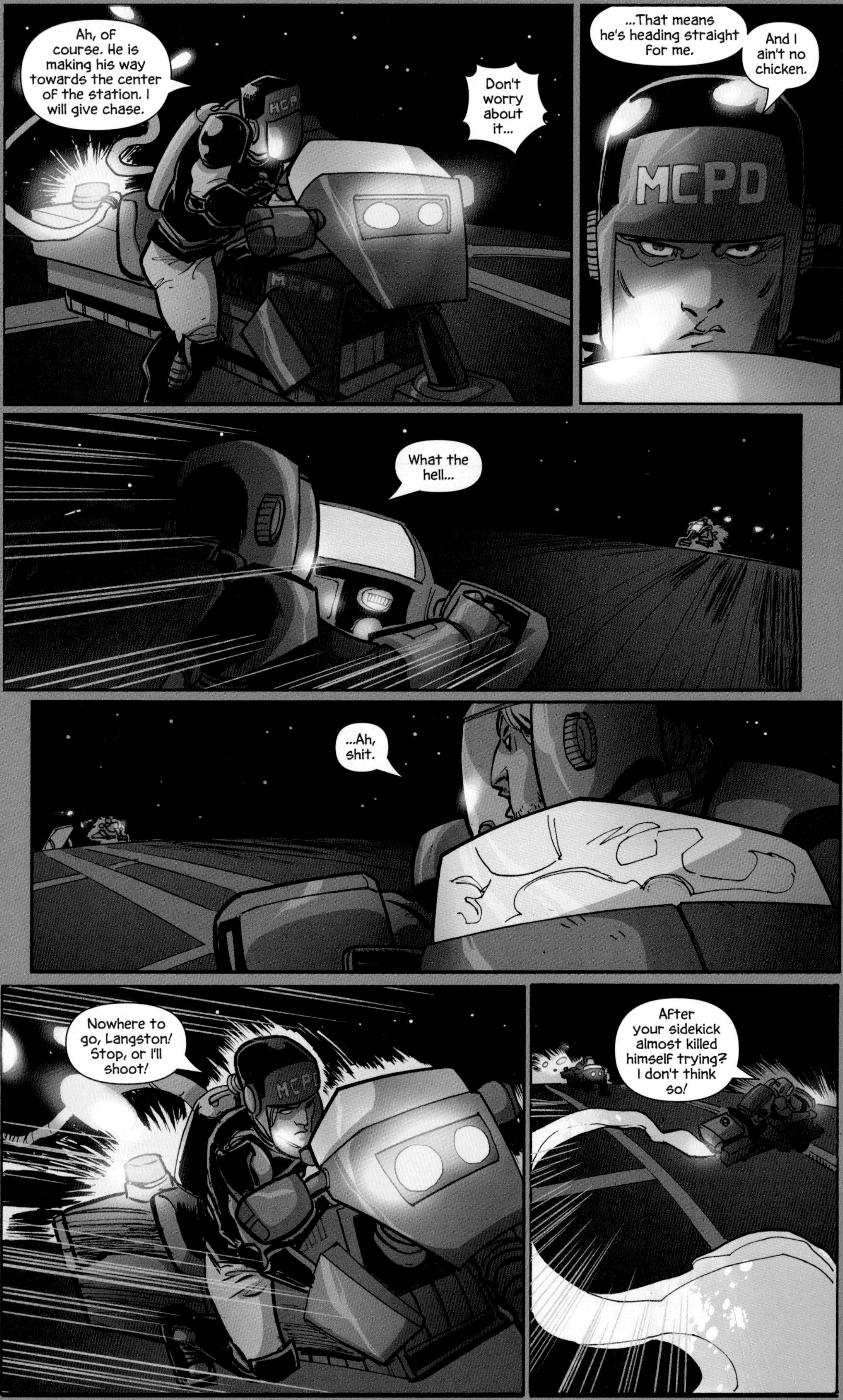
Ah, of course. He is making his way towards the center of the station. I will give chase.
Don't worry about it...
...That means he's heading straight for me.
And I ain't no chicken.
MCPD
What the hell...
...Ah, shit.
Nowhere to go, Langston! Stop, or I'll shoot!
MCPD
After your sidekick almost killed himself trying? I don't think so!

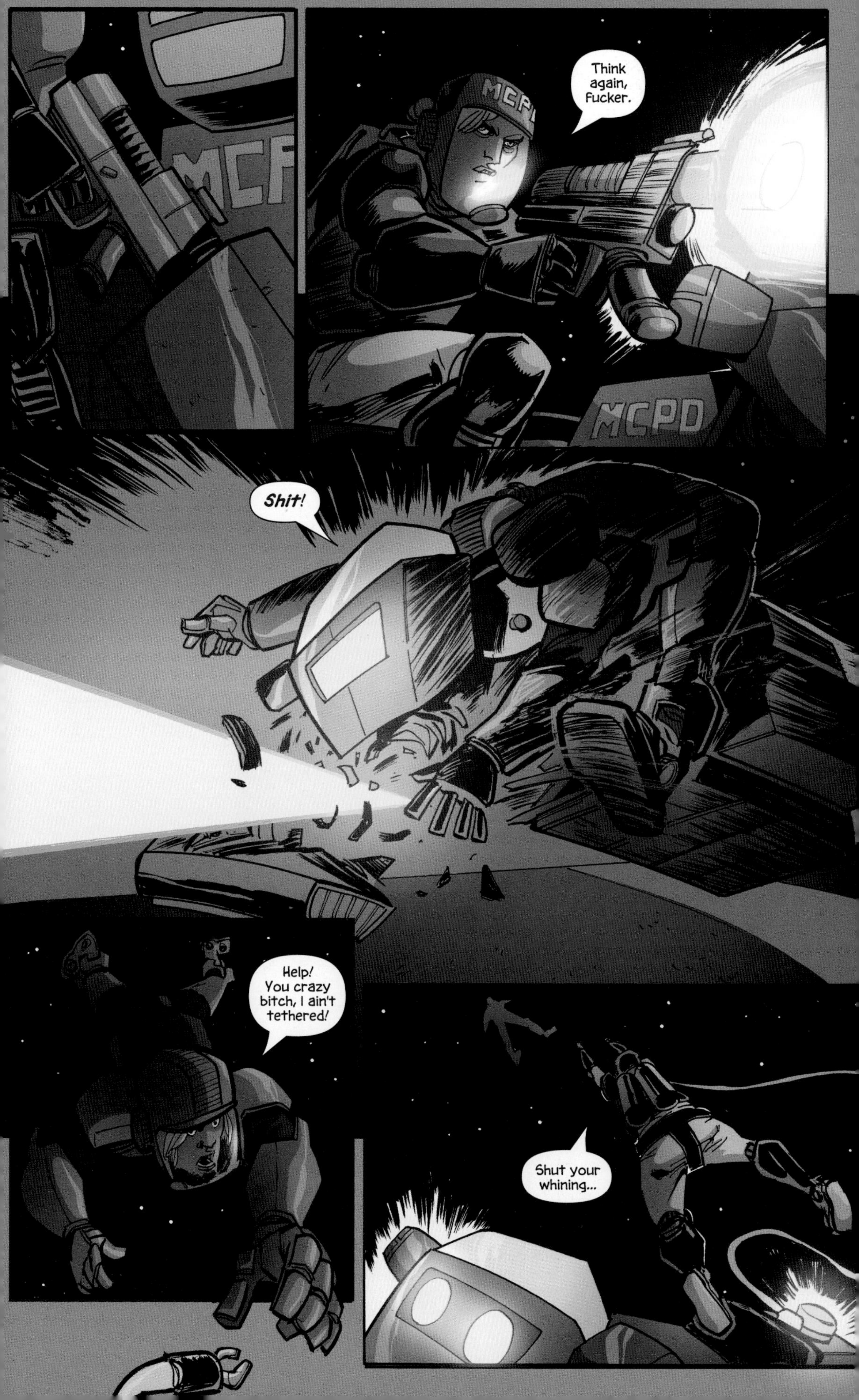
MCPD
Think again, fucker.
MCPD
Shit!
Help! You crazy bitch, I ain't tethered!
Shut your whining...

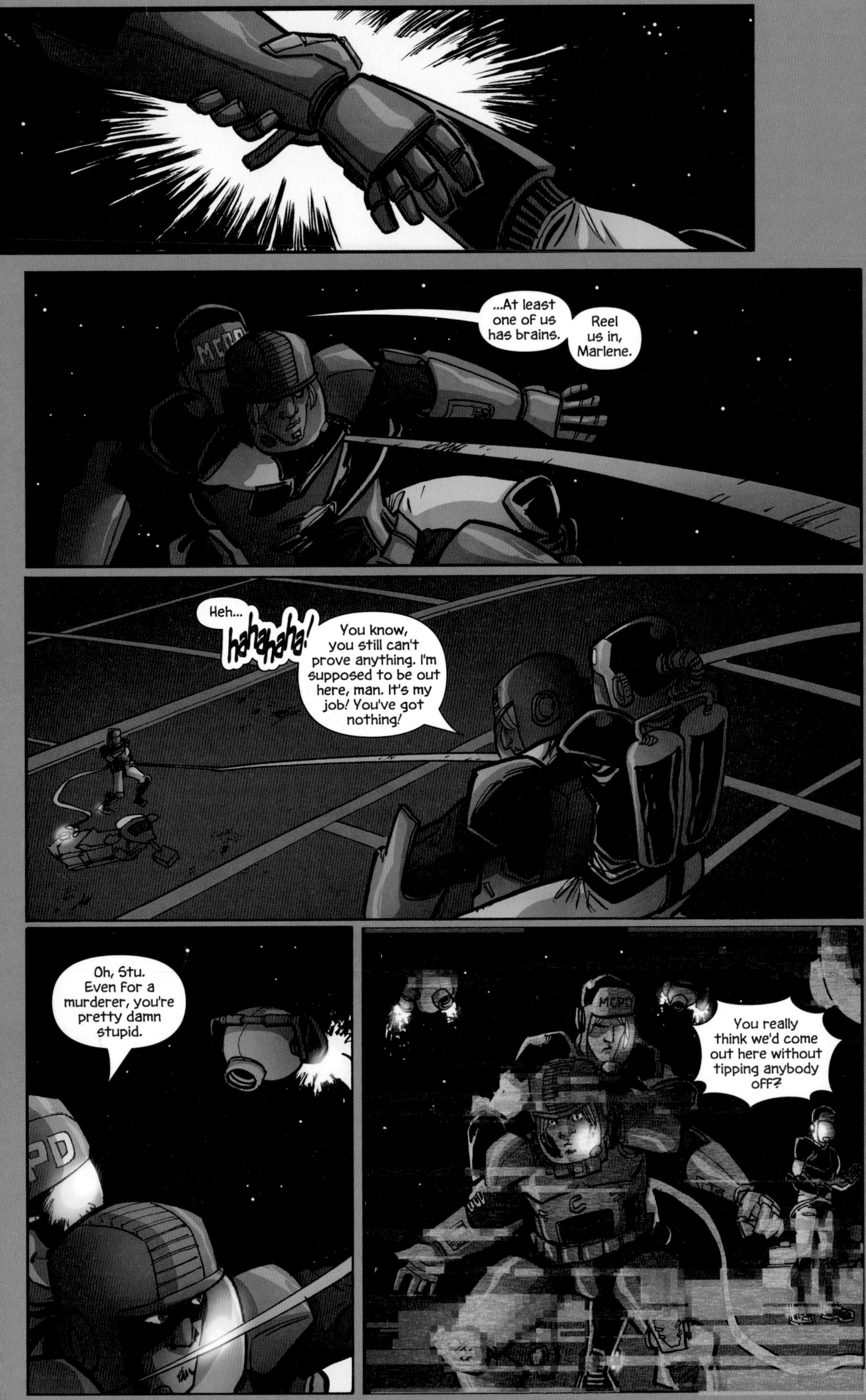
...At least one of us has brains.
Reel us in, Marlene.
Heh...
hahahaha!
You know, you still can't prove anything. I'm supposed to be out here, man. It's my job! You've got nothing!
Oh, Stu. Even for a murderer, you're pretty damn stupid.
You really think we'd come out here without tipping anybody off?

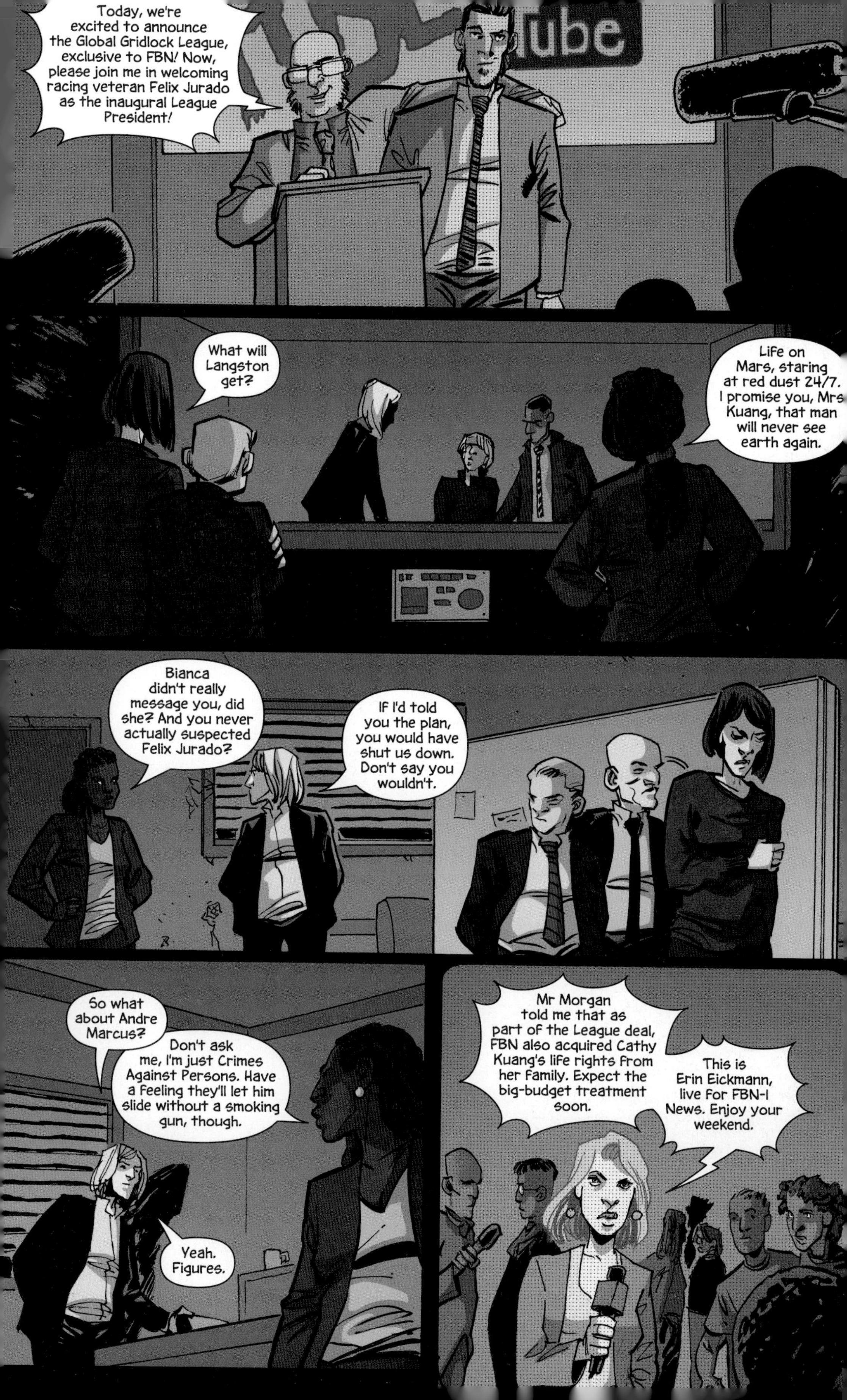
Today, we're excited to announce the Global Gridlock League, exclusive to FBN! Now, please join me in welcoming racing veteran Felix Jurado as the inaugural League President!
Tube
What will Langston get?
Life on Mars, staring at red dust 24/7. I promise you, Mrs Kuang, that man will never see earth again.
Bianca didn't really message you, did she? And you never actually suspected Felix Jurado?
If I'd told you the plan, you would have shut us down. Don't say you wouldn't.
So what about Andre Marcus?
Don't ask me, I'm just Crimes Against Persons. Have a feeling they'll let him slide without a smoking gun, though.
Yeah. Figures.
Mr Morgan told me that as part of the League deal, FBN also acquired Cathy Kuang's life rights from her family. Expect the big-budget treatment soon.
This is Erin Eickmann, live for FBN-1 News. Enjoy your weekend.

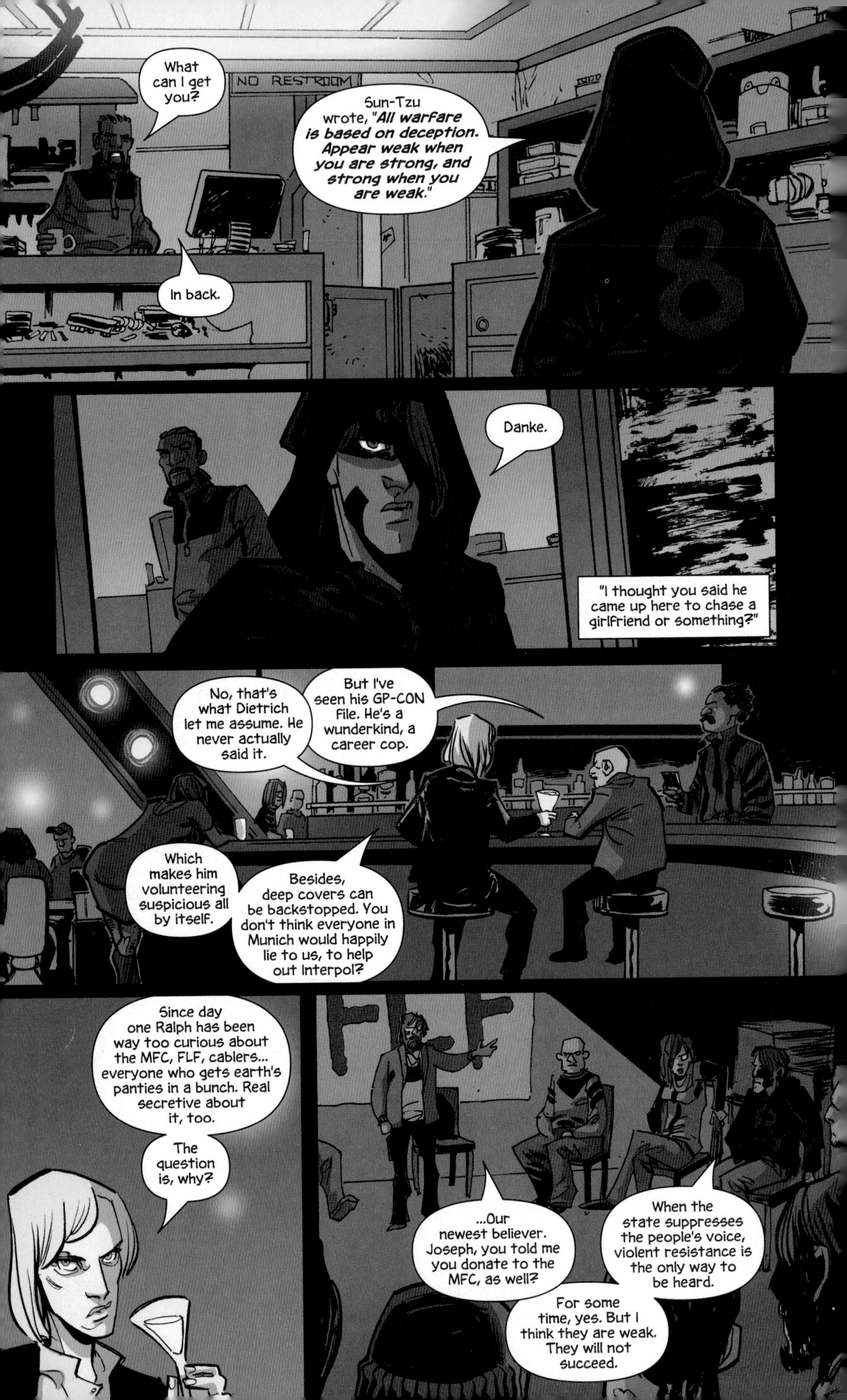

What can I get you?
NO RESTROOM
Sun-Tzu wrote, "All warfare is based on deception. Appear weak when you are strong, and strong when you are weak."
In back.
Danke.
"I thought you said he came up here to chase a girlfriend or something?"
No, that's what Dietrich let me assume. He never actually said it.
But I've seen his GP-CON file. He's a wunderkind, a career cop.
Which makes him volunteering suspicious all by itself.
Besides, deep covers can be backstopped. You don't think everyone in Munich would happily lie to us, to help out Interpol?
Since day one Ralph has been way too curious about the MFC, FLF, cablers... everyone who gets earth's panties in a bunch. Real secretive about it, too.
The question is, why?
...Our newest believer. Joseph, you told me you donate to the MFC, as well?
When the state suppresses the people's voice, violent resistance is the only way to be heard.
For some time, yes. But I think they are weak. They will not succeed.

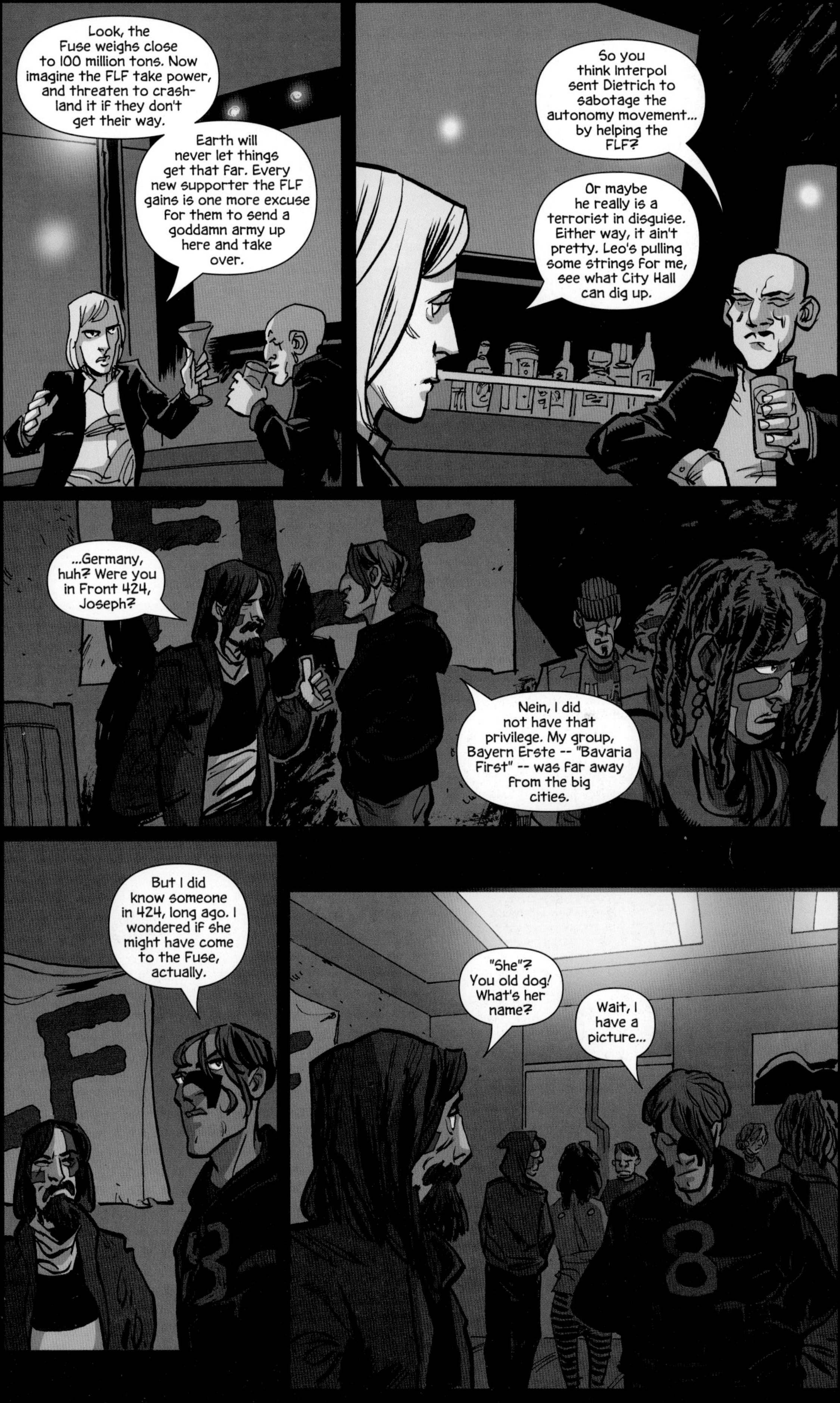

Look, the Fuse weighs close to 100 million tons. Now imagine the FLF take power, and threaten to crash-land it if they don't get their way.
Earth will never let things get that far. Every new supporter the FLF gains is one more excuse for them to send a goddamn army up here and take over.
So you think Interpol sent Dietrich to sabotage the autonomy movement... by helping the FLF?
Or maybe he really is a terrorist in disguise. Either way, it ain't pretty. Leo's pulling some strings for me, see what City Hall can dig up.
...Germany, huh? Were you in Front 424, Joseph?
Nein, I did not have that privilege. My group, Bayern Erste -- "Bavaria First" -- was far away from the big cities.
But I did know someone in 424, long ago. I wondered if she might have come to the Fuse, actually.
"She"? You old dog! What's her name?
Wait, I have a picture...

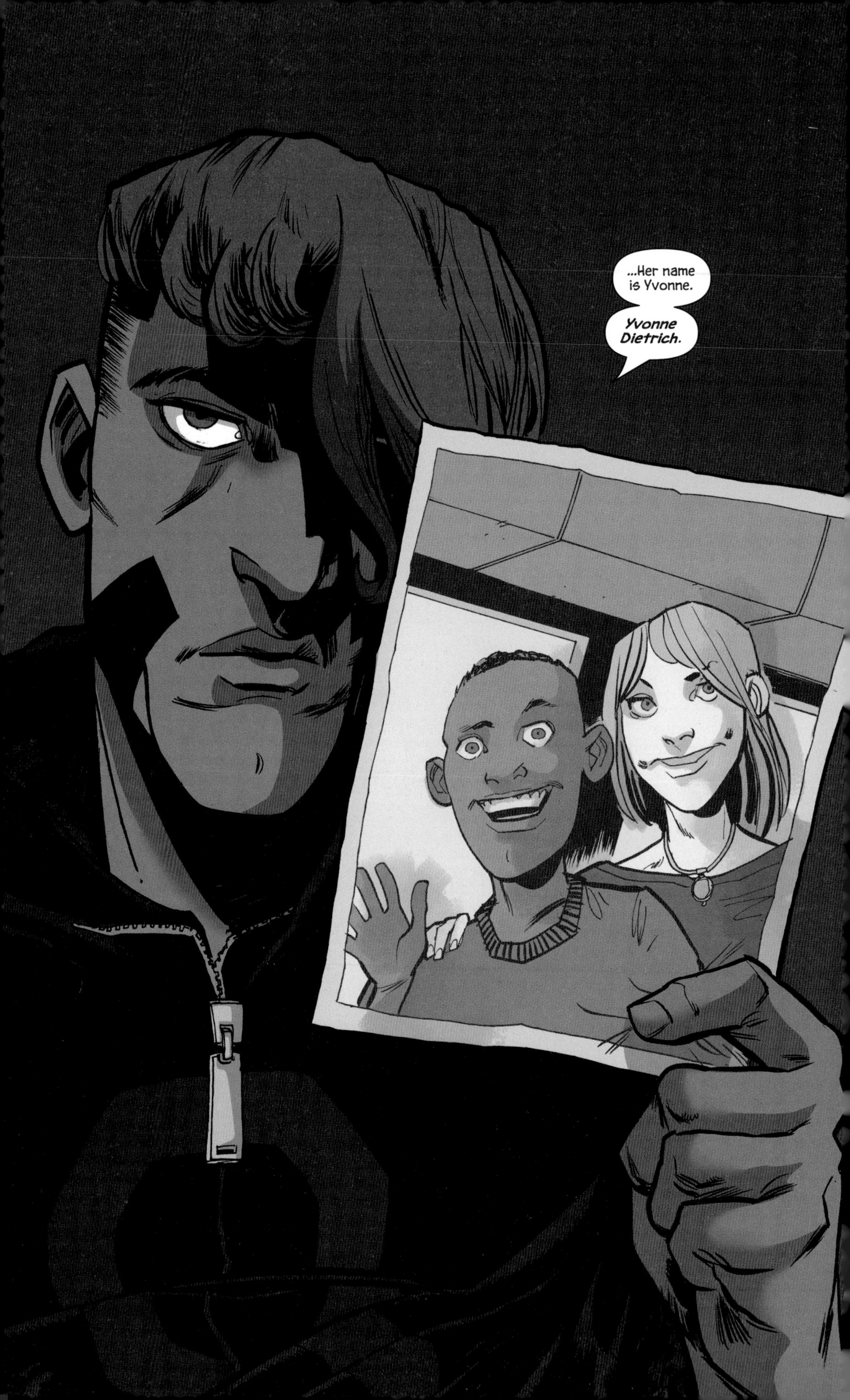
...Her name is Yvonne.
Yvonne Dietrich.

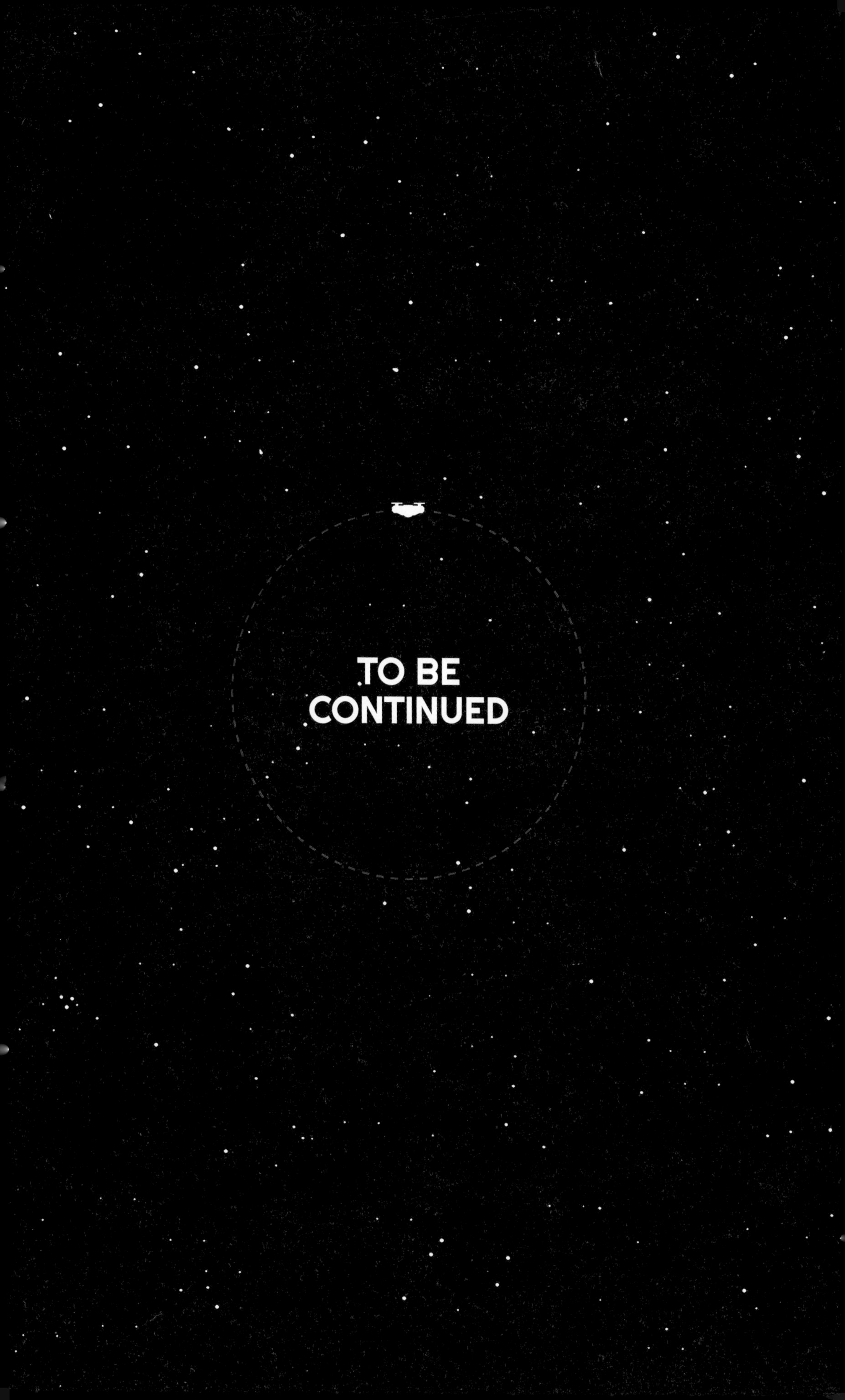
TO BE CONTINUED

GRIDLOCK

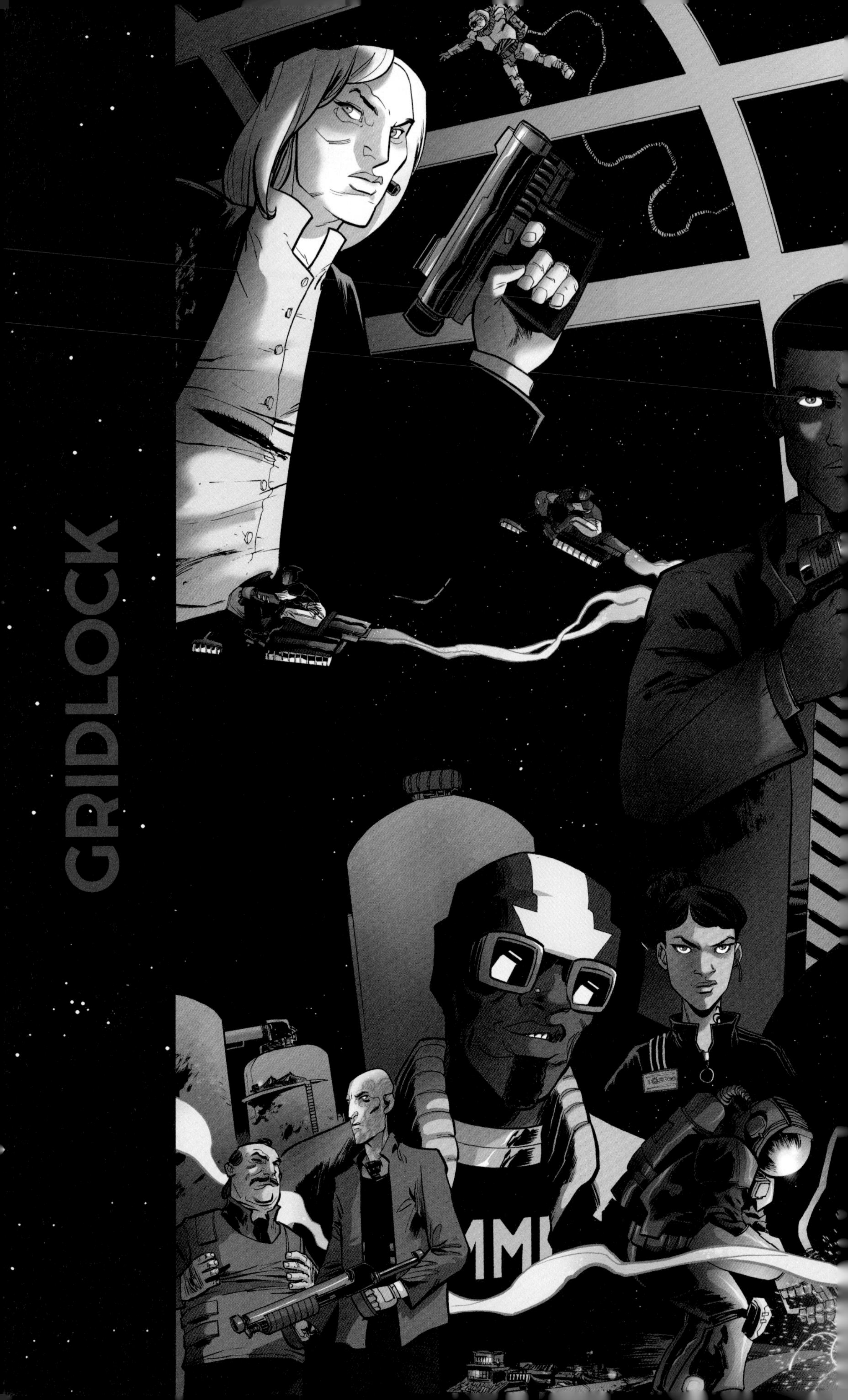

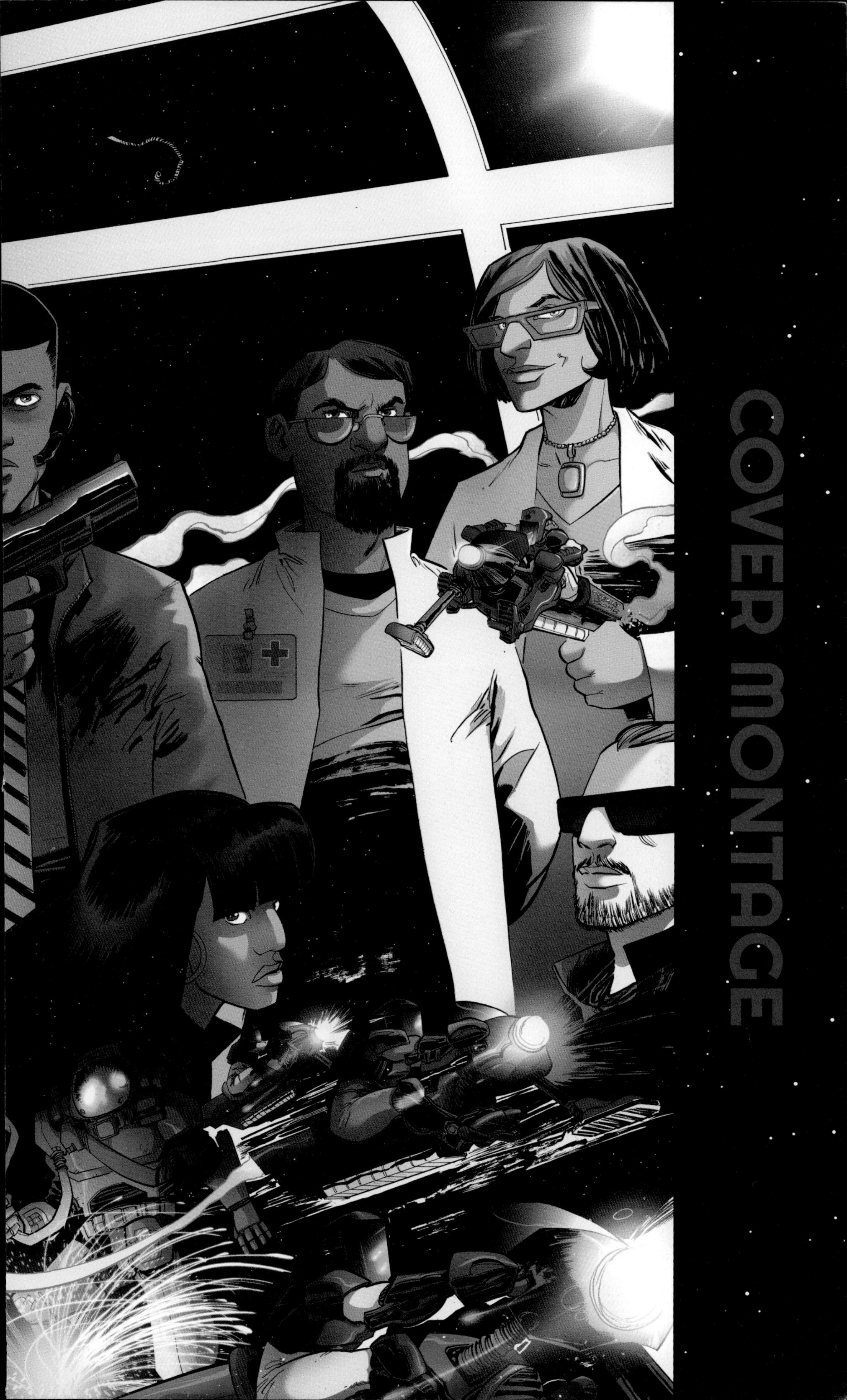

COVER MONTAGE

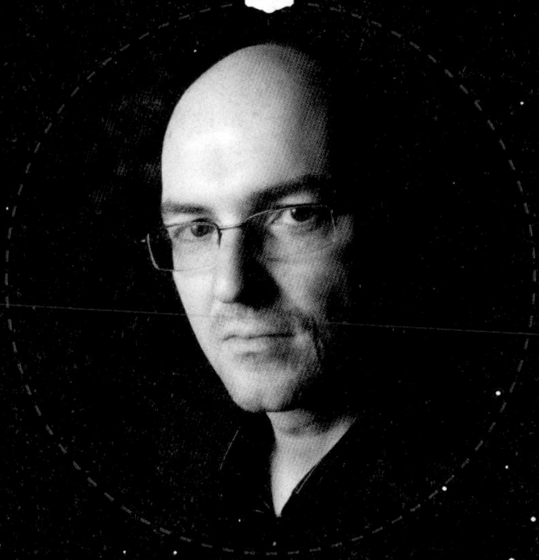

ANTONY JOHNSTON

Antony is an award-winning, *New York Times* bestselling author of comics, graphic novels, videogames, and books, with titles including *Wasteland*, *Umbral*, *Shadow of Mordor*, *Dead Space*, *The Coldest City*, *ZombiU*, and more. He has adapted books by bestselling novelist Anthony Horowitz, collaborated with comics legend Alan Moore, and reinvented Marvel's flagship character *Wolverine* for manga. His titles have been translated throughout the world, and optioned for film and TV. He lives and works in England.

ANTONYJOHNSTON.COM · @ANTONYJOHNSTON

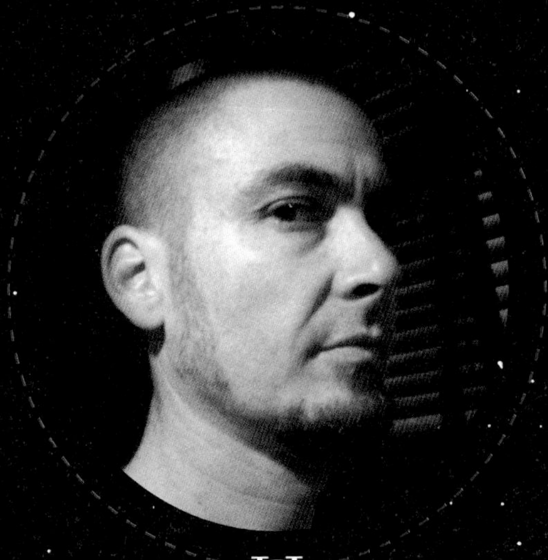

JUSTIN GREENWOOD

Justin is a finely tuned, comic makin' mammy jammy, with work on series like *Wasteland*, *Resurrection*, *Stumptown*, and *Stringers* from Oni Press, as well as projects like *Masks and Mobsters*, *Ghost Town*, and *Continuum: The War Files* under his belt. When not drawing, he can be found running around the East Bay with his wife Melissa and their dual wildlings, tracking down small produce markets and high intensity card games with equal vigor.

JUSTINGREENWOODART.COM · @JKGREENWOOD_ART

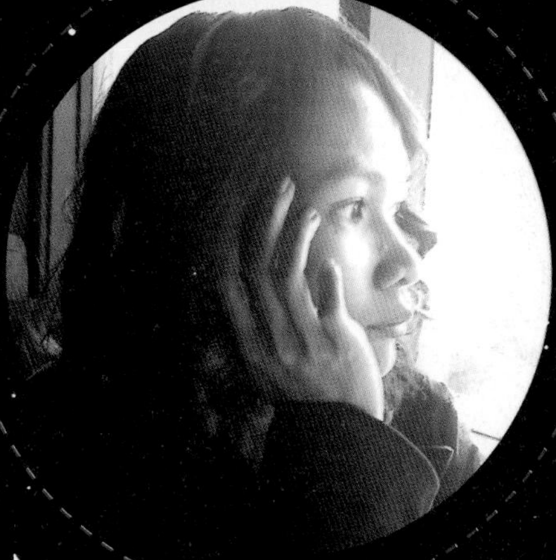

SHARI CHANKHAMMA

Shari lives in Thailand and has been working as a colorist for a while now. She previously wrote and illustrated creator-owned titles such as *The Sisters' Luck*, *The Clarence Principle*, *Pavlov's Dream*, and short stories in various anthologies. Besides comics, she enjoys wasting time on MMO and romance novels.

SHARII.COM · @SHARIHES

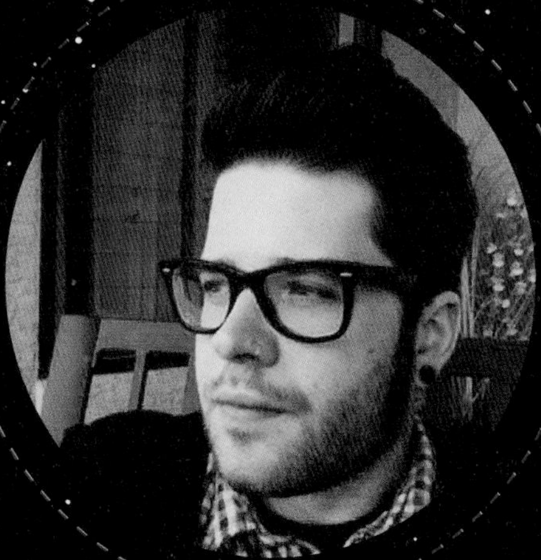

RYAN FERRIER

Ryan is a comic book letterer based in Alberta, Canada. He has lettered comics for Image, Dark Horse, Oni Press, BOOM! Studios, Black Mask, and Monkeybrain. Ryan also writes comics like *D4VE* and *Curb Stomp*.

READCHALLENGER.COM · @RYANWRITER

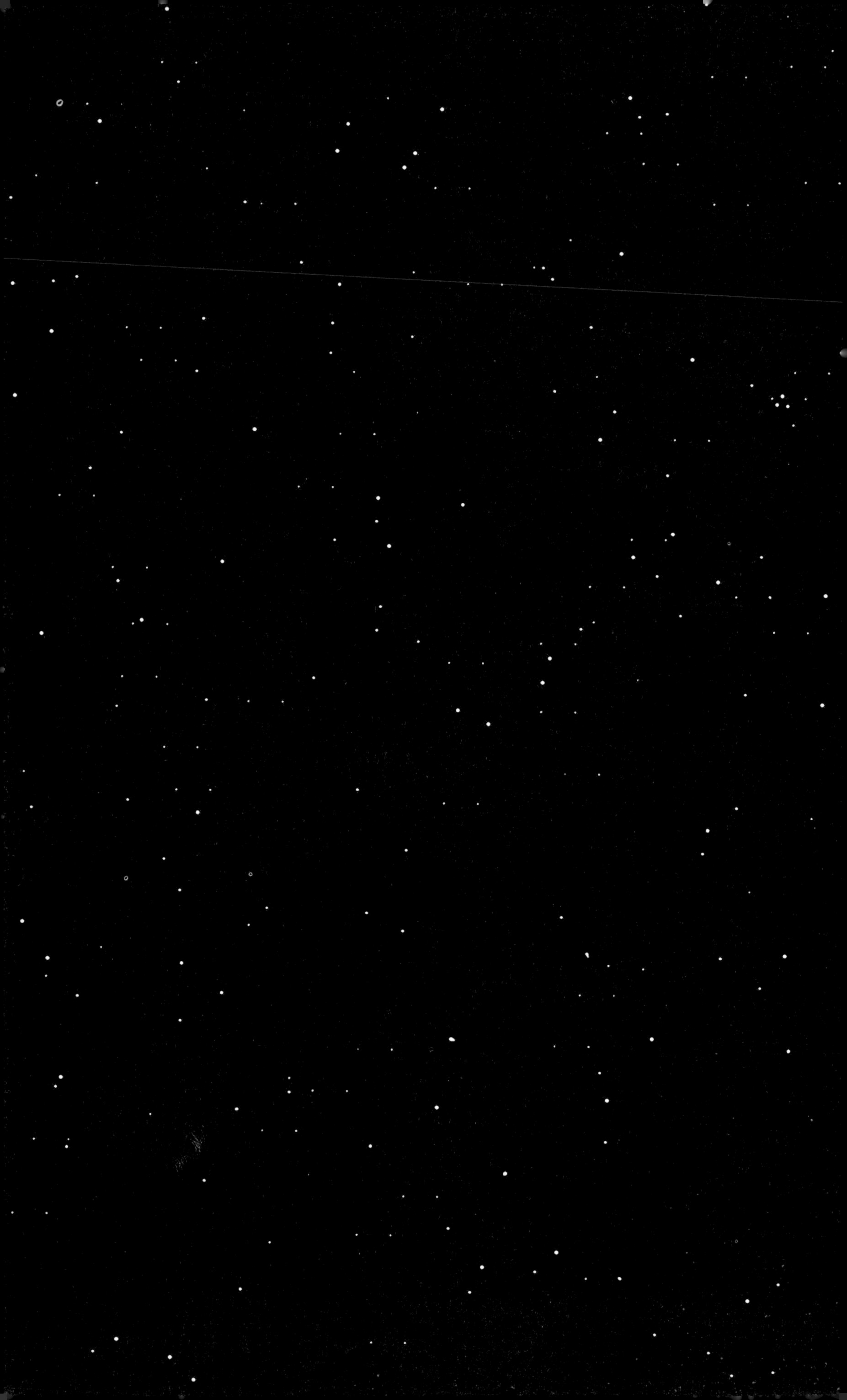